INTO THE BLUE

MEGAN O'LEARY

Megan O'Leary sold all her stuff in 2006 and bought a one-way ticket to St. Thomas, leaving behind her corporate job and Manhattan's East Village to give life in the Caribbean a go. After a four-year stint in St. Thomas that included working, cooking and living on boats, she went back to the continental U.S.— only to return to the Virgin Islands in 2016.

She transitioned her life to the Pacific in 2018 and currently lives on Maui with her boyfriend, Thomas, and their dog, Wiley. She still surfs on the same longboard she dragged all the way to St. Thomas and back.

A professional copywriter for more than 15 years, Megan holds a bachelor's degree in English and music from the University of Pennsylvania. *Into the Blue* is her first novel.

MeganOLeary.com

INTO THE BLUE

MEGAN O'LEARY

This is a work of fiction. Although the Virgin Islands are a
real place—and some of the events were loosely inspired by
real occurrences or rumors obtained through the coconut
telegraph—the names, characters, business, events and
incidents (and even some of the locations) in this book
are the products of the author's imagination.

ISBN: 978-0-578-87424-1 (paperback)

Cover Design by Laura Duffy
Interior Design by Alejandro Espinosa
Author Photo by Thomas Boeker

Published by Monstera Leaf Press
MonsteraLeafPress.com

For my mother, who always nurtured my creative side,
and for my father, who introduced me to Hemingway's
routine and put the novels of Tony Hillerman and
John D. MacDonald in my hands.

I couldn't have done this without your love and support.

AUTHOR'S NOTE

I first moved to St. Thomas in 2006. I have a specific sense of nostalgia for that era—and not just because I was in my mid-twenties and seemingly impervious to hangovers. My first stint on a tropical island had a certain charm. Smartphones had not been introduced yet, and social media was still in its infancy. In fact, Facebook was something only college students did. Even when the iPhone was introduced a year later, only a few people had one. Almost nobody thought we'd need smartphones at all, let alone to the level we've come to rely on them.

I've chosen to set this novel in 2009 to capture this era and its idiosyncrasies. I see this as the first of several Lizzie stories, which will move closer to present day. However, for now, I want to show you the St. Thomas where we knew people's first names and what they did—Peter who works at Budget Marine, Joseph from Iggie's, etc. It was also the era before Google Maps. You were told to turn right at the tree in the middle of the road or left after the Bridge to Nowhere. If the landmarks didn't appear as promised, you just wandered until you found the right place. Sometimes, you drove down a road only to discover it was someone's driveway. It was all a part of the experience.

I'm also very cognizant that this book represents a single viewpoint: that of a white person of privilege, born in the continental U.S. It has limitations for telling the full story of this island, but it is also a viewpoint I know well. I hope you find Lizzie Jordan's lens interesting. That said, there are many other lenses with which to view St. Thomas, those of resettled down islanders, native Virgin Islanders, some of whom are direct descendants of slaves, ancestral Virgin Islanders whose families have birthed new generations on the island and many more. The more I learn about the history of the Caribbean and its diverse islands, the more I realize that the echoes of conquest, colonialism and slavery are still reverberating today, some quite loudly. I hope someday to be able to do them full justice in print. For now, I offer this novel as one slice of life in the U.S. Virgin Islands in the early 2000s.

Finally, this book is a work of fiction. I've drawn inspiration from real life. However, nothing in this book happened quite the way it's described, and I've bent some features of island life to accommodate my storyline.

Or, as Lizzie would say, "I changed some stuff about St. Thomas to make the story better. Don't get yourself all twisted up about it."

1

Bring everyone back alive.

The first rule of working a tour boat in the Caribbean is pretty damn simple.

I thought following that rule was going to be an easy task today.

I stood on the back deck of the charter boat I work as first mate, sipping a fizzy Diet Coke. The sun was warm on my face, and the clear blue water of the British Virgin Islands lapped invitingly around the swim platform.

We had reached the quietest point in my twelve-hour day. The captain had nosed the 50' white whale of a powerboat to a mooring, where I tied her up. I passed out snorkel gear, and my guests, adults of all shapes and sizes with a sprinkling of kids, scattered to explore Diamond Reef.

The reef had supposedly gotten its name when a woman got pissed at her fiancé and pitched her huge diamond engagement ring into the water. Of course, the ring has never been found. Cue mysterious music.

Who knows if the story is true? It's dubious, but it's also fun to tell. I get to make my most theatrically enigmatic face at the end of the tale. Although, for the record, I do cringe inwardly when Larry, one of the other captains I work with, layers on a joke about maritime law requiring that you split all findings with the crew. Hilarious.

Putting up with captains' humor. It was all part of this glamorous gig.

Now all I had to do was make sure that no one died. Oh, and stop obsessing over Dave—also known as "the guy who's not my boyfriend"—and why he'd been such an ass last night.

It sounded so simple.

The family of four from Texas had found a sting ray. Mom had gotten in the water without one word about smearing her makeup—and there was a lot of it. The male halves of the two couples from San Diego sat on the back deck dangling their feet in the water, their sculpted shoulders flexing as they lifted their cans of Heineken to their mouths. Their girlfriends—only one of whom was California blonde, thank you very much—snorkeled to my left, their tanned and toned derrieres floating primly above the surface. A few more guests lay scattered across the boat's cushioned benches like seals on the beach. The rest floated calmly in front of me, snorkels peeking out of the water, fins flapping lazily.

It had been a good day so far. Uneventful, in other words. No one had gotten themselves lost during my tour of the Baths on Virgin Gorda.

You'd be surprised how many people separate themselves from the group while meandering through the house-sized granite boulders. Enough to give me a few mild heart attacks, for sure.

Next, all twenty-two of our guests received the cocktails and entrees they ordered at the restaurant on Marina Cay, which was not always a given. The island-style service on Marina Cay was alternatingly delightful and frustrating. We'd caught them on a good day.

Then, I'd solicited a few *oohs* and *aahs* by pointing out the photos of Sidney Poitier on the walls. His movie, *Our Virgin*

Island, was based on the story of the couple who had owned the tiny island for a time.

And, as of this very moment, I still hadn't broken that first golden rule. All twenty-two guests were alive and well. Several of them were even starting to develop a nice afternoon buzz from our open bar.

It was going to be easy to bring this group back to the United States Virgin Islands intact—and hopefully happy enough to tip us well.

But as I scanned back across the reef, I saw something that made my breath catch: a set of bamboo pole arms flailing above the water line. They conveyed the universal gesture that translated as, "This snorkeling may turn out to be the last thing that I do."

Shit. Shit. Shit.

All the safety training around scenarios like this urges you to stay calm above all. I set my Diet Coke down gently on the gunwale. To be honest, I wanted to chuck it behind me with a scream and dive into the water like a pig on fire. Instead, I settled for a calm call to the captain as I gathered my fins, mask and snorkel.

My heart, however, didn't get the memo. It thumped in my chest, its pace and strength increasing with a second sighting. The arms—and the person attached to them—were making a beeline for the exact place we'd told them NOT to go: the edge of the reef. There, a sly current was waiting to give the owner a fast-paced tour of the shoreline of Great Camanoe Island.

Pretty soon, my guest would be headed straight for the open Atlantic, if he could stay afloat long enough. If he happened to hit the tiny coral atoll of Anegada twenty miles away, he'd be lucky because the next thing he'd hit would be Bermuda, more than 900 miles north.

Realistically, though, the prevailing currents would likely drag him west, which is where we were headed in about half an hour. If he could just keep his head up, maybe we could pick him up along the way. Or throw a life ring over the side and drag him to our final stop, the island of Jost van Dyke, population 297.

Flippant thoughts while someone was drowning, I know, but that's just a taste of the way my sick mind works.

My name's Elizabeth Bower Jordan, by the way. Most people—including my drowning victim—know me as Lizzie.

I've never rescued a soul, but being a first mate on a tour boat requires you to play a lot of different roles—bartender, boat hand, psychologist, mediator, cruise director, bloodhound, psychic, DJ. You've just gotta run with whatever the day throws at you.

I fumbled to free my fins from the rubber band that bound them together. As my fingers flopped, my mind raced. Those long skinny old man arms could only belong to Herb, the septuagenarian from southern Connecticut whose life was about to be cut much shorter than even he imagined.

I jumped as a bright orange life ring appeared in my field of vision. I grabbed at it, my hand closing over the stiff foam in a death grip. I looked up at the captain on the other end, Ben.

"You gonna be okay?" he asked. Like the guys from San Diego, Ben was easy on the eyes, with blonde hair, blue eyes and white teeth that flashed frequently in his tanned face. A dimple on his chin and a slightly upturned nose gave his face a lighthearted look, bolstered by the fact that Ben was rarely serious. Even now, with one of our passengers fighting for his life, he was grinning at me, daring me to be scared.

Instead, I scowled at him. "Am I going to be okay? I wasn't aware there was a choice."

Ben opened his mouth to respond, but he got cut off.

"There's a man out there!" a female voice behind him exclaimed.

Aw, crap.

Now the boat was going to be in on it. There's nothing like having an audience for your first ocean rescue.

Ben held up a hand to me, indicating that he'd deal with it. I can only imagine how he planned to explain that I was the captain of the rescue squad, as improbable as it seemed. However, I knew he'd have that woman completely wrapped around his tan little pinky by the time I returned. Ben had a way with women.

He had a way of scorning them, too, but I had bigger things on my radar at the moment.

I was as ready as I'd ever be. I shuffled to the edge of the deck in my fins, pulled a mask over my face, threw the life ring off the back deck and stepped off.

The water wrapped my sun-warmed body in an chilly embrace, but I shook it off. I checked the location of Herb's arms, taking in a sharp breath as I noticed they were considerably lower in the water. I took off, scissor-kicking my legs furiously.

Even though I was cruising right over one of my favorite reefs in the British Virgin Islands, I didn't see the vivid green and pink parrotfish, their teeth scraping on the hard coral, or the school of twenty-five navy blue tang attacking an outcropping of algae or even the long, torpedo-shaped gray barracuda making slow circles through the reef, sending all of the little fish scattering into their nooks and crannies.

All I saw was the face of Herb's daughter, Lynn. She reminded me of Mrs. Lemon, my college roommate's mom. She was tall and thin with pale pink, freckled skin and short strawberry blonde hair. Lynn kept hers out of her face with a sensible haircut that framed kind green eyes couched in fine, elegant wrinkles.

I've noticed that people transform into two shapes as they age. They either acquire padding in strange places until they resemble a bean bag chair or continue to shed flesh until they resemble some variety of bird. Like her father, Lynn was on her way to becoming a stork. And not an unattractive one for her age.

On our way up to Virgin Gorda that morning, Lynn told me she'd brought Herb to St. Thomas because he used to love boats, but he'd been slowly making his world smaller and smaller since he hit his late seventies. She thought it might be one of their last vacations together. She wanted this one to be special.

The jury's still out on "special," but I'd bet today's entire tip that it would be unforgettable.

I took another sighting to locate Herb. I could see his arms cresting above the waterline, but just barely. I felt my breath catch in my throat. I kicked harder and faster.

My quads were starting to burn. I ignored them. I'd been conserving a little energy in case Herb proved to be a fighter. Right after they tell you to remain calm in an emergency, your rescue instructors will tell you that drowning victims will drown you if you're not smart about how you approach them. And then they remind you how important it is to remain calm. Helpful, that.

Considering Herb wanted to argue with just about every pirate story I told that morning—it was a first for me to have a guest raise his hand for Q&A as I was enthusiastically relaying the outrageous tale about the fisherman who found enough pirate gold in a cave to buy his own island—I figured he wouldn't be an easy rescue. I'd probably have to grab him hard. I felt a little flourish of sadistic pleasure at the thought.

I took another look at Herb, his face now completely underwater. However, I was heartened by the fact that his mask and snorkel were still on. Some people panic and tear their mask off in a desperate bid for oxygen. Chalk one up for Herbie.

I squinted through my mask. Had he gone horizontal in the water? Was he trying to float? He was kicking up a lot of whitewater, making it difficult to see exactly what he was doing. I'd have to just wing it. Wait—it looked like he was moving toward me. This complicated things.

I planned to go in life ring first, to see if he'd grab onto it. That would make my job easy. It would also keep him from closing bony claws on my shoulders, shoving me down to boost his own body upward, ducking me underwater in the process. I felt my shoulders tense as I prepared.

He looked even closer now. Was I seeing things? I'd have to get the life ring between us quickly before he shoved me below the surface—

I jerked upright as I realized he was too close for me to wedge the ring between us. I lifted my head out of the water, ready to fend him off. I had a life ring, and I was prepared to use it to save my life, as well as his.

But instead of trying to use my body as a rescue raft, Herb stopped short, pulled his head out of the water and let the snorkel drop from his mouth. "Is it time to come in?" he asked, his yellow teeth gritting between thin lips as he kicked to stay above the surface.

I was struck speechless.

Herb took this either as a sign of deafness or idiocy. He tapped his wrist with two gnarled arthritic fingers covered in brown liver spots. "What. Time. Is. It?" he asked in a booming voice that I was sure scared all of the fish off the reef below. Then I flinched as he brought his bony arms out of the water the way he had when I saw him on the boat, crossing them once over his head, then bringing them back down into the water. He bobbed as he did it, and I realized that the man was treading water.

Treading water. The man wasn't drowning. He was treading water.

It was all I could do to look at my own wrist and say, "2:30. Time to come in."

He nodded once, then put his head down and went horizontal again. His limbs started thrashing, and I thought for sure he was going to go down. I put my face in the water and realized that the man was just . . . swimming. And fast.

As I watched Herb's arms flail him back to the boat, I felt the energy drain from my body. I wanted to throw myself on the mercy of the life ring and rest. And I wanted a drink, preferably poured right down my snorkel.

However, a glance behind me revealed that I was drifting closer to the rip current at the edge of the island. I'd be the one in need of rescuing if I didn't start back for the boat, stat.

I maneuvered the life ring between the boat and me, then put my head down and started to kick. I cursed through my snorkel the whole way, my legs protesting and my lungs wheezing.

I arrived back at the boat bedraggled and irritable. Herb sat on one of the teal cushions on the back deck, his thin silver hair neatly slicked back, a green towel draped over his neck like a prizefighter. He was working on another Painkiller, our signature cocktail and a delightful blend of orange juice, pineapple juice, cream of coconut and plenty of rum. It was his fourth of the day if I was counting right. And here I was, looking like the creature from the black lagoon, breathing hard, face flushed, my auburn locks lying in hanks around my face, darkened to a dull brown by the salt water. At least my bikini was intact, which wasn't always a given.

My nerves were shot, so when a warm hand landed on my shoulder, I jumped like I'd been burned.

Lynn's face swam into view. "Thank you," she said. "He used to be a champion long-distance swimmer, but he hasn't swum like that in years. It was sweet of you to go out to him." She beamed at me, revealing a set of ever-so-slightly-buck teeth. Then she joined Herb on the cushion.

I just stared dully at them, my vision going in and out of focus, my hands and legs shaky from adrenaline and exertion. Had she seen him give the universal "help" gesture? Did she think I'd just casually stroked out there to share a sweet moment with Herb?

Later, this would all be hilarious. Or, at least, I sure as hell hoped so.

"Fresh water?" Ben said, the green nozzle of the hose in his hands. He was also in perfect array, his blue polo shirt tucked neatly into a pair of khaki shorts, his hair gently tousled.

I glared at him. He sprayed me, right in the face.

In case you've never worked on a boat, I'll let you in on a little secret. In addition to cheesy jokes, this is one of the things captains think are funny.

And I'll let you in on one other secret that most captains don't seem to know—or appreciate: Their mates rarely agree.

"Better?" he asked once the stream had stopped, the corners of his mouth tight with amusement. He knew better than to laugh outright. I think I would have charged him like a bull.

But, if nothing else, I was a professional. I stood stock still and gave him the best dead fish eye I could, then collected my strewn clothing from the back deck and vowed to get him back later.

And I vowed to have a drink that night after work.

Make that lots of drinks.

2

In the interest of full disclosure, I'll tell you that I rarely needed an excuse to head up to Island Time Pub after work.

You couldn't beat the location—or the view. It was perched right over one of the busiest harbors on the island, open to the balmy Caribbean air and gentle trade wind breezes. It also offered a perfect view of the second Virgin Island of St. John, barely four miles away, right across Pillsbury Sound. In fact, St. John was so close that you could see its weather patterns and, in turn, know exactly what was headed for you. When St. John completely disappeared behind a rain storm, you knew it was time to move away from the balcony rail or prepare for a good soaking.

In better weather, the rail offered you the chance to watch boats of all sizes return to harbor for the evening. You might be treated to the sight of a small powerboat returning with sunburned day trippers dancing drunken circles in their bathing suits around the captain as Jimmy Buffett blared; a weathered inflatable dinghy bearing a family of four back to shore after a day of monohull sailing to St. John, the father often in a khaki Columbia fishing shirt/hat combo—and sometimes the wife, too, or a fishing boat in pristine condition, its stainless gleaming even after a day at sea, its tall tuna tower bearing the little flags that report their marlin catches for the day and its crew tanned to a caramel crisp and ready for that night's dose of Jägermeister.

It all made for a very satisfying close to the day, especially with a cold beer in one's hand, preferably a Presidente.

Although the company at the bar wasn't nearly as breathtaking as the view, it was at least familiar. I saw the same faces at Island Time that I waved to out on the water, each with their own shade of tan betraying how often they'd been working lately.

Island Time was the place where the day's "yachting for dollars" stories got exchanged: whose boat hit the bottom in the shallows at Foxy's that day, who tied up their boat like a total idiot ("If you don't know how to tie knots, tie lots.") and who had taken bikini models/Playboy bunnies/hot cougar moms out for the day.

That sundowner beer was all I thought about as I cleaned the boat that night, especially when I checked my phone and saw no messages from Dave.

I shook my head. It wasn't like him, but maybe I didn't know him as well as I thought I did.

Ben and I divvied up the cash from that day—$200 each, not bad—but it didn't improve my mood for the drive to Red Hook.

I was at Island Time often enough that Detroit Jake, the tall gangly bartender from (you guessed it) Detroit, poured an Absolut Citron and soda, splash of cranberry, as soon as he saw me crest the top of the stairs.

Detroit Jake wasn't alone in his nickname. We don't do last names down here. We do occupations or affectations. In addition to Detroit Jake, we have Scuba Steve, Franklyn the Mechanic, Crash . . . the list goes on. I'm usually Redheaded Lizzie or Boatie Lizzie on my good days.

On my bad days, I don't want to know what they call me.

iPhones and Facebook were changing that to some degree, but everything moves on island time down here, even change.

"The look on your face," Jake said as he squeezed a lime wedge into my drink, "told me that it's not a Presidente kind of day." He pushed it toward me with long, spindly fingers.

Jake looked like he'd been stretched on a rack when he was shaped, his face long and gaunt no matter how many slices of pizza he ate from the kitchen, leaving his poor ears flapping out in the breeze. His skinny hips and bony butt hid under baggy cargo shorts, which always looked dangerously close to falling right off him. Like many of the bartenders on the island, his complexion remained a pale white from too many hours behind a bar and too few in the Caribbean sunshine.

He smiled at me. "Besides, a hero like you deserves a drink." His blue eyes sparkled.

I paused for a second, my straw an inch from my lips. There was no way they could already know about today.

Could they?

This was St. Thomas. Of course they could. The coconut telegraph, that informal person-to-person game of telephone which made everyone's private business public, was the fastest, most efficient thing on this island.

I dropped my head back and groaned. "How the hell did you hear about that? It's only 6:03."

He tilted his head toward a blue-shirted captain who was wearing the same outfit Ben had been wearing earlier, although he wore it a few sizes larger. I figured he also probably had to adjust his hat nightly to accommodate his ego, which was also constantly expanding.

He called himself Cappy. God only knows what his real name was. When his boat guests would ask whether that was short for "Captain," he'd always reply with, "Well, it ain't the name I was born with!" Then he would laugh a huge belly laugh and slap his knee.

That was Cappy, always full of non-sequiturs that he thought were hilarious but left everyone else puzzled.

Cappy was one of the many white boat captains who moved down from the continental U.S. to live in St. Thomas, as was Ben. On the boats we worked, there were only a few Virgin Islanders at the helm. By the way—and contrary to popular belief—arriving on island with an intention to stay didn't make you an instant Virgin Islander. Being "bahn here" pretty much did.

That said, those who were born on St. Thomas descended from people who arrived to these islands in all kinds of different ways. Some were the ancestors of Africans who had been brought to this island as slaves. Some were the children of people who moved from other Caribbean nations like St. Lucia, St. Barths and Dominica, while still other families arrived from elsewhere, with the U.S. and Europe leading the charge. On St. Thomas, I knew white people who were born on the island and black people from Texas. The island was a major intersection point for folks from all over, and if you wanted to know where someone was from, you had to ask. It made for interesting bar stool chatter, if you're into that sort of thing. (Which I happen to be.)

"I'll save you!" Cappy's poor imitation of what I could only assume was my voice dragged me back to Island Time. Then he looked at his buddies and laughed that laugh. He thought he was so hilarious—even more so after a few cocktails. His moon-shaped face was even ruddier than usual with glee.

I glared at him.

He continued with absolutely no regard for my mood. "Might want to read that article that's going around about how drowning don't look like you think. Might save you some trouble next time."

I opened my mouth to make a sharp reply, but I felt a tap on my shoulder.

I spun around and barked, "What?!?" into the face of the person who had touched me.

It was Ben. Jesus Christ, hadn't he done enough today?

"I gotta talk to you," he said, white knuckling his iPhone in his right hand while his other hand reached for a Heineken that Jake already had on the bar.

I jerked my thumb over at Cappy. "Sounds like you've talked enough today."

He looked over my shoulder, his eyes squinting. I took it as a sign of guilt. "Yeah, sorry."

"It's not like he needs more ammunition to give me a hard time."

He suddenly looked thoughtful. "Hey, how much did you give that old guy to drink today?"

"You mean Herb?" I took a hard hit of my drink and arched an eyebrow at him. "I didn't overdo it. You know some of the girls like to put an extra bottle in the mix, but I actually follow the recipe."

"One of your rules?"

"I just hate dealing with drunks," I said, staring at his beer.

He smirked at me and I could see his mouth start to open with a new retort. It shut quickly. Then I saw a small furrow appear between his sun-bleached eyebrows. "I really need to talk," he said.

I held back my most sarcastic reply. I needed to get better about that. Maturity and all. Preserving work relationships as sacred.

And, truly, it wasn't that I didn't like Ben. We were friends, and he was one of the captains I enjoyed working with. But there was no way I would ever tell him so. It would jack up his ego to ungodly levels. But I could make a small concession here.

I flipped my hand over, palm up. *Go ahead.*

"I met this girl two nights ago—"

I groaned. "Really? It's bad enough when I have to listen to the tourist-of-the-week story when I'm being paid to work with you. At the bar, it's strictly leisure time for me." I held up my pointer finger. "Actually, wait, when you start dating a girl who doesn't already have a ticket out of here, then—and only then—will I be your Dear Abby."

Ben put a hand on my shoulder. "Trust me, this is different."

I rolled my eyes and looked pointedly at his hand. "What, because you're in looooove? Does she have a ticket, or doesn't she?"

But before I could fire off another one, Ben's hand dropped listlessly off my shoulder, and I saw something change in his eyes. Maybe it was sincerity, or maybe I caught a glimpse of what all those girls were chasing: sad blue eyes under knitted eyebrows set against tanned skin. A sensitive man against the elements, tough on the outside, marshmallowy on the inside.

Barf.

Still, I let him continue.

Whatever overtook me, I just want to say this: I wish I could take it back and keep this whole mess from happening.

Instead, I actually *asked* him to continue. Big mistake.

Ben brightened considerably at the prospect of pouring his sad little heart out to me. "I met this girl at Duffy's yesterday. Andrea."

I groaned.

"No, no, no, wait," he said.

"Mmm-hmmm?"

"She was with her friends, visiting from D.C."

I waved my right hand in a circle impatiently. This was still sounding like the conquest stories of the old Ben.

"We were dancing, having fun, you know, and then I said, 'Let's go to XO so we can do something a little quieter.' She said okay, so we went in and had a drink. I asked her to come home with me—"

"The vomit is rising in the back of my throat."

"Lizzie."

"Get to the point."

"She went back over to Duffy's to tell her friends that she was coming home with me, and she never came back."

I waited for him to continue, but he just stood there and took another swig of his Heineken.

"Okay, so some girl ditched you at Duffy's. I'm sure rejection like that is hard for a stud like you. And . . . ?"

"I knew she was at the Ritz. I asked one of the towel guys on the beach to look for her today, just to make sure she was okay."

"You mean, 'just to stalk her,' right?"

"Lizzie."

"My patience is wearing thin." I sucked the last of my drink through the straw. I shook the plastic cup—affectionately known on the island as "Caribbean crystal"—at him. "And my drink is empty. We're at a delicate juncture."

He sighed, then grabbed the cup out of my hand. He upended his Heineken to finish it—in sympathy, I supposed—and nodded his head at Detroit Jake.

While Jake poured, I pulled out my phone, a laughably old, scarred pink Motorola Razr that belonged in a flip phone museum, and scrolled to the name "Dave." I cast a glance over at Ben to see if he was observing my texting, as he often did.

But he was staring over at St. John, lost in thought. That was a first.

My thumbs paused over the keypad for a second. Then, I dashed out a message: *What are you up to tonight?* I slammed my phone shut just in time to accept a new cocktail with my right hand.

Ben gave me a look. "Got better things to do?"

"Honestly? Yes."

"Will you just *listen*?"

"Mmmm-hmmm," I said as I sucked straight citrus vodka through the straw. I was having trouble finding the club soda or the cranberry juice in my drink. Apparently, Jake thought I was looking for a drink that packed a punch.

"So my friend at the Ritz saw her friends. Just the two of them on the beach today. No Andrea."

"So she went home with someone else and you're jealous." I shrugged.

He reached out and grabbed my shoulder hard. "Lizzie. He went and talked to them. They said she went home with me."

His grip tightened, and I knocked his hand away. "You're hurting me," I said. I took a step back, my body tensing like a runner at the starting line.

He raised his hand in apology. "I'm sorry, Lizzie. I'm sorry. I'm freaking out."

I took a breath. My heart was pounding, but, with some effort, I refocused my gaze. This was just Ben. He didn't mean anything by it. But knowing what he knew about me, he should be more careful.

He read me quickly. "Lizzie, I'm sorry. Please. You're the only person I can talk to about this."

I took a deep breath. *You're fine, Lizzie. You're with Ben. You're in St. Thomas.* I felt my heart slow again, and I resumed my place at the bar. However, I left a few extra inches between us.

I set my drink down on a coaster that Jake had so thoughtfully left for me. "So let me get this straight. This girl—"

"Andrea."

"Andrea. Her friends thought she went with you, and you thought she went with them."

He nodded.

"So no one knows where she is."

He nodded again.

"What did your towel guy say to them?"

"Nothing more than shooting the shit about their night. He told me he played it cool."

I rubbed my forehead with my left hand, willing my brain to think faster. The hamsters running the wheels in there were hitting the hard stuff right along with me. "Wait, her friends just left her and went home?"

"Because they thought she went home with me."

"Some friends."

"Lizzie, this was yesterday, and she still hasn't turned up."

"As far as you know."

"As far as I know."

"Ben, it's, what, twenty paces from XO to Duffy's? And how many people are there in the parking lot on any given night? There's always a crowd of spectators, leaning on cars and watching the action. It's not as though someone can just disappear against her will with no one noticing. My guess is that she ditched you."

He leaned forward, closing the distance between us, giving me a chance to look at his face in extreme close-up. He really was classically good-looking, although he did have a small scar on his upper lip. A car accident, if I remembered correctly. I think he told girls he got it on a motorcycle. He also had a couple of broken blood vessels in his right cheek that I'd never noticed before.

Even so, it was an earnest face that lacked for nothing in the charm department. The only flaw I saw in Ben—well, okay, besides the whole gunning-for-tourists thing—was that he could be a little too slick for his own good. When you watch the same smooth act day in and day out, it can get tiresome. I willed myself not to fall for it.

"Something's not right, Lizzie," he said. "Maybe I'm wrong. But if I'm not, you know this is all going to fall on me."

"Ben, come on. People don't disappear down here. This island is too small."

"Aruba. Natalee Holloway."

"If you're telling me that you're some kind of Joran van der Sloot, I don't want to know."

"Be serious. That wasn't that long ago."

"I am. Look, I'm sorry. What else can I say? It's probably just some big misunderstanding." I blinked twice. I could feel the top part of my head start to feel light. The vodka was talking to me now.

"Do me a favor?"

I lifted my eyebrows, but I didn't say anything.

"Go over there, and see if she's okay."

"What? No."

"I just need to know what I'm dealing with. Maybe she met someone else in the parking lot and went home with him, instead of me. Maybe she's rolling up to the Ritz right now with bed head from shacking up with him. Or maybe she's hiding out at the hotel, avoiding me. But I need to know because if she's not back, this is going to get bad fast. You know how the cops are down here."

"Why me? Why not just do it yourself?"

"I'd just make it worse."

"You know my rule. I don't get involved." I lifted my glass as though to toast him. "I just drink my drinks and go home. It's the only way to be, and I should know." My tone was light, but I felt my stomach do a little somersault, remembering the last time I decided to take a stand. It didn't end well.

His eyebrows came together and rose up like a pair of praying hands. "I just need you to take a quick look. Get a lay of the land. Maybe ask some questions. You're good with people, even though you like to fake like you're not." I scowled at him. This was flattery of the baldest kind. I'd like to believe it was true, but this was *Ben* who was talking. The man would say anything to a woman to get what he wanted. "Besides," he continued, "you're a girl. They'll open up to you."

"You're laying it on kind of thick."

"What about that time I helped you move? You told me two trips, max, and I spent all day moving your shit."

"That not the same thing at all."

"What do you mean?"

"We're talking about a missing girl, not team-lifting a crappy futon. Besides, I can't go, not in the state I'm about to be in."

He exhaled slowly. "Tomorrow morning. Bar tab with your name on it here at the end of the day. Just go and see if she's all right and report back. That's it." He checked his watch and tipped his Heineken up again. "I gotta go."

"If I were you, I'd probably head home, if this this week's track record is any indicator."

I heard a voice pipe up behind me. "He's coming to El Cubano with me to play some pool. You wanna come?" Cappy appeared on my left, just a little too close for comfort. Personal space wasn't a field in which he excelled.

"There are so many things wrong with that sentence."

Cappy laughed that laugh again. I had to hand it to the man. He almost never took my barbs personally. He mock saluted at Ben before starting toward the stairs to the garage. "See you there, chief."

Cappy paused at the top of the stairs and pointed a finger at me. "I'll send you that article. Gotta know what drowning people look like. Safety first!" He tipped his cap and laughed again. I sighed.

I reached out an arm to stop Ben before he followed Cappy like an eager puppy. "Ben, I don't know about this."

"El Cubano? We go there all the time."

I sighed. "No, these girls. Me going to the Ritz. I can't make any promises."

"Just think about it, Lizzie. Proof of life. Maybe a couple of questions. Turn on your Lizzie charm. That's it, no more."

I took one more sip of my drink to buy me some time. "No promises," I finally said. It was the best I could come up with.

He nodded once, but I could see the disappointment in his face.

"Just one more question, though," I said.

His eyebrows popped. "Nice move, Columbo. About Andrea?"

I shook my head. "No, no, no. Is 'playing pool' a euphemism for paying one of the ladies at El Cubano to make your night?"

He rolled his eyes.

"Don't roll your eyes at me. I really want to know what you guys do there. You say you just smoke cigars and shoot pool, but do you really need a bordello for a venue?"

"Best pool tables on island. Plus, Cappy always has Cubans. Nothing like a Cuban. Let me know what you find out."

I opened my mouth to protest, but he started to walk away.

"I'm texting you their hotel info," he said, and then he was gone before I could get in another word.

I leaned against the bar and drained the rest of my drink. Now it was my turn to stare at St. John and chew on everything Ben had told me. The music and the chatter were getting steadily louder around me, but I only noticed it in passing. My phone buzzed, and I jumped.

It was Ben, texting me the girls' room number.

I wondered briefly how he'd gotten it. *Ben's got friends all over the island*, I grumbled to myself.

I dialed into work to see if they needed me tomorrow. I felt a little trickle of anxiety in my chest. I'd managed to piss off the boat's owner after miscounting how many small souvenir T-shirts we had on the boat last week. They made a ton of money selling those things, so losing one was pretty much a felony in our world.

She kept reminding me of my offense by skipping me in the work rotation.

She'd allowed me to work today, though, so maybe I'd finally gotten out of first mate jail.

There was also a big part of me that wanted an excuse to avoid getting tangled in Ben's business.

I could already hear myself saying the words to him. "Sorry, man, I have to work." He would understand. It was the golden excuse down here. An extra shift meant extra money, and pretty much everyone needed money. Plus, when the owner gods offered you work, you took it, lest you anger them and find yourself seriously underemployed, as I had the last few days.

As the office manager cheerily told me I had the day off, the trickle did a little dance in my chest. I'd made rent for the month, but just barely. And my next credit card payment was coming up fast. Another shift on the boat would have really helped.

Finances aside, it looked like Ben's errand had bounced back in my court. That look on his face when I'd refused to commit hit me right in the guilty bone, one I hadn't really even realized I had before tonight.

I shook the ice in my drink, trying to dislodge a few extra molecules of vodka. I had the whole day tomorrow to either do Ben a solid or feel guilty about letting him down. I tried to look for a silver lining, something I hadn't really known how to do before I got here. Maybe playing Nancy Drew would suit me. It certainly was starting to feel like I'd worn out my welcome on the boat, at least where the owner was concerned.

A detective, I scoffed. I hated it when people poked into my business, but I'd always been a bit of a snoop, if I was honest about it. When I walked by a house with wide-open windows, you can bet I snuck a peek to see what my fellow humans were up to.

People also had a tendency to spill their secrets to me, either on the barstool or on the boat. I didn't know whether it was my face or my willingness to listen to the completely outrageous with nothing more than an affirmative murmur and a blank face. Or maybe it was the booze.

Someone slammed a can of beer down on the bar, and it brought me back to the bar. I cast a glance around and saw no real excuse to stick around.

I checked my own state of sobriety. The first drink had started to work on me, but the second cup of vodka was still humming in the distance, like a faraway freight train. I wanted to get home before it flattened me to the rails.

"How much do I owe you, Jake?" I asked as he passed by. He waved a hand in my direction, either meaning he'd decided to comp me or that he'd put my drinks on Ben's tab. I was a happy girl either way. I left a five on the bar, then headed down to the basement to retrieve the death trap I call a car.

The Suzuki was only ten years old, but it looked at least twenty. The body was dented on most of the panels as though it had been attacked by a crew of men wielding sledgehammers. All the gloss of the clear coat had weathered away by the sun and salt air, and the white body paint was peeling around the edges. The front right wheel threatened to fall off at any minute. Or, at least, that's how it looked to me, although my mechanic, Garfield, laughed at me when I told him so. Soon come, but not yet—or so he said.

My little Suzuki ran well, though, as long as I put a gallon of water into it at least once a month. Must have been a radiator leak somewhere, but who has the patience to track those things down? Oh, and I really had to stomp on the brakes to get her to stop. But that didn't matter. On this island, you rarely got up above thirty miles an hour.

I got in and fastened my seatbelt because that's what mattered down here. Go ahead and chat on your cell phone. And, if you're thirsty, drink a beer. Just make sure you've got your seatbelt on because they'll ticket you for that.

I guided my car slowly out of the marina parking lot,

dodging a herd of fisherman in their white, long-sleeved T-shirts.

I paused at the top of the driveway. The road home was left. The road to El Cubano was right, although I imagined I'd never set foot in there.

Another option sat straight in front of me: the graded driveway that led to the parking lot that housed Duffy's Love Shack, the scene of the girl's supposed disappearance.

Andrea, I reminded myself. *She has a name.*

That vodka freight train in my veins blew its whistle, and I knew it wouldn't be long before I needed to get off the road. But something compelled me to take a quick ride through the parking lot. I'm not sure if I was expecting Andrea to jump out and throw herself on my windshield, but I guess my curiosity got the better of me.

I coaxed my car up the steep grade, whose scarred blacktop told the tales of other cars who'd previously scratched their way to the summit.

The shopping center at the top of the driveway was a white concrete slab strip mall that would have looked at home in any 1980s American suburb.

By day, it bustled with people going in and out of the insurance agency, bank and homegrown mail center (because you certainly didn't want to suffer the official USPS down here if you didn't have to).

By night, its two bars dominated. At the end of the strip sat XO, the wine and martini bar where Ben and Andrea had their final drink. Smack dab in the middle of the parking lot, you'd find Duffy's, an open air tiki bar whose wooden tables and plastic lawn chairs sat directly on the black pavement.

It was still early, only 6:30 or so. By the time the dark rolled in, Duffy's would be pulsing with everything from Jimmy Buffett to the latest Rihanna hit, the tables crowded with tourists and a particular kind of man prowling around. Mostly the kind who liked watching young girls dance—the dirty old man crowd repackaged for Caribbean habitation.

I was also pretty sure the parking lot was a thinly disguised open air drug market, with pot the most likely drug of choice. Pot and drugs of any kind were not a part of my world anymore. No exceptions.

Well, alcohol was the exception, but that was different, in my book. Another one of my "little rules," I guess.

I rolled through the parking lot slowly, my gaze slipping over faces that ran the gamut of hues—just-got-off-the-plane white, dark brown with a copper cast, formerly white but sunburned to a crisp, light yellow-brown and dark, rich umber. I lifted a few fingers off the steering wheel to those I recognized.

There were plenty I didn't. If you worked on a boat out of the East End, I'd know you by sight, if not by name, and you'd probably get a finger wave. Boater's rules apply even on land, as far as I was concerned. But I rarely hung out with the people who lived and worked around the capital of Charlotte Amalie, just a few miles away. They were much more likely to catch a drink at Betsy's in Frenchtown or Sib's, rather than traveling all the way to Red Hook. St. Thomas was small town life made even smaller by the bizarre way that people stuck close to home.

As I drove, I scanned the sixty feet between Duffy's dance floor and the tinted door that led to XO. *Where did you go, girl?*

Nothing popped out at me. To the left, I saw the usual row of cars parked head-in with two shiny taxi vans blocking them in, waiting for tourists to stumble out and head back to their resorts. To the right, two white girls in tank tops and shorts were standing outside the XO door. (Insider tip: It looks like a "push" door, but it's really a "pull.")

They glanced at me as I cruised by. I was tempted to pull over and ask them if they'd been around last night, but I kept moving. The strip mall ended with a Banco Popular ATM, followed by a dumpster and three secluded parking spots, sometimes four if people were feeling bold enough to crowd the dumpster.

I found myself at the road. I paused. Should I go back and talk to those girls?

The vodka must be getting the better of me. Who did I think I was, Kojak? I hadn't even decided if I was going to do Ben's little errand tomorrow. And, besides, as far as I knew, Andrea might even be home now, telling the tale of some wildly charming island man she met in the Duffy's parking lot who whisked her away for an evening she'd never forget.

I fervently wished it to be true. I hoped it was all some big misunderstanding, like I'd suggested to Ben. But there was a part of me, a cynical one maybe, or one born of experience, that couldn't quite get on board.

I decided to turn home, guiding my car to the left side of the road, the side we drive on down here. They say it has to do with donkey carts. I'm pretty sure there's some stubbornness involved, too. The stickers inside the rental cars say it best: Keep left. Honk often.

As I headed out of Red Hook, my mind was already working on an unflattering picture of Andrea's friends. I imagined them in those skintight dresses that look like ace bandages, their faces affected with an expression that was half boredom, half contempt.

"They just left without her," I murmured. I usually listened to the radio. I favored 104.3, the Buzz, but I wasn't in the mood for rock tonight. I drove in silence.

I passed a fruit and fish stand on the right, a rickety booth made mostly of plywood and 2x4s coated with purple and yellow paint that had faded to pastels under the Caribbean sun.

I caught a snatch of raucous laughter from a guy called the Red Man as I drove by. It sent a shiver up my spine. All I knew about him was that he sold fish, that his skin was a reddish brown under a crown of spiky bleached dreadlocks—hence his nickname—and that he said hello to me like he knew me intimately every time we passed each other down at the docks. He might have been the nicest man in the world. I didn't know. But his overly familiar greetings hinted that I didn't want to know him any better than I already did.

I took the left turn right after his shack. I shivered again as I merged onto the empty road.

I was musing about how odd it is to catch a chill in 80-degree weather when something flashed at the right side of my car, streaking about a foot or so in front of my hood. I slammed on the brakes and felt that damn right wheel lock on me. I gritted my teeth and hoped for the best as I felt the back end of my car skid around in a half circle and finally shudder to a stop.

What the hell was that? My head swiveled from side to side. Nothing. My heart was banging against my chest. I had the whole road to myself. That was a good thing because my car was splayed across both lanes at an angle, pointing back toward Red Hook.

I flexed my hands on the steering wheel. My palms were wet. I took a deep breath and gauged my sobriety. Pretty okay—but I needed to get home as soon as I could.

I gripped the wheel with slick hands and gently tapped on the gas. The car shuddered forward. I gingerly coaxed the car into the left shoulder, made of packed dirt and stones, bordered by a wall of native Caribbean brush. I peered across the road and into the tangle. Because we use left-drive cars here, I was peering over the empty seat, then across the road. I couldn't see a thing.

I drummed my fingers on the steering wheel. Then I jumped out. I wanted to know what flashed by my car.

I stood on the shoulder, looking into the vegetation. I hesitated. The brush was dense here since this land bordered the tiny St. Thomas National Park. I saw skinny trees mixed with squat bushes whose branches stretched wildly in just about every direction available to them. I couldn't see it, but experience told me that there was also some kind of plant with secret spines just waiting to wrap its tentacles around my leg.

I listened for thrashing in the brush, but I heard nothing. The sun goes down quickly here in what we refer to as a "cartoon sunset," so it was getting hard to see more than a few feet ahead.

I realized my knees were shaking. I flexed my quads in a vain attempt to stop them, but the harder I flexed, the harder they knocked.

I heard a rustle and I jumped, but nothing appeared. I wrapped my arms around myself as the shakes engulfed me.

I opened my mouth. I thought I was going to say "hello?" but what came out was "Andrea?" There was no way whatever ran past my car could have been a person. Could it?

I took a few steps into the bush and hesitated. I thought I saw what looked like a small path amidst the tangle. At some point, it would probably become impassible—or I would simply end up with a leg full of stickers.

I took a step forward.

I heard a crackle ahead of me, and I froze.

"Andrea?" I whispered. Another crackle. I shivered again and tightened my arms around myself, my hands making the unpleasant discovery that my armpits were soaked. I still didn't release my aggressive hug.

What if I solved this problem right here and now through a piece of dumb luck? I imagined a girl emerging from the bush, her alabaster skin scratched and bruised, her dark hair in complete disarray, but otherwise fine. I noted that, in the absence of a picture of Andrea, she looked a little like Disney's Snow White in a sun dress. Maybe the seven Caribbean dwarves had been offering her shelter.

I took another step and called her name again—then I screamed as a doe plunged out into the open. It wheeled around in a mad turn, then bolted for the National Park and its mangroves.

I laughed manically, releasing my arms and covering my face with my hands. A deer. I had just been scared out of my mind by a deer.

Some detective I'd make. I rocked back and forth for a few minutes with nervous laughter, trying to catch my breath. The air felt thin and I was getting woozy. I sank to the ground, pulling my legs to my chest and feeling my heart pound against my thighs.

When I felt sure I wasn't going to pass out, I rose slowly and wiped my streaming eyes with the backs of my hands.

I reached the road as a beat-up maroon pickup rolled up on the opposite side of the street, next to my Suzuki. The driver, a white man with a weathered face that I didn't recognize, leaned across an empty passenger seat to ask if I was okay.

I wasn't sure, but I told him I was anyway.

He raised a hand and slipped down the hill. I trotted across the road and into my car, my hands still trembling.

Why had I called out Andrea's name? Andrea was at the Ritz, probably showering off the day's suntan lotion in a marble shower, her entire being focused on which sundress to wear to dinner that night.

But if I truly believed that, why hadn't I gone right up to the Ritz tonight? And why was I hedging with Ben?

I wasn't sober enough to answer these questions. It was time to get home.

I took a cautious U-turn. All the wheels seemed to be working, so I headed for my little cottage.

Time to figure out whether that bottle of whiskey at home still had a shot left in it.

3

I live down a road that looks like a driveway. By some twist of Virgin Islands logic, it's only paved for about twenty feet off the main road, then it turns to deeply rutted dirt with the occasional tire-eating volcanic rock strewn about. The brush along both sides constantly threatens to take the road back. Every now and then I get so tired of the branches whacking my car that I get out my own machete and beat back the long spindly fingers of the native greenery.

You might think I'm kidding about the machete, but no household in St. Thomas is complete without one, which people charmingly pronounce "ma-SHET." You know, no big deal. Just your garden variety, razor-sharp blade that's the size of your right arm.

They've got a stack of them at Home Depot. Might as well hand them out at the airport along with your shot of rum, as far as I'm concerned.

Bushwhacking my own driveway is the price I pay for seclusion. It's worth it.

This crazy road leads me right up to the guest cottage I occupy. No one sees me come and go. I can barely see the main house from mine because my landlord is letting the bush take over his back yard.

I found this place on the bulletin board at the mail service. After getting directions over the phone, I found the main house easily.

But that was only where the journey began. He was "out back" he'd told me, so I had started by weaving through an obstacle course of construction tools and detritus in the driveway—a table saw, a circular saw, a haphazard stack of 2x4s, a pile of warped tar paper roof shingles, a rusty axe head.

Next, I traversed a rickety wooden walkway—the boards rotting in places and the handrail unreliable—while dodging palm fronds and bougainvillea offshoots. I nearly turned back. There was no way I was going to live in Grey Gardens with this weirdo.

However, when I saw the orange sherbet cottage peek out from behind the bush, I felt my resolve soften. Orange wasn't a color I would have chosen, but it had a plucky charm.

I entered the cottage to find an almost completely open floor plan with a nook for my bed, a full kitchen with no roommates to fill the sink with dirty dishes, a vaulted ceiling, a wall of windows that overlooked the marina and my own personal bathroom with a huge shower. It also came with a few cobwebs, some resident flying cockroaches and a rat-sized hole behind the stove, but every rose has its thorn, right?

When I discovered that the cottage had a back entrance via the half-paved road, I gave my new landlord, Bernard, a deposit on the spot.

Once I moved in, I discovered a delicious seclusion I hadn't known in a while. I can barely hear Bernard, and Bernard can barely hear me. If I want to play that sad, depressing Sheryl Crow album, *The Globe Sessions*, and howl along with her at 2:00 am, it's my prerogative.

However, on a night like tonight, I wished for a little less seclusion and a little more company.

I pulled to the side of the road into the dirt patch that served as my parking spot. It was pitch black. I must have forgotten to leave the outside light on.

I did have a tiny little penlight attached to my keychain. Although it kept me from tripping on the uneven path that led up to the cottage, it didn't really illuminate my surroundings.

But, truly, I would have needed a set of floodlights to dispel the feeling that had descended upon me, one that was making my skin crawl.

My best friend in this situation would be speed. I grabbed my backpack and arranged my keys so that my penlight was shining forward, with my door key tucked in between my index and middle finger, a trick I'd learned in a women's self-defense class in high school.

Then I ran. I pushed my car door open, slammed it behind me and bolted up the rough-hewn path. I heard a rustling in the bush as I sprinted, but I rounded the corner without slowing down to investigate.

Mercifully, I didn't fumble the keys, and I got my door open quickly. When I slammed it shut behind me and threw the deadbolt, I exhaled. With bars on every window, I felt safe. Any stray deer with murder in its heart would have to look elsewhere to get its thrills tonight.

I flipped the main light on, illuminating the entire place. Nothing looked amiss. I checked behind the shower curtain and the couch—a Martha Stewart futon I bought from Kmart. Only then did I feel safe enough to search for that whiskey.

The aforementioned bottle turned out to be Dewar's, which is technically scotch and which is apparently different for reasons that make sense every time I Google it but slip right out of my mind as soon as I take my first sip.

I had two sad-looking ice cubes in my freezer, mere slivers of their former selves. I put them in a coffee mug, then poured myself about half a mug of scotch.

This left a whisper in the bottle, which I dispatched by slugging it.

I glanced at the television, which wasn't anything more than a box connected to my DVD player. I half-heartedly flipped through the discs I'd collected, many from friends who were leaving island and shedding possessions. Nothing caught my eye.

I wandered over to my desk. I turned on my laptop, which was the nicest thing I owned. I'd bought it after a great season the year before and treated myself to my very own Internet connection. Getting the Internet installed took almost as long as getting the laptop shipped down from the States—and the Internet was only as reliable as the power, which wasn't saying much. But at least I could use Facebook to stalk my stateside exes and the girls I went to high school with at my leisure.

I took a glance at my "coffee," thinking about the vodka in my belly. Mixing alcohols usually got me into trouble. I took a sip anyway, deciding that this would be an experiment for science, for America and for mankind—actually, make that womankind.

Yeah, I was getting a little loopy.

I brought up Google. I wasn't exactly sure what I was after, but I had some time on my hands, as well as a big question mark hanging in the air. Maybe Google had some answers. I typed in "girl missing on island." Natalee Holloway was the first story to come up. I knew that one pretty well, so I only skimmed the first article. She disappeared after a night of bar hopping with three guys. Her body hadn't yet been found.

I took another sip of scotch and contemplated that. What a way to go. You think you're going to a fun island to have a boozy graduation trip with your friends. You not only never come home, you disappear entirely. I started to wonder what my family would do. Would they fly down like the Holloways? Or would they just shrug and go on with their lives?

Probably the latter.

This was dangerous territory. I didn't want to think about my family, not in the state I was in. I felt the old feelings mill start to grind, and I tried putting it to a halt with a click on another article on Natalee's unfortunate disappearance.

As I scanned the words, my mind drifted toward places that van der Sloot could have ditched a body on an island. I felt the prickles of gooseflesh on my arms. I grabbed a sweatshirt off a nearby dining room chair, took another sip of scotch.

Back to the search results.

Google had taken the island part of my query literally, so I got a result from Staten Island, where a teenage girl went missing a few blocks from her house. She was apparently headed for a "behavioral health facility"—was that code for rehab?—and didn't want to go. She came home later that week. Case closed.

Ah, here was one from a tropical island like mine. A sixteen-year-old girl had gone missing in Hawai'i, only to turn up a month and a half later. The article gave no further explanation for either her disappearance or reappearance. I studied her photo. She had memorable features that could easily have made her a model. Her light brown face was framed with sun-streaked brown hair that flowed gracefully over her shoulders. There were a few freckles scattered across her nose and a dimple in her right cheek that showed as she gave the camera a bright smile. There was an ease about her that spoke of beauty without much of a regimen.

I stared at her face. *Where did you go? And why didn't you tell anyone? What made you run away from the people who loved you?*

Sometimes, the people who say they love you aren't always the best people for you, I guess. I should know. I took another big slug of scotch.

Before I knew it, I was on Facebook, looking at the profile picture of my sister, Julia. We weren't friends on Facebook, not anymore. Her public profile told the story she wanted people to see. She was one half of the perfect couple, at ease and in love. She and her husband, Jacob, smiled broadly, his arm slung over her shoulder. They stood on a bright green lawn at what looked like someone's backyard party. It could have been their backyard. I didn't know. And I could see the way his fingers gripped the cap of her shoulder. There was nothing casual about it.

Sometimes Julia did look like her picture, with pin-straight blonde hair falling perfectly to her jawline, ivory skin, her features delicate, almost pixie-like. I always wanted the big blue eyes she got from our mother's side, but mine came out brown.

We were only a year apart, but the distance felt much greater. She always seemed more put together than I was—effortlessly. If our lives were a musical theater production, she would have been the beautiful, dainty soprano. I couldn't compete, so I chose a different role: the brassy, belty alto who delivers the comic relief, sometimes at my own expense.

I was happy when she met Jacob a few years after college. I really was. "Julia and Jacob" just sounded right, almost perfect.

It wasn't. It became clear very quickly that he dealt drugs. And did drugs sometimes. Soon, Julia was doing them too.

Sure, I was at some of those parties, the ones they threw in the townhouse they bought just a few miles from my parents. I figured it was safe. If I was going to do drugs, why not do them around people I knew and loved?

I experimented. Julia fell down a hole. When I tried to talk to her about it, I was being uptight. I needed to chill out.

She gave me a pill once that she said would help me "chill out," in her words. She was my big sister, so I just swallowed it. I didn't know what it was and I didn't ask, not until my skin began to crawl about a half an hour later. With chills running up and down my body, I grabbed her arm and demanded to know what she'd given me.

"Relax, Lizzie, it's just a little Ecstasy."

I exploded. Why didn't she tell me it was Ecstasy? Did she think this was funny, to drug her sister?

She just laughed, and so did the friends draped on the couches around her like a pride of lions on the savannah.

All my rage over a lifetime of being cast as her funny man poured out.

They only laughed harder.

But that wasn't when I left. I stuck around to watch as she'd go on bender after bender, spending days in her basement, the lights on low, the TV on high, her hair lanky and unwashed. She'd call into work and tell them she was sick. It wasn't a lie, exactly.

"She'll pull out of it," Jacob would say, and he always seemed to have a pharmacological answer. Jacob only smoked pot, for the record. Never touched the hard stuff, but that didn't stop him from feeding it to Julia. I wasn't sure whether it was meth or heroin or what. I was afraid to ask.

He wasn't entirely wrong. She'd perk up suddenly, clean like a maniac and show up on time for work for a few weeks, sometimes even a few months. Then the cycle would begin again.

After a year of watching, I staged an intervention, sister to sister. Jacob was supposed to be out. I sat in the basement with her, trying not to make a face at the stink that wafted from her body. I offered to drive her to rehab. I offered to take her over to Mom and Dad's. They'd help us find a solution. I told her it didn't have to be like this.

Jacob heard the whole thing. He waited in the kitchen and jumped out at me, wrenching an arm behind my back and pulling me close. He growled threats in my ear, told me to leave his wife alone.

I wasn't in the mood to take anyone's shit, and I told him so. That's when he pulled the knife, putting its point under my jawline, right where the tips of Julia's beautiful hair rested on her. He told me he had people who could make me disappear if I kept bothering Julia.

I was stunned. I didn't fight. I couldn't flee. I froze.

I can't remember much of the rest of what he said to me, but I do remember the way he pushed me away from him. I stumbled and almost fell. A last-minute grab at a kitchen chair kept me from nosediving face-first into their tile floor. But I kept my feet under me, and I made it to my car, my hands too unsteady to turn the key in the ignition, so I just sat there.

I probably should have gone straight to my parents, showed them the tiny cut under my chin. But I went home instead and drank beer until I passed out.

The next day, I convinced myself it didn't matter.

It wasn't until family dinner at my parents' the next week that I discovered how much it did matter. I started shaking as soon as Jacob walked in the door. I couldn't look Julia in the eye. I kept getting up and leaving the room.

My father finally confronted me and asked what was going on. I broke down. I started crying so hard that I was incoherent.

He sat me down on the couch and took my hand. He knew all about it, he said. Jacob had called him after it happened.

Imagine my shock—and my relief. It kicked off a fresh round of tears, but these were different. I could feel the burden I'd been carrying start to lift.

But then, my world did a 180.

My father told me that it was time to recognize that I had a problem. Jacob and Julia were having a baby and I needed to sober up so I could be a good aunt.

The tears slowed, and I felt my face wrinkle in confusion. I didn't understand. Julia was the one on drugs, I said. I was just trying to help her, and Jacob held a knife to me.

That wasn't how it happened, Jacob said, with calm authority, striding into the room.

He'd found me with a stash of drugs and asked me to leave. That's when things got nasty.

It was all I could do to stare at them in turn as my mother and sister filed into the room. My dad looked disappointed. My mother, pinched and nervous. Julia wouldn't make eye contact. Jacob, however, locked eyes with me, sending me a message. *This was what would happen if I persisted.*

I left my parents' house right there and then.

A few weeks later, a bartender at a place I frequented told me she was moving to St. Thomas in a month. I packed a suitcase and cashed out my bank account. She didn't question why I wanted to go with her. We found an apartment together, shared a car for the first month until she found her own island cruiser. She introduced me to the man who gave me my first boat job. I brought friends to her bar. She taught me about the whole silver lining thing. I taught her how to make my famous key lime pie. We watched each other's backs. If one of us was short for the month, the other covered.

She left after a year for ski season in Colorado. There was big money to be had, she said. She invited me to come, but I didn't want to leave the Caribbean waters that had captivated me.

That was four years ago. I haven't been back home since I left. This place feels like home now. My dad calls every now and then. I used to answer sometimes. But I never felt better after talking to him, so I started dodging his calls. They're more intermittent now, but they still come every now and then. I haven't spoken to Julia or my mom since that day. Jacob, I don't even want to think about.

I closed the browser window displaying Julia's photo.

I took another long slug of scotch.

Only one person on this island knew my story: Ben.

The ache in my chest threatened to explode into tears, screaming—or worse.

I needed to do something. I turned back to my computer and typed in "missing person statistics." The words swam in front of me briefly as my eyes began to fill with water. I blinked a few times to clear them. I read that one-sixth of missing adults have psychiatric problems. I wondered if that was the case with Andrea.

Snap.

I twitched violently at a noise from outside. Apparently, that scotch was doing nothing to dull my senses. I sat still and listened for the tell-tale clucking that indicated a wild chicken at work. I heard nothing. I waited like a gazelle at the edge of a forest pond, and after a moment of silence so loud my ears started to ring, I turned back to my computer.

We have all kinds of animals running around here at night. You already know about the deer. Stray cats, pigs, goats, mongooses and iguanas also run freely. St. John has wild donkeys. That noise could have come from any one of these night stalkers.

But even as I skimmed a story about how parents often find it necessary to advocate passionately for their missing children, I felt the back of my neck crawl. I was being watched.

Slowly, I swiveled my knees around.

The beauty of my apartment is that the top half of the eastern wall is all screens. In the morning, I can see all the way to St. John. At night, though, the whole neighborhood can see me. This island is full of trade-offs.

In the state I was in tonight, I felt vulnerable and exposed.

The light from my humble apartment didn't penetrate beyond the screens, so all I saw was a deep indigo-tinted blackness with pinpoint lights from the harbor. Any kind of creepy person could stare back from inches away without being seen. There's even a half-finished porch on the back that provides them a perfect platform for viewing. Not my landlord's smartest creation.

I tried to dismiss my fears, and I turned back to my computer. Every one of my windows—even the wall of screens—had bars, so unless the creepers brought a welding torch, they weren't getting in.

I clicked in to the story of a Vermont girl who went missing. Years later, her parents were still fighting for help to find her.

"If you don't do all this yourself, it doesn't get done," was what her father said to the reporter. I clicked the link to the website they'd set up, but the domain had been forfeited. Nothing there. I wondered if that meant that Brianna had come home. Or had her parents just given up?

I heard another branch snap, and my patience snapped with it. Now I was pissed.

I shoved my chair back with a loud scrape, took four strides toward my front door and grabbed my heavy-duty flashlight. It was a big, black Maglite—half flashlight, half weapon.

I stalked back over to the corner of my cottage and shone the flashlight out the screen, toward the source of the noise. The porch was clear of humans and wild chickens, although it could use a good sweeping. I turned the beam around toward the path between my car and the cottage.

The light swept over a hunched body.

I couldn't help it. I screamed.

4

Of course, no one came running. And as soon as I let loose, the hunched body began to unfold itself from a crouch to a full standing position, hands extended toward the beam in the "stop" gesture.

I'd caught a prowler. I was awfully proud of myself. Now what the hell was I supposed to do with him?

"Lizzie, it's me," the prowler said and I saw a flash of teeth in the darkness. A smile.

Okay, not a prowler. And as I looked closer, I saw a pair of familiar board shorts—yellow with green and black stripes up the sides. "Goddamn it, Dave. What are you doing prowling around?"

Dave, the man I've been sleeping with for the last few months but is definitely NOT my boyfriend—the same Dave who had still not texted me back—extended his arms wide, his right hand holding a bottle of champagne.

"Surprise!" he said. "I made Master Scuba Diver Trainer today. Moving up in the world. Now I'm even with most of the other guys in the shop. They took me out to celebrate." His words spilled together as he spoke. Yeah, I bet those guys did take him out. Shots all around, most likely more than once.

I sighed. My voice came out flat. "Congratulations. Come on around." I turned on a bare heel to open the door for him.

Dave had his sights set on this certification for a while. I wanted to be happy for him, but I couldn't help but think about how weird he'd been acting in the last week. When we first started hooking up, I'd almost always have a text from him waiting when I got off the boat. Sometimes I would pretend not to see it because, well, have I mentioned that Dave isn't my boyfriend?

In the last few days, though, he hadn't been the reliable, affectionate Labrador he once was. But Dave almost always showed up eventually, sometimes in various states of inebriation.

I simmered as he rounded the corner, as annoyed with him as I was with myself for freaking out for the second time in a single night. As he approached, I flicked open the deadbolt and pulled the door inward. I didn't feel ready to make eye contact, lest I boil over and let some of those pesky emotions run out. Most of those had nothing to do with him, but it was tough to make that distinction after so much scotch.

He appeared in the doorway with his shaggy blonde hair and light green eyes, both of which looked like they'd been bleached by the sun, peach skin that flushed easily and face lit up with a pure excitement for life. The sight of him lifted the lid off my pot. I went right down to a very low simmer.

He had a boyish face, one that contrasted sharply with his size. Dave towered over me at 6'4". And yet, despite his size, Dave was often the magnet for bar fights in St. Thomas. Or maybe it was because of it. Men said outrageous things to him that they wouldn't say to a smaller man. Dave's arms didn't bulge like a bodybuilder's, but if you saw him casually lift two forty-pound scuba tanks without much effort, you'd know not to mess with him.

Despite the charm of Dave's looks, I wasn't ready to kiss and make up quite yet. I kept the door in between us and gave him a formal sweep of the arm to usher him in. I closed the door quickly after him, but not before a cloud of mosquitoes followed, circling his black backpack.

Dave was still wearing his dive shop T-shirt, so his story seemed to check out. I wondered how many shots he'd done. It would help me calculate the countdown to bed time.

He went right over to the kitchen and started disassembling the champagne bottle. It wasn't $2.99 André, which meant it was a meaningful night for him.

I heard a pop and looked up to see Dave get two coffee cups out of the cabinet. No champagne flutes in this shack, obviously.

"I'm sorry, babe," he said as he poured the cups full.

"Mmmm?" I asked, my eyes focusing on a lizard running up the kitchen wall. It was a common occurrence, but I pretended to find it fascinating.

"About last night," he said. He handed me my favorite mug, the white one with a faded blue palm tree on it. It was here when I moved in, and it would go with me when I left. Sorry, Bernard.

Ah, last night. Yeah, that one had kind of sucked, too, but in a different way. Dave hadn't returned my text messages once I got off the boat, so I figured I might as well drink. Why not? By the time the party had moved from Island Time down to Caribbean Saloon, he showed up just in time for me to start an argument that ended with him stalking off. I'm not proud to admit it, but I'd been belligerent enough that he had called me a "real bitch." What an ass, right?

He'd sheepishly shown up at my place at 1:30 am with a chickenshit explanation and I had been too tired to argue.

And now here we were again.

He reached out and clinked his mug with mine. I wondered if I was straying into "real bitch" territory again, so I looked up and made eye contact with him.

"Congratulations," I said, feeling myself soften a little more.

He looked down shyly, his shoulder shrugging up an inch. "Almost everyone at the dive shop has their MSDT. It just seemed so far away when I first moved down and now it's done."

"Worth celebrating, I'd say." I took a sip from the mug, a little cautiously. I wasn't sure if this was the kind of champagne I liked or the kind that tasted like perfume. And there was all that vodka and scotch to contend with.

But it went down easy. Before I knew it, Dave and I were back to our normal routine. I got him laughing with the story of my heroic ocean rescue that day. Unlike Cappy, he was appropriately sympathetic between belly laughs.

But his mood turned sober when I told him about Ben.

"Are you sure you want to get mixed up in that?" he asked, pouring the very last of the champagne into my cup despite my protests.

I bristled a little. After the last few days, Dave was the last person in my life who was allowed to weigh in. So I glossed over my own doubt and said breezily, "It's an hour of my time, max. Maybe I can just catch a glimpse of them at the beach. No big deal." I didn't meet his eyes.

He shrugged back, but I could tell that he wasn't satisfied with my answer.

But then he drained his coffee cup, set it on the table, then leaned over and kissed me gently. It was these kisses that got me in the first place. In spite of his size, Dave kissed with grace. As his lips tugged at my lower lip, I tasted a little bit of salt from his day on the boat and smelled that unique smell that was just his: a little sunscreen, a little sweat and a little something that reminded me of freshly baked bread.

When I finally pulled back from our kiss, I was a little dizzy. His eyes met mine and I couldn't help but grin broadly. I pulled my shirt over my head to reveal the bathing suit I'd been wearing that day. I watched his eyes run over my body. My pale skin was barely tanned—I tan to a color that most people consider a normal skin tone—and I wouldn't have won a beauty contest at home. Here, though, where there were rumored to be at least seven men for every woman, I was a valuable commodity.

I reached around behind me and undid the clasp to my top, tossing it at Dave. Then I popped to my feet. "Catch me if you can!"

I ran for my bed, squealing as he chased me around my tiny table and dove in bed next to me, the cheap springs groaning under the weight of our bodies. I turned on the fan to keep the mosquitoes away as Dave pulled off his own shirt and covered his body with mine. His skin pulsed with warmth. I drank it in.

And that's as far as that section of my story goes. Maybe twelve years of Catholic school warped my sensibilities just enough to make me a bit of a prude, but I don't kiss and tell. Another one of my rules.

Besides, you don't tell stories down here that you don't want repeated from bar stool to bar stool.

So suffice it to say that we found ourselves laying in my bed a bit later, the tree frogs chirping outside the window. I listened as one started his song, calling and waiting for another frog to respond. I heard the second frog answer, then they chirped back and forth, their calls drawing closer and closer in rhythm until they were finally chirping together in concert. And then, for whatever unknown reason, they stopped and started the whole damn thing again. Why couldn't they just chirp together for the rest of the night? Why did they have to stop chirping and mess the whole thing up?

"Are you sure you want to go to the Ritz tomorrow?" Dave asked, breaking into my tree frog reverie.

"Nope," I replied. I turned over on my side and snuggled as near to him as the 80-degree evening would allow.

I thought about saying more, but instead I focused on the black behind my eyes, willing sleep to bring an end to that conversation.

I woke up a few times in the night, my mind dancing around Dave's inquiry.

At one point, I resolved to call Ben in the morning and tell him it was off.

The next time I woke, I decided just to send him a text and tell him it was a no-go.

The third time I woke up, I decided I was being chickenshit. These favors were the kind of thing we did for each other down here. There was that time that my friend, Joe, dropped what he was doing and drove across the island to help me change a flat tire. And I'd only called to ask if he had the number for an honest tow company. He lives in Florida now.

As he reminded me, Ben had helped me move. And, as I reminded him, that favor didn't quite rise to the same level of his current ask. However, helping me move was only one of many solids he'd done me over the years. At the end of the day, this island was notoriously short of people who did what they said they were going to do. Timelines were slow, and follow-through was rare. However, there was also a small cache of good people down here who you could rely on in any weather. When I met one, I kept him or her close and did everything I could to repay their kindness.

Another one of my rules, I guess.

Before I could come to a final conclusion, I slipped into sleep again.

I woke up again at 7:17 am, thanks to a ferocious bite from a mosquito, right under my left eyebrow. When they go for the face, it's personal.

I killed it in mid-bite and felt the warm blood smear across my brow bone—*my* warm blood. Being mauled by a blood-sucking fiend is pretty much my least favorite way to wake up.

I took a second swipe at the blood with the back of my hand without opening my eyes. Tissues were $4.99 a box at Kmart, one of several luxury items I'd recently cut off my list.

But this was no time for thinking. I squeezed my eyes tightly to hang on to the last smoky wisps of my dream. Maybe, just maybe, I could turn over, go back to sleep and wake up to discover that it was creeping toward noon.

I heard the whir of the fan start to slow. I felt my pulse quicken as it wound to a stop. Dammit.

After a few seconds of panic, then denial, I opened my eyes to confirm what I already knew. The power had gone out. The cottage was suddenly silent except for the throaty morning calls of a nearby rooster and Dave's light breathing.

When most people think about living in the Caribbean, they think about lounging on a white sand beach with the sun warming their skin, water lapping around their toes and a cold Corona in their hand.

They never really considered things like random power outages, but they were the reality behind that fantasy.

I lay in bed, hoping against hope that the power would come right back on. Occasionally, it did. The moist air was thick in my mouth, my throat, my lungs. My skin felt sticky, like I'd missed too many showers. The sheet began to grow heavy. It trapped the hot air around me, incubating me like an egg. I took another breath. I thought I would choke on the humidity. I breathed in again. I wasn't getting enough oxygen. I could feel my throat start to close up.

I gave up on sleep and rolled out of bed. I glanced out the window over at nearby St. John, wondering if their power was out, or if this was more of the Water and Power Authority's rolling blackout program. We threw around their acronym, WAPA, like a curse. Many insisted it stood for "We Atta Power Always." Today, it seemed true.

I left Dave sleeping in the bed.

My last long-think on the topic of Ben's errand had been inconclusive, but I wasn't going to sit around here. Fans kept the mosquitos away and the full-body sweat at bay. I started getting dressed. To go where, I wasn't entirely sure. I finger-walked through every one of my tank tops before picking a purple one. I flossed my teeth. I plucked a few stray hairs from my eyebrows, even though they were light enough that no one would notice.

I took a long look at myself in the mirror. I probably looked frightful for mainland living. For St. Thomas, I looked average, if a little pale. My nose was a little toastier than usual, practically a strawberry at this point. I had to be more vigilant, or I'd end up like one of those leathery ladies the men so charmingly call "sea hags."

I gingerly slathered some sunscreen over the bridge of my nose. I'd always wanted a ski-slope nose like Julia, but I'd gotten the Roman variety instead. It was balanced by a pair of good-size brown eyes, the batting of which has gotten me out of a few sticky situations. To be a woman is, in most cases, divine, if not helpful. I wrestled my hair into a messy bun. It would do.

But still I didn't leave. I contemplated a drive into Red Hook for an iced coffee.

What, was I scared of those girls? Ridiculous. All I had to do was go do a quick favor for a friend. It was the way we did things here in St. Thomas. One good turn deserves another. Right?

I pushed myself away from the counter and set my mouth in a determined line.

Before I left, I peeked into the bed nook to check on Dave. There was a small part of me that wished I would find him awake, that he would give me a reason not to head up the hill.

But he was sound asleep. I decided to leave him that way. I tiptoed out of the house, putting on my flip flops once I'd closed the door quietly behind me.

As I walked down to my car, I knew I was going to go to the Ritz, even as any and all earthly reasons that could keep me away flashed through my mind. A flat tire? A trip to the doctor?

Or maybe just an emergency sea salt soak, followed by an IV drip of Corona? Just in case, I thoroughly checked my tires. No dice; it was go time.

I reached for the ignition and noticed that my hand was shaking. I looked at it in disbelief. These weren't the alcohol shakes, were they? I did a quick body scan and found myself taut as a bow, my muscles tensed and ready as though I were about to go to battle with a saber-toothed tiger who was threatening my cave family.

I thought I'd left this crap back in the States. I rubbed my face with my hands. What was going on?

It was Ben, I realized. I was worried about Ben.

Frankly, it felt a little weird. Ben was the golden boy. Ben always took home the prettiest girls who always fell madly in love with him. Ben miscounted T-shirts and never got dinged by our boss. Ben's smile had gotten him more free drinks than I could count.

If I knew one thing about Ben, it was that Ben knew how to take care of himself.

And a few times, he'd taken care of me.

But this felt different somehow. If I got to the Ritz-Carlton and a stateside girl was missing, would Ben know how to get himself out of that?

Part of the charm of moving down to a place like St. Thomas was how much it felt like home—and, yet, it didn't. It was comfortable, with a little thrill thrown in.

Our roads were a perfect example. We all drove left-hand drive vehicles here, the same as you would in the continental U.S. But—plot twist—we drove them on the left-hand side of the road.

The same was true when it came to crime and justice down here. We had police officers, ones who looked pretty much the same as our officers back home. Their cars and uniforms were familiar enough. But I'd heard enough stories to suspect that a white boy like Ben could very easily become a scapegoat for Andrea's disappearance, truth be damned.

I wasn't sure this was a situation Ben would be able to get himself out of.

And if I went up to the Ritz, would I get myself tangled in this mess too?

I started the car. I was getting ahead of myself. What if Andrea was safely at the Ritz, working on her tan? Maybe she was just a girl who'd found an easy way to slide out of Ben's arms. All I had to do was set eyes on her, and this would all be over with.

I tried to puff myself up by imagining a few lounge chairs' worth of supermodels in perfect bikinis laughing callously at my inquiries. I'd just look like a ridiculous worrywart—especially when Andrea turned out to be one of those supermodels.

I don't know why I found that comforting, but I did. Let them laugh at me, as long as that meant that Ben was in the clear.

Because innocence doesn't really matter down here, not really. This might have been a U.S. territory, but it wasn't the U. S. of A. Not by a long shot.

But as I sat there in the driveway that morning, I can't say that I let logic run the show. I didn't make one of Ben Franklin's famous pros and cons lists. There was a feeling in my gut, a heaviness that I knew would start churning in a few hours. If I turned away, if I didn't make that simple drive to the Ritz for my friend, one of the few real friends I had on this island, I knew I'd have to drink the day away in order to tamp it down. And if Ben went to jail, that feeling that I could have done something to help would be nearly impossible to get rid of.

And in the end, there was one single thought that prevailed: *Fuck it. What's the worst that could happen?*

My heart took up a faster beat as I hit the gas.

5

There are two ways to get to the Ritz-Carlton on St. Thomas. The first is the way the tourists go: winding up the hill through Estate Nazareth, the terror of its blind hairpin turns contrasting sharply with increasingly stunning views of St. John and St. Thomas's close cays (we pronounce them "keys" here, by the way, just like the ones in Florida), each ringed with impossibly vivid shades of blue water.

A captain I worked with once told me that Nazareth was a pretty tough neighborhood until Hurricane Marilyn leveled it in 1995.

I don't know if that's true. And "tough" by whose standards? People tell a lot of stories down here. Some of them are outrageous fabrications created by bored islanders, and yet people still try to pass them off as the God's honest truth. Michael Jordan does not own a house on this island. Neither does Oprah—and don't let any taxi driver or boat captain tell you otherwise.

Other stories get repeated so often that they *become* true, or at least find their way into the canon. You'll also hear some tales that are so outrageous that they seem like total bullshit, but as the bumper sticker says, "St. Thomas: You Can't Make This Shit Up."

Off the boat, I don't repeat anything I don't know personally to be true. Another one of my rules. I also believe in karma and, on an island this small, it's much more instant than even John Lennon would have believed.

Today, Nazareth is where a lot of people live when they first move to St. Thomas. I've lived here my entire four years on the island. When you close down Caribbean Saloon with the hardcore drinkers at 4:00 am, you're happy to be home in three minutes flat, just before the blackout hits.

The second route to the Ritz-Carlton requires navigating what used to be the worst road in St. Thomas. Its potholes are big enough to swallow my Suzuki or, at the very least, snap its toothpick axles. The road is so famous that it's documented on its own island bumper sticker ("I survived the road to Latitude 18 to see the Sun Mountain Fiddler").

If you make it past the potholes, you'll pass along the back end of the Ritz property, where you can park on a sandy stretch and waltz right onto the Ritz beach, past a guard who's either sleeping or eyeing you with great intensity, depending on the day. All the beaches in the U.S. Virgin Islands are public up to the waterline, and most resort agreements include a public access provision. Not that they like it—or encourage it.

I wouldn't be going the locals' way today. I judged myself to be on official Ritz business. Plus, I wanted to get this over with. I didn't want to nurse my car down a questionable road. I wanted to throw it in the first spot available, jam it into park and wash my hands of this whole thing as soon as I could.

A whisper of anxiety in my chest suggested that I might be making a terrible mistake. I ignored it. I probably shouldn't have, knowing what I know now.

I waved at the guard in the shack at the entrance to the parking lot. Even though my beat-up car marked me as a local and not a resort guest, he merely peered at me over his *Virgin Islands Daily News*. I could only see the round top of his brown head, shaved clean, his eyes flicking at me over red half-moon glasses then quickly returning to his newspaper.

There's a lot you can get done on this island by acting friendly and pretending you know the deal.

I parked between a bright yellow Jeep Wrangler (probably a rental) and a beaten-up powder blue Toyota Camry whose paint had gone chalky under the Caribbean sun (definitely an island car).

I peered in my rearview mirror and did my best to tidy my bun before getting out. I always feel conspicuous on the Ritz property, much more than any other hotel on the island. The guests give off an aura of such squeaky cleanliness.

I admit it. I covet the look. The men wear neatly-pressed golf shirts over spotless, iron-smooth khakis, their foreheads shiny-clean from a recent shower, their slightly sunburnt noses worn like a badge of pride. The women carry big expensive bags that dwarf their tiny perfect bodies, which are foolishly disguised under oversized wraps or sarongs. They tote gorgeous children wearing clothes that would cost me a month of tips. They dine on $30 hamburgers for lunch and snack on sushi in the twilight hours. God, it must be nice.

My awareness that I was the thing that was not like the others only quickened my pace through the resort.

I felt my phone buzz. I slipped it out to see that my father had called. As was typical of our crappy phone service, the phone didn't ring but sent him straight to voicemail. I paused to delete the message without listening to it. Then I headed toward the Lily building where the girls were staying.

The rooms at the Ritz are named first by flower, then by a four-digit numbering system. I swear that's just to throw off any locals pretending to belong. If someone asks your room number and you're not ready to spit out "Lily 4301," their beefy security guards are happy to escort you right off the property before you even think of looking at a well-groomed hibiscus bush the wrong way.

I cut through the main building, past its Signature Shop full of Ritz-Carlton goodies like branded golf shirts and scented bath sets. I passed outside again and slowed my pace down the main set of beige stone stairs, taking in the view of Great Bay, the Ritz's protected beach. Half of it was natural and half was man-made.

The man-made side was my favorite. Perfect white sand like granulated sugar had been trucked in to cover what was once a gray, rocky beach that would have tortured your bare feet. The result? A postcard-worthy beach that gave way to tranquil turquoise waters lapping tastefully at the shore. It was one example of the way that money and desire can bend nature to their will. Maybe a hurricane would rip it all to pieces again and restore the craggy shoreline, but it hadn't happened yet.

I glanced out at the water, smooth as glass. Just yesterday, the surface had been choppy and rough. How things change in twenty-four hours. It was a terrible day for kitesurfing, but a great day for taking pictures.

My eyes traveled over to St. John, right across the way, then back to the water between the islands. The water was the reason I was here. I loved to be on it, in it, under it—you name it. I watched as two small white power boats crossed Pillsbury Sound toward St. John. I suddenly wished to be on one of them, instead of stuck on land.

No time for this kind of lollygagging. I had a job to do.

I started my march again, past an infinity pool, a beach-side restaurant and a collection of carefully-aligned beach chairs, all of which were still empty at this time of the morning.

I'd miscalculated. If this ghost town was any indication, the girls were probably not out on the beach yet.

I'd hoped I could just play paparazzi and run, but that plan was likely a bust.

I'd have to play it by ear, I decided. I continued along a path that skirted an outcropping of volcanic rock that separated the resort's hotel from its Members' Club. The path wound around the point, past an open-air cabana where they give massages overlooking the bay. The khaki-colored cabana was tied up tight, but a lizard lounged in the sun in the entryway. His turn next, I supposed.

The resort was huge, which I think was supposed to be a perk, but it was always a pain in the ass to get around for both staff and tourists alike—and, I suppose, for first mates playing at detective.

As I reached the Members' side where the girls were staying, I saw the servers and bartenders setting up the poolside restaurant and bar for the day. "Members' Club" is Ritz-speak for "timeshares," by the way, but don't tell the residents. I think they'll be shocked by such coarse language.

I slowed my pace to see if I knew the bartender. He was an older man of about fifty, with a shaved head and a rich, dark brown complexion. He wore the classic island server uniform: an orange flowered shirt over khakis.

I don't drink that many $14 rum punches, so I guess I shouldn't have expected him to look familiar. However, most of the people down here work more than one job. I thought I might recognize him from my time waitressing at another resort restaurant a few nights a week. No dice.

I was sorely tempted to pause at the bar and while away a few hours. Maybe the girls would walk right by me, and I could get my money shot without even leaving a bar stool.

But momentum kept my feet moving forward, my flip flops hammering the cement sidewalk. I'd just pop up to their room, then I'd be on my way.

I felt my breath catch in my chest. *Please be there. Please be there so I can just go home and go back to bed.* My chest was too tight. I took another gulp of air and walked faster.

After a few wrong turns, I found the girls' room. I checked my watch. It was barely 8:30 am. If they really were Andrea's friends, I supposed they probably wouldn't be sleeping well anyway. *Unless she was already home*, an optimistic voice whispered in my head.

My hand hung in the air for a second, then it dropped to my side.

What was I doing? I asked myself.

Paying a debt.

I lifted my hand and rang the bell.

6

No one answered my first ring. Of course.

As the Westminster Abbey chime echoed through the room loudly enough for me to hear it on my side of the door, I fantasized about running back down the stairs and up the hill, slamming my car door and driving away.

But I knew there was no way I could look Ben in the face and tell him I'd chickened out.

I rang the bell and listened to the pleasant chimes echo again.

A minute later, the door opened. A slim girl with long, straight brown hair that hung past her shoulders and equally straight bangs—the kind of bangs that must have been tended to by a stylist weekly because they lined up perfectly with the center of her dark eyebrows—stood in the doorway. She wore pink cotton shorts and a white camisole. She was skinny enough that the bony bumps of her clavicles stood out on the tops of her shoulders.

A little wrinkle appeared between her dark eyebrows, barely visible underneath the perfect wall of bangs. I couldn't say what shade of white her face would be normally. Today, it was overlaid with that rosy, too-shiny look of someone who'd overstayed her welcome in the sun. Two smudges at the inner corners of her eyes suggested that she hadn't been sleeping. That didn't bode well.

"Hello?" she said. The fingers of one hand were wrapped around the edge of the door.

"Good morning," I said. I paused, waiting for her to return the greeting.

She obviously hadn't been here long enough to adopt our peculiar island ritual. Nothing gets done in St. Thomas until you say, "good morning," "good afternoon," or, my favorite, "good night." (That last one is not a dismissal, if you're curious. It's a greeting, one that creates a great deal of confusion for tourists. But it also comes with a great deal of old-world charm, in my opinion.)

She didn't speak.

After a beat of awkward silence, I forged ahead. "My name's Lizzie. I'm a friend of Ben's." I cringed. Why had I said that? *Name, rank, serial number, Lizzie. And then get gone.*

No response.

I took a more direct tack. "Is Andrea here?" I blurted out.

The girl's eyebrows shot up and a light went into her big, dark eyes. She would have made an excellent megafauna. "You know Andrea? Have you seen her?"

I felt ice in my stomach despite the heat. "No. She hasn't come home yet?"

The girl's eyebrows dropped. "No."

I pressed my lips together and turned my head away. Painful as it is to admit, I thought of myself first. I had the sinking sense I'd stepped right in the middle of something that was way above my pay grade.

My second thought went to the missing girl. If Andrea wasn't here, where was she?

I looked back at the girl I assumed to be her friend, at least in name, if not in spirit. After all, she had to be one of the girls who left Andrea to fend for herself in Red Hook. The wrinkle between the girl's eyebrows deepened. Straight white teeth chewed on a thin lower lip.

I raised a hand and started to back away. "Well, then, I, uh, guess I'll go." I turned away from the door and took a few steps in the direction of the nearest stairwell.

Something cold wrapped itself around my right wrist like a tentacle.

I wheeled around. My wrist was released and the dark-haired girl stepped back, her eyes refusing to meet mine.

What the hell was going on here?

"Are you okay?" I asked.

She opened her mouth, then closed it, pressing her hand over her eyes.

I heard another voice from inside the room.

"Becky, who is it?" a deeper female voice asked. Becky shrunk out of the door frame as an even taller blonde girl appeared, her hair almost the same style as Becky's—long with long bangs—but in a shade of honey blonde. The second girl wore navy blue running shorts with white stripes down the sides and a white tank top, a serviceable white sports bra strap peeking out of one side.

As she examined me, I examined her. I saw a face that was a mash-up of memorable features: a long nose with a prominent upside-down triangle at its finish, a pouty upper lip that stuck out beyond its lower companion and a set of smallish blue eyes set so deeply in her face that they looked like doll eyes. I couldn't decide if she was pretty or ugly, but the effect was striking. It was a face you wouldn't forget. Unlike her friend, she'd kept her cream-colored skin from getting sunburned. But she did have a sprinkling of what looked like acne scars across the tops of her cheeks.

Whereas the other girl sported arms like toothpicks, this girl was broader, more solid. I would have bet money that she was a swimmer in college. I was also sure that I was looking at the den mother of the group. Any boy who wanted to talk to these girls probably had to go through this one.

Her affect was in better shape than her friend's. I didn't see evidence of tears or lost sleep. But maybe she played the role of the strong friend everyone could lean on.

Her silence felt like a question mark.

I kept Ben out of it this time. "I'm Lizzie. I just wanted to know if Andrea was here."

I watched her top lip tighten down on the lower one, pressing them into a line. Her expression quickly dissolved into something more neutral. "She isn't here now." Whereas the other girl, Becky, had been almost lethargic, this girl's words were quick and tight, charged with an electricity that extended to her bright blue eyes.

"She hasn't come home?"

"Who are you?" Her eyebrows plummeted to a deep knit, her tone dismissive.

I bristled. I clapped my hands together and bent forward in a mock bow. "It's been a pleasure, ladies. Best of luck finding your friend." I was just about to rotate on my right flip flop and head out. In fact, my mind was already paging through my beach options for the day.

But then I caught the eyes of the girl with the dark hair. Becky—the one who had grabbed my wrist when I tried to leave earlier. She was pressed up against the open door, her shoulders hunched, her arms holding opposite elbows so tightly that her knuckles were white. I would swear that the look I saw in her face was a plea.

I felt myself soften, and I couldn't turn away. "What did her parents say?"

The blonde girl said nothing, so my eyes shifted to Becky, who dropped her gaze. She spoke to the marble floor. "We haven't told them."

My sunglasses nearly fell right off my face.

"Have you told *anybody*?"

"It's only been a day." The blonde girl crossed her arms.

"A day and a *half*. You haven't told anyone that your friend is *missing*?" I shook my head. "You girls are unbelievable. What, afraid it's going to ruin your vacation?" I turned around and looked down the open-air hallway, my anger building. Who lets a friend go missing on a strange island and tells no one?

I turned back to the girls, intending to give them the full brunt of my indignation. The looks on their faces stopped me. Both of them were now staring at the ground. Becky's face was flushed as though she was about to bawl like a toddler. The taller girl was doing that lip pressing thing again, the energy gone from her face.

"Listen, I think you need to call the police. This has gone on too long—"

But before I could even finish my sentence, they were both sobbing.

I sighed. I hoped these girls were book smart, because they certainly weren't street smart.

I saw Becky start to sway, and I cast a quick glance at the blonde girl. She was too deep in her own tears to notice. I stepped forward and grabbed the thin girl a second before she pitched forward onto the tile floor.

"Let's find you a place to sit down," I said, and before I knew it, we were sweeping into their room. I heard the door click behind me, and I had the sense that there was no turning back now.

Like it or not, I'd broken one of my golden rules. I was now involved. A sense of loyalty had brought me here, a desire to do right by a friend, and now that continued desire to do right was only drawing me deeper. I wondered how soon I'd regret it.

But, in that moment, I was less focused on repercussions and more focused on staying upright until I could safely get Becky to a horizontal surface.

It had been a while since I'd been in one of the Ritz Member's Club residences. I took it all in as we staggered through—the staid beige marble floors, the steel-appliance kitchen, the glass-top dining room table with seating for six, the framed pen-and-ink drawings of Caribbean fruits and flowers. It made my shack look pretty shack-y. Not for the first time, I wished I'd been born rich. Maybe my next reincarnation would have better luck.

Becky collapsed like a sack of flour onto the couch, and Jessie sank down on the opposite end. I backtracked to the kitchen, found water glasses in the cabinet and filled two of them, marveling at the stainless steel fridge that dispensed both ice and filtered water. I bought my drinking water in gallon jugs at the grocery store and hauled them up my stairs, cursing the whole way.

When I returned, Becky had slumped down even further. She was looking almost catatonic.

"Are you okay?" I asked her for the second time this morning.

I got one barely perceptible nod in response.

"Maybe you should lie down."

The girl curled herself up in a fetal position on one end of the couch. Her companion scooted an inch or two to make room, but not that much. Typical, I thought. These girls were turning out to be just as self-involved as I'd imagined them.

Now if I could just wheedle a little information out of them, enough so that I wasn't returning from my errand empty-handed, then I could be on my way.

I set their waters on the coffee table, then sat myself in a demure green armchair that looked more comfortable than it was. I wiggled my rear to see if I could convince the cushion to give a little, but it held firm. Very firm.

"Okay, let's start again. I'm Lizzie. I met Becky." I gestured to her, although she didn't look at me. She seemed stable for the moment, but I got the sense another crying jag was just underneath the surface.

I turned to the blonde girl, the presumptive leader of this group.

"I'm Jessie," she said, sniffing once, her face still flushed.

I nodded at them. "Okay, I think it's time to make a call here, either to Andrea's parents or to the police."

All I got was a blank stare from Jessie.

"I assume you've tried her cell phone?"

Jessie paused, taking a beat to reach for the tissue box, which was neatly hidden in a decorative metal container. She dabbed at her nose, then eyed me. "Who are you again?"

She was suspicious. Understandable, given the circumstances. I didn't want to spook her, so I merely repeated myself. "I'm Lizzie." As far as she knew, I didn't know Ben from Adam and I wanted to keep it that way.

"And why are you here?" she asked.

"I'm asking myself the same question." I paused, trying to phrase the next bit delicately. "But I think the point is that Andrea hasn't come home, has she?"

Silence.

Then, a thin voice spoke from the couch. "We were just at a bar, having a few drinks. And now—"

I could see tears leaking sideways down Becky's face.

"Where was this?" I asked.

"Duffy's." The answer came from the other side of the couch.

I nodded, hoping Jessie would continue, but we sat in silence for a moment.

"Wednesday is Ladies' Night, right?" I prompted. "Free drinks?"

Jessie jumped in, waving her hand dismissively. "They're so disgusting. They don't even use Cruzan rum."

She made a face.

I made note that she pronounced Cruzan correctly, as CROO-zhian, not croo-ZAN, as many statesiders do. I also noted that Jessie seemed like she needed to be the smartest person in the room. Maybe I could use that to my advantage.

"Then you must not have had a lot to drink that night if the drinks were that bad." I tried to keep my tone light and casual. I wanted to keep her talking.

Jessie looked at me sharply. Then she shrugged as though the question was no big deal. "Not really." She looked at Becky, who didn't react. "A few Bushwackers, that's all."

My eyes flicked to Becky, her face still wet with tears. Finally, her head barely nodded once.

"Did Andrea talk to anyone that night?"

"You've been to Duffy's, right?" Jessie's expression hinted, rather strongly, that I wasn't the sharpest. While I was pleased that I had her talking, I could also tell that her manner was shifting, and it set off an alarm bell deep in my brain. This girl was no longer the devastated damsel who'd sobbed at the door. She was getting defensive again, and if she went on the offensive, I thought I might be in trouble.

I answered her cautiously. "Once or twice." *When I was new to the island and didn't know any better.*

"We couldn't get rid of them. There were guys everywhere. White guys and . . . locals."

My eyebrows went up, but I didn't comment.

"They wanted to get us drinks, dance with us. They were mostly sketchy. Not the kind of guys we usually hang out with."

"Andrew was with the Coast Guard," Becky said quietly.

I looked at Jessie, who shrugged at me. There I had it. Andrew was with the Coast Guard, whoever the hell Andrew was.

The conversation ground to a halt, and I felt like Jessie was examining me once again, closely enough to make my skin crawl. I'd probably worn out my welcome.

I gestured toward the phone. "Look, I think it's time to get some help here. The police, Andrea's parents, then your parents—"

Jessie cut me off. "Then this guy Ben showed up." Her face darkened. She shook her head twice. I was surprised she didn't take out her index finger and wag it around like a schoolmarm.

"He came over and started talking to all of us, but he and Andrea really hit it off." Her shoulders shrugged, and she blew out a burst of air. Clearly, she'd be sending out the lynch mob for Ben at any moment. This wasn't good.

She went on, her voice tight, "Ben had another guy with him. They talked for a few minutes, then Andrea said they were going across the parking lot to another bar."

"What was his name, the other guy?"

Jessie fixed her eyes on me. They were clear blue like the bay outside, but they looked cold. She didn't blink as she spoke. "He told me his name was Dave."

7

I shivered. The air conditioning that had felt like such a treat only a few minutes ago now felt like an arctic blast. I tried to keep my voice steady as I spoke. "And what did this 'Dave' look like?"

"He was a big guy. Blonde. He told us he worked at a dive shop."

I felt a little woozy. I tried to casually plant a hand on the arm of the chair to steady myself, but the gesture came out clumsy. I knew Jessie saw it.

I guess I now knew where Dave was when he wasn't responding to my flurry of texts from Caribbean Saloon.

Silence fell.

My mind was shuffling through my memories of that evening—the same evening Dave and I had our big fight. How had he acted when he arrived at Saloon, *hours* after I'd first texted him? Was that before or after Andrea disappeared? I flipped frantically through my memories from that evening, but my recollections were few and hazy. I felt a flush of heat so intense that even the Ritz air conditioning couldn't keep a bloom of sweat from breaking out on my lower back.

And what was Dave doing hanging out with Ben? As far as I knew, their relationship was defined by a nod of acknowledgement when they passed each other. In fact, Dave had made a few snide comments to me about Ben's flavors of the week. As for Ben, I don't know that he really thought about Dave at all. So what were they both doing hanging out together with the tourists at Duffy's?

With sheer strength of will, I wrenched my attention back to the girls on the couch. The mixture of hot anger and cold fear that now swirled in my gut was hard to ignore, but I had to deal with what was in front of me.

Becky was still in her own little world. She was idly staring at her hands, which sat in a careless pile in front of her face. I flicked over to Jessie, who was staring at me, her arms crossed over her chest.

Something about her stance just pissed me off. She'd taken me by surprise, penetrated my defenses. It was time to go on the offensive—poke the bear and see what I could get.

"So let me get this straight," I said, leaning forward. "You just *left* your friend?"

"We didn't just leave her. We went over to XO to see if we could find her but they'd already gone," Jessie said.

I shook my head. Was it possible that they just didn't get it—that they'd just left their friend with a stranger on a strange island?

I've seen tourists do some dumb things. I've had people ask me if they could swim under the islands. I've seen people who haven't exercised in ten years drink five mimosas then try to snorkel a mile in a strong current. But these girls' lack of regard for their friend, not just that night, but continuing into now? That just stoked the flames that were already building.

"So, this was what time?" I asked, knowing full well that my annoyance was showing. I decided to wear it like a flag while I gathered some key details.

"A little before midnight."

"For sure?"

"I remember getting in bed and the clock said almost 12:30," Jessie said. "It's not like I'm wearing my watch down here. Besides, I took an Ambien right after, so I was out until the morning."

Becky remained mute.

I couldn't help it. My mind flicked back to Ben and Dave at Duffy's. Had they made a plan to troll for the island's finest tourists at Ladies' Night? Had they discussed what a bitch I could be over a pair of Heinekens, clicking the necks of their bottles together and laughing about just how fucked I was going to be in life with that attitude?

I had to focus. The way it sounded, one of them was going to be on the hook for Andrea's disappearance.

I myself had never had a run-in with the USVI's finest, but everything I'd heard from friends and acquaintances pointed to an "arrest first, ask questions later" policy. Especially toward white boys. And as to whether or not one of them was actually responsible . . .

I couldn't even broach that at the moment. Not in front of these girls.

But what was the real likelihood that Andrea was dead? The island did have its share of gun violence, but a kidnapping? Especially in the short distance between XO and Duffy's?

On this island, it was tough—if not impossible—to keep a secret. Someone had to have seen something.

"You with us?" Jessie asked.

She'd caught me thinking. I tried to cover my embarrassment with a nod, but I could feel a blush creeping over my cheeks.

I was starting to unravel. I decided to make one more run at squeezing a little more out of these girls, and then I needed to make myself scarce.

I scanned the mahogany end-tables until I found a Ritz-Carlton pen and pad. They lay right next to a hideous brass lamp that featured two long-legged birds, one standing right behind the other. Well, the one seemed to be partially on top of the other. I blinked. Were those birds . . . mating? If they weren't mating, the bird in the back definitely needed to hit the brakes and give his buddy some personal space.

I turned back to the girls, the birds still haunting me, and scribbled some notes.

"What was Andrea wearing when she disappeared?"

There was a long pause.

"Anyone?"

The silence stretched. Maybe my sources had dried up.

I decided to leverage the weakest link. I looked pointedly at Becky. Then she spoke softly. "A blue halter dress."

"Okay . . ."

"And silver strappy sandals," Becky added.

"Not like Havaianas," Jessie added. The girl just couldn't bear to be left out. "It's a brand," she said, the tilt of her head suggesting that I clearly knew very little of the world. "They were real shoes."

I nodded. "Did you see if she talked to anyone else besides Ben?"

"Andrew and Frank," Becky said. "They were nice. They're with the Coast Guard."

I scribbled down their names. "Is that it?" I asked, hoping my taunt would lure Jessie back in.

"There was a man with red skin," Jessie said.

I shivered involuntarily. The Red Man. I didn't want anything to do with him, but it looked like our paths were going to cross. I wrote his name down.

"There was also a really large guy," Jessie said. "I didn't talk to him, but Andrea definitely did. And so did Becky."

I looked over at Becky, but she had gone from gazing at her hands to picking at a hangnail. It looked like she had a good grip, and she would draw blood soon.

I averted my eyes, swallowed through a tight throat and asked, "What do you remember about him?"

"He liked to dance," Becky said, her voice sounded soft. "He had long yellow dreadlocks."

I nodded. I knew Magnus. I also knew he liked to dance at Duffy's. He'd always seemed like a gentle soul, but maybe I was terribly, horribly wrong about that.

"Anyone else?"

"Ben talked to her the most," Jessie said. "He pretty much monopolized her time that night."

"That night? There were other nights?"

Jessie closed her eyes and shook her head slowly in disdain.

I waved a dismissive hand in her direction and tried to set my patter back to the "smart" setting. "Tell me about the other places you went."

"On which day?" she asked smartly. I've never really itched to slap anyone, but she was getting me close.

"The night before. Uh—" Andrea had disappeared on a Wednesday, so: "Tuesday."

"We went to Caribbean Saloon. It's usually fun over there, but it was totally dead. I wanted to leave as soon as we walked in, but Andrea wanted to stay. We didn't even finish our beers. The taxi driver wouldn't take us in his van with the beers and some weird guy who was hanging around asked if he could have them. It was gross."

"Did you talk to anyone that night?"

"Just one guy. He looked like a boatie or something. He had on one of those fishing shirts. He was really tan, tall, with short brown hair. He was still wearing board shorts—and he was pretty into Andrea."

I stared at her. "Boatie" was a pretty local word. The country singer Kenny Chesney might have introduced her to it, but, given her ease with the word "Cruzan," I voiced a suspicion. "You've been here before." It came out as a statement.

Jessie nodded crisply. "My parents have been Ritz members since 1999."

Well. In THAT case.

I returned to the "boatie" in question. Unfortunately, they'd pretty much described most of the men in Red Hook, which housed one of the busier harbors on the island. "What did he say to you?"

"He offered to buy us all Jägermeister shots. I told him that I don't do Jäger. He said the bartender would make me anything I wanted. Not interested. Like I said, I wanted to go. Plus, he had one of those ridiculous straw hats on a string around his neck." She rolled her eyes.

Bingo. There were a few guys on this island douchey enough to wear one of those hats. I was pretty sure they were talking about a guy named Duncan.

I scribbled another note, pleased with myself. I didn't quite know how I'd done it, but I'd kept the girls talking, and I'd gotten some good info. Nothing to clear either Ben or Dave, but I'd done what I could.

Then Becky's faint voice cut into my thoughts. "Andrea did a shot with him while you were in the bathroom."

Jessie's eye twitched once. She said nothing.

Becky's voice lowered to almost a whisper. "She said it tasted just like Nyquil." Becky's eyes were unfocused again, her hangnail forgotten.

Jessie now stared out the glass doors. Despite the mood in the room, the sky was still a solid bright blue, interrupted only occasionally by a puffy white cloud. The features of Jessie's face hardened the longer she looked, revealing future frown lines running down from her nose to the corners of her mouth.

It was one of the great ironies of St. Thomas. It was a place of awe-inspiring natural beauty.

But when your mood didn't match the view, it only made you feel worse.

I asked about their other nights and the only other place they added to the list was the poolside bar I'd passed on the way in. They had spent Monday night eating dinner under the care of a bartender named Grady.

I glanced at the two girls on the couch. They could have been in separate rooms, for all that they acknowledged each other. "How do you girls know each other anyway?"

Jessie's head swiveled sharply. "Why?" she asked, her eyes narrowing.

I shrugged. It was a nosy question, but I'd gotten them to tell me this much. Why not press my luck a little?

"Jessie and I went to high school together," Becky said.

Jessie jumped in. "And college. Andrea was our suite mate. We became friends. I wanted to bring the girls down and show them around. They'd never been here before."

I wondered if Andrea was regretting that decision. Becky looked like she was.

I gazed down at the pad. I felt tired all of a sudden, even though it was barely 9:00 am.

I wanted yesterday's problems back. Worrying about whether the guy in my life had moved on from me was quite different from wondering if he'd killed a girl. I didn't want to be Andrea's only hope, I didn't want to be these girls' keeper and I didn't want to be Ben's savior—or Dave's.

But if I didn't do something, who else would?

I heard a cell phone begin to bleat in that familiar but annoying way from the kitchen. Jessie flew off the couch and picked it up from the granite breakfast bar.

As she saw the screen, her eyebrows popped briefly, then her face went slack, her cheeks hanging loose, their acne scars set in relief from the glow of the phone.

She turned the phone screen to face us.

"It's Andrea," she said, her voice a harsh whisper.

"Answer it." I leapt up to join her.

Jessie slid her thumb along the screen then took a few steps away from me to answer. Obviously, the girl didn't trust me. Maybe she was smarter than I'd initially thought.

"Hello?" she said, her voice barely audible.

I watched her shoulders set from behind, the muscles flexing. When she turned back to me, her face was blank, unreadable. "It's not her. It's some guy."

She looked like she was about to hang up on the person, but I lunged and grabbed the phone out of her hand.

It looked like "Andrea" was still on the line. "Hello?" I asked. My voice quavered. Adrenaline had me jacked up like a triple espresso.

I heard Jessie protest in the background, but I ignored her.

"Who is this?" the voice on the phone asked. Jessie was right—definitely masculine.

"I'd ask you the same question. What're you doing with a missing girl's phone?"

"Lizzie?"

I squinted. How in the hell did this person know *me*?

"Who *is* this?"

"It's Ben."

The wind went completely out of me, as though I'd been punched in the gut. "Jesus," I gasped.

"It's not what you think," he said. His voice sounded sheepish and I felt my knees go weak. I reached out a hand to steady myself on the granite countertop, wedging the cool stone into the webbing between my thumb and first finger. If I lost my grip, I'd go straight to the ground.

"I don't even know what to think right now, Ben."

"Is that Ben?" Jessie's voice rang shrilly behind me. "Oh my god, he's got Andrea's phone—" I could feel her coming up behind me and I knew we only had a minute.

"Where are you?" I asked.

"I'm in Red Hook at the coffee cart. We need to talk."

"Five minutes. Don't go anywhere."

Jessie wrenched the phone out of my hand and I sagged against the counter.

"What is the matter with you?" she demanded. "And who are you anyway?"

My mind swirled around Ben. Maybe it was an accident. Maybe not. Maybe she was one of the first girls to really say no to him. I tried to imagine him dragging her across the Duffy's parking lot by her arm—way too many witnesses. Maybe he'd taken her home. But what had he done with the body?

I heard Becky's wan voice from the couch. "She's a friend of Ben's."

Jessie shrieked and whipped her head around at me, her blue eyes flashing.

I couldn't stay here. I pushed off the countertop and looked at the two girls. Jessie was screaming at me, but I wasn't hearing the words, just noise. Becky had flipped over, her face pressed deep into the couch cushions.

I started backing away, my eyes on the blonde girl, who was still hurling curses at me.

I held up a hand. "I didn't mean to—"

I started as the shrill ring of a phone cut into the noise. This time, it was the main Ritz-Carlton phone, its bell deafeningly loud and startlingly old-fashioned. It was the kind of ring you'd hear when staying with your grandmother for the weekend— or at the Bates Motel.

This time, Jessie didn't need a prompt. She ran to the phone and pulled it off the cradle as I continued backing out of the apartment. "Hello?" she said.

Then she held the phone up triumphantly.

"It's the police."

8

They say only guilty people run. I didn't need another excuse to make my exit, but the fact that the VI's finest were on their way quickened my pace out the door. I didn't want to sit around and answer questions about who I was and what I was doing there. All I was guilty of at that moment was naïvely stepping into a missing persons case that was none of my business. But if Andrea didn't turn up, the police might cast a wide net of blame that ensnared me, too.

So I took the easy way out. I ran.

I ran all the way down the stairs, then halfway up the steep hill to the parking lot, walking the rest of the hill like one of those suburban housewives on a mission to lose ten pounds by next week. To their credit, I could see how it might have some effect. I pumped my arms and legs as fast as I could, trying to control my ragged breathing. The accompanying monologue in my head was laced with expletives.

I passed two women in housekeeping uniforms who were on their way to work. They were too involved in their conversation to give me more than a rote "good morning" that must have been required by the handbook. I nodded them and kept my eyes averted in order to keep a low profile.

After they passed, I stopped long enough to swipe my

forehead with the bottom of my tank top.

A man appeared at the top of the hill. I probably would have dismissed him as a resort guest, except for the fact that he was dressed in a gray suit. His skin was the color of mahogany. His crisp shirt, white. Was he a security officer? Most of the Ritz employees wore uniforms, but maybe they had someone in plain clothes in house. Although, let's be clear, there was nothing "plain" about a suit in this weather.

Act like a guest, Lizzie. He has no idea who you are—and nothing on this island moves that fast. Besides, what have you really done, anyway, other than being a certified busybody? I started up the hill again, waiting for my new friend to veer off our collision course and soothe my fears.

Wouldn't you like a nice game of tennis this morning, sir? But he passed the tennis courts without a glance in their direction. In fact, it seemed like he might be looking at me.

It was at this point in my life that I wished I truly grasped what "act cool" meant. My brain understood the concept, but none of the rest of my body did. I felt my senses go hyper-aware. I heard the distant sound of a truck, then the clucking of a chicken in the bushes. I took in my surroundings casually, pretending I was admiring the flamingo pink Ixora, each spray of pink flowers forming their own mini bouquet, when I was actually looking for a subtle way to change my route.

I swore I still felt the man's eyes on me. Who was he and why was he so seemingly interested in me?

At that point, we were only about twenty feet apart. I ventured a peek, hoping I was just paranoid after this morning's events.

Our eyes met. *Damn.* For once, I feverishly wished he were looking at my boobs.

I had to pull myself together. I could be anyone, for all he knew. I looked up at him, trying to project a pleasantness I didn't feel. I was startled to find my adversary strangely handsome. He kept his black hair in short twists at the top of his head, with the sides and back neatly trimmed. I could see his dark eyes searching my face. A small smile played over his lips, as though he walked through life constantly amused.

"Good morning," I croaked out—then I cursed myself. I was a tourist. Tourists didn't do that.

"Good morning," he said, nodding briskly. The amusement dropped from his face.

I took a breath in and held it as we passed. We were moving so quickly in opposing directions that I actually felt the passing breeze fan my feverish face. After we passed, I gulped in air like I was coming up after being underwater for too long.

He let me pass.

After ten paces, high on adrenaline, I recovered my old spunk. I felt a smile spread across my face. Time to toss out my tinfoil hat. There was clearly no need for this level of paranoia.

My confidence restored, I couldn't resist looking back. I swiveled my head over my shoulder and felt a jolt of electricity when our eyes met once more. Apparently, he was as curious about me as I was him.

Fuck.

I tried to turn forward casually. It was all I could do to keep myself from breaking into a full-on sprint. I kept my body at housewife-power-walk speed, even as the spark of my fears threatened to build into a full-on fire.

I gave the guard house a wide berth. I had always seen it as a mere prop to keep the local riff-raff out—myself included—but now it took on a more sinister cast. Would the guard stop me if I tried to leave? Had the police called in orders like "no one in or out"? What if they had one of those wooden black-and-white striped arms that dropped down to block my way? Would I run my little Suzuki straight through it? And would it possibly break my car, instead of the other way around?

Focus, Lizzie. Just get to your car.

I made it to my Suzuki and it started, much to my relief. I cautiously guided the car out of its spot, headed toward the exit. I knew I looked like a sweaty mess, but I plastered on my brightest smile as I came around the curve and pulled even with the guard shack.

There was a wooden arm to bar my exit—but it was up. My path to freedom was wide open in front of me.

I slowly turned my head to speak to the guard, my head filling with excuses that didn't involve those girls. I was applying for a job with the water sports desk. I was delivering a cake. I was meeting a friend for tennis in 90-degree weather. I was—

My eyes fell on the guard at the shack, the same one I'd seen reading the paper on the way in. The paper lay slack in his lap and his head was bowed slightly forward. He didn't move as I pulled up.

The most outrageous thought ran through my head: *Is he dead?*

The paper in his hand twitched and I bit back a scream. Not dead. Asleep. And not interested in me.

I hit the gas, jerking the car forward—and nearly taking out one of the gardeners, who was dragging a pile of palm fronds across the driveway.

I put my hand out to apologize. He just shook his head at me to remind me, as if I didn't already know in the moment, what a crazy white girl I was. My left leg jiggled up and down as he moved his bundle slowly but surely, his khaki uniform dark with sweat around his throat and chest. I couldn't tell you what his face looked like because I was too scared to make eye contact. I just needed to get the hell out of dodge with my sanity intact. As it was, I was on the verge of bursting out into hysterical laughter, and my body was humming with enough electricity to power this island for a few days.

When he finally cleared the front of my car, I crept forward enough to look right, then left.

Then I jammed down on the accelerator to get to Red Hook as fast as I possibly could.

I kept an eye out for VIPD cruisers coming the other way.

If the girls hadn't called the police as they claimed, who had? Either way, it seemed like a good idea to make myself scarce lest they set their beady little sights on me. I had a feeling that Jessie would pull out that finger wag of hers again and tell tales of not just Ben, but also the redheaded girl who identified herself as Lizzie.

If the VIPD were as incompetent as rumor said they were, maybe they wouldn't follow up on that lead. But then where did that leave Ben—and Dave?

And now I found myself on my way to Red Hook to figure out why Ben had a missing girl's cell phone. What a mess.

If he's guilty, will I turn him in?

The thought blanked out my mind. I owed Ben, but if he'd hurt that girl or, Jesus, killed her . . . I couldn't think about that. I just needed to get to Red Hook.

It was a bustling day in the marina. I had to circle the parking lot twice to find a spot. Most of the charter boats had gone out for the day, and their owners and crew had parked up the lot, leaving slim pickings for little old me. I finally found a semi-legal spot at the very end of a row that seemed made for a Suzuki. Sure, the sign said "no parking," but it said that all over the marina. We mostly ignored those signs. (You probably could, too.)

I caught myself tip-toeing up the stairs to the coffee cart, and a bubble of laughter burst out of my throat.

Not only were the police likely not searching for me, but, even if they were, they probably had very little idea where to look.

I was just not cut out for this stuff.

I paused on a landing and gave my face a quick rub with hot hands, plus a little pep talk that involved a lot of curse words. Then I continued up the stairs. I was just Lizzie Jordan, ordinary island-dwelling citizen.

At the top, I stopped dead.

Ben stood at the edge of a table occupied by a handful of fifty-to-seventy-year-old sailors. I thought of them as the Old Pirates Club. Several of the club's members happened to be white New Englanders who spent summers in places like Nantucket and Providence, although a Californian, a southerner and a native St. Thomian named Paul who never touched the cart's coffee also belonged. They snagged this same table every morning to discuss today's paper and yesterday's boating news: who struggled to dock in thirty-knot gusts, whose boat was on the wrong mooring, yadda yadda. That's what passed for news down here. That and the thieves at the power company who kept raising our rates and cutting off our electricity.

This morning, though, their focus wasn't yesterday's news. It was Ben, who stood at the end of the table, white coffee cup in his left hand, eyes bulging, gesturing wildly with his other hand while a salt-and-pepper head sporting a long sailor's braid nodded along. The woman next to him, a blonde in her fifties, her white skin florid from the sun, rolled her eyes. She'd clearly heard Ben's stories before.

So much for Ben keeping a low profile—and if he was telling my story from yesterday, God help him. I'd turn him over to the police myself.

I cleared my throat once and the head with the braid swiveled in my direction. I knew its owner well—a jolly soul who served a killer cocktail and was at least fifteen years sober himself. I wanted to give him more than a tight smile, but it was all I had in the moment.

Ben continued on, oblivious to my presence.

I tried again, my throat-clearing now theatrical in its emphasis and volume.

Ben snapped out of his performance and gave his usual 120-watt smile. It froze in place when he saw my expression, my eyebrows hiked high and my mouth pursed tight.

He turned to the Old Pirates. "Duty calls, guys." He sauntered over to me, again offering a cautious smile—his defense mechanism, I noted. I grabbed his arm and hauled him toward the stairs.

"Go," I commanded, giving his back a shove to get him moving.

The look he gave me over his shoulder was pure hurt little boy. But he complied, heading to the parking lot where I commanded him into my Suzuki with a glare.

"Where are we going?" he asked.

I didn't answer. I turned my wheel hard left to maneuver out of my semi-legal spot, then hit the gas, weaving through the marina toward the exit.

"Lizzie, where—"

I stopped the car abruptly, jerking both of us forward. "I don't know!" I said. "Just—just sit back and shut up for a minute."

I saw his face neutralize before he turned forward. That was enough for me. I guided the car to the end of the driveway, then made a right turn, my tires chirping as we took off.

I wasn't sure where I was taking Ben, but I wanted him—and me—away from prying eyes. Red Hook wasn't going to do the trick. That place was too full of gossips who had nothing more to do than talk.

The next resort, Sapphire Beach, was a little more private, but it just wasn't the kind of place I wanted to discuss a potential kidnapping—or murder. Some days, taxis dropped off cruise ship guests by the hundreds. Not what you'd call a quiet spot.

As we twisted around past the resorts on the eastern side of the island, I marveled at Ben's silence. Maybe he finally realized that he was in deep doo-doo and that he might have dragged me in, too.

As we pulled around a tight curve, I noticed that the chain was down in front of the path that led to Lindqvist Beach. I didn't hesitate to wonder who had opened up the entrance. I just turned right and pulled down the path. We went over a grassy hill, then down into the trees and scrub that ringed the beach.

Beaches here are public to the high-water mark, but, when it comes to private property, owners don't have to provide access unless it's written into their deed. In other words, you can theoretically enjoy every beach on the island—but you have to get to it first.

I'd heard a million rumors about Lindqvist and why the property was usually chained off. I never heard the same story twice, so I won't repeat any of them here. All I knew was that sometimes it was okay to go down to the beach, and sometimes it wasn't.

Lindqvist appeared to be open today, although it might be a bitch to get out if the owner decided to put the chain back up. I'd worry about that later. For now, it would be a good place to regroup. My car would be hidden from the road, and we could plot our next move on a beach that would remind us why we lived here in the first place.

I stopped in the shade of a palm tree and looked over at Ben. His face was blank, his eyes inscrutable behind his Ray Bans.

"Out," I said. I opened my door and traced a goat path that led around a sea grape tree. The dirt and stones of the parking area turned into sand under my flip flops.

I came around the bush, and, even in my angry state, Lindqvist Beach took my breath away. We were just a three-minute walk from the busy road to Smith Bay, but I felt light years away from the hustle and bustle of St. Thomas.

A line of palm trees, scrub and sea grapes ringed a crescent-moon-shaped white sand beach. Clear water surged gently against the shore, then extended over to St. John in deepening bands of turquoise. With only a little imagination, you could be on your own deserted island, especially on a quiet day when there was no one else around.

I sighed and suddenly wanted to be in a bikini, toting a chest of Corona and a new novel.

Unfortunately, I had other items to deal with at the moment, so my "I live in a place where most people vacation" moment would just have to wait.

I didn't see any sign of whoever had unbolted the chain, so I plopped down in the shade of a tall palm tree, the sand cool against my rear. Ben sat down beside me unbidden, which I took as a good sign.

"So—" I started, but Ben cut in.

"Lizzie, you are being *ridiculous*." And then he laughed. He *laughed*. Any tranquility I'd been gifted by the scenery melted into anger.

I cut right into his outburst. "Andrea's gone. And do you know who called *right after you called from a missing girl's cell phone*?" I didn't give him a chance to answer. "The police."

His coffee cup slid from his hand, landing sideways on the sand. I watched its milky brown contents spill out. Although my love for order begged me to right it, I let the coffee make rivulets in the sand as Ben's face sank into his hands.

"This is your reality, my friend," I said. "Correction: *our* reality."

"Oh, God. You serious?" he asked through his fingers.

"How the hell did you get her cell phone? And you better not bullshit me because now you've got *me* mixed up in this cluster."

He looked up, startled by the anger in my voice, that innocent boyish look back again.

But I wasn't having this anymore. I slammed my right fist against my open palm.

"Goddamn it, Ben. Stop fucking around. You aren't going to be able to skate by on your looks and your charm on this one."

He sat up straight, exhaling a long breath. "What do you want to know?"

I locked my eyes with his. Then his gaze skittered away, out over the water.

"Did you hurt her?" I demanded.

His whole body jolted as if I'd hit him. "No. I don't know how you could ask me that."

I paused.

I knew Ben better than I knew most people down here. When you spend twelve hours a day together, sometimes for as many as twenty days in a row, you get to know someone inside and out—or you think you do. And of course, there was that night when he'd actually seen me, listened to me and helped me lighten the load I carried about my family. But I couldn't think about that now. It was too much. How had we gotten to this point—where I believed he might have something to do with a girl's disappearance?

My mind snapped back to the moment I'd heard Ben's voice on Jessie's phone that morning.

"Time to explain Andrea's phone, then," I said. "And it's time to explain Dave."

His face took on a knowing look. "Ah, now I know why you're upset. Dave."

I banged my fist in my hand again. "No, Ben. I'm angry because you lied to me. You dragged me into whatever you have going on, and now we might both be completely fucked. How did you get Andrea's phone? I think you at least owe me the full truth."

I saw a muscle twitch in his jaw.

I wanted to look away. I wished I could let my eyes drift over the startling beauty of Lindqvist and forget everything. But I couldn't. I kept my eyes on Ben, shooting daggers into the side of his face to keep the pressure on.

Finally, a nod. "I didn't tell you the whole truth last night."

I felt my heart drop in my chest. And now the police had a name and a description of yet another person who might have been involved—me. How stupid could I have been? I shoved myself up off the sand and began pacing the beach, my mind clicking.

It was a take-prisoners-first, ask-questions-later kind of police state down here. Just ask my friend who was rear-ended by a police car last year. The police officer accused her of stopping short on purpose. Then he threatened to take her to jail for assault on a police officer. When she requested to return to her car to call her lawyer, she was arrested for a hit-and-run attempt.

Even though she was eventually released, that same officer miraculously appeared at all the same and bars and restaurants she frequented. He never spoke to her, just sat and stared. She finally left island when he started following her home with his lights flashing. Did she report it? Of course she did. However, that officer was married to the cousin of someone higher up, and her complaints went nowhere.

What lay in store for Ben—and for me—I could only imagine.

"When we left Duffy's, we didn't go over to XO," he said. "We went back to my car first."

"And?"

"And she gave me a blow job."

I groaned. "In your *car*? In the busiest parking lot on island?"

"There's this little corner over near the dumpster. No one looks over there."

"Jesus. I'm guessing you've done this before."

He didn't answer, which I took as an affirmative.

"You better hope they don't have a CSI team worth their salt down here." I shook my head. "What then?"

"The rest was true. I swear to you. We did go into XO and have a drink. She told me she wanted to come home with me, but she had to go tell her friends first. She never came back. I really thought she ditched me."

"Still doesn't explain the phone."

"I found her phone this morning. She must have dropped it in my car while we were—"

I held up a hand. I needed details, but not *those* details. "But what on earth possessed you to use her phone to call?"

"I wanted to know the last person she called. When I saw it was Jessie, I just called. I dunno. I guess I hoped Andrea would be there."

I shook my head in frustration. "I really thought you were smarter than that. Of course her last call was to one of the girls she was on vacation with. You just made it worse."

"I'm making it worse?" he asked. "You're the one that got the police involved."

"Me? What are you talking about? Why would I call the police?"

"You're the only one I told."

"And I didn't tell anyone except those girls who already knew their friend was missing."

"That's it?"

"That's it." I paused. "Well, okay. I did tell Dave." I stopped pacing. "But Dave wouldn't—wait, what was he doing with you at Duffy's the other night?"

Ben held up his hands. "Ask him," he said. "But if he called the police . . ." Ben shook his head, his face dark.

The sand sucked at my feet as I paced. My mind flashed to the possibilities: an investigation, jail, a trial. My life here would never be the same. I felt my throat tighten. "Ben, what are we going to do?"

He heard the shift in my voice and stood. I saw something different in the way he carried himself. His shoulders were square, his jaw set. This was the Ben who'd calmly handed me the life ring yesterday, the one who believed I could handle a drowning victim. This was the guy who'd helped me start to trust other people again. This was the Ben I knew. This was the Ben I did the favor for.

"We find her," he said.

"Interesting use of the word 'we.'"

"You said it yourself. You're in this now, whether you like it or not. And I can't do it on my own."

"What are we going to do, go door to door? Even the Postal Service doesn't do door to door down here. There's a reason."

"Did you get anything out of the girls?"

I gestured toward the car. "I've got some notes in my glove box. Somehow, I talked them into giving me some highlights of their vacation so far. It wasn't that interesting. They went a few places—Duffy's, Saloon—met some people, some weird, some douchebags—you know, island life. Nothing that really stood out to me."

Ben put a hand on my shoulder. I didn't stop to question its sincerity, like I usually would. I needed its weight and warmth.

"The person who took her has got to be here, Lizzie. This is a small island. Someone had to see *something*."

"Except if it happened near the dumpsters behind XO." I tried a weak smile. It didn't fit right, like a shoe one size too small, so I let it drop from my face. "What about you? You were there. Anything weird happen that night with Andrea?"

"Except for what I told you? Not much."

I put a hand on top of his to get his attention. "Think. It could be really important."

A sheepish grin grew on his face.

"I was pretty wasted, Liz. I only remember flashes. Like I wasn't near the front at XO. I was in the back. I saw her go out the door, but I didn't watch every step." His voice cracked. "I didn't think I had to."

"Any creeps hanging around at Duffy's? Anyone exchange words with you or the girls?"

He shrugged. "It was the usual Ladies' Night crowd. Bunch of West Indians, bunch of white guys, bunch of tourists. No one who stood out to me."

"What about the girls?"

"Jessie was not a happy girl that night. She seemed pissed Andrea was leaving with me, but . . ." He grimaced.

"Girls on their vacations," I said. We nodded in unison. They could be bitches. We'd seen it a million times on the boat, especially with three. It was a tough number that almost always left someone in the cold.

"Becky mentioned some Coasties?"

"I was kinda focused on Andrea. I mean, I saw Dave because he came up and talked to me, but that was it."

I looked sharply at him at the mention of Dave, but he raised his hands again. "Not touching that. You're gonna have to handle that yourself. Oh, your boy Magnus was there." He snorted. "He's hard to miss. I've never liked that guy."

"Well, then, bring out the handcuffs. I'm sure he's guilty if *you* don't like him. This from the guy who went to El Cubano the other night with Cappy. Face it. You don't get along with most dudes. You're a ladies' man."

"And you don't get along with that many girls," he said sharply. "So maybe we're not that different."

I could feel heat rise in my cheeks and I was about to make a retort when I felt Ben squeeze my shoulder.

"I'm sorry," he said. "I'm freaking out."

I nodded.

A rustling in the bushes caught my attention.

A man in ragged black pants shredded to threads halfway down his calves stumbled out of the sea grape trees down the beach. A faded purple shirt hung on his bony frame. He had shaggy hair with a few stray salt-and-pepper dreadlocks pointing from his head like spikes. The lower half of his deep brown face was covered with a scraggly white beard.

In his right hand, he held a machete.

For all I knew, he could be doing maintenance with that blade. But then his eyes swung in a loop-de-loop and he started shouting unintelligibly, the machete swaying back and forth as he walked.

Unlike most villains in scary movies, the guy was moving at a pretty brisk clip toward us, his feet kicking up plumes of sand as he strode. Maybe he was the person who had taken out the chain to the beach. I certainly wasn't going to ask him.

I turned back to Ben, but I realized he was already moving toward the car.

"Coward," I muttered under my breath. I tried to move back to the car in a casual, I'm-not-nervous-at-all kind of way so as not to provoke the machete man. My courage broke about five feet from the car. I ran the last few paces and slammed the door shut behind me hard enough to shake the car.

When I got the car started, I jammed the accelerator hard and the car jerked backward. I thought I caught a glimpse of the machete around a tree as I put the car back in drive, but I didn't look back. I swore I could hear the man yelling as the Suzuki bounced over the rough terrain.

"Careful there, Jeff Gordon. You're gonna pop a tire," Ben said, bracing himself on the dashboard.

We reached the road and, mercifully, the chain was still down. I knew I had to turn right and get us farther away from the visibility of Red Hook. I hit the gas and we sped away from the madman on the beach.

"Turn around," Ben said.

"No way."

"TURN AROUND."

"No."

"I want to go home."

"Are you crazy?! That's the first place they'll look."

"And I have some stuff that I don't want them to find."

I snuck a peek at the soon-to-be-accused kidnapper in the seat beside me, but I had to look away quickly. Although it was one of the wider, better-paved roads on the island, the road through Smith Bay was still a series of sharp curves. It wasn't a road you could relax on, not that I thought I'd be doing that any time soon.

From the quick glance I took, I could see that his shoulders had caved in and all the confidence I'd seen on the beach had drained away.

"This is probably the worst idea you've had yet," I said. I kept the car moving forward, away from Ben's apartment.

"I can just take the safari bus."

"Yeah, that's a better idea. Just wait on the side of the road in the open for the safari to pick you up. Sounds smart."

"You don't have to get involved. Just drop me at the lower resort area," he said. "I'll figure it out from there."

"Are you sure there's not a cute girl on the Northside you could hole up with for a few days?"

He nodded. "Yeah, there is. I just have some stuff I want to get first."

"Like what?" *A missing girl?*

He didn't respond immediately.

"More secrets, huh, Ben?"

"Fine," he said. "It's pot. I know you don't approve."

"You think a little bit of pot is going to be a problem when a girl's gone missing?"

Out of the corner of my eye, I saw him shift in his seat.

"We're not talking about a little bit of pot, are we?"

His silence told me what I needed to know.

"Christ. Are you dealing?"

He ruffled his hair with one hand. "I'm doing a friend a favor. A one-time thing."

"Stop right there. I don't want to know any more."

"You don't have to approve, Lizzie. I'm just asking you to drop me off."

I blew out a long breath. We rode a few more minutes. Neither of us spoke. I guess I hadn't known Ben as well as I thought I did.

I pulled into one of the many resorts that lined this road, one with an ancient guard shack that hadn't seen a guard in years. I hung a left into the first parking lot, scattering a flock of dumpster chickens who squawked their displeasure.

My breathing was shallow. I tried to control it, but I couldn't. I felt Jacob's hand gripping my arm. I saw my mother's face, her disappointment clear as a bell. Drugs had cost me my family—

A hand landed on my arm, and I jumped. I was in such a fog, I'd almost forgotten Ben was in the car.

"Lizzie, you okay?"

"It's just that the last drug dealer I knew . . ."

"I know," he said. "But it's me, Ben. I'm the guy who helped in your ocean rescue yesterday. Remember me? In fact, I should have gotten half credit for saving that guy. If, of course, he'd really been drowning."

I snorted. "Half credit? For what?"

"Handing you that life ring. Vital piece of equipment."

"Ridiculous."

"At least a supporting role. Like the Oscars. Best Supporting Actor in a Caribbean Rescue."

I started to laugh, a deep laugh I felt all the way to my belly. It brought me back to my Suzuki, to the feeling of the slick sweat in my armpits, to the sound of a mosquito buzzing near my left ear. I gave it a half-hearted swipe.

Once again, Ben had brought me back.

"Thanks," I said.

He nodded, and we sat for a moment, watching a rooster strut across the cracked asphalt. The sun lit up his cloak of flame-colored feathers, their intensity underscored by the dark, almost-black emerald plumage on the lower half of his body. Their throaty calls were annoying as hell, and rumor had it they were too stringy to eat, but, at the very least, some of these roosters were damn good-looking birds.

I turned to Ben. "This is what you really want?" I asked. "To go home? For sure?"

He smiled weakly. "Drop me, and you're free to go about your normal Lizzie business."

I wasn't so sure about that. But I knew I was either going to drive him home, or he was going to find his way there himself. I might as well do him this one last favor.

I checked for chickens behind me, then I backed up and maneuvered back toward the road. I didn't like this at all. My stomach agreed, and it did a flip-flop as I turned left, toward Ben's home.

Seven minutes later, I pulled into the Sapphire Resort, making a quick left toward the lower part of the resort. The long-term condos, where Ben lived, were perched on the hill above.

The vacation rental side of the property had definitely seen better days. The white retaining wall along the road was cracked in several places, its paint flaking to reveal dull, gray cement below. We passed the tennis court whose green surface was bleached to gray and riddled with fissures that sprouted native greenery. Who ever decided St. Thomas wasn't suited for agriculture apparently hadn't tried abandoning a tennis court. Rumor was that the condo board was in a legal battle with the owners, and both sides were refusing to pay for upkeep. Whatever the dispute, it was obvious throughout the resort.

I pulled into the dirt lot designated for public beach parking. I looked over at Ben. A slight sheen had broken out on his forehead, but it could have been the heat.

"You going to go see Dave now?" he asked.

I punched him on the arm, faking an air joviality that I didn't feel in the least. "Like you care," I said. "You've never showed one ounce of interest in Dave, and you're starting now?"

"You know that's not true."

I didn't say anything. I wanted to apologize, but the words just wouldn't come. Instead, I put my hand on Ben's shoulder.

We sat in silence for a moment, then I heard Ben say, "I'm gonna be okay." I gave his shoulder a squeeze and took my hand back. The corners of his mouth turned up slightly.

Seeing him smile should have made me feel better. Instead, it made my stomach clench. Then he twisted in his seat, gave me a kiss on the cheek and slid out of my car. I could feel a cool spot on my face where he'd left a trace of sweat. Instead of being disgusted, I was, well, kind of touched. For two emotional basket cases, we'd really extended ourselves.

"Eleven seventeen," he said.

"What?"

"Her birthday. One day before mine."

I nodded as though I understood, but I didn't.

I watched him walk across the dirt lot, then he disappeared behind a tall bush. I felt a small burst in my chest, strong enough that I put my hand to my heart, just in case something did explode out, *Alien*-style.

I didn't know it then, but the next time I'd see Ben, he'd be almost unrecognizable.

I backed out of my parking spot. As I reached the top of the driveway, I let my car roll to a slow halt.

Left led toward Dave. Not an option right now. I needed to roll in there like an Army tank, ready to deflect enemy fire and demand the truth.

In the state I was in, I would burst into tears before getting a single word out.

I turned the wheel right with no particular destination in mind. I passed a few scattered resorts, including the closed Marriott Renaissance whose abandoned pool was rumored to be a Caribbean wildlife version of Hieronymus Bosch's *Garden of Earthly Delights*. I'd never had the guts to check it out myself. The sheer idea gave me the shivers.

I drove on through Smith Bay.

The neighborhood was the unlikely home to the best restaurant on island. Romano's was an elegant northern Italian restaurant that operated out of an old house, which was tucked away in a neighborhood that also featured a Crown Fried Chicken, the infamous El Cubano and several small stores housed in cement bunkers with small, barred windows. Romano's hired a guard to stand watch over everyone's cars while they ate.

I probably could have stress-eaten my weight in lasagna with béchamel, followed by a few shots of their house-made limoncello, but they didn't open until five o'clock. I kept rolling.

After Smith Bay, my little Suzuki whined up a huge hill, then I made a nearly-180-degree right turn onto the road that headed to the Northside of the island.

I couldn't tell you the name of the road. We called it "the road to the Northside." Clever, no?

It wasn't a road for the claustrophobic. It was carved into the side of a steep mountain with just enough room for two cars between the volcanic rock face on the left and the steel guard rail protecting you from a sheer drop-off on the right.

The road wound through residential neighborhoods, and I passed houses perched precariously on the side of the drop-off.

Sometimes all you would see to indicate a house below was a glimpse of the top of the driveway, with the characteristically roughed-up cement that gives cars the traction they need to climb and descend.

I made another right and a quick left, giving me a brief glimpse of Magen's Bay, the horseshoe-shaped cove that lived at the top of every magazine's top ten beaches list. It was a stunner, no question, with verdant green hills surrounding a bay that sported every stunning shade of blue you could imagine. The beach itself hosted a boisterously fun bar, but also a ton of cruise ship visitors. I liked the view from up here best.

Six open-air taxis were parked in the Drake's Seat overlook today, their benches temporarily empty while cruise shippers snapped their photos. I kept going.

This road had some of the toughest curves on the island. I wanted to give it my full concentration but my mind kept wandering back to Ben—and Andrea. It bothered me that Ben had lied to me. Twice. It didn't seem like a good sign.

But, then again, did I truly believe that he was capable of killing a girl? What if it had all been some kind of horrible accident? Movie scenarios ran in quadruple time on the screen in my head. Maybe she slipped on his shower tiles and hit her head, then he panicked and dumped the body in the ocean. Maybe he called Dave in a blind panic, and they'd taken her out in his little boat, where they'd weighed her down and dumped her in the middle of Pillsbury Sound.

I paused for a moment. Was I really writing a mental movie in which Ben was the killer, with Dave as his accomplice? What was the matter with me?

I felt something like panic begin to well up in my chest with such force that my vision blurred. I had to pull over. I had to pull over now, or I was going to drive right off the damn road.

The trouble was that I was on a tight road with barely enough room for two cars and a ton of blind corners, so unless I wanted to end this whole charade permanently, I was going to have to find the road to Hull Bay where I knew I could stop and take a breather. And I needed to find it fast.

I didn't think I'd passed the turn yet, but I'd been so focused on imagining the worst that I was disoriented. The bush-lined road didn't offer many landmarks. My breathing grew shallow, and I could feel my palms get damp. My vision got cloudy again. If I passed out, my Suzuki and I would be in big trouble. I tried to gulp a few breaths of air to keep myself going.

I rounded the corner and saw E&M Market, a staple bodega for the Northside that sold a few fresh items and plenty of booze. Now I knew where I was. As I got closer, I saw two older men standing outside of the market. One was leaning against his car as he chatted with the other man. I wondered if they were Frenchies, a group of people on St. Thomas whose origins and culture fascinated me. I didn't know much about them, only that many of them came to St. Thomas from France via St. Barth's. I also knew many were fishermen, and that their culture tended toward insular.

I didn't have time to think about the Frenchies, though, because I felt my chest squeeze again.

I didn't want to have a breakdown in front of these guys. A rim of white appeared at the corner of my eyes and began creeping inward, but I kept going, searching desperately for the next road so I could pull over. I flexed my eyes wider, but that didn't make any difference.

Just as a layer of white snow began to overlay my view of the road, I saw a cut-off to the right. I wasn't sure if it was a road or someone's driveway, but I didn't care.

I hung a sharp right in front of a red pickup who beeped angrily at me. Shit. I hadn't even seen that guy.

I drove about thirty feet and stopped the car. The brush crowded in my window, scratching my left arm. My heart was pounding. I tried to suck more air in, but I just couldn't get enough, no matter how much I heaved my chest in and out.

My brain raced.

The air was dead still outside my windows. Sweat sprung out on my face, and a drop rolled down my nose. I tried to gulp some more humid air, but I still felt like I was drowning above water.

I blinked as the snow continued to take over my vision. I frantically looked around my car for something that could help me. I had snorkel gear and a faded blue beach chair in the way back. No help. Two old beer bottles nestled on the floor of the back seat. No help. My eyes searched the passenger seat, then I felt underneath. Nothing. Never had my car been so clean—or so unhelpful.

My field of vision was almost fully snowed in at this point. I grabbed for the glove box and flung it open. Inside, I found a small bottle of water about a quarter full. The label was faded and peeling, but I twisted off the cap and downed it. My head was now pounding right along with my heart. I'd need some aspirin, too, but that was asking way too much in the moment.

The water tasted vaguely like mold and it was hot in my mouth, but my lips grabbed greedily at each drop. I felt the pounding in my chest start to ease.

I leaned my head back against the headrest, closed my eyes and waited. If this was someone's driveway, they would have to wait. It was all I could do to simply sit and feel the panic that gripped my body recede.

Finally, I felt stable enough to sit up straight and open my eyes. I checked my vision by rolling my eyes in my head like an angry bull. My skin felt sticky, and I desperately needed a shower.

A flash in the glove box caught my attention. I leaned over and there, on top of a stack of those St. Thomas maps they give you at the airport, was an iPhone. I picked it up and turned it over in my hand.

My mind couldn't grasp what it was doing there.

It certainly wasn't mine.

It felt like some kind of alien device planted in my car.

The phone was turned off, the screen blank no matter how many times I pressed that center button.

Even so, I knew whose it was. I put a hand to my throbbing head as it began to pulse to a faster pattern. It was Andrea's. Ben had left Andrea's cell phone in my car.

I did the only thing I was capable of in that moment.

I screamed a blood-curdling scream that made my temples bulge.

Then I leaned on my steering wheel and sobbed.

9

After feeling sorry for myself for exactly nine minutes—that was all I'd allow myself—I did the logical next thing. I wiped off my face with the bottom of my tank top, then I backed up to the road.

I guided my car back toward E&M Market, walked past the two men who were still chatting in that particular dialect the Frenchies have. (It sounds to my untrained ears like Creole.) Then I bought a six pack of Presidente and a bottle of Advil.

I asked the guy behind the counter to pop the first beer for me, and he obliged with an opener he kept near the cash register for just that purpose. As I walked out, I downed about a third of it, washing down three Advil with my first swallow. One of the men, who was tall and skinny with a little beer paunch that announced itself through the unbuttoned front of his white shirt, winked at me from an olive-toned face as if to say, "I been there before."

I nodded at him and raised my bottle in a salute before pulling back out the way I came.

When I finished that bottle, I tossed it in the backseat where it clinked against the other two.

I bargained with myself before popping a second one. I'd have a second one, but I'd drink it slow.

And it would be my last. For now.

Someone once told me once that bargaining with yourself is one of the signs of alcoholism. I needed to walk a fine line right now. I had to stay sober enough to keep my car on the road but numb enough to keep my panic down and stay functional.

I started to feel steadier. My eyes still looked a little red in the rearview mirror, but I didn't think anyone would notice. I brushed at my sweaty hairline, but I was sure that had everything to do with the humidity and nothing to do with having a missing girl's cell phone in my possession. Right.

I took another long swig—just one more to keep me going—and I dropped the bottle in the cup holder. It was almost empty. I had to slow down.

I reached for my own cell phone. I kept one eye on the road and one eye on my cell as I paged through to find who I was looking for—my great white hope, in this situation.

"Lucas," I said when he picked up the phone. "It's Lizzie. I need your help in a big, big way."

I got the answer I'd hoped for and continued driving toward Lucas's house.

I told you that we all look out for each other down here, didn't I?

Lucas lived on the western side of the island, the middle of nowhere as far as I was concerned. It's odd that any place on a thirteen-mile-long and four-mile-wide island could feel so isolated, but the western side always felt eerie to me, despite the fact that it's home to two big institutions: the airport and the University of the Virgin Islands.

Part of it was the deceptive size of some of the neighborhoods. You'd drive for a while and see nothing but coastline and brush. Then a small sign would pop up, hinting at maybe three to five houses beyond. It told you nothing of the twisty one-lane tracks, lined on all sides with modest Caribbean-style cement houses.

I once went home with a bartender I worked with—a tale for another time. He lived over in Fortuna, one of the popular neighborhoods in the West End. When leaving his house the next morning, I took a wrong turn. Instead of finding the main road, I spent twenty minutes turning onto smaller and smaller roads until I realized the "road" I was on was someone's driveway. My little Suzuki came face to face with a pit bull that was all too happy to yank against the frayed rope that held him to a tree. I couldn't help but think that every deep-throated bark conveyed how happy he would be to sink his teeth into my flesh.

I nearly pissed myself on that "adventure," and frankly, I felt like I got off easy. I've never been so relieved to see a two-lane paved road in my life.

Lucas lived in a development on the West End called Shibui, a little strip of condos that overlook the airport, originally designed as a Japanese-style hotel. He was one of the few people I knew who had an office job on St. Thomas, and that position had given him the cash to buy his place.

Lucas was the IT manager for a hedge fund that had chosen St. Thomas for its tax generous incentives. It was easy to spot someone who worked at Everest because they were overdressed for just about every bar on island. They were the guys in button-down shirts and dress pants, the ones running the biggest tab in the place.

Lucas was different, though. Like many IT guys I'd known, he did his own thing, which today included not going to work, apparently. Not that I was criticizing, by any means. He was right where I needed him to be.

I eyed the other four Presidentes on the seat beside me. I didn't have a buzz on quite yet, but I was starting to feel mellow. Two for me and two for Lucas seemed kind of paltry. Although I rarely showed up on anyone's door step asking for help—actually, it was the first time I could recall in a while—it seemed rude to bring only four beers, two of which I intended to drink myself. I came around a bend and hung a left. The brief detour allowed me to grab a second six-pack of Presidentes from a gas station.

I thought my act of generosity deserved a reward, so I cracked another beer, but I promised myself I'd only drink half before I arrived at Lucas's house.

One beer later, I reached the gate at Shibui. Lucas buzzed me in. I parked next to his blue Jeep Grand Cherokee. It looked a hell of a lot better than my shit heap, but his Jeep bore its own share of scratches and dents, including what looked like a fresh one in the quarter panel over the left rear tire, where the body was crinkled in. Even the nicer cars on the island looked like they'd been through a war zone.

"Kmart parking lot," a voice said from above.

I jumped a little, not realizing Lucas was already on his porch. With all the juice running in my veins, I probably would have screamed bloody murder had it not been for those three beers.

I felt a flush of embarrassment. I didn't want Lucas to think I was coming unhinged. I focused on the car. "That parking lot is a magnet for accidents. Although, to be fair, my car wouldn't even show the damage."

He nodded and smiled lazily. Lucas always looked to me as though he was about to fall asleep or he'd just finished the world's biggest blunt. He was about my height but much more substantial—big shoulders, barrel-chested around the middle, legs like tree trunks sticking out of his black mesh basketball shorts. Today, he wore a black Slayer shirt with the sleeves ripped off, its color faded to a brownish-gray by the Caribbean sun. He leaned his thick pale white forearms on the black wooden railing. It was about as faded as his shirt.

His hair was a sandy brown color, cut close to the scalp all around. I'm pretty sure he did it himself with a trimmer. At least he hadn't grown it out to the long, stringy island-boy style that so many guys favored down here, a style that made me want to snatch up a pair of scissors more often than not.

Lucas had a nice, white smile, and I often thought he would be kind of attractive if he cared a little more about his appearance instead of, say, letting his patchy facial hair grow for indeterminate periods of time. But Lucas didn't seem to care about things like that. In fact, I wouldn't be surprised if he went into the office dressed like this.

He waved his arm in a "come on in" gesture and headed back inside.

I stuck the phone in my back pocket and grabbed both six pack cartons from my seat.

I walked up the red wooden steps, my eyes tracing the angled, red Japanese-style roof. From the exterior, you might think you were stepping onto the set of *Shogun*.

However, the interior of Lucas's place was almost completely modern, with dark wood cabinets in the open kitchen and stainless steel appliances. I happened to know that he also had a sunken tub right in the center of the floor of the master bathroom. Wander around in there in the dark and you might just break a leg.

Because Lucas was a dude, the place was a mess. Every possible surface was occupied with old mail, pizza boxes, a collection of empty bottles and more detritus of the bachelor lifestyle.

Lucas was sitting on a futon in his living room, clearing some papers off his mahogany wood coffee table. It looked like something my mother would have owned, with thick, intricately carved legs. However, the top had been scarred by years of abuse. Most notable were the rings in the finish from sweating drinks that had not been afforded coasters. I saw a burn mark from a cigarette, too. My mother would have had a heart attack.

In deference to the table's future, I set the six packs on the floor. I held a beer out to Lucas. He nodded and took it, popping the top with a bottle opener he kept at close reach. He passed the opener to me and I popped one too. This was my fourth beer, right? I had to keep it tight if I wanted my head about me—and if I wanted to get back on the road home.

Lucas's cat, Arthur, appeared from the bedroom. He sniffed the remaining Presidentes and took an experimental lick at one of the bottles. He rubbed his black and white body against the edges of the cardboard carrier. Then he wound through my legs in a tight figure eight that threatened to take me out. I sat on the futon quickly to avoid falling. I couldn't let a cat get the better of me.

Arthur was awfully friendly today. He was part Maine Coon, Lucas had told me once, and he had a personality as big as his twenty-pound body, whose apparent size was amplified by his fluffy coat.

Once I sat, Arthur jumped up on the couch with me, walking indifferently across my bare legs, his bottle-brush tail tickling the underside of my chin. He stopped between Lucas and me, then, without warning, he plopped down against my leg, twisting his neck to rest his chin on my thigh.

The underside of Arthur's chin was hot—too hot. I was sure Arthur would move at any minute, realizing his mistake. Instead, he rearranged himself so he could add a mitt-like paw to my leg. Then he appeared to go to sleep. I could feel my lower back start to sweat in sympathy. I hope Lucas worked fast.

"He likes you," Lucas said.

I nodded. Bully for me.

"You have it?" he asked.

I leaned forward and pulled the iPhone out from my pocket. Arthur twitched a whisker but stayed in position. I placed the phone on the newly-cleared table, next to Lucas's laptop. I noticed a tiny crack in the phone's screen in the upper right corner. Had that happened during a struggle?

Lucas wasn't the kind to ask questions, but I wanted him to know what he was getting into. So I told him.

As was his habit, Lucas's expression stayed constant—until I told him that I was 99% sure that this cell phone belonged to a missing girl. His sleepy eyes widened a few millimeters. They looked down at the phone and back up at me, and I could see light flicker in them. This was probably the most animated I'd seen him in a long time.

"And this is the phone? This is her phone?"

"I can't get it to turn on. Are you—" I swallowed. "Are you okay with doing this?"

He shrugged. "Don't think it can hurt."

"I'm hoping it can help Ben."

Lucas tilted his head at me. "How'd you get yourself mixed up in this again?"

I took a long draw of Presidente. "I did a favor for Ben."

Lucas didn't say anything.

"I owed him."

"You and Ben . . . ?"

I felt my face flush. "Oh God. No. I'm not another one of his love-sick conquests."

No response from Lucas.

"Suffice it to say that it started as a favor to him, but now the police are involved. I'm afraid they're going to think I'm involved, too. But if I can find Andrea or at least figure out what happened to her . . ."

We both looked at the phone on the table. I took another swig of beer, as did Lucas.

Finally, he nodded. "We gotta know what's on it. Passcode?"

"I don't know. Is there any way to get around it?"

He tilted his head from side to side. "Maybe. It's a little tricky and involves almost calling the police." He paused.

"You know anything more about her? People use stuff they'll remember easily."

"Like what?"

"Dates, birthdays, anniversaries, zip codes, house numbers, stuff like that."

"God, I wish I did. I don't even know where she's from. Just that she wasn't wearing Havaianas the night she went missing, if that's even how you say it."

Lucas squinted at me.

I waved a hand in the air. "Forget it." I chewed on the inside of my cheek. "Okay. Birthdays, anniversaries, zip codes—what else? Can we Google her?"

"Of course. I've got some pretty good databases. You know her last name?"

Crap.

Lucas shook his head. "You know these things matter in the real world."

"Last names?"

"Yup."

We sat in silence for a second, each taking a swig of Presidente. Arthur flexed his paw and I felt the gentle prick of his claws. Any more of that and he'd have to move.

I wondered whether the cops had caught up to Ben yet.

I sat bolt upright, eliciting a meow of protest from Arthur. "November 17th. That's her birthday."

Lucas squinted at me. "Where'd that come from?"

"Ben told me, right before he got out of my car. I didn't know what he meant at the time, but . . ." I trailed off, replaying the moment he'd walked away, his blue shirt soaked through with sweat in the middle of his back. I snapped back to reality. "That idiot used her phone to call me."

Lucas's eyes widened briefly. That was twice in one day.

"I know. Not the smartest move he's made. I told him to find some lady to hole up with on the Northside."

Lucas took a long swig of his Presidente. "Ben. Man."

I nodded and took another swig in solidarity. I think it was safe to assume that we were both thinking the same thing. Was it possible that Ben had made Andrea disappear? And if he had, how could he have been so goddamn stupid about the whole thing?

Lucas picked up the phone and looked at it.

"Can they find us here, tracking that phone?" I asked.

"Nah. I don't think they have the tech. When I got robbed last year? The cops who showed up could barely write their own names. I asked if they could dust for fingerprints and they looked at me like I was a time traveler. But either way, I'm going to clone her phone and put it on a spare I keep around." He pushed himself up from the couch and went to his kitchen, rummaged through a drawer and came back with an almost identical phone, minus the crack at the edge of the screen. He put it on the coffee table along with a few white cables. Then, he leaned forward to work without another word.

I leaned back on the couch and took another long draw of my Presidente while I watched Lucas work, his large body compacted in half as he tapped, clicked and pushed buttons. He finished his first beer and grabbed another from the six-pack, holding it out to offer it to me first. He was a gentleman, that one.

I shook my head. I was feeling that tell-tale lightness in my head. I had to slow down.

He shrugged then popped the top and went back to tapping.

I dropped my head back and looked at the dark wooden beams crisscrossing Lucas's ceiling. Here and there, I spotted a feathery white spider web. I put my right hand on Arthur's body. He was still hot to the touch, but I tried to take comfort in his warmth.

"Alright, you ready to hold your breath?"

Lucas broke into my cat-induced reverie. His face wore a slightly impish grin.

I sat up quickly and winced as Arthur flexed his claw into my flesh again. "Wait, why?"

"I'm turning on that girl's phone. But just long enough to make a copy. Just in case they're tracking it. Backup plan if we hear them coming is to throw it into the bush down the hill. It would take them HOURS to find it there. If they'd even bother."

"Wait, wait," I said, putting out my arm. "I thought you said they couldn't track it."

"I'm pretty sure."

"Pretty sure?"

"This island surprises me every day."

He had a point there. I put my beer to my forehead. "Are you sure we should do this?"

"What else you gonna do? Like you said, those girls know who you are. You're already in the shit, Lizzie. Best thing you can do is find some info to get you out of it. You just gonna wait at home until the police come for you?"

I took a sip of Presidente. Score two points for Lucas. I was probably already a known person to the police. There was no turning back on that one. If I had some capital to work with, I'd be in a much better position. And maybe, just maybe if I could find Andrea, I could put everything right again.

"How long will it take?"

"Depends on the phone and what's on it. I'm hoping less than ten minutes. Main police station is in town. Even if they pick up the signal immediately, we should be done before they get here. Take them a while to even get the gate open."

I nodded. Although my body ached to lean back and take a breather, I couldn't. I stayed ramrod upright, the side of my leg pressing into Arthur who was now nearly nuclear on the heat scale.

"Hold on to your butts," he said, and pressed the side of the phone.

I held my breath as the screen lit up with an icon of an Apple.

Lucas hit a few buttons and I watched a blue progress bar on his screen begin to inch to the right. I checked my watch. 10:34. Ten more minutes and I'd have answers—or I'd be carted off to jail.

I didn't know much about the jail in St. Thomas. I passed the jail in Tortola, in the British Virgin Islands, every day that I worked. It was a lime green building, high on the hill on the northeastern tip of the island. It looked lonely to me. The views from the prison cells—lush green islands with white sand beaches at their shorelines, lined by palm trees that swayed in the cool Atlantic breeze—must have been torture.

I looked at my watch: 10:37 and the bar had only moved a tiny bit. "What gives?" I asked.

Lucas was leaning back on the couch, finishing his second beer. "Relax, Lizzie. It sometimes takes longer. All good."

I tried to mimic his posture in hopes that it would help me mimic his attitude, but it didn't work. I kept twitching every few seconds. Lucas picked up the remote to turn on the television.

"Don't," I said.

He raised his eyebrows in a question.

"We won't be able to hear the sirens."

The edges of his mouth curled up in a smile, but he said nothing.

"You think I'm paranoid?"

"Probably." His smile deepened briefly. Then he put his head back and shut his eyes.

My arms and legs begged for motion. For the first time in my life, I felt like maybe I should go to a rave and dance through the night. As it was, my knees twitched at intervals as I watched the progress bar continue to turtle forward.

After a particularly violent twitch of my leg, Arthur gave me a reproachful look. He gathered himself and stood, heading for Lucas's lap. Lucas barely moved as Arthur settled himself in. They certainly made a pair.

I cocked my head to the side. Did I hear something? Maybe it was just a ferry blowing its horn. I sat stock still. A rooster crowed. Nothing else. I needed to calm down.

I checked the progress bar. It sat at about 50%. I begged it to move faster.

I stretched my legs in an effort to quiet them, then laid my head back again. I felt movement on the couch, then paws on my legs. A fluffy body plopped itself on my bare legs. Arthur was back. I laid a hand in his fur. Might as well embrace it. I let my eyes drift closed—then I heard it.

I leapt to my feet, spilling Arthur on the floor. He yowled angrily. "Lucas, they're coming."

"What?" he said, his eyes blinking. He had clearly fallen deeply asleep.

"Don't you hear it?" There it was again. At the edge of my hearing, I clearly and distinctly heard a siren.

"Lizzie, you've got to chill."

I listened again, but the sound seemed to have disappeared. I couldn't sit. I paced around the room and checked the progress bar. Maybe 60%. *Move faster.*

I felt a breeze blow through Lucas's apartment, and the siren blew in with it.

I saw Lucas sit up. We exchanged glances.

Arthur stood at my feet and howled at me. "Cut it out," I told him, but he continued to berate me.

I could feel my chest start to tighten again, just like it had this morning. I grabbed my beer and took a swig as though it were medicine.

Over Arthur's yowling, it was impossible to tell if those sirens were getting closer.

"Seriously, Lucas. We gotta hear. How can I get Arthur to can it?"

He pointed toward an open door. "Put him in there and shut the door." He was now leaning forward, staring intently at the computer screen, his lips pursed. More than the vague siren, that worried me. I had never seen Lucas show any kind of emotion.

I slammed my beer on the table and bent over to lift Arthur. His protests continued as I picked him up. Twenty pounds at least, I guessed. He twisted his head around to nip at my hands, but I managed to avoid his little teeth with a few turns of my wrists. I plopped him on an unmade bed—black sheets, black comforter, figured—then quickly shut the wooden door behind him. It was one of those cheap hollow wooden doors, so I could still hear his cries, although now the sirens were louder than he was.

"Shit," Lucas said, the meaty fingers of his right hand drumming on his knee.

"How close?"

"The cops?"

"The progress bar, Lucas! You're not equipped with GPS," I snapped.

Lucas held up his hands in surrender. "Jesus, Lizzie. We don't even know if they're coming for us."

"You think it's a coincidence?"

"The police found out about this two hours ago, and they're up on the phone already?"

He had a point. I took another swig and listened. The sirens seemed to fade a little. I breathed a little easier.

But then, just as I was about to sit down on the couch, they started up again with their full vigor. "What the hell?" I asked, aborting my descent to the couch.

"Winding roads. Changes the sound."

"Fuck."

"Almost there," Lucas said, but the sirens sounded closer than ever. I trotted to the door and opened it a crack.

"Can't see the gate from there," he said.

"What are we going to do with the phone?"

"Throw it into the bush."

"Maybe I should hand it over to them, explain that I found it in my car?"

Lucas just looked at me as though I'd grown a second head.

I sighed. "Yeah, bad idea."

The sirens were getting louder and louder. They sounded as though they would scream into view any second. Even Arthur had shut up. I was so wired that I was ready to jump out of my skin. "Is it done yet?"

"It's hung up on the last bit. Does this sometimes."

"Fuck. Fuck. Can you pull it?"

"Wouldn't recommend it. You won't get anything if it doesn't do a full download."

I blew out a sharp breath of air and kept pacing.

"Done!" Lucas called triumphantly and yanked the phone out of the cord. I watched the screen go black as he turned it off. Then, before I could stop him—and faster than I'd ever seen him move—he ran to the back of his apartment and chucked the old phone out his window. "Now you hide," he said. "If they come here and see you, it's bad news."

"Where?"

"Closet," he said, pointing to his room.

"Are you fucking serious?"

"I'll get 'em to go away."

What choice did I have? I took my Presidente and yanked open the door to his bedroom.

"Keep Arthur in there," he said.

I didn't have time to ask questions.

The sirens were piercingly close. I stepped over more discarded pieces of black clothing, then threw open the sliding door to Lucas's closet. There was a duffel bag in the bottom. I put down my beer and yanked it out with effort. Apparently, Lucas collected boulders and kept them in the bottom of his closet.

I ducked into the small space, sat on the tiled floor and slid the door shut. But not without first grabbing my beer.

I heard a large vehicle drive up, then the sirens went silent.

A pair of pants tickled my nose. I couldn't afford to sniffle or sneeze. I bent my head awkwardly, worried my neck would cramp soon.

I heard a muffled *plop*. Arthur had jumped off the bed. I held my breath, anticipating a yowl yet to be released.

I twitched as I heard scratching sounds against the closet door. I saw the black tip of his paw dart under the door. Arthur didn't want to get out. He wanted to get in.

I tried to ignore him.

Thud. I jumped as the giant paw of the Maine Coon whacked against the outside of the door. Shit. "Stop," I hissed.

He must have taken that as encouragement because he did it again.

What the hell was I going to do with this cat, other than skin him later? He obviously wasn't going to be deterred.

I slid open the door as quietly as I could, grabbed him by the scruff and hauled him onto my lap without spilling a drop of Presidente. Far from crying out, he settled into the crook between my drawn-up knees and my chest. I was tempted to clamp his mouth shut, but I figured that would only make him more ornery.

The damn cat actually started to purr, if you can believe it. He had zero barometer for disaster. Or, perhaps, like most cats, Arthur just didn't give a shit.

All that was left was to wait and listen.

I took one more sip of beer for courage.

Over Arthur's loud purrs, I thought I heard Lucas open his front door and say something. It was too muffled to make out. I felt my butt cheeks tighten against the cold tiles.

Arthur continued to purr away as though this was the best day of his life.

I heard Lucas speaking, but it was still too garbled to understand. I put my ear to the wall—but pulled back when I heard a set of steps headed my way. Crap. He'd sold me out.

How could I have been so stupid? Gullible, that's what I was. Could I blame him? If the situation was reversed, would I have gone to bat for Lucas?

I weighed my options. Even if I could dump Arthur and unfold myself, where was I going to go? I briefly imagined myself running through the wall of the condo and leaving a Lizzie-shaped hole, like Wile E. Coyote.

It was over. I took a long swig of beer, knowing it was my last for a long time.

The door to the bedroom opened. My body tensed. Then I had the terrible realization that I needed to pee, right then. I tightened my pelvic muscles. It was already going to be humiliating enough to be discovered crouching in a closet with a cat. If I wanted to maintain any shred of dignity, I had to hold it.

The footsteps stopped at the closet. Little did I think when I moved down to St. Thomas that this was how it would end. I must have tightened up on Arthur because he began to wiggle.

The door slid open abruptly, the light blinding me briefly. I blinked a few times, expecting to see the royal blue pants of the VIPD. I shrank back into the corner.

Instead, I saw a pair of meaty, hairy shins. It was Lucas. My bladder reminded me it was holding on by a thread, but I tightened down again.

He let out a bray of laughter. And trust me, it was a bray. Lucas could look kind of tough if you didn't know him, but that laugh gave him away as pure geek. "What is this?"

"You said get in the closet."

He took a few steps back and sat down on the bed, the laughter building. "You planning on taking Arthur to the clink?"

Now I was pissed.

I stowed my beer on the floor. Then I used one hand like a shovel to dislodge Arthur. He looked back at me reproachfully for disturbing our special moment. I toppled myself forward out of the closet onto hands and knees. Lucas was still laughing on the bed, his face shaking in soundless laughter.

I rose to stand in front of him, hands on my hips. "So? What the hell? Where are the police? What did you say?"

But Lucas was lost to me. His face went red, and he couldn't speak. I wanted to beat the crap out of him with my now-empty beer bottle. But first, I had to use the bathroom, or this day was going to turn worse.

When I emerged, he and Arthur were back on the couch. He extended the new phone to me, and I walked over and took it. I knew that my face still looked sour.

"It was an ambulance," he said. "Person in #5 had a damn heart attack."

10

I couldn't really stand to look at Lucas's face anymore, and I told him so. It only made him laugh harder. They say that on a small island you have to make your own fun. I thought Lucas was taking this bit of wisdom a little too far.

I gave him a gruff thank you as I gathered my belongings. When I tried to huff out, Lucas managed to get a gentle but firm hand on my arm. He was quicker than he looked when he wanted to be.

"Lizzie, be careful," he said. "You know how it is down here. Don't want them to lock you up and throw away the key."

He looked at me earnestly and, for a moment, I thought he was going to guide me back to his bedroom and make sweet, slow love to me all afternoon in a haze of pot and Presidente. I had never seriously considered making out with Lucas before. For a brief moment, the idea of escaping what lay in front of me felt tempting.

But I couldn't. I knew myself better than that. I couldn't wait for things to just catch up with me. I'm not sure if it was my conscience or some form of masochism. Whatever it was, it made me lean in and give Lucas a quick hug with a firm release.

As I walked to my car, Andrea's cloned iPhone felt heavy in my pocket.

I left the Presidentes at Lucas's house as my thank you. I also added another entry in my mental book of debts to pay. I knew the day would come, but I hoped returning Lucas's favor wouldn't be as dramatic as returning Ben's.

It was time to regroup. The incident with the ambulance had sobered me up—or so it felt. I needed a quiet place to gather myself. A bar wouldn't do. Instead, I turned my Suzuki in the direction of a small coffee shop in Yacht Haven Grande. I also knew almost no one would recognize me there, since this wasn't my usual side of the island.

Yacht Haven, as its name implied, was a marina that played host to the bigger yachts that made their way to St. Thomas. Its shopping area was designed for the kind of people who could pay $60,000 for a week on a boat—or a few million for a boat of their own. The price tags at many of the retail stores reflected the clientele, which meant that I almost never went there.

The place often felt nearly empty, which seemed like a shame. The grounds were beautiful: fresh, yellow buildings set around brick walks, manicured tropical landscaping that rivaled the Ritz-Carlton and air-conditioned public bathrooms that were cool enough to make you want to stay long beyond the time you'd finished your business.

I was a little shaky from adrenaline—and, to be fair, beer. By the time I pulled into the parking lot, I was just about ready to crash. My limbs felt heavy. I suppressed a yawn as I turned off the ignition. I considered leaning my seat back for a few minutes and catching a snooze, but I imagined that would only draw attention to myself in this ritzy neighborhood. No one in Red Hook would have batted an eye.

Instead, I made my way to Bad Ass Coffee. I shivered a little at the chilly air-conditioning—and the cheesy Hawaiian décor, including a fake palm tree and a vintage travel poster for Pan-Am airlines, featuring a smiling beach babe with a coconut bra, a grass skirt and a hibiscus behind her ear.

I ordered the largest iced coffee they had. As I waited for my hit of caffeine, I looked around, surprised by how many people were in the shop, either tapping on laptops or sitting in conversation. The people of this island clearly needed their caffeine.

I took the proffered coffee, added milk and a heap of sugar, then posted myself under the Hawaiian babe. Maybe some of her gentle tranquility would rub off on me.

I slid the cloned phone out of my purse slowly, looking left and right to see if anyone was watching. I drew absolutely zero notice. Then I rolled my eyes at myself. As far as these people knew, the iPhone might as well be my own. Lizzie Jordan, irrationally paranoid.

I pushed the only visible button and a picture of the Ritz beach appeared on the screen. So this was what it was like to own an iPhone.

Then, as the phone instructed, I slid my thumb left to right over the screen and entered Andrea's passcode.

I felt an extra kick of adrenaline, either from the caffeine or the prospect of getting some answers I desperately needed. Plus, there was something titillating about snooping through someone's private life.

My eyes swam as I looked at all the little icons in front of me. I should have stuck around and made Lucas show me how to use this damn thing. My Motorola flip phone might have been ancient, but it was also pretty darn simple.

In the upper left, I saw a green button marked "Messages." That seemed like a good place to start. At the top of the list, I saw "Ben St. Thomas." Seemed about right. I tapped in.

Wednesday night at 11:30: "U get lost? :)" I wasn't surprised that Ben was too lazy to type out "you." Disappointed, but not surprised.

Thursday afternoon at 2:05pm, right around when we'd stopped at Jost van Dyke and picked up a U.S. cell signal again:

"What happened to u last night?"

The messages seemed to corroborate Ben's story. Of course, he could have sent those messages after he'd brutally killed Andrea and disposed of her body, but I wasn't sure he was capable of such guile. The guy had simply called her cell phone earlier. And he couldn't even bother with three letters when one incorrect one would do.

I expected that to be the beginning and the end of their communications, but there seemed to be texts before then. I thought Ben had said they met at Duffy's? Here they were at 3:37 pm on Wednesday—way before Ladies' Night got started—coyly discussing plans to meet up for the night. I scrolled clumsily up to their first message. Tuesday: "It's Ben. Let's hang."

Tuesday. What the hell had happened Tuesday? I took a long hit of my coffee. That made yet another lie Ben had told me. I needed to start documenting this stuff. I pulled out the four pieces of paper I had from the Ritz-Carlton, but I couldn't for the life of me find the pen. Damn. I had to work on this detecting thing, obviously.

I glanced over at the girl behind the counter. She was at a lull in her shift, readjusting the rolled purple bandana that was acting as a headband. I plastered on my nicest smile and sidled over to the register. I was hoping that dollar tip I'd placed in her jar might work its magic.

I can't say it was magic, but she did hand over a pen that read, "Bad Ass Coffee" with a little donkey on it. Score. She wasn't getting this one back.

I returned to my perch and scribbled on the back of a sheet. "Lies Ben Told Me." Then, underneath it: "Tuesday?" Then, for good measure, I added, "Blow job" and "Dealing"? I turned my attention back to the phone quickly. I didn't want to think too much more about that one.

That was the end of the messages they'd exchanged.

The next set was from Jessie.

Wednesday night, she had sent a flurry of messages. I scrolled back a bit to read that night's communications in order. 10:30 pm: "Where are you?" 10:45: "Are you even still at Duffy's?" 11:00: "Did you go off with BEN!!?!?"

Jessie's mood was clearly escalating as the night went on. She seemed awfully concerned about Andrea's whereabouts, in stark contrast to the way she'd behaved that morning. Had shock made her numb?

Then, at 11:15: "We need to know where you are." That was the last message for the evening.

Huh. Those thoughtless bitches didn't even tell her they were leaving. I imagined Jessie storming off in a huff, thinking she would teach Andrea a lesson. Some lesson.

Where had Becky been in all of this? I imagined Jessie clamping a hand around her toothpick arm and hauling her through the parking lot. I could see it.

I went back and scrolled down Andrea's main list of text messages, looking for Becky's name. I found her way at the bottom, wishing Andrea a happy birthday the November before. Huh. I guess they weren't close. Maybe Jessie was the nerve center of this group.

I went back to the message chain from Jessie to see if I could understand anything more about this dynamic trio.

There was one message from Thursday morning at 10:04 am, after Andrea hadn't come home: "Where are you? Call me." Another similar one at noon, then nothing more.

I scrolled back down Jessie's messages to see what had happened before Wednesday. The previous set of messages was from Monday, showing a few tiny pictures.

Even though they were small, I could tell that they were beach pictures, probably the kind every tourist takes of the Virgin Islands. Nothing new there.

I was about to tap away, but I noticed something that made my eyebrows pop.

There were more pictures above, but they looked entirely different. They weren't vacation photos. They looked like mini versions of text messages. I assumed that if I tapped on them, they would get bigger. I was delighted at myself when I discovered I was right.

They appeared to be screenshots of text messages between someone and a person named Zack.

Zack: *What are U wearing?*
Mystery Text Recipient: *Naughty, naughty ;)*
Zack: *I like to imagine you in those little red panties*

I felt my mouth twist as though I'd taken a swig of milk gone sour. I swallowed my distaste for both the use of "U" and the word "panties" and waded back into the text string.

MTR: *Ewwwww. You know girls hate that word*
Zack: *Sorry. :(When do I get to see you again?*
MTR: *What were you thinking?*
Zack: *Tonight?*
MTR: *Ummmmm . . . is this a booty call?*
Zack: *Just want to see you*
MTR: *You know I'm not that kind of girl. I expect dinner first ;)*
Zack: *Tomorrow?*
MTR: *Sorry, babe. Have plans :(*

Zack, who were you talking to? And why had Andrea sent these screenshots to Jessie? I wished I could see the date of the original texts, but that information didn't seem to be on the screen.

The exchange itself puzzled me, too. This Zack guy seemed to be out of his league. Whoever was texting him seemed to be getting the better of him, and he was still coming back for more.

Had I missed anything?

I went back to the photos I'd dismissed as boring vacation photos. Once I tapped on them, I realized that the girls had made a trip to the British side of the Virgin Islands. I recognized Sandy Spit, a white sand island with a single palm tree and nothing else. People called it "Corona Island" because it could easily have been the setting for one of their ads. However, as far as I knew, no Corona commercial had ever been photographed on that island. Like I said, lotta BS stories down here.

The next photos showed me the north shore of Tortola and St. John's pristine beaches from the water.

Then I saw a picture of the three girls with unfocused eyes, leaning up against a wooden bar staffed by a bartender with deep brown skin. I'd recognize Zeus and his lecherous look anywhere. With his dark, flashing eyes and salt-and-pepper goatee, he looked like an impish satyr. In this picture, he stuck out his tongue like Gene Simmons from KISS. It was a classic Zeus pose.

Zeus was the bartender at the Willy T, a floating pirate ship bar that was permanently located in the Bight of Norman Island in the British Virgin Islands. The island had been notorious as a hangout for pirates back in the day. The Willy T had created its own infamy with its promise that girls who jumped off the ship naked would receive a free T-shirt. I didn't see any naked pictures, so maybe the girls hadn't jumped.

That was the end of the pictures. I went back to the main messages folder. My snooping was turning up some interesting stuff, although I had no clue how it all fit together.

I scanned the list of names and I felt my scalp tighten. There was a correspondent in Andrea's message folder named "Zack." Could this be the same Zack from the screenshots? My heart hit an extra beat and I tapped my finger on the row to open the messages.

I guess I tapped wrong, because the whole column dragged left and I saw a red button that said, "Delete." I let out a little yelp that turned a few heads in the shop. I held my breath, but everyone turned back to their business quickly once they realized the show was over.

I took a deep breath and went back to the screen. I looked for some kind of cancel button, a little X—whatever. I didn't see one, and I felt my hand start to shake. Maybe it was the caffeine, but I was pretty sure it was iPhone anxiety. I needed to calm down. I took two deep breaths, then I hit the phone's only button.

The phone went back to the main screen, which I now realized featured a background with a cute silver car, a VW. Andrea's?

I located the messages icon again and pushed it, hoping desperately that the weird red button would be gone.

Everything had gone back to normal. I breathed out. Carefully—very carefully—I tapped on the messages between Zack and Andrea.

Whoever this Zack guy was, he was sending updates from wherever he was. Apparently, it had rained for an entire day (imagine that!) and his kickball team was headed for the championship (woo!). To be fair to poor Zack and his conversational skills, he wasn't getting much material to work with. When he asked, "How's the trip?" he got in return, "Great! :)" When he asked, "What are u up to?" she replied, "Beach!"

He could be quite verbose, sending two and three messages at a time. Andrea's answers were almost always pretty lackluster, with a picture or two to punctuate the conversation. Sometimes, she only sent a picture in response, no caption.

As I continued reading their banal exchanges, I was stumped. Why did these two bother texting each other? It was clear that she wasn't that interested, yet she kept responding. It was also evident to me that she was putting in the minimum effort required, and yet he kept sending updates. These girls were only a few years younger than me, but their peculiar rituals seemed positively foreign.

The longest message Andrea sent was in response to a message she'd received on Sunday. Zack had written, "How's paradise?"

Andrea sent back a picture from the Ritz beach with its Windex-colored water and its view of St. John in the distance. Then, she wrote, "Our cruise director is getting a little annoying."

I re-read the message, wondering who the "cruise director" could be—although I could guess. I scrolled for Zack's response. "You know Jessie likes to be in charge."

Confirmed. I scrolled for Andrea's response, but she hadn't written back. Instead, Zack had checked in on Tuesday and was once again relegated to one-word answers.

I scrolled further up to see if I could find the exchange that had been screenshotted. There it was, plain as day. But why had it been deemed so important as to be texted around on vacation? Huh.

I pulled out another piece of paper and started another list: "Questions for the Girls." (If I ever got to talk to them again, of course.) Underneath, I wrote: "Ben – Tuesday?" and "Zack Texts." On a whim, I also scribbled, "Becky, where on Weds night?"

I went back to the main message screen. There was another recent one from a 954 area code. The message simply read, "Salsa." Salsa? Was that a grocery list? Or a request at the store—but from an unknown number? I had to file that one away.

The next set of messages was between Andrea and "Dad," with the typical stuff. There were a few pictures of the resort and a note that her plane arrived safely. I scrolled through the rest of the messages between them, but most were mundane texts that applied to stateside life.

I made one final scan of the main list of messages. I did find a thread for Mom, but the messages were at least two weeks old. Andrea sent short missives like "Miss you" and "Love you." Some went unanswered, but Andrea persisted. Maybe half the time, she was rewarded with a return message back, like "I love you too."

I took a sip of my coffee. It seemed odd that Andrea's mother was so reluctant to answer her messages.

My mind flicked to the unanswered voicemails from my father. A stranger would think me cruel. But every inaction has its reasons. I wondered what Andrea's mother's were. Maybe she wasn't yet as adept at text messaging as her daughter, or maybe there was something more there.

I hit the main button and started the search for Andrea's photos. I scanned all the little icons until I saw something that looked like a camera. It turned out to be the camera. Whoops.

I went back. Right next to it was a rainbow flower icon that was supposedly evocative of a photo, hence the word "Photos" underneath. Okay.

I tapped into the photos and felt myself blanch at a selfie of Ben and Andrea in Duffy's.

Here they were, in all their grainy glory. The photo was dark, but I was able to make out their faces in the disco lights that accompanied whatever Pitbull song I assumed was throbbing in the background.

I studied their faces for signs of anger or distress. I saw none, just two people having a good time, their smiles wide and their eyes agreeing. I scanned the background for creepers, but the poor quality made it hard to make anyone out, let alone anyone who displayed an unhealthy interest in Andrea.

After a few clumsy attempts to scroll, I dragged my finger right and found myself moving backward through time. Andrea had taken a few more shots at Duffy's that night. The next was a group shot of the girls, maybe taken by Ben. Jessie had spread her lips to show her teeth, but her attempt at a smile looked pasted on, especially with her shoulders slumped in displeasure. Becky was making a much better effort, her smile wide but a little crooked, her eyes unfocused. She looked drunk. Maybe that explained where the hell Becky was that night. She was too tipsy to be of any use to anybody.

I swiped again and we were gone from Duffy's to a shot of Andrea's feet on the beach, then a series of palm tree outlines against a cloudless sky—the usuals. When I came to a photo of all three girls on their Ritz balcony, I spent an agonizing few minutes trying to figure out how to text it to myself. When I finally heard my ancient phone burr, I started swiping again.

I stopped abruptly when one photo caught my eye. I saw a Hobie Cat, its rainbow sail bright against a blue sky. I peered at it closer. The boat looked to be pulled up on the Ritz beach. In front of the boat was Ben, plus the girls posing in orange life jackets.

Met at Duffy's, my ass. When was this? Tuesday?

I put the phone down on my lap again and sighed. Was there anyone who wasn't lying to me? I reached out blindly for my coffee and felt my hand brush it, nearly tipping it onto the floor. I snatched it quickly. Then I cradled it in my hands, sipping the cold liquid as my mind ticked.

What did I have? On the face of it, not much. A few white lies. A weird text conversation screenshotted and sent to Jessie from Andrea. I had a single word (a command?): Salsa. And then I had evidence that Ben, Jessie and Becky were not telling the full truth about their relationship. What the hell was Ben doing taking these girls out on a Hobie Cat? Maybe it could be explained away, but I couldn't help but feel a profound disturbance that things were clearly more complicated than they initially seemed.

And here I was, smack dab in the middle of it.

My stomach took a dip. Today, I'd aided a fugitive. I wouldn't say I'd gone so far as to flee from the cops, but I was definitely making a grand attempt at avoiding them. And despite packing all that drama into these morning hours, all I had to show for my efforts were a few lies about what happened a few days ago. Big whoop.

I had finished my coffee, my straw creating that particular sucking sound that my mother chastised me for making when I was a child. She wasn't here now, so I did it again to suck up every last drop of coffee.

There was no one to scold me now, and it felt damn good.

But my joy was quickly replaced by a grim realization. It was sounding less and less likely that my original fantasy of Andrea being holed up with a fisherman was going to come to fruition. Sure, she had lost her phone, but she also hadn't tried to call it, text it or recover it in any way, as far as I could tell. It didn't bode well.

I picked up Andrea's phone again, scrolling through the rest of her photos. I was no expert, but it seemed like they were dominated by an inordinate number of pictures of Andrea by herself.

There was Andrea in the driver's seat of a pristine car, her face obscured with sunglasses and her lips pursed in a pout. Right before that picture was one of her standing by a silver Volkswagen. I wonder who had taken this photo.

Then, there was Andrea photographed in what looked like a cubicle at work. She sat in an office chair, dressed in a chic white silk blouse that set off the olive undertones of her skin, and a dark skirt.

Finally, I found some shots with other people. Andrea sandwiched in between two fresh-faced guys in a bar, their faces grainy in the dark but their teeth blindingly white as they flashed for the camera. Andrea at the head of a table of girls at a Chinese restaurant in a black halter top. I scanned for the other two girls. I almost missed Jessie, who loomed over the shoulder of a smiling blonde. No Becky.

I found myself looking for flaws in Andrea's photos, a hair out of place, an excess of chub in her backside. They were hard to find. If you believed her pictures, her life was much more glamorous and fabulous than mine.

I started thumbing through the photos faster and faster, looking for deviations. I came to a stop on a self-portrait taken in a bathroom mirror. Andrea stared into the glass, her phone held up next to her—no makeup, the skin under her eyes puffy. Her eyes looked much smaller, and I could see red blotches on her cheeks. I scrolled backward and found four more photos in this series. She looked like she'd just finished a hell of a good cry. I wondered what had caused it. I flipped back one more photo and found one of her smiling with an older man and woman. Based on the facial similarities, I assumed they were her parents.

Her father towered over Andrea, filling out his Polo shirt and khakis. His hair was dark like hers, slicked back from a slightly receding hairline. He shared Andrea's olive-toned skin. I hoped in five years he would shave his head instead of going the Bozo the Clown route.

Her mother wore a pink floral dress that gave her skin a sickly yellow cast. Her dark hair was thinning at the crown, and her smile seemed to hold echoes of strain. Her arms and legs looked trim, but she was thick around the middle, maybe unnaturally thick in proportion to the rest of her body. Something about it spoke to ill health, rather than simple weight gain. Had she been sick? I made a note.

I tried to check the date on the photo, but despite tapping, shaking, double-tapping—pretty much everything but throwing the damn thing across the room—I couldn't figure anything out. I'd have to wait, I guessed.

I backed out of her photos, stumbled into her calendar (empty), the calculator (oops) and I was just about to check if she was on Facebook when I felt my own phone buzz.

I flipped it open to see a message from Dave. "We need to talk. At the shop," it read.

Jesus. I had gotten so wrapped up in my own drama that I'd nearly forgotten that Dave was tangled up in this mess, too. My stomach tightened as I wondered what he had been doing at Duffy's. And why had Ben been so mysterious about it? Whatever the answer, I wanted to know. I felt heartache peeking over the horizon, but I dismissed the thought quickly. I didn't have the emotional bandwidth.

I was turning Andrea's phone over in my hand, contemplating a response to Dave when I heard someone call my name.

I dropped the phone on the ground with a smack.

My head swiveled up to see an acquaintance—a girl I'd met on a boat trip six months ago. She looked really good in a bikini, and, yeah, when I met her, I hated her just a little for that. What can I say? I can get awfully petty sometimes.

But then she bought me a Dark & Stormy and a shot of something delicious at a beach bar on Jost van Dyke. Once the booze took effect, we had a surprising heart to heart. (Isn't that how it always works?)

I still have a picture of us taking the shot with Mic, the bartender, in the background, holding a fake stethoscope to his heart and swooning. I don't know where the prop came from, but that was classic Mic—always full of surprises.

Afterward, we both leaned heavily on the wooden bar, and she revealed to me that she'd had a brief fling with Ben. She'd wanted more, and he didn't. Surprise, surprise.

But I still felt for her. She wasn't the only lovelorn victim left behind in the swath Ben cut through the island. The confession created a weird bond between as we both realized that we thought he was scum when it came to women, but we couldn't bring ourselves to hate him entirely.

In the here and now, Ellie was bending over to retrieve my phone from the tile floor, and, from her expression, I could tell something was wrong. What did she know?

I watched her face carefully as she stood up. She sold timeshares at one of the nearby hotels, so she was dressed better than most. She wore a white flowered dress that flattered her trim figure, plus makeup that made her lightly tanned skin look dewy and perfect. Despite the humidity, her blonde hair draped over her shoulders in perfect waves. In my grubby outfit, stiff from multiple rounds of dried flop sweat, I felt like the ugly little sister. Lizzie Jordan, fashion "don't."

I stood to greet her, less out of courtesy and more because I was jumpy.

I drew my lips back from my teeth in what I hoped was a grin. "Hi, Ellie."

She handed over the phone with a grimace that, on her, looked adorably pert. "Sorry about your phone."

I took it from her—perhaps a little too quickly, like a hungry dog snatching a piece of meat. The screen had spiderwebbed into an intricate series of cracks. Well, I guess Lucas wasn't getting his phone back. Add another mark in his book. I owed him a new one now.

"What are you doing over here? You sticking around? Have lunch plans?" she asked.

She enveloped me in a hug of perfume. She smelled great. I wondered if I smelled how I felt—*eau de fear*. She probably regretted wrapping her arms around my sweaty self.

I wanted to say *I'm in a bit of a mess,* but I managed to blurt out, "I'm on the move" instead.

She put her hands on her hips. "I'm so glad to see you've joined this century." She gestured to the phone.

I sputtered a bit. "It's not really mine. Just a loaner."

"Well, looks like you owe them a new screen. There's a guy next to Pizza Amoré who does them. He's kind of a perv. He always stares at my boobs when he talks to me, but he'll get it done fast."

"Thanks for the tip," I said. I was probably going to throw it in the ocean, but, hey, the more you know.

She smiled, and I felt the conversation grind to a halt. Time to make my exit. A few words tumbled out of my mouth that might have been a lunch promise for the future. I started to move past her, but she put a cool hand on my arm.

I jumped a little at the contact and saw her brows knit together.

"Sorry." I shook my empty coffee cup. "Too much of this."

She leaned a little closer. "Are you okay, Lizzie?"

I nodded, but nothing came out of my mouth. It wasn't convincing. Ellie's hand stayed on my arm.

"Don't go back through Red Hook," she warned me.

I froze. *She knew.* Was it all over the island? If I drove straight to the airport, could I get on a flight? We're a U.S. territory so I wouldn't even need the passport I keep in my underwear drawer.

I couldn't stop my voice from shaking.

"W-what's going on in Red Hook?" I asked. I searched her face desperately for some indication of her intentions, but I couldn't glean anything other than the fact that she was way better at makeup than I would ever be.

Her shoulders went up and down. "Something's going on in Red Hook, at the marina. Tons of cops. Traffic is the worst."

I relaxed a fraction. Okay, so there wasn't some kind of island-wide bulletin out about me. I really needed to get this hyper-vigilance of mine under control. The police might not have even hadn't arrived at the Ritz yet. I had no reason to believe they operated on anything other than island time.

That being said, everything was still far from okay.

I tried to feign a light tone but winced when my voice hit the approximate tone and pitch of Mickey Mouse. "Really? What's going on?"

"Probably some drug bust. They caught one of the DPNR guys last week."

Ordinarily, that was a story I'd stick around to hear, but I knew I was going to need all of my mental resources to get me into Red Hook to find Dave. I suppose I could ask him to meet me somewhere else, but I wasn't going to give him the satisfaction of doing me a favor. And besides, I wanted to know what was going on at AYH—and whether it connected to Andrea. The thought sent a shiver up my spine. I needed to get out of this air conditioning.

I gave Ellie one last tooth flash and turned toward the door.

But then I thought of something and turned back. "Ellie, can I ask you something?" I didn't wait for her answer. "Didn't you go out with Ben for a while?"

"Ben? You mean boat captain Ben?"

I didn't have time to marvel at the fact that Ellie must have dated more than one Ben or revel in how we identified people on this small island.

Instead, I just nodded.

"Yes," she said hesitantly.

"Why do you say it like that?"

"Well, I wasn't his girlfriend or anything."

I waved her words away. "We both know that Ben doesn't have girlfriends. That wasn't what I was getting at. I just wanted to know if he ever did anything, well, you know, weird."

"Weird how?" I saw a small vertical line appear between her eyebrows.

I was really screwing this up. What was I going to ask? *Did he ever, well, try to kill you?*

She squinted at me. "Lizzie, why are you asking me this?"

"Never mind. He called me this morning and—I don't know—" I raised both hands in both surrender and placation. "I'm sorry, Ellie. Thanks for letting me know about Red Hook."

She nodded, then a shadow crossed her face. I paused and looked at her.

"What?" I asked.

"He did, um . . ."

I felt my eyebrows rise by themselves. "Yes?"

She leaned in so close that I could smell her perfume again.

"He did try to, um, choke me once. In a romantic way," she whispered into the space between us.

I tried to keep my face neutral. That one was hell of a way to describe it. I nodded and tried to look sympathetic. Inside, though, my blood had started pumping again.

What the hell was that called? Auto-erotic asphyxiation? No, no, no—that was when people did it to themselves. I think it was just erotic asphyxiation, although I'd still like to argue with the "erotic" part. I think of myself as a pretty open-minded person, but I value my airway pretty fiercely.

Ellie pulled back and I watched her face color with embarrassment. "Was that what you meant?"

I grimaced and nodded.

"Did he try to do it to you?" she asked in a low voice.

I was a little flattered that she would count me on her level, even though I was sure I was several rungs below her on the feminine scale.

"Oh, um, no," I said. "He and I are just friends. I just had heard some rumors and I—"

She shook her head, her face dark again. "Well, whatever they're saying about him, they're probably right. He wasn't at all who I thought he was going to be."

The door to the coffee shop banged open and a tall man in a faded blue jumpsuit and mirrored sunglasses walked in, his black dreadlocks tied back away from his deep brown face. "Traffic in the country outta control!" he yelled at no one in particular.

Red Hook was the "country" at one point during this island's development. Today, it was the center of my universe. I needed to get out there—fast.

"I'll see you soon, Ellie."

"Let's have lunch!" I heard her call after me.

If for no other reason than she seemed to be a font of information today—oh, and that delightful perfume of hers—I gave her a nod and a smile.

I wondered if we'd have to have that rendezvous with steel bars between us.

Lizzie Jordan, eternal pessimist.

11

Other than the fact that I squealed around St. Thomas's tight corners a little faster than usual, my ride across the island was relatively quiet.

The fact that Red Hook was a mess turned out to be a blessing in disguise. I would normally drive straight through Tutu, the central shopping area of the island, right by the police station. I knew I was probably being overly suspicious, but I decided to take an early right turn down what was called "the road to Kmart"—even on government signage. (Seriously.)

I ticked off the landmarks as I drove through a mix of residential and industrial neighborhoods, passing the Red Lantern laundry in Nadir, which was rumored to also be a brothel. I couldn't tell you for sure, though. I'd only ever used their wash-and-fold service.

I came around a sharp turn and slammed on my brakes, praying they would hold. The backup to Red Hook was worse than I thought. The line stretched all the way back to the entrance to Compass Point Marina, about a mile from Red Hook.

There we sat. What started as a simple tapping of my fingers on the steering wheel kept building in speed and pressure.

Finally, the line started creeping, only to stop dead again.

We were inching toward the single traffic light on this side of the island. Its erratic cycles probably weren't helping the traffic situation. All I needed was to get to that light and I could wind through the surrounding neighborhoods to get back to my place. From there, I could sneak into Red Hook on foot.

The light sat at the top of a steep hill, and I saw it turn green. Finally. The line lurched forward a few feet only to stop again. I knew it would probably go red again before more cars could pass through.

We cycled like that a few times until my body was practically humming. Finally, the light turned green. I said a quick prayer and made a quick illegal right-hand turn into the heart of Nazareth.

If I kept going straight, I'd end up down by the water, near the almost completely derelict white concrete building known as the Dolphin House. I was sure the next hurricane would bring it down entirely. The entire bottom floor of the house was designed to allow the adjacent sea water in. In the '60s, the US government funded a project in which humans and dolphins lived together, with the goal of teaching the dolphins to speak English. A woman lived on the first floor with a dolphin named Peter. Apparently, Peter loved her, and when the experiment was over, Peter committed suicide.

Pretty heavy stuff.

I hung a left to take the road parallel to the main one, this one studded with speed bumps my shocks weren't entirely equipped to handle.

Someday, this car was going to die on me. I desperately hoped today wasn't the day. I took it easy on the old girl, just in case.

After five speedbumps and two more twists in the road, I turned down my little lane. I pulled into my dirt parking pad, jammed the shifter in park and dashed up to my little cottage.

I threw open my closet doors and pulled out a red and black flowered dress. It came out of the closet maybe once a year for Christmas parties. I sniffed it—not bad, maybe a touch moldy—then stripped down, discarding my clothes on the floor. My underwear and bra were damp. I changed those, too, relishing the feel of dry fabric on my sensitive areas. Then I pulled the dress over my head and took a quick turn to look in a mirror. It would do.

I reached up to the top shelf and pulled down a Baltimore Orioles hat. There weren't many redheads on this island, so a hat would ensure I stayed incognito, just in case anyone was looking for me. This morning's mention of the police was my first brush with the possibility down here, and it clearly had me spooked.

I put the hat on, looked in the mirror again and made a face. I don't claim to know anything about fashion, but I knew that a flowered dress and a grungy baseball cap would probably draw more attention than not.

I went back to the closet and started pulling things off the top shelf. Out came old T-shirts from boats I worked once, faded board shorts with their metal grommets pitted from salt water, an old snorkel mask that leaked and then, bingo, a wide-brimmed straw hat that a friend from college had brought down and left with me.

Pro tip: Down here, you almost never want to throw anything away. We're an island of limited resources, and you never know when you'll be able to repurpose yesterday's discards.

I shook the hat once to clear the dust, then tucked my hair under and secured it on my head.

I took one more look in the mirror and nodded at myself. Game time.

I grabbed a purse from the top of my dresser.

I rummaged through it with one hand while my mind

churned about what I wanted to say to Dave. I had a lot of questions about that night at Duffy's, and my mind kept pulling scenarios from that night.

Our shouting match at Saloon.

Dave sheepishly appearing at my door later that night. Lately, it had become a pattern with him.

So was the subsequent makeup sex, although, that night it had been greedy, almost rough.

Then I flashed back to one of our happier days on Dave's boat, a calm day in which his little craft neatly cut through the navy blue water between St. Thomas and Jost van Dyke. Us sitting in the warm sand, rum running in our veins and smiles on our faces as we watched the boats come in and out of the busy bay.

I felt tightness rise in my chest. That was enough of that. I zipped my purse and headed out the door.

I gave the back quarter panel of my Suzuki a little pat as I passed her. She'd done well today, but it was time to go stealth.

I walked down my lane about ten paces, then found what looked like a game trail in the bush. It was also a local shortcut to the main road.

Ten more paces and one sandspur in my dress later, I was on the main road, not far from where I'd spotted the deer the night before.

I looked both ways and dashed across, then made my way down the shoulder, watching for crazy taxi drivers and even more insane water truck operators. I didn't think there was any such thing as a cistern-filling emergency, but they certainly drove their cement-truck-sized vehicles as though someone's life depended on getting their shower in the next fifteen minutes.

At the intersection, I turned right toward Red Hook and began to put my story together. I was Elizabeth Morgan, visiting from the great city of Washington, D.C. I was staying at Secret Harbour resort. I had popped into town to pick up a new mask for snorkeling. ("They tell me it's wonderful off the beach at the resort!")

Traffic was still bad. Cars were moving at a crawl, if at all. A beat-up army green jeep that looked like a relic of some war slowed to let me cross. I lifted a hand in thanks and trotted to the other side, where a sidewalk had been installed—a rarity in St. Thomas.

"Lizzie Jordan!" I stopped short. No one used last names down here. Was I busted?

Then I berated myself. I didn't know a Lizzie Jordan. I was Elizabeth Morgan, currently of the Secret Harbour Resort. I took a tentative step forward, desperately hoping I had misheard.

"Lizzie! Over here," the voice called again. I cringed as my name rang out again.

The voice clearly wasn't going to go away, so I turned slowly and saw the man in the green Jeep waving to me. His baseball hat obscured his features, but as I looked more carefully, I could see a blonde thatch of a ponytail sticking out the back. It was Lenny, my old landlord. In addition to being an extremely friendly guy, Lenny was also a mechanic employed on a private island right off the coast of St. Thomas. Rumor had it that the man who owned the island liked young girls. Lenny wasn't one to gossip, and I was also too chicken to ask him directly, so it remained an unconfirmed rumor until the man was finally convicted in a Florida court.

I didn't know whether Lenny still worked for him, and, once again, I was too chicken to ask. I guess I liked Lenny, and I wanted him to like me. Strange, I know.

I gave a small smile and waved back. "Hi, Lenny." Although I would usually stop and at least exchange a pleasantry or two, I desperately needed to stay under the radar. I could already feel my shoulders curving inward to make myself smaller. I cast a glance around to see if we were attracting any attention.

I turned away to put a polite end to the conversation.

"Need a ride?" he asked.

I looked over my shoulder, keeping my body pointed toward the marina. "Just going into Red Hook."

"Hop in and I'll get you there." He waved a white arm speckled with freckles at me in a welcoming gesture.

I scanned the line of cars. Was anyone watching? There was a black sedan a few cars back, its windows tinted too dark for me to tell if it was a cop car. It looked a little too shiny to be a civilian vehicle.

Although getting off the street would have been good, I was pretty sure that would blow my disguise. I also didn't want to get Lenny tangled in whatever mess I was creating for myself.

I held a palm up. "Need to stretch my legs," I replied. "But thank you."

Ordinarily, I would be cheered by this island kindness. For every immovable woman at the Bureau of Motor Vehicles who refused to issue your license because your Social Security card had your middle initial only while your passport spelled it out, there was someone who was willing to step up to make your life a little easier.

Well, maybe it wasn't that even-steven, but the rush I got from seeing one human help another was enough to smooth a lot of bumps in the road. Then again, it might have been that philosophy that got me into this in the first place, so I might have to reconsider—once I could think with a clear head.

As I walked away from Lenny, trying to get as much distance between us as possible in case he decided to holler out my full name again, I felt something slowing my steps.

Was it dread over confronting Dave? Was it a desire to hole up in my little cabin and let the storm roll by on its own? Whatever it was, it was creating a tug of war within my body that made every step feel first like a relief, then a mistake.

"Whatcha up to in Red Hook?" I heard Lenny's voice ask.

Crap. My head snapped around. It appeared that the lane of cars was moving at just about the same pace I was.

I looked back at the black sedan again. It now looked like the driver's side window had been cracked an inch or two.

I turned my head forward and swallowed. I needed to get rid of Lenny fast.

Casual was the way to go, right? I shrugged, swallowed the rising lump in my throat and managed to squawk out a few words. "Just a cup of coffee."

He winked. "Haven't seen you in a dress in a while."

Now who was the freaking detective? I took a deep breath to keep myself calm and jerked the corners of my mouth upward. "Just got to keep them guessing."

The conversation stalled, although Lenny's vehicle kept rolling forward beside me. This wasn't good.

I could just imagine Lenny leaning out the side of his Jeep and yelling, "Bye, Lizzie Jordan!" right in front of a cop. Knowing my full name was the kind of thing he would have thought was funny. I used to find it funny, too, until I was worried that the cops might be looking for me.

Before you ask, yes, it did occur to me that I could be overreacting. Lucas had confirmed that we weren't dealing with the world's most technically proficient cops. Maybe they'd even ignore Jessie if she tried to tell them about me.

But if I was wrong, I was done. Better paranoid than sorry. Another one of my rules.

I was almost past the high school just outside of Red Hook, Ivanna Eudora Kean, whose student uniforms inexplicably consisted of pink shirts and maroon pants.

My mind ponders strange things in times of stress.

I took a sharp breath at the sight of a dark blue police SUV parked across the entrance to the marina parking lot. I didn't look to confirm, but I could still feel Lenny rolling along beside me. The time for action was now.

I touched my lumpy purse to take inventory. I had two phones clanking around—why in god's name had I brought Andrea's phone along with me?—plus a wallet that identified me as Lizzie Jordan. I think I had about $80 in cash and a pack of gum that had long gone squishy from the heat and humidity. I hung onto it only for the direst of emergencies. In this case, it was zero help.

In terms of assets, I was screwed.

I took a look at the officer outside the car. From what I could see, he was tall and built strong, his biceps bulging underneath the sky blue short sleeves of his uniform. I couldn't see his eyes. Dark sunglasses covered the top of his face. Sweat was pouring down his mahogany skin, but he looked immovable. The heat wouldn't get the best of this guy. I glanced at Lenny, who shot me another grin. Shoot.

I gazed around quickly and inspiration struck. The East End Café. They had a back exit that would drop me in spitting distance of the dive shop. I could slip in there, slip out the back and avoid the roadblock entirely.

I took one more glance at Lenny and figured surprise was my best friend. I lifted a hand to him and dashed behind his vehicle, hoping to get in the door before he yelled my name. I thundered up the wooden stairs and pulled the door for the East End Café. Mercifully, it was unlocked. I slipped in. The door banged shut behind me.

If Lenny shouted my name, I didn't hear it.

I took off my sunglasses and hat, then blinked a few times in the dark vestibule. They kept the lights low in here, and I was practically blind until my eyes adjusted.

The place was decorated in dark wood, offering the classic traditional Italian restaurant atmosphere you can find in many towns in America. Like Romano's, their lasagna was also excellent.

If you're wondering why the island can support so many Italian restaurants, I can't help you there. But I can tell you I helped keep both of them open.

I peered around for signs of life. Nothing. I glanced at my watch. I thought they'd be open by now.

I had two options here. I could just dash through the restaurant, stroll through the back kitchen like I owned the place and scuttle down the stairs. Or I could try to go legit. Who did I know who worked here these days—

"Hello?"

I felt my flip flops leave the ground at the unexpected sound of the female voice behind me.

I turned around and saw a woman with an oval face and a pointed chin, her blonde hair hanging long and straight. Unlike so many women who lived here, her eyes were carefully made up, so they leapt out from her pale white face. Like Jake the bartender from Detroit, she hadn't spent a lot of time in the sun recently, either.

I didn't know her name, but I knew her face. She had always looked like she might be a kind person. I hoped I was right.

"Good morning," I said. I transferred my hat and glasses to my left hand and reached out my right. "I'm Lizzie."

Her brows knitted together, but she shook my hand. "Good morning. I'm Christie." She paused. "We're not open until noon."

I shook my head. "I have a HUGE favor to ask you. Will you let me use your back exit?" I felt my hand clench on the brim of my straw hat. The appropriateness of the gesture wasn't lost on me. All day long, I'd been appearing at people's doorsteps, asking for help, offering nothing in return and now literally my hat was in my hand. My list of paybacks was growing. It made me distinctly uncomfortable, like an itch I couldn't reach.

She paused and glanced over toward where the police

officer would be outside the restaurant. I saw her eyes travel over me, giving me the once-over. "Um," she said.

I thought a little local knowledge might grease the situation. "Please. I just need to get over to see Dave in the dive shop really quickly."

I saw a flash of something in her face. Maybe she knew Dave. But still she didn't move.

We stood there for a long minute. It was so quiet in the restaurant that I swore I could hear my heart beating. Even my breath sounded ragged. I tried to slow it down, hoping that a veneer of decorum might buy me a little with this Christie person.

It didn't. We still stood there, me looking into her face while she avoided eye contact and shifted from one foot to another.

I couldn't take the silence anymore. All those emotions that had been swimming around in me gathered, swarmed and attacked.

I led with the truth. "Look, this isn't my usual MO," I blurted. "I've had a crazy day running around the island, and I really just need to see Dave because I'm pretty sure we're going to break up, and I just need to know because I have some pretty big fish to fry today."

And then I sealed it with a lie, gesturing in the general direction of the officer at the mouth of the marina. "I just can't deal with the police. I called them after a robbery a few years ago. They came and tore my place apart and blamed me for being stupid enough to have a window right next to the door even though I obviously didn't even build the place. And I get traumatized all over again every time I have to deal with them."

Now I was really gathering steam, although I was veering dangerously into bullshit territory. If I kept going, I thought I could even muster a few tears.

Too much. Instead, I added one final flourish. "And so I just want to get to Dave so I can finish this crappy day already."

Christie's expression didn't change.

I felt myself deflate a little.

Maybe I'd have to muster those tears after all.

Then, miracle of miracles, she crooked a finger and turned toward the kitchen.

I followed on her heels. At the two swinging shutters, she turned to me and held a hand up, the palm toward me. I paused obediently, but she didn't speak.

I actually heard her swallow, then she opened her mouth. At this point, my body was positively humming with the desire to be through those swinging doors and out the other side.

Finally, her hand dropped and she spoke: "He was with me the other night."

"Excuse me?" I said, as though I didn't understand.

But I did. I felt an icy chill run down my spine.

"Dave," I said, numbly.

"The other night, whatever it was. Wednesday."

My head nodded, but it felt like it was floating far above my body—a balloon tethered to a string. I didn't speak. I wasn't sure I could.

She went on, color rising in her pale skin. It gave her a delicate look, like the Madame Alexander doll I got for my fifth birthday. "Nothing happened, even though he said you two weren't really together, just . . ." She trailed off. Then she looked at the swinging doors again, her voice small now. "Did you really come in to use the exit?"

My balloon head bobbed silently.

"Like I said, nothing happened . . ." She trailed off and searched my face for something. Permission? Absolution?

My gas tank was empty. I didn't have anything to give, not rage or even a shred of disappointment.

"Yeah," was all I could come up with.

My whole body felt numb with shock.

We stood there for a few seconds, studiously avoiding each other's eyes.

Finally, I couldn't stand it anymore. I flexed my fingers to see if they would move. When they responded, I used them to place my floppy hat back on, then my sunglasses.

I parted the shutter doors and willed my feet forward, leaving Christie on the other side.

A short woman with light brown skin, wearing checkered chef's pants, a white chef's coat and an orange handkerchief tied over her braided hair looked at me, then went back to chopping an onion.

"Good morning," I said, as though waltzing through her kitchen was the most natural thing in the world.

"Good morning." The rhythm of her chopping didn't change.

I walked toward the back of the kitchen, past a few other staff members who I didn't fully register, toward the metal door marked "Exit." I pushed through and found myself once again flooded in sunlight.

The door slammed closed behind me. I didn't even flinch.

What were the odds?

I stood in place for a moment, my mind ticking.

My eyes traveled down the stairs, across the small alley and right to the front door of the dive shop, which sat about ten paces from where I stood.

I was staring at the geography of a romance.

Proximity was a powerful thing.

So was real, unbridled, unrestrained emotion. I felt a taste of it then, like a bucket of water dumped over my head. It dripped down my face, over my shoulders, down my back. For a second, I wanted to scream. Or cry. Or rip something to shreds. Or get so completely wasted that I could barely remember my own name.

Instead, I just stood in the sun and let it bake my skin. I let my gaze wander up to the intense blue sky. It was a sight that usually filled me with joy. Not today.

But the desire to scream, rip and cry began to recede, as though the sun had evaporated it.

I eyed Molly Molone's, the Irish bar just below me. They were doing bottomless mimosas today. Who was I kidding? They did them every day. But, today, I had an excuse.

Or I could just turn around, stomp back to my apartment and let all these crazy people sort everything out for themselves. Forget Dave. Forget Ben. Forget Andrea. Focus on Lizzie.

I didn't have time to consider. A quick squawk of a police siren and a shout from the street brought me back to reality.

Ben was on the lam.

I might be as well.

I took a quick look around for anyone in a blue police uniform. The coast was clear. I headed down the steps toward Dave, toward uncertainty and toward the close of a chapter of my island life.

12

The alley was ripe with the tang of spoiled garbage, mixed with the aroma of cooking hamburger from Molly Malone's kitchen, an odd combination that left me both nauseated and hungry.

I saw Rick standing outside the door to the dive shop. His attention was fixed on the iron gate that led to D-dock. He had his black wetsuit peeled halfway down. His tanned arms were crossed over his pale chest, his bony frame and farmer's tan on full display. At fifty-two, Rick was far from being an old man, but you could already see the kind he'd be: a bird, the skinny kind with the caved-in chest and rounded back.

His right leg was jiggling all the way down to his flip flop. This made me stop short. Rick had spent fifteen years as a white cop in the Bronx, and he still kept his gray hair short with almost military precision. I'd seen him haul a half-drowned twelve-year-old from the water and perform CPR without an iota of hesitation. Rick never jiggled.

I stood and watched him for a second, feeling a fat drop of sweat trickle down my neck. I moved quickly into the shade in front of the shop and said softly, "Rick, what's going on?"

He swiveled his head, his startling blue eyes peering at me out of a long, thin and tan face.

Without speaking, he pointed a finger at me, then walked into the dive shop.

I'd trained with him as a dive student long enough to know that I was expected to follow him.

Once inside, he shut the door behind me and locked it.

This was also strange behavior.

"What are you doing?" I asked.

In response, he only looked at me with those piercing blue eyes and headed toward the back of the shop. I took off my hat and sunglasses and trotted behind him to keep up.

As I followed him, my hip bumped the edge of a table of T-shirts, upsetting one of the stacks. I paused to straighten it again, knowing I would never get the stack quite as precisely neat as Rick. Then I followed him into the back of the dive shop, where the gear was stored and repairs were made.

I braced myself to see Dave, a sight that I knew would be a jolt to the system.

However, when we got to the work area, it was empty. I exhaled with relief. Rick pulled the lone stool out from under the workbench and gave it to me. I shot him a look of gratitude and sank into it only seconds before he would have needed to hold me up.

Lizzie Jordan, unexpected weakling.

I breathed in the smell of the room—wood from a cabinet Rick had just built and grease from the tools he used to keep dive gear in tip-top shape. Usually, I found it reassuring. In Rick's world, everything had its place.

But today, even the smell of the workshop couldn't steady me, even as my feet rested on the metal rungs of the stool.

Rick left me for a moment, exiting through the back door. I saw him peel off his wetsuit and throw it in a large tub. Then he sprayed himself down with fresh water from the hose. Usually, the navy Speedo he wears under his wetsuit makes me snicker, but not today. I didn't have it in me.

My unfocused eyes settled on the aluminum tanks sitting against the wall that waited to be filled.

The door opened and shut. Rick was back, wearing a pair of board shorts and a dive shop T-shirt. He leaned his hip against the workbench and folded his arms across his chest.

"What's going on out there?" I asked.

He paused a second, appraising me. Then he spoke. "Whatever it is, it's not good. There are all sorts of rumors flying around, but nothing reliable." He waved his hand as though swatting at a mosquito.

"Rumors like what?"

Rick just shook his head.

Then he fixed his gaze pointedly on me, his face set.

I expected him to speak, but when the silence began to stretch, I blurted, "Rick, what do you know about Dave?"

Rick's eyebrows went up, but the rest of his expression stayed the same. "You're asking me?" he said. "I just work with the guy. You, on the other hand . . ."

I twisted my mouth, but I didn't reply.

He lifted his chin at me. "Spill it, kid. What's going on?"

I spilled. The whole story, including Jessie's mention of Dave's presence at Duffy's, Dave's omission of that particular detail and my chance meeting with his other girl. I wanted to skip my encounter with Christie, but once I got rolling, I couldn't stop. I told him everything.

It wasn't the first time we'd had a heart-to-heart in the back of the dive shop. Asshole bosses, guys who loved me and left me, car trouble—Rick and I had talked about it all. I almost told him about my family once, but we got interrupted by another instructor who couldn't get the dive boat started.

Rick took it all in without interrupting my rambling narrative. He considered everything for a long moment, as was his way. Then, he finally spoke. "Lizzie, I have to ask: Why the hell did you mix yourself up in this?"

"A misguided sense of loyalty? An altruistic desire to give back to my fellow residents?"

Rick just shook his head at me. Here, in the light of day, my words sounded weak. How could I have been so stupid?

"She's been missing for thirty six hours?"

I nodded.

I could see him doing some calculations in his head. I froze on the stool. I suspected that Rick knew more about what was going on in this marina than he was telling me.

Rick exhaled. He uncrossed his arms and picked up a piece of the disassembled second-stage Scuba regulator he was working on. He flicked at something imperceptible with the tip of his fingernail, then he put the part back on the counter.

He opened his mouth to speak and I felt myself leaning forward, desperate to know what he did. Had they found Andrea's body?

"I know someone at the police department," he said. "He helped me out when my house got robbed a few years ago. A good guy." Before I could argue, he held up a finger. I shut my mouth. "I think you should talk to him. It doesn't have to be at the police station. And then you need to stop messing around in things that are over your head. Amateur detective days are over for you."

I was already shaking my head *no*. "I know your intentions are good, Rick, but you know what happened to Georgia. She had to leave island because that cop wouldn't leave her alone."

"You've been listening to too many stories up at Island Time."

"What about Dave?" I asked.

Rick tilted his head back and forth. "Just because he was at the bar doesn't mean anything. If he's the guy I think he is, he'll be fine. But you two obviously have some other issues to work out."

"Has he—"

I didn't get a chance to finish my sentence when I heard a voice behind me. "Lizzie," it said.

I started violently right off the stool, my momentum carrying me halfway across the shop. I got my feet under me a few inches from the neat row of aluminum tanks, narrowly avoiding a round of dive tank bowling.

I could feel Rick's eyes on me. How I'd turned into a jumpy little mouse in a few short hours was beyond me, too.

Dave was standing at the entrance to the back room, a hard look on his face. His signature smile was nowhere to be found.

I tried a joke. "Amateur detective? More like professional wimp."

No one laughed.

Rick put a hand up. "I'm going to leave you two to it." His blue eyes were stern as they bored into me. "Think about what I said."

I nodded once, then tried to find some kind of purchase to lean on, just in case my legs went out again. My hand closed on the top of Rick's work bench as Dave started speaking.

"I understand you met Christie," he said.

I dug the pads of my fingers into the rough wood for courage. "By accident," I countered.

"Lizzie, things haven't been great between us—"

"I want to know what you were doing at Duffy's and why you didn't tell me about it."

He shook his head in what looked like frustration.

When he didn't answer, I prompted him. "Well?"

He shrugged. "This is your problem. This missing girl is more important than us. And you don't even know her." He pursed his lips together for a moment. "Besides, what does it matter?"

"What does it *matter*?" I felt a flash of anger. "You let me tell you all about Ben's predicament, and you just didn't think it mattered that you were *there*? Right exactly where Andrea went missing?"

Dave's face hardened further. "Andrea," he said, turning the girl's name over in his mouth.

"So you're telling me you know nothing."

"Look, I was there."

"And?"

"I did meet some girls Ben was talking to."

"But you and Ben don't even like each other."

He made a face. "I don't know where you're getting that. Look, I saw him, I said 'hi.' I kept moving."

"Because you had to meet Christie."

He didn't answer. I saw a small smile creep up on his face, but it wasn't that Dave special smile. It was a grimace.

"Liz, I just want more than you do, more than you ever did."

He had me there.

But that didn't extinguish the fire that burned in me. So I kept at it, my tone accusatory. "So you have no idea what happened with those girls."

"I stopped to talk to Ben because I thought I could talk to him about you. But he was too intent on hooking up that night to be distracted, and the last thing I wanted to do was entertain tourists."

"That's it?" I asked. "I want to know the truth, Dave."

I saw his body shift, and I knew there was more.

I felt a connection click into place. "You were buying pot from him."

And just like that, the fire in me winked out.

He didn't need to tell me more. I guessed that he had continued through the Duffy's parking lot, then back across the street to the East End Café, where he found Christie. But why had he found his way to my door that night?

"So you went to Christie," I said.

"Yeah, but she encouraged me to give it one last try to make sure I was sure."

I realized I was holding my breath, waiting for the sentence to be delivered.

He met my eyes again. "I'm sure."

I exhaled. Then I felt my eyes turning toward the exit. It was ludicrous, I knew. All I wanted for the last half hour was to get here, and now I couldn't wait to get away. Maybe I could just dig myself a hole and crawl in it.

It had to feel better than this.

Rick's voice floated in from the shop. "Are you two done yet?"

"Yep," Dave said, his voice tight.

I wasn't, not by a mile. My boyfriend had been doing drugs behind my back—by the way, was everyone on this island involved with drugs for God's sake?!—oh, and he'd already moved on to someone else. I couldn't even begin to process it all.

The air seemed to shimmer. Was it possible this was a bad dream? A girl was gone. Ben might be guilty of killing her. He was certainly guilty of selling pot to Dave. And Dave was done with me. It seemed unreal.

Just yesterday, I was scrambling over giant boulders in the Baths, making tourists laugh, lining them up to take pictures and pouring enough Painkillers to get them drunk. And, today, I was dealing with death—the death of a young woman and the death of my relationship.

Rick reappeared around the corner, his blue eyes looking particularly bright in his solemn face.

"They found a body in the harbor."

I felt the air leave my lungs in a *whoosh*.

"It was a young woman, probably the one you're looking for."

I closed my eyes.

I wanted it to be silent, but Rick kept talking. "And, Lizzie, my friend is coming over now. I suggest you tell him what you know. It's better to deal with this now than to have them show up at your door unannounced."

I felt my head start to shake in the negative again. Whether the cops had been looking for me before, they were certainly looking for me now, thanks to Rick.

Rick started to talk, but I couldn't make out the words he was saying.

Even in my weakened state, my endangered body knew what to do. I turned and ran for the back door. I threw it open and heard it slam against the concrete wall. This was no time to worry about breakage.

Once I was out in the open, I had no choice but to act natural or risk calling attention to myself. I planted my floppy hat firmly on my head, slid my sunglasses over my ears and tried, as casually as I could, to stroll up the driveway toward the street.

I tried to make my gait easy and unaffected. My mind sung with the desperate wish to take off running. I struggled to keep my steps even. My arms swung stiffly.

I waited to hear the sound of Rick calling my name, or the rhythm of heavy footfalls behind me. My muscles twitched as they anticipated being grabbed from behind as I headed toward the marina exit, even if it was just for a "friendly talk."

But somehow, I was allowed to continue.

However, even if I was able to scoot up the driveway without being caught, I was far from safe. I still had to walk past the officer who guarded the entrance to the marina.

I started up the steep driveway. I tried to look carefree, but I could feel massive tension at the base of my skull. The officer stood to the left of his car, his eyes fixed on traffic. I kept my eyes pinned to his body, gauging his state of mind. I waited for him to yawn or lean against his patrol car, but he stood ramrod straight, his arms crossed his chest, his chiseled triceps reminding me how screwed I was if the police decided I was a person of interest.

I wanted to look back to see if Rick or his police officer friend was after me, but I didn't dare. I just kept my feet moving forward, desperately hoping I could get out to the road and slip away. My mind screamed at me to move faster, to simply break and run. To use the adrenaline pumping through my veins as fuel. But I held the reins of my body tightly, knowing that calmness was my most useful disguise.

Each step was a small celebration. And by the time I hit the top of the driveway, I felt a glimmer of real hope. *I was free.*

Then I saw a figure at the very edge of my right-hand peripheral vision, and I felt a jolt of recognition. But not a pleasant one. It was the man in the gray suit from the Ritz.

My brain resumed its pleas for me to run, hide, do *something*, but with great effort, I willed my feet to move forward at the same measured pace. I had to stay in character. I was Elizabeth Morgan, tourist.

The man in the suit continued forward.

In a few seconds, we would all come together: the unwitting amateur Nancy Drew, the gray suit who had to be suspicious of me at this point and the officer who would take me off to jail for aiding and abetting a fugitive and accessory after the fact.

I wished I had a god to pray to at that moment.

Instead, I had a brain flash. Across the road lay Duffy's. What if I could just keep going right across the street, just like any tourist would, to get a piña colada and, in my case, gather my wits after scattering them about Red Hook?

As our paths carried us closer and closer, my right eye straining with the effort of watching Gray Suit out of its extreme edge, I repeated my story to myself. *I am Elizabeth Morgan. I'm staying at Secret Harbour. I came to get fins for snorkeling, but instead I'm going to Duffy's to drink the most innocent piña colada a person can have.*

A small breeze fluttered the hair that lay down my back and I felt an icy wave of realization. I'd forgotten to tuck my hair under my hat when I left the shop, so my red hair was hanging loose, ready for any Gray Suit worth his salt to recognize it from the Ritz. Crap, crap, crap.

I took small sips of air. I wasn't capable of normal breaths anymore.

We would have collided, Gray Suit and I. But I took a hop step forward and raised my hand in apology, as I hoped any considerate tourist would have done to avoid colliding with another person. That quick step allowed me to pass right in front of him, just before we both reached the officer.

It felt like Gray Suit's head turned to follow my path as I passed him. I was so close I could smell his cologne. It was a nice change from the usual smell of Red Hook. Clean and understated—or maybe it was the smell of fresh laundry. For a second, I was tempted to throw myself into the man's arms, bury my face in his chest and confess everything.

In other words, I needed a drink.

But my faithful legs kept me moving forward. Everything told me that I'd made it. I'd flown under the radar and I was free—for now.

And then I was forced to stop short, just a few steps away from the officer and Gray Suit. Traffic was still heavy through Red Hook. Not a break in sight.

I continued to breathe shallow gasps while I scanned the line of cars. I was close enough to hear them talking behind me, but not close enough to make out the words.

I could swear my vision was starting to crowd with the same snow I'd seen this morning. I blinked hard, even though I knew it wouldn't make a whit of difference.

Just get across the street, Lizzie. Get across the street.

No one would stop for me. Screw the guy in the giant black pickup truck with three Haitian workers in the back. Screw the woman with "Miss Nice Guy" in decal letters at the top of her gold Acura's windshield. Liar. And screw the white kid in the aqua blue Corolla that looked like it came from a junk yard.

I was ready to dash across the street in spite of the traffic when a maroon taxi van finally stopped and gave a small honk, which either meant, "Do you need a ride?" or "Go ahead, you crazy white lady."

I didn't care. I took it as the latter, raised a hand and sprinted across the intersection, making a space in front of a white pick-up that apparently belonged to a local plumber. He honked and I cringed. So much for flying under the radar.

I was safely across the street. I felt like I'd run a marathon. I wanted to stop and lean my hands on my thighs, but I knew I had to keep moving. I looked at the regular security guard who was sitting on an old wooden stool in the corner of the lot, in the shade. I nearly raised my hand to him as I usually did, but I pinned it to my side instead. Elizabeth Morgan would not be so friendly.

I veered right toward the wooden shack where this whole mess began.

A tiki bar in the middle of a parking lot might not seem like a recipe for success, but Duffy's Love Shack made it work. Today, it looked barely open, even though it was just after noon. The shutter doors on the yellow clapboard building sagged on their hinges, hanging half ajar. The usual top-volume boisterous music—an eternal rotation of the B-52's, Jimmy Buffett, Rihanna and top 40 hits from five years ago—wasn't on yet. I checked my watch. The place officially opened about an hour ago. Whoever was working must have gotten *really* drunk last night.

To be fair, it wasn't much of a daytime place. The tables that sat in the parking lot at night were neatly stacked in a corner until around 5:00 pm. A few people did shuffle in for lunch or a frozen nooner, but it was the dancing at night—and the resulting parking lot scene—that really attracted the tourists.

Sarcasm aside, there's something vaguely charming about partying in a parking lot. It can be strangely magical, especially when rum is involved. Maybe you had to be here to experience it, but I'd felt it once or twice.

At the moment, I wasn't looking for magic. I just needed to get a stool under my ass before I collapsed. I staggered into the bar, my nose crinkling at the smell of stale beer.

A tall white guy in cargo shorts and a tie-dyed Duffy's shirt was in front of the bar, arranging stools so slowly and carefully that you might have thought he was building a house of cards.

This was Chuck, the bartender who had served the girls on Wednesday night. Without really meaning to be, I was back in the game. I felt a tiny surge of energy, one that propelled my feet forward.

Even with his back to me, I could see that Chuck held himself like a man who'd had a barrel chest and stomach to match for many years, his weight in the heels of his long, skinny legs.

I wondered how those cargo shorts of his held on, balanced under his stomach with no real ass to hold them up. Then again, I'm sure men could wonder similarly about the physics of strapless bras. Hell, I wondered about the physics of strapless bras, often while wearing one.

I shuffled to a newly arranged stool and sank onto it, my elbows hitting the bar hard. I sat there for a few breaths, panting like a fat dog who'd just climbed a long set of stairs.

"Good morning," I said in between huffs.

"Afternoon by now," Chuck said, continuing his task without skipping a beat. Chuck was a lifer if I ever knew one. Oh, he might announce he was leaving, throw a going away party and spend a few months in Key West or Fort Lauderdale, but he'd be back.

A friend of mine calls this "Plan B."

Go ahead, leave island. Buy a ticket to another place you're sure must be better than here. Chase your dreams. St. Thomas is always here for you when nothing else works out.

Maybe it sounds depressing. I always found it comforting. St. Thomas will open her arms to you, even after you've forsaken her.

Finally, Chuck placed his last bar stool and looked over his shoulder slowly, his eyelids at half-mast. "Get you something?"

Lord, did I want something. A small voice suggested that maybe I should keep my wits about me with the police right across the street, but those earlier Presidentes had stopped working their magic. I could feel a sour stomach set in.

"Absolut Citron and soda with a splash of cran," I said. "And a bottle of water."

He nodded and took a mid-speed meander around the other side of the bar, which, like everything else, was decked out in full tiki regalia. The base of the bar was covered with a façade of split bamboo poles. A small "roof" hung over the bar, covered in long grass strands that looked like they'd been stolen from a hula girl's skirt—many, many years ago.

Behind the bar were shelf after shelf of the supplies that made up Duffy's signature drinks. There were ceramic glasses shaped like Shamu—I believe the drink you sipped out of his wide open mouth was called the Whale of a Tale—alongside monkeys, parrots, coconuts, pirates, schooners and other whimsical nautical items. In the daylight, they just seemed garish as they grinned toward an empty bar.

One shelf caught my eye, the one that held the small goldfish bowls the bartenders used to make their Shark Tank cocktails. They came complete with a small plastic shark toy filled with a shot of rum. Every time a Shark Tank was served, the speakers blared Jimmy Buffett's "Fins." It was quite the event. I was surprised the girls hadn't gone for one of those.

Or maybe they had, and they'd lied about it.

Because I'd simply ordered a regular drink, it got delivered in Caribbean crystal, next to a bottle of water, both of which merited their own coaster. Classy. I twisted off the top to the bottle of water and downed the whole thing in one messy chug, wiping my mouth with the back of my hand when I was done.

"You live here, don't you?" Chuck asked.

I barked a laugh, surprising myself. "What gave me away? My delicate, ladylike manners?"

Chuck's expression didn't change. It must have been too early for humor. His features showed his time behind a bar. His cheeks were puffy under dark stubble. His dark eyes were shot with red. A scruffy soul patch threatened to take over his chin. His olive face was rimmed by two long, unruly sideburns and a mop of chin-length curly black hair, which he brushed away from his eyes at regular intervals.

"I'm surprised you recognized me through my stateside disguise. Lizzie." I held out my hand.

He looked at it for a beat, then touched it briefly. He returned to arranging bottles behind the bar. His expression never changed. The Lizzie comedy show was not going over so well.

Bullheaded girl that I am, I tried again. "I don't usually dress like this. I've just had a hell of a day—"

He was barely looking at me. I trailed off. Chuck was clearly not interested in much about me, let alone the minutiae of my very strange morning. In fact, it looked like it was taking all of his focus to stay upright. He rubbed his face sleepily. I wondered if he'd closed down Saloon that morning. You could find most of the bartenders and servers on the island there after their shifts were done. Drinking until 4:00 am seems like a good idea in the moment, but it rarely turns out that way.

"Rough one?" I offered. I had to get this conversation moving somehow.

"Pretty crazy one." He started setting out blenders for their specialty drinks, almost all of which were frozen.

I didn't know how the guys at Duffy's did it. Most of the bartenders I knew would give you a hairy eyeball for ordering a piña colada in the middle of a busy shift. But the guys at Duffy's made them all night long, and they had to do it while listening to the B52's sing "Love Shack" three times a night. Not an easy job, by any stretch. Maybe that explained Chuck's demeanor.

"You work Ladies' Night this week?"

A nod.

"You hear about that girl who went missing?"

Chuck's motions paused. "Yeah, I heard." He tilted his head over at the marina. "Probably what's going on over there. Took me an extra twenty minutes to get to work this morning." He shook his head in annoyance.

Real compassionate one, this guy. I bit back an acid reply. He might know something that I could use.

Keep it casual, Lizzie.

"Did you know she was in here with you before she disappeared?"

Chuck's face darkened and his eyes finally focused on me. For a moment, I thought he was going to cock his arm back and hit me with the blender he held in his right hand.

Well, I'd finally gotten Chuck's attention.

Now I needed to diffuse it. I put a hand up. "Hey, it's not like that. I just want to know if you remember her."

The anger drained from his face quickly, and I watched him put the blender down. I marveled why a guy with such a short fuse would work at Duffy's. It was a busy bar, packed with tourists who each wanted their own frozen drink, in its cheesy ceramic cup, right NOW. I wondered how he handled it—if he handled it at all.

Could he have come around the bar, grabbed Andrea's bicep with his hand and forced her across the parking lot to the secret storage room where Duffy's bartenders were known to have trysts with their best-looking customers (and each other)? Maybe those red eyes meant something else. Maybe he'd been up all night, wracked with guilt.

Instead of answering my question, Chuck had dropped his focus to the ground. A corner of the black rubber floor mat had curled under itself. Instead of leaning down to free the corner with his hand, Chuck tried to slide the toe of his dirty black sneaker underneath the edge, his tongue peeking out from between his lips in concentration. He made little progress, but he kept at it stubbornly. I took a long draw of my drink to give my mouth something to do, other than delivering a snide observation.

Finally, his toe got purchase and the mat flopped into place.

I dismissed him as Andrea's killer. He was too lazy to bend over to straighten a floor mat, let alone kill a girl and dump her in the harbor.

I dug in my purse for my cell phone and flipped it open to show him the picture I had texted myself earlier. "She's the one on the left. Do you recognize her?"

He gave me another look, a warning that his patience for this kind of thing was limited.

The vodka he'd given me kept my resolve steady. I had dogged persistence on my side, and he knew it.

Finally, he looked at the picture of the three girls on the balcony at the Ritz.

I took another look myself. They were leaning against the rail with the resort behind them. All three were smiling brightly at the camera. Andrea was the only one of the three who didn't have long hair and straight bangs, her dark hair in waves that hit her shoulders. Where Becky was long and lean and Jessie long and solid, Andrea was short and curvy, even in her ski slope nose and the twist of her smiling mouth.

Chuck said nothing, but he did continue to stare. I prompted him. "They ordered Bushwackers."

He shook his head and turned away, busying himself with a cup of drink toothpicks with tinsel on top. "Fuck do I know?" he said.

I said nothing.

"I mean, maybe."

That was something. "A lot of girls order Bushwackers?"

"Know how many Bushwackers I make a night?" He reached into a cooler and pulled out a gallon jug of housemade mix, labeled in sloppy lettering with a Sharpie. "I go through four of these a night. 'Less they stiffed me or left me a $50, I wouldn't remember them."

"Who else was working that night?"

"Jeannine. She's useless. That night, she got wasted early with a group of guys who kept ordering shots. She passed out in the back storage room for about an hour." He shook his head. "You know she passed out in the walk-in last week? Girl is lucky I found her."

"Anyone else in here who caught your attention?"

A pained look crossed his face. My time with Chuck was winding down, no doubt. "I was talking to Pete most of the night. You know Pete, right? Bartender at Saloon. He's been having some girl trouble." He paused and ran a hand through his hair. "Who isn't?" His face looked pained again, and I wondered if Chuck's present state was due to an island girl.

Not that I cared that much. I had my own girl to find, and he wasn't being much help.

I tried again. "I heard there were some creepy Coasties in here that night."

"Those guys?" Chuck shrugged. "You think they did this?" He snorted. "Can barely tie their shoes. Not likely."

I must have looked a little crestfallen because he grabbed my half-full drink, dumped it into a pint glass and topped it off with mostly vodka. Then he put it back in front of me.

"On me. Talk to Jeannine. She comes in at three."

Then he retreated to rearrange bar mats featuring the Cruzan rum logo. Apparently, our conversation was over. If I had any doubt, Chuck stalked over to the computer in the corner, and "Margaritaville" came blasting out of the speakers at a deafening volume. I guess I wasn't going to be waiting for Jeannine here, unless I wanted to hear about Jimmy Buffett's tattoo of a Mexican cutie at approximately a million decibels.

I reached in my purse and put a $5 on the bar. I didn't get that much from Chuck other than vodka, but I wasn't an animal. Tips mattered here, more than any other place I've lived. Almost everyone lived off them. You could be an asshole and be forgiven, but a bad tipper? Heaven help you.

Drink in hand, I drifted into the sunshine. I squinted painfully before dropping my sunglasses down on my nose, then stuffing my hat on my head.

Well, that was a pretty big waste of time.

At any other bar on the East End, the bartender probably would know more. Duffy's was so busy that things often didn't get personal. Just my luck—and Andrea's.

I glanced over to the left and saw the police SUV still sitting in front of the marina.

If I wanted to play on the safe side, I had more time to kill.

First stop was the drug store. I crossed the lot and pushed in the swinging glass door, keeping my drink at my hip. They probably wouldn't hassle me, but I didn't feel like taking my chances.

I turned down the tiny aisle where office supplies were mixed with children's art supplies and toys. I grabbed a small notebook and a backup pen, noting that St. Thomas is the only place in the world where such a small purchase will set you back $7.35.

At least the woman who sold it to me wished me a "blessed day." It made me feel a little lighter. Or maybe that was the vodka. I left the drug store and peered over at the marina. My friend, Officer Statue, was still in place, so took a right turn toward XO, where Andrea and Ben had the second phase of their first date.

Correction—the third phase, counting Ben's car. I shook my head.

As I walked by XO's plate glass windows, I felt a buzz in my purse. I froze. Was it my phone or Andrea's? Did phones with cracked screens even still work? I quickly maneuvered behind a pillar and parted the top of my purse with two fingers.

I breathed a sigh of relief as I saw the outside screen of my crappy flip phone light up. I glanced at the number. 216 area code. No idea. I let the top of my purse fall shut, took another hit of vodka and headed for XO.

I felt the phone buzz again, and I pulled it back out of my purse. Same phone number *Leave a message, buddy.*

I pulled open the door to the bar. XO used to be a tiny place, more a hallway than a bar. They'd expanded a couple of years ago, knocking out a wall and continuing the bar out and around in a handsome curve into what used to be the shop next door. All the walls were still painted the color of cabernet. The new booths were a rich brown. Maybe it sounds too dark for a bar in the Caribbean, but I had always found it a welcome change, and an air conditioned one at that.

It was also the most reliable place on the East End to get a good glass of wine while wearing the khaki shorts and T-shirt you'd worked in that day. Even though the wine list tended toward fancy at XO, it was still a "come as you are" kind of place, which I always found a relief.

I scanned the bar. Maybe Jeannine had come in for a meal before her shift, and I could quiz her about her night at Duffy's.

I didn't see her.

Instead, the seats were dotted with a few older men, some of whom were fishermen and some of whom were tradesmen in work clothes. I nodded to a boat mechanic I recognized, and he nodded back.

My eye strayed to the corner booths. Two women were laughing over salads and iced teas. Behind them, in the corner, sat a man who looked massive even from his seated position. His powerful shoulders sat on top of a torso as thick as a Redwood tree, swathed in a faded yellow T-shirt that advertised a St. Thomas Carnival long gone.

When I'd first met him a few years ago, his hair had been a wild, curly blonde halo, with corkscrew tendrils that fell alongside his round baby face. He told me that had a St. Thomian father and a Norwegian mother to thank for his looks. These days, long blonde dreads had become his trademark. His smile stayed the same. It lit up his fawn-colored face, making him look like the biggest cherub you'd ever seen.

This was the dancing man the girls had mentioned: Magnus.

He had a book in front of him and I could see his head bobbing in time to the Sade song playing over the bar's sound system.

I had met Magnus over a six-hour marathon of pool at a long-gone bar called the Poorman's, where you could pour your own drinks for $3. We'd exchanged astrological signs, then beaten half the island in a performance that I was sure I'd never be able to duplicate. At the end of the night, I went home with someone else. I knew he'd been disappointed, but he still shined me a smile as I bid him good night.

Magnus was a prince among men, if such things existed on St. Thomas.

"Magnus, how are you?"

His head popped up from his book. It snapped shut to reveal itself to be a copy of James Michener's *Caribbean*.

He flashed me that smile and dipped his head in a mock bow. "Well, well, well. Miss Aquarius, how are you?"

I pointed to the book. "Better than you. That thing is a nightmare."

He grinned. "I know it. I've been fighting with it all week and have nothing to show for it. My fault for being curious about what a crusty old white man had to say about these islands." He dropped his hand onto the battered white hard hat on the seat next to him, gripped it with his palm and lifted it to the other side. He gestured to the empty space with his open hand.

That same hand could probably grab my face and crush it without much effort, but I also knew that kind of thing was the farthest thing from Magnus's mind.

I sat, resting my half-empty pint glass on the table. I sighed audibly. As long as Magnus didn't turn into a potential killer or a cheater, I could rest for a short time.

I glanced at the Presidente in front of him.

"You have troubles written all over you," he said, ordering another beer as the waitress came by. I ordered one myself, as well as a chicken, Brie and apple sandwich—my go-to at XO. My stomach growled in approval.

I looked at Magnus and opened my mouth to ask him about the girls, but I let my lips drop shut silently. When I opened them again, I asked, "How are you these days, Magnus?"

The corners of his mouth turned up. He knew what I was doing, but he was willing to play along.

He held out one hand flat, then shifted it from side to side and shrugged. A slight grimace on his face indicated that he might be worse off than he let on. He looked fairly healthy, but pushing 275, he would always look healthy. There was a bit of roundness to Magnus, but underneath that softness was pure muscle.

Most people were scared of him, probably because they didn't know what to make of this giant mixed-race man with blonde dreadlocks. Let's say that I had a healthy respect for what he was capable of, but that I knew him to be a mostly-gentle Sagittarius.

"How's the construction business?" I asked.

"That's not really what you came over to talk about."

I could feel all the relief I felt at sitting down drain away. "No, it's not." I picked up the beer bottle the waitress placed on the table and took a sip. I chased it with a sip of vodka and made a face.

"What have you got yourself mixed up in, Miss Aquarius? And can you get yourself un-mixed? You've got a gorgeous smile and I haven't seen it once since you came over."

That garnered half a smile from me. From anyone else, that line would have rung false, but there was something so sincere about Magnus that even the cheesiest lines worked for him.

I met his light brown eyes. "I have a question for you."

He smiled broadly, those cheeks puffing up in their strangely endearing way. They were speckled in a few places with freckles and what might have been acne scars. No one would call Magnus conventionally attractive, but his charisma was off the charts. "If the question is, 'Will you go home with me?' you know the answer is 'yes.'"

"Ah, you don't want to get mixed up with me right now."

"You still seeing Dave?"

Now I held out my hand as he had before, but instead of tilting it side to side, I dive bombed it like an airplane into the deep red Naugahyde seat.

Magnus didn't laugh. "I always thought you could do better."

I was surprised to feel a smile creep onto my face as I formulated a retort. Magnus's playful energy was working on me. "You mean, like you?"

His smile radiated. "Like me."

"You're incorrigible."

He shrugged, then we clinked beer bottles and drank. His sandwich arrived, sliced beef on a French baguette with a side of *au jus*. I rarely regretted my CBA, but the smell of the beef was almost too much to bear. A moment later, my stomach's anxieties were quieted by the arrival of my sandwich.

We spent a few moments in silence. I demolished the first half of my sandwich like a wolf who'd gone without a kill for days. Magnus dipped his sandwich delicately in the side bowl and chewed thoughtfully.

I left the other half for the moment and drained my vodka glass. I looked at the half-empty beer bottle next to the now-empty pint glass and knew I needed to slow down. I would nurse this beer, I promised myself.

Finally, Magnus swallowed the last of his sandwich, wiped his hands on his napkin and looked at me. "Now what can I *really* do for you?"

"A couple of days ago, a group of three girls went to Duffy's for Ladies' Night. Tourists. They thought they saw you there." I flipped open my phone and showed him the picture of the girls. "Did you see them?"

"Ben was all over that one," he said, pointing to Andrea.

I nodded. "She's dead."

"I know."

I raised my eyebrows at him.

He shrugged. "Why do you think I'm in here eating a leisurely lunch on a perfectly good work day? We were working on some of the more decrepit plaster along the second-level balcony at AYH when the cops kicked us out."

I nodded.

"I talked with her that night," he said.

"You talk with all the pretty girls."

A smile and a shrug. "I try. She was a Scorpio."

"What did you think of her?"

"Sweet girl. Independent streak. A little bit sad. Just my type. Remind you of anyone?"

I felt myself blush briefly and I was grateful I had a moment to recover as Magnus ordered another round. I didn't protest.

"I'm not sure anyone has described me as 'sweet' since kindergarten."

"Their mistake."

I ducked my head and felt the heat from my face spread down my body. To distract myself, I rooted in my purse and pulled out my new notebook and pen.

"Was she looking for trouble?" I asked Magnus, who was still grinning at me, undeterred by my obvious embarrassment.

He shook his head. "Nah." He pointed to Jessie's face. "That one was watching her like a hawk. Maybe Andrea wanted a little island flavor, but that's all. Just a taste."

"You called her 'sweet.' That wasn't really the word I was thinking. 'Wild,' maybe?"

"'Wild,' compared to what?"

"She gave Ben a blow job in his car by the dumpsters."

Magnus made a face. "According to Ben. He's been known to exaggerate the magnitude of his conquests." He scanned the bar and lifted his nose to point out Jeannine as she walked into the bar, already in her Duffy's uniform. As she sat, she received a pint glass that looked like rum with a splash of Coke. He continued. "Compared to that one? Andrea was a pussy cat. But compared to . . ." He gestured at my phone again.

"This one?" I asked, tapping Jessie's face.

"Yep. That one was on the prowl. She wouldn't talk to me, but she was definitely looking to work it that night. Scorpio maybe, or an Aries."

"Jessie?" I asked, tapping her image again to be sure.

"Miss Aquarius, you know I'm a better judge of character than you are. She was trying to make something happen, but the poor thing had no idea how to pull it off. Then with Ben all over Andrea, it activated her mama bear instincts."

He put the tip of a thick finger under Becky's face. "Now, this one, I'd bet she's a Cancer," he said. "I did get her to dance to *Love Shack* but then she got bird dogged right out from me."

He shook his head. "Couldn't get a real bead on her. All the energy from the other two ladies. She ended up a satellite."

My eyebrows wrinkled. The way the girls had relayed their evening at Duffy's, I imagined them huddled together like a pack of vulnerable wildebeests while the lions circled. At least, that was Jessie's version. Then again, there had been that incident with Duncan and the shot—and the alleged blow job. Maybe Andrea wasn't as innocent as she seemed. But from what Magnus was saying, Andrea wasn't a predator. Jessie was.

"This was not quite how the girls told me it went down," I said aloud.

Magnus shrugged. "Everyone's got their own truth."

"It feels like they wanted me to think Andrea was the one looking for fun."

"Miss Aquarius, we're all looking for fun. Some of us know how to have it better than others. Andrea knew how to get hers. Too well, maybe."

He paused and I felt my mind wander to the body I imagined they were pulling out of the harbor.

Magnus tapped Jessie's face again with a finger with white plaster in its creases. "That girl has all the fire, but she has no clue how to direct it. "

I nodded, taking in Magnus's barroom psychology with another swig of Presidente. "I just can't understand how those girls just *left* Andrea."

"Ben's harmless." He pointed his thumbs at his chest. "Now, me, they wouldn't leave her with."

"Ben, harmless? I think that's still TBD."

"You can't think he did this."

"Magnus, it's been a weird, weird day."

Magnus frowned. "He doesn't have it in him. The guy doesn't even have it in him to commit to dating a woman, let alone killing her. No chance. At the end of the day, Ben's just a little boy who hasn't grown up."

"I just can't help but think that if her friends had been more responsible, Andrea would be alive instead of being pulled out of the harbor right now. How could they just leave her?"

Magnus put a hand on my shoulder and squeezed gently. "You expect a lot from people, Miss Aquarius. Not everyone is as conscientious as you."

"It's not about being conscientious. It's about basic decency."

"Why are you here, asking me about Andrea?" His eyes twinkled. "This isn't really your mess, but here you are, trying to clean it up."

My mouth opened, but nothing came out. I tried to cover my speechlessness by digging into the second half of my sandwich, but Magnus saw right through me. He chuckled as he accepted a new beer from the waitress. I hadn't even seen him order it.

I spoke through a mouthful of warm brie and chicken. "Ben needed help. It's that simple."

"Nothing is ever that simple."

It was apparently my turn for a psychology session with Magnus, only I didn't want to be the patient.

"You know how it is down here, Magnus. If a friend of yours was in trouble, you'd do the same, wouldn't you?"

He shook his head. "The police down here don't play. They may seem like they don't do much, but when they get someone in their crosshairs . . . You better watch your back."

My mind flicked back to the officer at the mouth of the marina. I hoped he would move on soon.

I moved the conversation back to the girls. "Did they talk to anyone else while they were at Duffy's?"

Magnus nodded. "Frick and Frack. You know them? Coasties. That's who bird dogged me out of another dance with the cute little satellite."

"Frick and Frack?"

"I don't know their real names. They'll talk to anything that moves."

My mind flicked back to the "Andrew" that Becky had mentioned.

Magnus continued. "They're almost as bad as your Ben when it comes to women. But I like Ben. And I don't think he did anything to Andrea."

"Why is he 'my' Ben?"

Magnus smiled slowly, the kind of smile you'd give a child who wasn't catching on. "You're the one who's out here asking questions on his behalf."

"I told you—"

"Settle down, firecracker. I'm just giving you a hard time."

I gave him a hard look in exchange for his hard time, but he just laughed at me. I broke it off, feeling a little wounded. I took another bite of my sandwich to cover it up.

Magnus looked thoughtful. "You know, there was a rumor earlier this year that a girl had accused Frick or Frack of rape. But nothing came of it. Probably just one of those coconut telephone rumors."

"Did you see anything hinky go down with the girls?"

"Just the usual Duffy's hijinks—drinking and dancing. But once Ben showed up, the tension really skyrocketed. Lots of pouting from the fiery one. If mama ain't happy, ain't nobody happy."

"Meaning?"

"She seemed to take the budding romance between Ben and Andrea to heart. If she wasn't getting her fun, she didn't want anyone to have their fun. Maybe she had designs on our Mr. Ben."

My eyebrows lifted and I thought back to those photos of Ben on the beach with that Hobie cat. Jessie and Ben? I couldn't see it, but maybe it was because of all the vitriol she'd sprayed about him that morning. Hell hath no fury.

"What about the Red Man?" I asked. "The girls mentioned him."

"You mean Luke?"

"His name is Luke?"

"That's the name he was born with."

"Huh."

"He's harmless."

"He gives me the creeps."

Magnus gave me a long side look. "You might think the same about me, had we not shared that fateful night at the Poorman's."

"He barely speaks."

"He's shy."

"And he leers. I never understood that phrase 'undressing her with his eyes' until I met him."

Magnus tilted his head. "He may not be a country gentleman, I'll give you that."

"Dave was there, too."

"I saw him." Magnus was quiet for a moment. "That done between you?"

"He's got another girl."

"You're too wild for him, Miss Aquarius. Dave's a swan, wants a life partner. That's not you at all."

I nodded, and I knew he was right. But even though my brain agreed with him, I felt a pain in my chest, like someone had plunged his hand in there and given my heart a squeeze. I took a long draw of Presidente.

I thought Magnus was going to make a crack about me being single again, but he stayed quiet.

I put one hand on his bicep, noting that it would probably take three to grab all the way around. "Keep an ear out?"

"You know I will."

He gave me a single nod and that smile again. "Anytime. And the next time you're ready to beat the entire island in pool, you know where to find me."

13

After Magnus left, I moved from our commodious booth to a stool at the bar. I pulled out my little notebook. I had a lot floating around in my head and I wanted to get it down before the vodka and the Presidente chasers blurred my recollections.

I felt my phone buzz again. That same number again—the 216 area code. Once the call went to voicemail, I checked my list of missed calls. Six missed calls total, no message. I raised my eyebrows, but I made no motion to call the mysterious number. People who didn't leave messages don't get return calls. Another one of my rules.

I navigated away from my missed calls, over to the picture of the three girls. My eyes lit on Andrea and that twisty little smile of hers. What did I know about her? She'd done a shot with Duncan. She'd given Ben a blow job in his car after apparently meeting him at the resort a few days earlier. I started a fresh page in my notebook, wrote Andrea's name at the top and underneath wrote "boy crazy?" It was a phrase I hadn't heard since reading pre-teen fiction, but after hearing about Zack and Ben, it was rattling around in my head and I wanted to get it down.

"Another beer?" the bartender asked. I looked up at her. I

didn't know her name, but that wasn't unusual. In addition to its regular staff, XO seemed to have one or two slots reserved for girls who came in one week and left the next. She didn't have the look of someone who'd been here long. Her tanned skin looked fresh, and expertly curled dark hair fell over her shoulders in waves. She wore a green silk tank top over tiny cutoffs that displayed toned legs. No beer weight in sight. I sighed inwardly. Maybe in my next life, I'd get to come back as an XO bartender.

I didn't really need a beer, so I ordered a Corona Light as a compromise. When she came back, I asked if she had been working Wednesday. She had, but she didn't remember seeing Andrea. "We got all the runoff from Duffy's. And we were slammed that night," she said, her eyes flitting to one of the fishermen on the other side of the bar who had lifted his hand to get her attention.

I nodded and went back to my notebook.

I was about to put pen to paper when I felt an ice cold hand land on my shoulder. I twitched, then turned to see Jeannine, the Duffy's waitress, standing next to me, her eyes a little unfocused.

"I hear you were looking for me," she said. "What do you want?"

She had a reputation for being a fun server, mostly because she'd drink with you, shot for shot. Today, though, no one would have accused her of anything close to that. Her thin lips were set in a hard line. Despite the air conditioning, I could see a line of beaded sweat in the pale white skin at her hairline. She smelled like soap, but there was something else rancid around the edges. Vomit? Maybe her rum-and-Coke routine was a hair-of-the-dog remedy.

"Did you serve these girls on Wednesday?" I aimed my phone screen at her.

"That bitchy blonde. That's who I remember."

"Did you talk to them at all?"

"Not a hell of a lot. Busy night and I'd been helping Chuck test some new shots at the start of the shift."

If that's what you want to call it, sure.

"Besides, even though she was sitting at one of my tables, she wanted nothing to do with me. She was all about Chuck, who couldn't give a rat's ass about anyone, let alone her."

Then Jeannine turned on her heel, her ponytail swishing, and left.

I stared after her, wondering what the hell had just happened.

Were she and Chuck dipping their nibs in the office ink? Was that what set Jeannine off? Simply the idea of dating Chuck set me off, but who am I to judge? It's a small island. You have to make your decisions accordingly.

I flipped to the next page in my notebook and wrote "Jessie" at the top. I recorded Jeannine's note that she was "all about Chuck"—with a big question mark, due to the source—then Magnus's suspicion that she liked Ben. Maybe she was the boy crazy one, and I had it all wrong. Magnus had said she was full of fire.

I reached in my bag for Andrea's phone, looking both ways to see if anyone was watching. No one was even remotely interested.

I tried to unlock the phone again. But as many times as I drew my finger carefully across the cracked screen, it wouldn't open.

I'd have to rely on my less-than-stellar memory. I thought back to that one picture of the three girls in front of the Hobie cat.

As I recalled, Jessie was on one side of Ben, Andrea on the other. Becky, as Magnus had noted, was indeed a satellite, even in this picture. Ben in the middle of two girls. Exactly where he loved to be. I wondered if his ways with women had finally caught up to him.

I flipped through my loose papers to look at my notes around Andrea's texts. I still didn't know who that Zack was, or why Andrea had sent those weird screenshots of other texts. If I wanted to know more, I would have to go back and talk to the girls. Maybe they could tell me who had the burning passion for salsa.

I lifted my head from my notebook and the room spun a little. I needed to get home and take a nap.

I left some money on the bar, along with the three-quarters of the beer. I stood carefully, making sure both phones and my notebook were stowed securely. I wrapped my hand tightly around the Duffy's pint glass and stuffed it in my purse. No way was I going to leave that gem behind. I tucked my hair carefully under my hat and waltzed out of XO, my steps slow and deliberate.

The security guard was missing from his post under the tree. I would have loved to pick his brain, but I'd missed my window.

I took a quick glance at Officer Statue to make sure he wasn't interested in me. He was more interested in the traffic inching through Red Hook. His body remained ramrod straight, even as he flicked two impatient fingers at the line of cars to encourage them forward.

Nothing for me to worry about. I turned right, toward home.

I kept my eyes forward, my mind churning on the events of the day.

And then it happened. I felt my world drop out from under me.

It was like a bad dream. One minute, I was perfectly vertical. The next, my flip flop found a crack in the sidewalk. I felt my horizon shift as I began to pitch forward. In a state of lesser intoxication, I might have been able to catch myself, but the booze caught up to me, and I watched the pavement speed toward my face.

I had just enough time to bemoan the fact that I'd actually started to like my unique beak of a nose and wonder what the rhinoplasty services were like on island. My face and I were about to find out.

At the last minute, I put my hands in front of me. I cried out as they skidded against the concrete. I ended up on my hands and knees, right in the middle of Red Hook.

Lizzie Jordan, dexterous drunk.

I paused for a moment in an exquisitely embarrassing tabletop position to gather my scattered wits, then I sat back on my heels to assess the damage. My knees had caught the worst of it, the right one now bright red with blood. I was just about to consider standing, when I heard a voice behind me.

"Good afternoon. Are you alright?"

Someone had come to my rescue. How charming. Maybe Magnus had stuck around after leaving me. I prepared a smile for him as I turned.

I turned and found myself looking at the royal blue pants of a police officer.

Oh God. It was Officer Statue.

He held out his hand and I prayed for stability as I took it. His hand was surprisingly soft and gentle. I could feel my chest tighten as I came up to the level of his clean-shaven mahogany face. Even though he still wore his sunglasses, I could see that he looked young, his face unlined. His hair was neatly trimmed close to his scalp. His nametag read "Chinnery."

We stood face to face, his hovering a few inches above mine. His physical bulk was even more apparent at close range. This man could snap me like a twig.

I searched his face for signs of malice—or recognition of my unlawful status—but the lenses of his sunglasses were too dark for me to make out anything.

I thought I heard the radio in his car squawk from across the street, but I couldn't be sure. As we stood in silence, it squawked a second time and I saw him incline his head slightly to hear it. I knew that this was my chance to run. If I could make it as far as the National Park, I could probably disappear into the bush, or hole up in the storage room at Latitude 18, if a sympathetic bartender were working.

But I knew I couldn't make that run in the state I was in, and the moment was gone quickly. He turned his attention back to me. Sweat trickled into my eyes and I found myself wondering if they had showers in prison.

Chinnery peered at me, his eyebrows crinkling. "Miss, you alright?"

"I'm so sorry. I . . . I tripped." I tripped? Lizzie Jordan, brilliant under pressure.

He nodded once, crisply. "You been drinking?"

I shook my head, then I realized there was no way I could pull off a lie like that. *What would Elizabeth Morgan say?*

"I had a few Bushwackers at Duffy's," I stammered and forced a small laugh. "They were a little stronger than I expected."

One more brisk nod. He bought it. I felt a tingling in my fingers.

"The heat can get to you down here. You drink enough water? You're not driving?"

That last sentence was more a statement than a question and I shook my head. "No, I'm going to walk back to Secret Harbour."

One more nod from him. And then he turned away.

I suddenly felt so light, I could have flown back to my little shack. Either my disguise or my drunkenness was working in my favor because the officer had no idea that I was the person his boss wanted to talk with.

I turned back in my original direction, then bent and picked up my purse. Even my pint glass seemed to be intact. I grabbed my hat off the sidewalk, and stuffed it back on my head. I flexed my feet in my sandals, and I felt the skin pull taut around my right knee. I grimaced. *First casualty.*

Then I thought of Andrea and felt a stab of guilt. I was the second, if mine even counted.

Behind me, I heard the short whoop of a siren.

I froze.

I knew I couldn't run. I was too tired and too drunk. The best thing I could do right now was maintain my dignity.

Start walking, Lizzie.

By sheer will, I moved one foot forward, then the other. My head was starting to throb in time with my knee. This might be the end of the line for me, but, dammit, I was going to keep shuffling.

The whoop sounded again, this time right next to me. I jumped about a foot in the air, but still I didn't turn. I was pretty sure that the SUV with its lights on had pulled up next to me.

If they wanted me, they were going to have to come get me.

"Hello?" I heard the voice of Officer Chinnery, but still I didn't turn. I pretended that maybe, just maybe, he was calling to someone else.

"Hello, miss?"

I saw the SUV pull up into my left peripheral vision, its lights flashing.

No mistaking it now.

I turned slowly, my legs tensing.

Officer Chinnery's SUV was across the street, and he had to lean across his front seat to call out to me.

What would Elizabeth Morgan say? "Yes, officer?"

"Is it your intention to return to Secret Harbour?" he asked. He fumbled around with something in the car, and I was desperate to know what it was. A pair of handcuffs?

"Yes," I heard Elizabeth Morgan answer for me.

I heard a switch flip and the lights on his patrol car went off. "I'm going off duty. I'll take you there."

And that was how I got my first ride in a St. Thomas patrol car.

I can't remember a single thing I said. My mind was dominated by sheer terror, although I can tell you that we didn't talk much. I simply wasn't capable. I twitched every time his radio went off, but he seemed not to be interested in what they were saying.

I must have made up some very convincing bullshit because he left me in the Secret Harbour parking lot with a final nod. There was a point when I got out of the car that I thought he might ask me out, but I kept myself moving before anything like that could happen.

I didn't have the strength to walk home yet, so I took a few steps to the beach and collapsed on a plastic lounge chair. The slats dug into my legs, but I didn't care.

I hadn't been lying there thirty seconds when I felt my phone buzz.

I rooted around in my bag, marveling at the fact that I was stupid enough to still have Andrea's phone in my possession. Dumb luck was apparently on my side in a big way.

It was that same number that had been trying me all day. I probably should have been excited by the intrigue of these mysterious calls, but my gas tank was empty. Besides, given the fact that I thought I was on the lam but had, instead, been given a pleasant ride in a police car suggested that the call wasn't nearly as sinister as my imagination might have believed. It was probably someone trying to sell me a timeshare.

I sent whoever it was to voicemail.

From under a palm tree, I spent a few minutes looking at the calm bay at Secret Harbour. I watched a couple wade into the clear, shallow water, hand in hand. They looked young, and I guessed they were on their honeymoon. I felt a pang in my chest. That wasn't going to be me for a long, long time.

That was enough of that. I rolled off the chair and somehow got myself into an upright position.

I walked into the bar and gave Andrea's phone to Tower, the bartender on duty and also a friend. I asked him to put it in his drawer under the bar and hold it for me for a while. He did so without question.

Good bartender that he is, he asked me if I wanted a drink for the road. I shook my head mutely. He looked surprised, but he didn't say anything.

Then I made the short walk home and emptied my hot water heater in the greediest shower I'd taken in years. The water stung my knee like a motherfucker.

After I'd dried myself off, I put some Neosporin on the hamburger meat that was my kneecap. I didn't have a band aid big enough to cover it, so I left my cut open to the Caribbean air. My mind danced with fears about staph, but I'd deal with that later.

I grabbed a pair of underwear from the top drawer of my sagging dresser. I didn't bother with anything else. No one was coming home to me tonight. Then I downed a glass of water from the gallon jug in the fridge and collapsed into bed.

I was startled awake in the darkness by a pounding at the door. An angry pounding, by the sound of it. My head felt stuffed with cotton.

The pounding paused, then started up again. I covered my naked chest with my sheet, feeling vulnerable. All I had was a pair of purple bikini underwear between me and whoever was at my door.

I instinctively reached over for Dave, but the bed was empty. Then the day's events came back to me.

Never there when you need them, are they?

The pounding started again. I counted five bangs.

"Dave?" I hissed, hoping it was him knocking—overzealously, I'll grant you.

No response.

I jolted as the banging started up again in earnest.

I debated getting back in bed and pulling the covers over my head. I'd had a friend install a heavy-duty lock a year ago. It might hold. Of course, it all depended on the integrity of the wood of the door jamb, which had been steeped in the Caribbean humidity for God knows how long.

It wasn't a great plan, but I didn't know what else I could muster.

I was just pulling the sheet over my head when I heard a voice.

"Lizzie?"

A male voice. Damn. And more to the point, a male voice who knew my name. Double damn.

I crept out of bed, my hands searching the cool tile floor for the clothes I'd discarded earlier. I found my dress where I had left it. The pounding and yelling started again in earnest as I continued my low crouch. *The police would announce themselves, right?* I debated as I tried to turn my dress inside out and figure which way was front—all in the dark.

Once I had it over my head—no bra, because that would have taken both thought and coordination—I realized how ridiculous this all was. Here I was, in my own apartment, cowering on the floor because some asshole was trying to bang down my door.

These were strange times indeed.

I stood up and bellowed back, "What the hell? Who is it?"

The pounding and yelling stopped. I felt immensely proud of myself.

"Lizzie," a voice croaked. "It's Ben. You have to let me in."

My bravado winked out. Why was Ben pounding on my door like Freddy Kreuger was hot on his heels?

My instincts told me not to open the door.

Then I found myself taking a tentative step toward it. *This was Ben. I knew Ben. What did I have to be afraid of?*

I turned on the outdoor light, flipped my heavy-duty bolt and opened the door.

The man who stood there looked ghastly.

It was Ben, but a Ben who looked like he'd been sleeping in a dumpster for a week. His eyes were swollen and red. Their gaze darted back and forth like a wild animal. His hair stuck out in greasy patches. He also seemed to have grown an unusual amount of stubble since I'd seen him this morning.

"What happened to you?" I gasped. I didn't step back from the door to let him in. I wasn't sure that I wanted this thing that only vaguely resembled Ben in my cottage.

"She's dead. Andrea's *dead.* They found her body in the marina." Ben rubbed his face fiercely with his right hand. "I didn't do it, Lizzie. They're after me. You have to help me."

His eyes looked glassy in the dim yellow light. Was he crying? Or was he on something?

His eyelids were beginning to droop and I caught a strong whiff of whiskey. Knowing him, Jack and Coke. "Let me in."

"Uh," I stammered, searching for some kind of excuse. "It's kind of a mess in here—" I just couldn't turn off my Spidey sense. Something wasn't right. Ben suddenly seemed taller than I remembered him, and I knew he'd be able to overpower me easily, even after a few shots of Jack. And the fact that I was even sizing him up told me that I needed to keep a door between him and me.

Times like these, I wished I were a guy. A big, strong one.

As I stammered, I saw his eyebrows crinkle. He leaned closer to me, the sour smell of alcohol even stronger than before. "C'mon, Lizzie. What the fuck?"

It took everything I had not to flinch and give him the advantage.

"You're drunk."

"That's never been a problem before."

He was right. I'd brought him home with me—platonically—several times when he was too wasted to function. It wasn't a big deal then, but as he loomed closer and closer to my personal space, it seemed like a big deal now.

Ben began to move forward, pushing his weight against the door. I sprung to action, pushing back. I was lucky I'd sobered up. I was just able to keep control. We could only play this game so long, though. I felt my feet struggling for purchase on the tile floor.

I seized upon sudden inspiration. "Dave wouldn't like it."

Ben lurched back, freeing the door. "Dave?" He snorted. "Dave's fucking that girl over at East End. If you don't know it by now, you should."

It probably shouldn't have, but it hit me like a gut punch. Did everyone know? Were they laughing behind my back? How had I missed all the signs? And how long had Ben kept that secret from me?

I should have just shut the door right there and then and washed my hands of the whole thing, but I guess my ego got the best of me. "Oh, so St. Thomas's one-man tourism welcome committee is now telling me what's what? Please."

He held up a finger an inch from my face. "Let me tell you something, Lizzie—"

The heat of anger still radiated from him and I began to wonder why I had scoffed at the local custom of keeping a machete at the door. If he took another run at the door, I didn't think I could hold it.

Was this the Ben that Andrea had met on the last night of her life? I braced my legs in preparation for him to make a run at me. Was this going to be the fight of my life?

Ben hadn't yet finished his sentence and his eyelids had drooped to three-quarters mast. I wondered what else had been in the mix with the Jack.

His mouth moved a few more times, but he couldn't get any more words out. His hand dropped. Then his legs crumpled underneath him and he staggered. Ordinarily, I would have moved to catch him. Tonight, I simply stood and watched as he collapsed onto my stone walk.

I looked at Ben's prostrate form. Then I shut the door, locked it and bolted it.

I sagged against the door, gulping in air with relief. My hands were shaking. I wanted a drink. I double-checked the door locks, then flew into the kitchen.

I threw open my cabinets and found a small bottle of port I'd gotten at a Christmas party. At the time, I'd been annoyed, but I was grateful to see it now.

I took a long slug.

Now I could think. I took one more drink, just for good measure, then put the bottle back on the counter. My hand fluttered back to it for a third round, but I retracted it. I had to think.

I tiptoed back to the door. I slid the bolt back slowly and gently turned the knob lock, then inched the door open quietly.

Ben still lay prostrate on the concrete outside my door.

He was so still. My eyes scanned his chest to see if he was breathing. The idea he was hurt—or dead—made my throat tighten, but I didn't open the door any wider. How was I supposed to be sure that he wasn't faking it, that the minute I leaned down to check his breathing, he wouldn't grab me in a bear hug and toss me in Red Hook harbor?

With one eye on Ben, I left the door open a few inches and crept backward to my cell phone. I prayed that my phone would behave for this critical call.

As I picked up the phone, it started ringing with that same 216 number again. I was tired of playing games. I hit the green button.

"What," I said quietly, my eyes still locked on Ben's form, ready to bolt if he moved a muscle.

"This is Darren Milliken, Andrea Milliken's father. I'm here in St. Thomas. I'd like to speak with you." His voice was loud, brash. It sounded like the voice of someone who was used to giving orders. I bristled a little.

I heard Ben groan. I twitched toward the door and grabbed the handle with my free hand, ready to slam it.

"This really isn't a good time." I started as Ben's right hand twitched. "And I'm not sure it's a good idea in general."

"Come to the Ritz tomorrow morning at 9:00. Blue Water Grill. We'll talk over breakfast."

"What exactly are we going to chat about, Mister, ah . . . ?"

"Milliken."

"Yes, Mr. Milliken." Mr. Milliken? What was I, five years old? Ben's right arm shifted again and my body tensed. I pushed the door closed until I could only see Ben through a two-inch crack.

"How did you even get this number?" I asked.

He ignored me. "The girls say you've been asking questions. Investigating, as it were."

"What? 'Investigating' is a pretty strong word for it. I just—"

"We need to talk. I'll see you then," he said and hung up the phone.

I had been strong-armed. I didn't have time to dwell on it, and I knew I had at least twelve hours to figure out how to dodge the meeting.

In the meantime, I had a more pressing item on the agenda. I needed help, but I really, really didn't want to ask. That said, I didn't have much of a choice.

I scrolled to a name in my contact list. Wasn't there someone else I could call? Rick would have been on that list once. After running from him today, I couldn't face him.

Screw it. I took the kind of breath you take before stepping off a high dive, and I dialed Dave.

It rang once, then twice. I heard a rustling sound and saw Ben's hand reach around the door jamb.

"I swear to God, I will cut it off."

"What?"

"I swear to fucking God that I will cut your goddamned hand off if you do not remove it from my doorway. Now."

The hand paused for a second, regarded me, then retreated.

"Lizzie?" a voice said in my ear.

"Oh, thank God. I need you here. NOW."

"Lizzie, we can't keep—"

"Stop. Listen. It's Ben. He's here. He's drunk, and I'm . . . well, I've never seen him like this." I paused, hating the next words, but knowing I needed to say them: "I'm scared."

"Be there in five."

I hung up and kicked the door completely shut. I reached up and drove the bolt home with a satisfying click. Then I turned my back to the door and slid down to the floor against it, relishing the feel of the tile against the backs of my sweaty legs.

What a day.

I heard a moan outside the door and my body tensed. I listened like a deer at the edge of a pond, eyes alert, ears twitching.

I heard only the quiet tut-tut-tut of a nearby wild chicken.

The tension drained from my body, and I nearly laughed. It was all so absurd. Yesterday, he'd handed me a life ring to save what we believed was a drowning man. And now?

I flashed back to the look on Ellie's face when she had talked about Ben. I understood that expression now. Ben had given me the willies tonight, no question, and no matter how I tried to justify it, my gut told me that something was very wrong.

I sat and waited.

"Jesus Christ. Lizzie?"

I leapt to my feet at the sound of Dave's voice.

"What happened?" I heard him say. I unbolted the door and opened it.

"He showed up drunk and scared the shit out of me is what happened."

"So you laid him out?" he asked. I couldn't tell if he was horrified or impressed.

"He did all the work for me. He's drunk or on something."

Dave's eyebrows shot up, and he shook his head in disapproval.

"I get it. This is weird," I snapped.

Dave's eyes traveled to my dress, and then to my obviously non-bra-sporting chest. His eyebrows raised another half an inch.

"Stop," I said, wrapping my arms around my body. "He woke me out of a dead sleep. I didn't have time to put on the full uniform." I flung an arm at Ben in a wild gesture. "What are we going to do with him?"

"Call the police?" Dave reached for his phone.

"We can't do that."

Dave gave me one of Rick's looks. I guess the old man was wearing off on him. "Lizzie, enough. You've got to stop covering for him. This isn't Ben stumbling in to work with a hangover. This is murder."

"So you think he's guilty."

"You called *me*. You're obviously afraid of him. Why didn't you just let him in and put him on the couch? Or even your bed for that matter?" I tried to speak, but Dave cut me off. "Did you know that he was accused of rape a few months ago?"

"That wasn't him. That was Frick and Frack."

Dave screwed his face up in disbelief. "What are you talking about? Are you drunk too?"

"No. I've been asleep." I could feel the heat starting to rise in my face. "It wasn't Ben who was accused. It was someone else, some Coastie."

"That's not what I heard. This is not Ben's first go-round."

Ellie's face flashed in my mind again, but it was too much. It fried my circuits. "So what do we do now?"

"We?"

"Dave, please, I need your help."

He looked at me and his eyes softened. I thought for a moment that he was going to scoop me up in a hug. We'd figure it out together. I knew we would.

But then I remembered why he met Ben in the parking lot a few nights ago, and where he went afterward. I felt my body stiffen.

When I looked back at him, his expression was cool. Once this assist was over, we were, indeed, done.

I threw up my hands. "Just put him on the couch. I'll— I'll find somewhere else to go." I contemplated calling Lucas and asking for one more favor. I knew Arthur would enjoy the company.

Dave shrugged, and the casual nature of his response cut me to the bone. I wrapped my arms tight around myself again as Dave nudged Ben with his foot. "Ben. Dude."

Ben didn't move.

Dave tried again, bending to his knees and shaking Ben's shoulder.

I leaned closer. "Oh, God, is he dead?"

I'll be brutally honest with you. I felt a brief second of relief. It meant I could call the police and simply go back to being Lizzie again. No meeting with Andrea's dad. No spike in adrenaline every time I saw a police officer.

Just my simple, island existence returned to me, unharmed.

Dave nudged Ben again with his foot.

"At least check that he's breathing," I said.

Dave shook his head at me, annoyed at this new level of drama. But, still, he squatted next to Ben, putting the tips of his fingers under Ben's nose. "He's breathing. Help me get him up, will you?"

I felt a twinge of uncertainty as we settled Ben on my futon. This seemed like a terrible idea.

However, I couldn't think of an alternative and Dave wasn't volunteering a thing, damn him.

Once we had Ben settled, Dave and I shuffled around each other awkwardly. I settled on one of my dining room chairs. My other option was a butterfly chair in the corner that tended to trap me in its deep seat. It didn't seem like much of an option. With both Dave and Ben in my apartment, I wanted maximum mobility.

Dave eyed me carefully as he chose the other dining room chair. I knew he was trying to read me.

I stood and walked to the fridge, then opened the bottom drawer. A Miller Lite can and a bottle of Presidente rolled loosely in the bottom. I grabbed them both, passing Dave the Presidente. I am nothing if not a gracious host, both to ex-boyfriends and suspected murderers.

I sat back down again, hoping the beer would break Dave's laser gaze on me. At the very least, I knew it would distract me.

"He looks like he's out for the count," Dave said, breaking the long silence.

"I hope so."

"You're not going to stay here tonight."

I shook my head.

We looked at Ben, whose limbs hung loose like strands of spaghetti. His mouth was open slightly and I could hear his breathing from across the room. I wondered if those tourist girls would find him half as attractive if they could see him now.

"Ben couldn't have done something like this, right?" I said.

"What, get drunk and show up at your place?"

I stole a glance at him to see if he was kidding, but his face looked grim. Where was that goofy, happy Dave who'd shown up just last night with a huge grin and a bottle of champagne?

I shook my head. "Andrea."

"So you don't think Ben could have done it, but you think I could have?"

Ouch. I took a long swallow of beer. "It just didn't sit right with me, you not telling me that you were there that night." I paused. "And, the pot—"

He nodded, but he didn't offer a defense. I guess we would agree to disagree on that one. And, yet, there was a moment there where I felt like we were on the same side, two messy humans shaking our heads in wonder at what a weird existence this was.

Ben chose that moment to turn over and slur a few loud words. It made me start so violently that I nearly knocked my beer.

When I looked back up at Dave, his face had shut like a swinging door. Any emotion was gone. We were somehow on opposite sides again, with a gulf of things between us, one of them a huge deal breaker for me.

My shoulders sagged. I knew if I sat here and stewed, I'd probably cry and then things would get weird. Or I'd end up betraying myself to try and keep a modicum of comfort in my life.

So I did what most people on St. Thomas do when things are about to go sideways: I decided to go to a bar and get drunk.

I shooed Dave out of the house first with a few words of thanks and a disingenuous "see you around," then I strapped on my bra for courage, one eye on Ben the whole time. I'd decided I'd rather show him my boobs than turn my back on him. Where I was planning to go that night, I wasn't sure. I'd figure that out after I had a drink.

As I left, I didn't see Ben's car. I wondered how he'd gotten to my place, and how I'd get him out of there. I also asked myself for what felt like the hundredth time whether he was capable of hurting Andrea.

I left all of those questions open for now.

I drove my little Suzuki into Red Hook and squeezed into yet another semi-legal space in the marina parking lot. As I got out of my car, I felt a magnetic force pulling me toward the water where Andrea had been found that morning.

I walked out of the fluorescent lights of the garage and into the dark, toward the water. In the dim light, I crossed the driveway and stepped through the iron gate to the series of wooden docks that made up American Yacht Harbor.

I scanned up and down the boards. All was quiet except for the faint sound of jolly voices from a nearby boat. At least someone was having fun tonight. I looked for any trace of police presence, but all I found was some yellow police tape hanging out of the trash can near C-Dock.

I hugged my arms around myself. Andrea had gone into the blue here—and she'd never come back. I wondered if she'd been scared, or whether she'd even known what was happening.

I couldn't imagine ending my life in this harbor. But, in a way, what happened in the marina had taken me into the blue, too. I'd gone beneath this island's surface appearance, and I'd seen what was underneath. St. Thomas wasn't just a playground for tourists made up of raucous bars, white sand beaches and turquoise waters. It wasn't just an easy-breezy place where someone like me could start over. It also was a place where an innocent night of fun could turn very dark. It was a place where a girl lost her life.

Then, another thought: *If I stepped off the dock now, how long would it take someone to look for me?* Now that Dave was gone, I could go missing for several days—or even a week—before anyone raised the alarm.

Before I knew it, my nose stung and I felt tears in my eyes. I wasn't crying for Andrea. I was crying for me—and it had to stop. I wiped my eyes roughly and sniffed hard.

I heard a rustling in the bushes that ringed the marina and froze.

No threats visible, but also no one to help me. What was my safest bet? Back to the gate, or farther down the dock, maybe duck behind a dock box for cover?

I heard the crunching of the bushes again, and I veered wildly to the left, away from the noise. Something hard struck the dock, and I let out a yelp. Maybe I wouldn't have to wonder how Andrea felt much longer.

I looked back and stopped in my tracks. I felt all the air go out of my lungs, and I nearly doubled over with relief.

There on the docks was a damn iguana, probably four feet long including his tail. It was dark, but I could just barely see him leaning on his stubby forearms, his spiky head cocked sideways like a curious dog.

I had to get out of here before I frightened myself to death.

I left the iguana to his night business. Before I exited at the next gate, I looked back. The iguana still sat squat in the middle of the pathway. I swear he was looking at me. It gave me goosebumps.

I quickened my pace and stood under a streetlight to catch my breath.

With Ben at my apartment, I was likely now aiding and abetting. That said, if the police were actually looking for me, they were taking their sweet time. But if they found Ben at my apartment . . . what a mess I'd made for myself. Better for me to stay away from home for a bit. I bet I'd find Duncan lurking around Red Hook, and maybe happy hour would have loosened his tongue.

In for a penny, in for a pound. And what else did I have to do?

I sucked at relationships, but maybe I could redeem myself by catching a killer.

14

I struck out at Molly Molone's in more ways than one. No Duncan at the bar. Then, when I ordered a Presidente to bolster my spirits, I apparently didn't say "thank you" loud enough to the bartender. This prompted a woman with frizzy hair dyed a flat black to grouse, "Don't let the door hit you on the ass on the way out."

I flipped her the bird and stalked away.

I took a long chug for courage, then I glanced back over my shoulder at the woman, just in time to see her slide right off her stool. She hit the floor with a thud. I felt a mean flash of righteousness and took another long swig.

I finished the beer by the time I reached the cement stairs and slammed the bottle in the nearest trash can for two points. I huffed up two sets of stairs, which brought me back to where this whole clusterfuck got started.

Island Time was noisy tonight, with nearly every seat filled in both the bar and the surrounding picnic tables. It was one of those places where hardcore drunks mixed with the families who came for the pizza. Usually everyone managed to keep their peace, but I wasn't interested in social dynamics tonight. I was on a mission.

I hit the jackpot. As I scanned the backs of the people sitting at the bar, I saw a straw hat peeking out. I walked down the line toward Duncan, returning a murmured greeting from one of the more grizzled regulars, his BYO insulated tumbler half-full of dark rum and Coke.

I stopped behind the man in question, taking in his permanently sunburned neck and head of disarrayed black hair. He had on his usual uniform: a white Columbia fishing shirt, splotched with the sweat of the day, and red-and-white striped board shorts.

I tapped him on the shoulder. "You know, if you'd put that hat on your head instead of wearing it like a handbag, you might not get so sunburned."

He turned to reveal a tan face with a stripe of white across his eyes where his sunglasses sat.

He smiled, and I tried not to look at him too hard. Duncan looked like I imagined the devil would, with a killer smile that revealed even white teeth and dark, mischievous eyes under dark eyebrows. Those eyes always seemed to be laughing, even when his mouth was not. He was a sly one. I'd have to keep my guard up.

"Well, well, Miss Lizzie. What can I do for you? Or are you just here to heckle me?"

"Would that I had the time."

He grinned. "Busiest girl on the Rock."

"More than you know."

Another voice entered our conversation, a female voice. "Lizzie? You want a drink?" I looked to the right and saw the bartender, a sunny girl with curly blonde hair named Ellen.

I glanced at Duncan's mostly-empty Presidente. "I guess we'll take two of those."

"You want me to put it on your tab?" she asked.

"Sure."

We accepted our beers and, as I took my first swig, Duncan asked, "So, to what do I owe this kindness?"

"I do have an ulterior motive."

"I figured. Girls like you always do."

I gave him my best Lizzie Death Stare, but he only raised his eyebrows and smirked. I think he got off on that kind of thing.

"A few nights ago—Monday, to be exact—you were in Caribbean Saloon."

The smile flashed. "Probably."

"Not probably. I need you to be exact. That's what the beer is for. No dicking around."

"You're wound pretty tight today, girl."

"There's a lot at stake."

We locked eyes.

He broke off first. "Okay, okay." Duncan made a show of raising his eyes skyward in thought. "Monday. I had an all-day charter. Hot girls, barely legal—"

"Duncan—"

He held up his index finger. *Wait.* "Yes, I finished the day at Caribbean Saloon. I had chicken fingers for dinner." His eyes rolled back to me and he looked quite pleased with himself. "What about it?"

"There were three girls there that night, tourists. One blonde. Two brunettes." I pulled out my phone and showed him a picture. "They said you offered to buy them Jäger shots."

"Where are you going with this?"

"Did you see them or not?"

"Couldn't miss them. Three good-looking girls walk into Caribbean Saloon and you expect me not to notice?" His voice got harder. "Where are you going with this, Lizzie?"

"I just want to know what you saw of them and if anything unusual happened while they were there."

He shrugged.

"One of those girls is gone now."

"You mean . . . ?" He tilted his head toward the harbor where Andrea had been found.

Maybe it was my imagination, but I thought I heard several conversations around the bar stop. This probably wasn't the place to have this discussion. I gave a very small nod.

Duncan's face froze in place. His eyes hardened into black marbles. He turned his head to look out over the water and we both watched a wide catamaran glide into the harbor under power, its sails rolled up for the night. I wondered if it was a rental. Normally, I'd be up for watching the show as they tried to dock in the dark. Tonight, I turned back to Duncan.

He wouldn't look at me. "I don't have anything to say to you."

"Do I look like VIPD? I'm not accusing you of anything. I just want to know what happened at Saloon that night."

All the flirtatiousness in his manner was gone. His body was stiff, and I could see a muscle working in his jaw. Still, I waited. I felt the eyes of the people around us on me, too. We wouldn't make the headlines in tomorrow's coconut telegraph, but we would probably be worth a mention.

"Nothing," he said finally. "Nothing happened."

"What, were you off your game that night?"

He shook his head in annoyance. "That blonde girl was like a sucker fish. She just latched on to me and kept talking and talking. I bought the other girl a shot just to get her away from me." He sighed. "The short one. There was something about her I liked. Is she the one . . . ?"

I nodded.

"I bought her a shot. I didn't have anything to do with her after that. They left. Happy now?" He put his beer down and shifted his body away from me.

"Did—"

He cut me off, his voice getting loud. "Lizzie, leave me alone. We all know what this is about."

"What do you mean?"

"Ben's your boy. You're trying to get him out of trouble and put someone else in his place."

"Whoa, whoa, whoa." I held up a hand and leaned toward him. We were going to have to get a few things straight here. "I just want to know the truth about what happened that night. And what do you mean, he's 'my boy?'"

"You know, you get lonely, he gets lucky." He shrugged. "We all have one."

I recoiled. "What are you talking about? I've never slept with Ben."

Duncan shrugged.

I resisted the urge to grab the hat and strangle Duncan until he begged for mercy.

"What, my word doesn't matter?" I asked.

"I've seen his car outside your house."

"Okay, stalker. He slept on my couch a couple of times." I could feel the heat of anger rising in me, too.

"Not my business." He held up a hand between us. "I'm done talking."

"Jeez, Duncan—"

He stood suddenly. He towered over me by a few inches. I also couldn't help but notice that he outweighed me by a good fifty pounds. He leaned over me and shouted in my face. "Just leave me the FUCK alone. I don't want anything to do with this."

Discussion in the bar dropped to near silence.

"Do you hear me?!" he continued. I could feel the hot breath from his mouth move the hair beside my face. "Leave. Me. ALONE."

I stood frozen as he grabbed his beer and stalked out of the bar. For once, I was at a loss for a sharp retort. I could feel my face flush.

Now we'd definitely be the topic of discussion at the coffee shop tomorrow morning.

I gathered myself by looking down at my beer.

Lizzie Jordan, public spectacle.

I heard the voices around me begin to return to normal and, before I could get my bearings, I felt someone come up next to me.

I turned sharply to see a sunburned, blonde man with bleary blue eyes, threaded with red lines. "Anyone sittin' there?" he slurred, gesturing to Duncan's seat.

I shook my head mutely, and he slid into the seat as though nothing had happened.

"What an asshole," Ellen said, as she appeared across the bar. "He walks out on his tab all the time. I'll get him tomorrow. Want another?"

I shook my head, still processing.

She shrugged. "Those two are on Ben anyway."

My head snapped up. "Ben? Is he here *now*?" The end of my sentence came out with a squeak.

"Now? Not that I know of. You okay, Lizzie?" she asked.

I had to get out of there. I fumbled in my purse to tip her. I laid a five on the bar, grabbed my beer and started to make a hasty exit. I barely heard her voice over my shoulder. "He left you a $50 tab earlier today."

It probably should have slowed my steps, but it didn't.

That damn tab. The reason this whole damn thing started. Well, not really—not if I were honest with myself.

My feet carried me back to the docks again, iguanas and killers on the loose be damned. I sat on a rectangular dock box and played with the beer bottle in my hand.

As I brooded, something Duncan said came back to me. He called Jessie a "sucker fish." And he said he bought Andrea a shot just to throw Jessie off the scent. It jibed with what Magnus had told me, that Jessie had a lot of fire and no clue how to direct it. I couldn't quite get a grasp on the dynamic between those girls.

Once again, I had absolutely nothing.

I pushed myself off the dock box, wobbling slightly. It was the second time that day that I found myself unstable on my feet. I had visions of pitching into the black water. With all the boats, holding tanks and diesel in this water, I'd have a nasty case of staph in my still-raw knee in no time.

I needed to eat something, but I wasn't quite ready to wander back into the fray yet.

I stared out at the dark water and the lights beyond. St. John was lit up like a Christmas tree. It looked peaceful in the distance. To the left, a light blinked on Two Brothers, a navigational hazard that had snagged its share of boats at night. "Steer clear," the light said, over and over again. Advice I probably could have used—and heeded—earlier.

I wished I could go home and curl up in bed, but I couldn't, not with the belligerent drunk and suspected murderer on my couch. I'd shuffled Dave out too quickly. I should have asked him to take Ben with him and leave him on a beach to sleep it off.

I decided to head to XO for the second time that day, visions of the French dip that Magnus had eaten earlier drawing me in.

The French dip was as delicious as it had looked earlier. So delicious in fact, that an Absolut dirty martini sounded like a good idea.

Then a man appeared at my elbow and offered to buy me my next one. I couldn't help but notice that he wasn't at all physically like Dave. He was one of the new assistant managers at the Marriott, and he had a body that had been shaped by the office, not a dive boat. His face was a little bit round where Dave's had been chiseled. His hair cut looked like an expensive stateside job. But he had a kind smile and knew how to string words together, so we drank a martini together. Then we split another one.

I drove us back to his house. I probably shouldn't have gotten behind the wheel, but he didn't have a car yet and I wasn't in the mood to deal with a taxi driver.

He set me up on his porch with a beer that I didn't plan to drink, then excused himself to tidy up his bedroom. My mind turned to Andrea. Where had she gone that her night ended all wrong?

I took a sip of my beer, reflexively. Then I made a face. I never liked Heineken, never understood why so many guys ordered it. Mystery of the universe, I guess. It just tasted flat and heavy on my tongue.

Still no work tomorrow, which made me nervous. The T-shirt embargo continued. Hopefully it would be over before I had to hand over my rent check. And hopefully Ben wasn't raiding my house. If he found that Ziploc of cash at the bottom of my T-shirt drawer, that would really set me back.

I peered over my shoulder through the screen door. Still no sign of . . . Jesus, what was his name? Joshua, not Josh.

I took another sip of Heineken and shuddered, then set it down on the floor. I've heard that it tastes much better in Amsterdam, but what wouldn't?

A fleeting thought ran through my head: I was supposed to meet Andrea's father at 9:00 am at the Ritz.

The screen door opened and closed. I shrugged that thought away as I felt Joshua's hand slide around my shoulder and down my arm.

I'll tell you what. This guy might not be able to haul dive tanks down a long dock with ease, but he had already shown me that he sure as hell could kiss. I stood up and pressed myself against him, tilting my head back to receive his lips.

I shuddered slightly as he kissed me and I felt some knot inside me begin to come loose.

He lifted his lips from mine about an inch. "Are you cold?"

"No, just—" How could I explain that I needed this right now so badly that it was like a current running through my body? That I'd just realized it was possible to put down the burden of the day, to forget for a few minutes the fact that a friend of mine might have murdered a girl and I might be mixed up enough in it enough to be of interest to the police— and that I would do absolutely anything to let it slide from my shoulders, even just for a few minutes?

I figured words wouldn't do it, so I reached around him for the screen door and headed inside. I peeled my dress over my head and dropped it on the floor, headed for the doorway to his bedroom. He got the message.

And, as you might guess, that's all I've got for you on this subject. I'm sure you can make up the rest on your own. Maybe it would be juicier than the reality. But I doubt it.

15

Lest you think this was going to turn into a love story, I rose a little after the sun at 7:15 am, which was precisely one hour and fifteen minutes after I would usually report for work. I should have relished the extra sleep, but it left me feeling sluggish.

I looked over at my bed companion, who was curled away from me on his side, the back of his hair mussed from sleep, the white sheet draped over his naked figure.

I slid out of bed to use the bathroom, then gathered my clothes. This dress of mine had gotten more mileage in the last twenty four hours than it had in the last six months. It was damp to the touch. Gross. I'd drop it in my hamper as soon as I got home.

I looked back at the bed. Joshua hadn't stirred an inch.

I picked up my flip flops in my hand and walked out.

Okay, I crept out. I snuck out like a thief in the night, but I'd text him later. I pinky-swear promised myself I would.

A few minutes later, I was driving down the road, right past the marina where my co-workers would be welcoming guests on board for the day. I felt a stab of jealousy. Even though we often groused that our job was like herding cats, I'd have accepted the task gladly.

I cruised easily through Red Hook, which was still quiet in the morning hours.

I took the left toward my cottage. It also happened to be the direction of the Ritz, reminding me of my breakfast date this morning with Mr. Milliken. I didn't think I'd keep it.

I took the next right and proceeded along quietly until I got to the top of the lane where I lived.

There, the thought hit me like a lightning bolt: Ben was in my house.

I felt a stab of fear.

My mind skipped to the strong grip he put on my arm at the bar when he first told me about Andrea. Then it flipped to an image of Ellie with Ben's hands around her throat. It was enough to make me lift my foot from the gas pedal and coast to a stop in the middle of the lane.

Where could I go?

Dave's? Nope.

Back to Joshua's? It was a little early for that, and I didn't want to give him the impression that last night was anything more than fun.

What about Rick? He was probably still angry with me for running out on his policeman friend. He'd let me in, but I'd get a stern lecture.

Lucas? Two favors in less than twenty-four hours felt excessive.

I shifted in my seat, the dress sticking to my skin. I wanted new clothes. I wanted a shower. And I wasn't going to let some guy, let alone Ben, chase me away from my own cottage. I paid $900 a month for the privilege of calling it my sanctuary, cockroaches, rats, tiny water heater and all. He needed to get gone.

I put my foot back on the gas and pulled up to my apartment. I was the only car in sight, but I already knew Ben hadn't driven himself to my place. I peered up at my cottage, perched on the hill above. I couldn't see a damn thing.

My palms were damp. I reached under the passenger seat, delighted to feel the weight of my foot-long Maglite. These babies were worth every dollar.

I shut the car door as quietly as I could, then wrapped my hand around the flared head of the Maglite, ready to swing.

I left my flip flops at the bottom of the stone staircase. That turned out to be a huge mistake. I thought bare feet would allow me to creep silently up the walk. For the first two steps, it did. Then I stepped on a broken shell—a discard from one of my hermit crab residents, I was sure—and I nearly cried out in shock when it pierced the bottom of my foot. Great. Now I was really going to get a case of staph. I picked up my foot, removed the sharp piece of shell and tossed it into the bushes.

I'd have to rethink my approach. I glanced back at my flip flops and discarded the idea. Still too risky. I wanted the upper hand.

Instead, I crouched and leaned forward onto my toes. Slowly, I picked my way up the walk, avoiding scattered rocks, broken shells and sandspurs—nasty little plant balls made entirely out of spikes. My foot hurt like a mother, but there was nothing I could do about it.

The whole time, I kept my eyes on the bank of screens, knowing that it was much easier to see out than it was to see in.Ben could be standing there, watching this whole dance and positioning himself perfectly to grab me.

I paused, mid-crouch. Why was I doing this again? Oh, right, because I had nowhere else to go.

I felt a gentle breeze start to blow. It offered some relief from the building heat of the day, but it gave me no joy. As the screens over my windows flapped, I thought I saw a shadow pass.

I froze, straining to hear. It was silent except for the low rumbling of a large truck laboring up the main road 50 yards away.

I resumed my creep.

Once I passed the corner of the cottage, there were no more windows until I got to the door, so I ducked down and made a run for it, taking the side of the house quickly and crouching to the right of the door.

I sat there, my ass on the cold concrete, breathless from the exertion and the rush of adrenaline, trying to keep my ragged gasps quiet while my body begged for more oxygen.

What was my plan? I wanted him gone, that I knew. So maybe I bang the door open, then demand that he leave. Swipe him with the Maglite if he gets too close. Or maybe I run for the kitchen and grab a butcher's knife, too. Then I have two weapons to ward him off with.

The reasonable side of my brain popped up to offer its input. *This is Ben. Remember Ben? He's not a killer . . . right?*

I shook off those thoughts. They weren't going to help me get Ben out of the apartment, which is what I needed, first and foremost.

I tipped forward until I could get myself in a crouch. I reached up with my left hand to try the doorknob. I felt it begin to turn easily in my hand. Now, if he hadn't thrown the bolt, I was ready to run in and surprise him.

I pressed myself soundlessly up to standing, my back against the door, my Maglite gripped in my right hand.

I rotated the handle slowly, then pushed at the door gently, my right arm tensed to swipe.

The door didn't move. Was the bolt engaged?

I breathed out slowly. I waited, listening for sounds inside. Nothing.

I took another breath in and applied gentle pressure to the wood with my shoulder.

Then I felt the door slip over the sash faster than I anticipated. As it swung inward, my damp hand slipped off the knob, knocking me off balance. The breath whooshed out of my lungs as I stumbled forward. I came down hard on my injured foot in a burst of pain. I staggered to a crouch in my best "ready" posture and swung my gaze around the apartment.

Ben wasn't in sight.

I went with Plan B. I ran into the kitchen, took an overhand grip on my largest kitchen knife and drew it quickly out of the block. I reeled around, both arms ready deliver blows as needed.

I still couldn't see him. "Get out!" I yelled in my biggest, bravest voice. I hoped I would roar like a lion, but my voice squeaked with fear.

Lizzie Jordan, scared little lamb.

I waited. All I heard was silence.

My eyes began to scan crazily for any sign of movement. I saw nothing.

I took a few tentative steps forward, my muscles stretched tight with tension. I peered over the dividing wall to where my bed sat in its alcove, expecting to see Ben's body tangled in my sheets.

It was empty.

I snapped my head back around and scanned for hiding places. The most obvious was the bathroom. I crept over, feeling the wet blood on the bottom of my foot smear across the smooth tile. It still hurt like the dickens, but I couldn't think about that now. I crossed foot over foot, leaning on the wall next to the door like I'd seen FBI agents do on television. I cocked my head and listened, but I only heard the leaves of a tree outside rustling in the breeze.

I eased my nose across the opening, then one eye. No one in front of the sink or on the toilet, but the damned shower curtain was closed. My worst nightmare.

I took two steps in. I waited, the sound of my breathing deafeningly loud in my ears.

Move the curtain with the Maglite, then threaten with the knife, I told myself.

And yet some part of me whined that I should just run away. *Go to Dave's*, it said. *Go to a bar. Go to a beach. Go anywhere but here.* A memory flashed in front of my eyes. A silver switchblade, its cold tip poking just under my jawline. *Not now*, I told everything—the voices, the memory. *Not now.*

I blinked to clear my vision.

I was back in front of my shower curtain. I steeled myself, then reached the Maglite forward. I sucked a noisy breath in. Then I slid the shower curtain aside in a whoosh. I squared for battle.

The shower was empty.

I spun around. Could he have crept up behind me?

The apartment was as bare as when I'd walked in.

There was only one hiding place left: behind the futon. It was in disarray, the few cushions I had scattered on the floor, the covering wrinkled. I crept across my little apartment, trying to keep my bloody foot from dragging all over the floor. It had started to throb, and I knew I needed to get it cleaned out soon.

My foot and heart beat in near-unison as I stalked my prey.

I leaped knee-first onto the couch and gave my best battle cry, plunging the butcher's knife down at anyone who might be unfortunate enough to be waiting behind my couch.

A nearly translucent beige lizard skittered away in terror. Otherwise, the area behind my futon was empty.

I breathed a sigh of relief and slouched on the couch, dropping the Maglite and the butcher's knife on the mussed cover.

I sat there, letting the growing heat of the day press on me. I waited for my breathing to return to normal, but it kept huffing in and out, as though in preparation for a sneeze.

Then, I felt something somersault in my chest, and I let out a crazy laugh. I lost all control. I felt like someone else was pumping my chest. I was left to observe dumbfounded as the shaking began to take over my body. I struggled to get a gasp in between each cycle of giggles. Finally, I surrendered to hysterical laughter. When I was done, my cheeks were wet with tears. I was exhausted, my body limp in nearly the same position Ben had taken last night.

I checked my watch. It was almost 8:00 am. I wanted a shower and I wanted to get back in bed. I peeled my dress over my head. This time, it went straight into the hamper, not to be seen for a month—or until I managed to get back into Red Hook to do my laundry.

I glanced at the smears of blood on floor. They were at their worst near the door and in the kitchen. I'd clean that up later.

In the bathroom, I dropped my underwear on my bathmat and turned the hot water up as high as it would go.

There are some crazies down here who argue that there's no need for hot water in a tropical climate. I am not one of them. The only thing I wanted right then was warmth on my skin.

As I let the water run—cistern level be damned—I felt my shoulders drop an inch. I scrubbed my scalp, feeling the slick bubbles of my shampoo build under my fingers. I dipped my head back and let the water course down my head, taking all of yesterday's dirt and sweat with it. I felt like I could stand there all day, letting hot water and soft bubbles slide down my skin.

I was jolted out of my reverie by three sharp bangs on my front door.

My feet scrabbled for purchase on the slick tiles. I grabbed desperately for the window ledge, knocking all my plastic bottles to the floor with a clatter.

I managed to keep myself upright. Just as I was congratulating myself for avoiding death by shower tile, the shower spray hit the back of my head, sending soap down my face and right into my eyes. Crap.

Another set of knocks, again in triplicate. Who the hell was after me now? I tried not to jump to disaster scenarios, but my heart was double-thudding in my chest. I put my face in the shower spray to clear it.

I twitched again as the banging became more insistent.

I worried my hair under the spray, trying to move all the shampoo out in a hurry. My mind flicked to the bolt at the door. Had I slid it home? Did I even lock the knob?

I cursed myself and pawed at my eyes. They were bleary, but I could see. Now, it was time to see who the hell was banging my door down at 8:15 in the Goddamn morning.

Then I heard a word that made me stiffen in place: "Police."

Numbly, I turned off the taps and simply listened. For a moment, there was only silence, then I heard the banging again and a distinct voice that called, "Open up! Police!"

My mind spun. I had nowhere to go. I glanced at the small window over my shower that had saved my life only seconds earlier. It started at shoulder level and was probably the size of a sheet of legal paper. Even if I could make it out, I'd be naked with no keys, no car and no money and no shoes. I picked up my foot and looked at the cut from the shell. It was white and puckered from the shower, but clean of blood for now. I would definitely get staph.

The only other way out led straight into the arms of the police—and who knew what they wanted?

I stood naked and shivering, my mind clacking away. I wrapped my arms tightly around myself. I swear I felt that cold blade right under my chin again. I was so cold, cold to the core. I was tempted to let my knees buckle, scoot into the corner of the shower and bawl.

That thought was fleeting.

The next sound I heard was splintering wood as my door was kicked open. It banged against the opposite wall. I involuntarily stepped back in horror, into the corner of the shower, the tile frigid against my skin, my mind howling with syllables of fear.

I heard a barrage of footsteps and yells of "Police! Police! Clear!"

It hit me. They broke my door. They broke my fucking door.

Now I was pissed.

I nearly drew back the curtain and stalked out, stark naked, to confront them.

Then I came to my senses.

I took a deep breath, which went in shaky. I steadied myself, then called, "I'm in here. But I'm sure as hell not coming out without a towel."

I heard one set of light footsteps walk toward me. I'd left the bathroom door open, so the footsteps continued into the room—and around my underwear, I hoped. I vowed to be neater with my delicates in the future.

It was so quiet that I heard the fabric of the towel scrape against the bar as it was removed. The shower curtain was pulled back an inch by a brown hand attached to a white shirt cuff. The hand retreated, then offered a gray towel. I grabbed it and shut the curtain with my other hand. I squeezed my hair with the towel first, then quickly dried the rest of my body parts.

"Miss Jordan," the voice said from the other side of the curtain. "I need to ask about the blood on your floor. That was the reason for us entering your apartment by force. Is someone injured here?"

I wrapped the towel around my midsection and secured it tightly. I hoped that the swath of fabric would hold in the fear I felt, the rippling in my gut and the light tickling of adrenaline in my legs and arms. This trusty towel was all I had for a façade.

I'd need it.

I steeled myself, channeled my indignation over my door, then ripped the shower curtain back.

Gray Suit was standing in front of my miniature sink, his brown lace-up oxfords tastefully arranged around my discarded underwear. Today, he was wearing a beige suit that fit his shoulders and his trim waist so precisely that I wondered if he had it custom made. *Elegant*, I thought, in spite of myself.

I raised my eyebrows at him, trying to summon dignity despite my mostly undressed state. I pointed my foot forward delicately like a ballet dancer. "That's my blood. I stepped on a shell on the way up my walk."

His expression didn't change. "Then perhaps you might consider wearing your shoes all the way up to your house instead of leaving them at the bottom of the walk."

This guy didn't miss a trick. "May I please get dressed so we can discuss why you're here and why you broke my door?"

I saw his eyes stray to the small window behind me, then back to me. No way was I getting away from him.

He stepped out of the bathroom, holding his arm out as though to usher me through.

I kept my expression frosty to make it clear that his mock chivalry fell flat with me.

First, I shut my front door, noticing with dismay that they had pulled the doorknob plate right out of the molding. I apparently hadn't thrown my deadbolt, which was lucky. It probably would have given way, too.

I pulled open my underwear drawer and cast a glance around the apartment. Two tall officers in crisp uniforms stood ramrod straight next to my dining room table. They both had dark brown skin, but that of the officer on the left was just a shade lighter than that of his companion. Both watched me intently, their hands dangling free, just in case I tried to jackrabbit away, I assumed.

I rooted around for one of my favorites, a red pair with pink tigers. I felt one officer take a step forward as I dug, which bugged the crap out of me. I turned around in triumph and held up the underwear. "Just trying to get dressed, gentlemen. I promise there's nothing dangerous in this apartment, apart from the Maglite on the couch and the machete near the potted palm."

No one spoke, so I grabbed a bra, a pair of shorts and a tank top that said, "Don't bother me, I'm crabby," over a cartoon of a red crab, a relic of a former life. I marched back to the bathroom, and with a glance at Gray Suit, I shut the door.

Through the thin wood, I heard him say something, then I heard the front door open and close. He was probably sending one of the officers outside to cover his bases. I shook my head. Lizzie Jordan, flight risk.

Once I was properly dressed, I squeezed my hair once more in the towel, gave it a quick comb with my fingers, then hung up my towel. I also reached for my deodorant. It slipped through my fingers and fell to the floor with a clatter.

I leaned my weight forward on the sink. All my paranoid fears had finally come true. The police were here. Were they going to take me to jail? Who could I call? Alex, the tax lawyer? What else could I do? Andrea's phone was locked away in Tower's drawer at Secret Harbour, but if they had gone through my purse, they'd find all the notes they needed to suggest I'd had it in my possession. If I could just—

There was a knock at the door. "Miss Jordan?"

Crap. "Coming," I said, trying to keep my voice light, as though Gray Suit were merely the next person in line for the facilities. I picked up my deodorant from the floor and gave my underarms a careful application. I was going to need it.

I took one last look at myself in the mirror, strawberry nose and all. I hardened my eyes, set my mouth and banged out of the bathroom.

One officer was still gone, but the other still stood in my apartment. I noticed for the first time that the snap holding his gun in place was undone. I swallowed, my mouth dry.

"Miss Jordan, I have some questions for you." Gray Suit took a step toward me, a notebook in his right hand and a silver pen in his left.

"I'd like to see some identification, please, from both of you," I said.

It was a ploy. I knew they were legit. They knew I knew. But if they wanted to dance, we were going to dance. In fact, I wasn't going to offer them the option to sit. We would do this entire interview standing up, by God.

I inspected the ID cards they handed forward. The officer was Lyle Gumbs and Gray Suit's real name was Adán Christopher. He was a detective. His ID came in its own wallet with a badge on the opposite side, its gold plating polished to a shine.

Once I nodded at his ID, Detective Christopher spoke. "May we sit?" he asked, gesturing to my Martha Stewart dining set.

Something about those official IDs took the fire out of me. I felt my resolve crumble. I nodded as I poured myself into a chair.

"Full name, please." His silver pen was poised on the top of a fresh notebook page, waiting for my answer.

I took another look at Detective Christopher and wondered whether this was what all of the island's Kojaks looked like. While Officer Gumbs sported a close fade, the detective's twists stuck out from his head more defiantly. His eyes were deep brown, maybe a single shade lighter than his skin. He had a slight accent, but it wasn't one I could place. He didn't quite sound like the down-islanders I knew from Dominica and St. Lucia. He also didn't quite sound like a St. Thomian, either.

I flicked my eyes to Officer Gumbs, whose eyes were roaming over the cabinets of my kitchen. He looked bored. I felt hopeful. If he didn't think I was a master criminal, maybe I wasn't one.

"Miss Jordan?"

"I think you already know my full name."

His gaze didn't flicker, but I saw that touch of amusement at his mouth that I'd seen at the Ritz. It was gone quickly. "This will be a lot easier on you if you can just answer my questions," he said, his voice hard.

"Elizabeth Bower Jordan," I blurted. I was *such* a marshmallow.

"ID?"

I pointed to my purse, which I had discarded on the floor next to the table. He nodded. I thanked whatever bureaucratic god was watching over me that I had my Virgin Islands license. After three months on the island, you were supposed to surrender your stateside license to get your VI license. Most people didn't bother. Today, it would mark me as a law-abiding girl—which was mostly true.

He handed it back without a word, silver pen flashing as he assumed note-taking position again. "Alright, Miss Jordan. I heard that you've been around the island asking questions about a girl named Andrea Milliken."

I didn't say anything at first. Should I ask to call Alex? Some kind of attorney had to be better than no attorney. I thought back to the legal education I'd garnered from many a *Law & Order* marathon. "Am I under arrest?"

"Should you be under arrest?"

"I don't think so."

"The thing is, Miss Jordan, I'm working on a very serious case. A homicide. And wherever I go to investigate this homicide, you seem to appear. I saw you first at the Ritz-

Carlton yesterday and then at the marina yesterday. Why were you at the Ritz?"

In that moment, it became painfully clear to me that all my posturing had been just that. The detective—the real detective—was on to me.

What else did he know? Should I talk? Should I refuse to talk? If he had something on me, wouldn't he have taken me straight to the station?

He banged his fist on the table and I flinched.

"You're going to get yourself into worse trouble if you don't speak up, Miss Jordan. You're clever, but you're not so clever enough to avoid trouble."

I put a protective hand on my table. I felt my spine begin to stiffen. "Haven't you done enough?" I asked, my temper flaring. "First, you break my door and now you start beating on my table. I got it at Kmart. It can't take much of a beating."

Again, the mouth twist of amusement. He recomposed himself quickly and leaned forward, his voice softer now. "Just answer me honestly. You've probably heard a lot of stories about the police down here. I know. I've heard them, too. I'm not here to put you in jail unless I need to. In fact, I've come here for a favor."

"A favor?"

"But first, it's time to 'fess up."

"To what?"

"The fact that you've been messing about in this case." His voice started to rise. "I could arrest you for tampering with an investigation." He raised his eyebrows and looked at me indignantly.

I tried to keep my face neutral. "If you already know what I've been doing, why are you asking me?"

"Because I know *some* things. I don't know everything."

He had me there. I paused, calculating my next move.

He spoke first. "Do you think your friend Ben killed Andrea?"

I didn't stop to marvel at how much he'd already figured out about me. I simply shook my head vehemently. "I don't. I really don't. That's why I agreed to go see the girls—"

I stopped as Detective Christopher started scribbling on his pad. Dammit. Me and my big mouth.

Since I'd already lost this maneuver, I figured I might as well spill. "I agreed to go see the girls to make sure Andrea was okay. Ben thought she went home with someone else."

A nod and more scribbles from the left-handed detective. In another context, I would have been tickled by the contortions of his hand.

"Do you know where he is now? You're obligated to tell me if you do."

"I don't," I said, my voice flat. That, at least, was true, a fact for which I was grateful.

"Did you ever see him get angry or violent with anyone?" he asked, his head still down on his notes.

I shook my head again, but with less conviction. I wasn't sure Christopher picked up on it, but he did lift his head. "Was that a no?"

"Yes—no." I stammered. "Yes, that's a 'no.'" I felt myself flushing, my cheeks hot. I hoped Christopher would put it down to nervousness. What I knew from Ellie was just coconut telegraph chatter, anyway, wasn't it? Or did Ben's visit last night qualify?

I was sweating so badly now that moisture had trickled down my inner arm, making the contact between my elbow and the table both slippery and precarious.

Clearly, it was time to switch deodorants—or go back to being an ordinary citizen. My pores weren't cut out for this.

"Where is Andrea's phone?" he asked.

I felt a jolt of electricity. Damn, this guy was good. After the initial quick wave of panic, I felt my brain kick back in. There was his pattern, I realized. Make a few innocuous moves, then go in for the kill.

I had to strike back, but I wasn't yet sure how. I made a cautious move. "I don't have it."

"But you know where it is."

He locked eyes with me. I guessed that he was in his mid-thirties at least, but his eyes didn't have a single line around them. I wondered if he stayed out of the sun.

I wrenched my eyes away from his and realized that the length of my silence had already given me away. Double damn.

I nodded.

He leaned forward in his seat, and I could smell his cologne again, a fresh scent that was rather pleasant, despite our circumstances. "Miss Jordan, I need to find out who killed Andrea Milliken. I don't want to put it on your friend if he didn't do it. But I need everything I can get to piece this case together. We have equipment back at the station that can uncover a great deal of information from her cell phone."

"I thought you guys didn't have that stuff."

He moved only his eyebrows upward toward his hairline, the rest of his body perfectly still. "I can assure you that we do."

I nodded. So much for what Lucas knew.

Surreptitiously, I caught myself taking in another whiff of his cologne. I had to get ahold of myself.

I pulled myself out of his gravitational orbit and leaned back. I still had a few moves of my own to make.

"You said you had a favor to ask of me." I kept my tone cool.

He matched my posture, leaning back in his chair. "Two, actually."

"Two," I said, putting surprise in my voice. "Sounds like you need a lot from me."

He shrugged, but I didn't feel much conviction behind it.

"Was breaking my door part of the plan? I wouldn't say something like that generally inspires cooperation. It certainly hasn't put me in the mood to do you *two* favors."

Maybe it was my imagination, but he looked uncomfortable for a moment, his left eye squinting slightly. "It was the blood on the floor. I thought there was someone hurt inside."

I paused, as though chewing that over. "The phone is the first favor, I gather. What's the second favor?"

"You have a meeting with Mr. Milliken this morning."

I froze for a microsecond. Score another point for the detective. This guy really did know everything. I waved my hand in a dismissive gesture, trying to cover my shock. "I'm not going."

Christopher pointed at me. "That's where you're wrong."

"Wait, what?"

He sat forward and pointed at the cartoon crab on my chest. "You're going to have to change your shirt. It's not quite up to the Ritz standards, wouldn't you say?"

I felt the game slipping through my grasp. "Who says I want to measure up to the Ritz's standards? And who says I'm going to go?" I folded my arms.

Christopher merely appraised me. Then, he shrugged, the corners of his mouth turning down in a grimace. "Officer Gumbs here would be happy to take you down to jail right now. I can easily hold you on obstruction of justice, interfering with an investigation—any number of charges. It's Saturday. You won't even get a hearing until Monday, and I suspect the company you'd be keeping in jail wouldn't be particularly pleasant for a woman like you."

My mouth opened, but a sharp gesture with his hand cut me off.

"Or, Miss Jordan, you can do these two things for me. I know you've been going around, asking questions about Miss

Milliken's whereabouts. I think you've been doing it out of a misplaced sense of loyalty for your friend, but it's got to stop. In exchange for my turning a blind eye, I want you to turn in Miss Milliken's cell phone to me, *and* I want you to keep your meeting with Mr. Milliken and report back to me as to what he tells you."

"I don't get it. Is he a suspect?"

No answer.

"How could he be? Didn't he just get here?"

The detective only looked at me pityingly. It was clear that he thought my Nancy Drew days were fleeting, if they'd ever even begun.

I sat for a moment, mulling over what he'd offered me. I didn't really have a choice. Jail didn't seem like a good option merely in the name of righteousness. And maybe Detective Christopher really would search for the truth. Maybe the cell phone, spider webbed screen and all, would somehow clear Ben's name. And as for the meeting, it was a free breakfast, right? Maybe my last meal, if the detective had his way.

I heard a metal clanking sound and turned to see that Officer Gumbs had pulled out his handcuffs and placed them on the table.

The sight made my breath catch in my throat, but I didn't dare reveal my true feelings. Instead, I rolled my eyes. "You two are the fastest-acting government employees I've met in St. Thomas. Okay, I'll do it. But I want to tell you something first because I'm sure you've already gotten an earful from Jessie."

"Just the phone, Miss Jordan. I don't need—"

"Hang on, I'm getting there. Yes, I know where Andrea's phone is, and, yes, it was in Ben's possession. But he found it in his car. He said that it was because she gave him a—"

I paused and felt my face flush. Both men were now staring at me intently. My mouth opened and closed. Maybe I didn't have to go into that much detail.

"She gave him what?" Christopher asked.

I bit my lower lip. I guess the Catholic school girl in me was rearing her prudish head.

Christopher looked impatient. I guess I'd been working his nerves because he reached over, picked up the handcuffs and rattled them at me. "Gave him what?"

I raised an eyebrow at him, but he raised his right back at me.

I huffed for a moment, just to regain my dignity. Then, I spoke. "Well, they were around the corner in the Duffy's parking lot, where the dumpster is, where no one could see them and Andrea, well, she apparently—"

"She what?"

Officer Gumbs let out a high-pitched chuckle. He got where this was going. He covered his hand with his eyes, shaking his head.

This only made the detective more impatient. "She did WHAT?!" he bellowed.

"She gave him a blowjob," I said meekly.

And then I couldn't help it. I giggled. I was sure I heard Officer Gumbs continue to join me.

"I don't know if she put her phone in his car on purpose, maybe to give herself a reason to get in touch with Ben again, just in case. But they were in his car together. That's how Ben got the phone."

The detective looked up at the ceiling and sighed. "And where is the phone now?"

"At Secret Harbour, in the drawer behind the bar."

Christopher nodded at Gumbs, who stood and went to the door, his head turned toward the radio microphone on his shoulder.

My mind flicked to the original phone in the bush behind Lucas's place. I decided to keep a lid on that one. I didn't want to get Lucas tangled in this mess.

Christopher looked at his watch. "Not long now," he said. "You'll want to change."

I looked at him blankly, then felt my eyes shift down to the handcuffs that still sat on my table. I could nearly feel their weight against my wrists.

I stood, the chair legs scraping loudly against the tiles. I trudged over to my closet. I'd already used up my one good dress yesterday. I pawed past my rain jacket and a few hooded sweatshirts until I came to a black silky tank top Dave had given me for Christmas last year. I'd gotten him a book.

Girlfriend of the year, I was not.

I pulled it off the hanger with a sigh. I noticed a few wrinkles—probably the result of the single wearing last New Year's Eve. My brain flashed to a few images of our celebration together—happy times, fueled by cheap champagne, followed by a hell of a headache the next day. I pushed the memories aside, along with the small catch in my chest that came with them. No time for that. I had work to do.

I shuffled over to my dresser and sorted through maybe ten pair of khakis in various states of presentability until I came to a red pair of shorts. I glanced behind me and, sure enough, Detective Christopher was tracking my every movement. I was tempted to make a face at him, but those handcuffs winked at me in the sunlight. I restrained myself.

I rooted around for a racerback bra to go with the tank top. Call me "rough around the edges," "uncivilized" or simply "not girly," but there was one thing I didn't do, and that was walk around with my bra straps hanging out. A girl's got to have her rules, and that was another of mine.

I took the pile of clothes into the bathroom without asking for permission.

Before getting dressed, I turned on the spray of the shower. I stepped in and gave myself a quick rinse. I needed to wash off the stink of that morning's interrogation.

I dried myself quickly and put on the new clothes, applying two layers of deodorant once I'd slipped the tank top over my head.

I checked myself in the mirror. I looked paler than usual. I considered adding some mascara to my eyelashes, but I decided against it. Besides, I was pretty sure the one tube of mascara I owned was all dried up.

My hair was still wet, so I gathered it all in a bun on top of my head. It would do.

I came out of the bathroom to find the table empty.

I started and jumped a foot to my right when the detective's voice boomed from the kitchen. "May I have a glass of water?"

I peered around the wall into my kitchen. "What are you doing?" One cabinet door hung wide open. The detective was riffling through its contents.

"Looking for a glass."

"I'm sensing a distinct lack of respect here. I certainly wouldn't break into your house and start snooping around your kitchen."

He turned, a smile flashing across his face. He had nice teeth, I noticed. Very even and very white. "Actually, Miss Jordan, given your activities of the last twenty-four hours, I think that's exactly what you'd do."

I scowled at him and stalked over to the closet, throwing my balled-up clothes in the hamper. When I turned, he was standing in the kitchen, looking at me with that same amused look I'd seen several times before.

"One more cabinet over," I growled. "Jug is in the fridge."

With slow, deliberate movements, he brought out two pint glasses, then filled them both with water from the plastic gallon jug in the fridge. We met at the table and seated ourselves like civilized human beings.

"Thank you," I said. I took a swallow of the water. I wished it were a cold fizzy beer.

Christopher shifted in his seat and put his left hand in his pocket. He pulled out a black ballpoint pen whose barrel was a little thicker than usual.

"Let's talk about how this is going to go down."

I took a breath. *Bring it on.*

And, yet, underneath that crust of determination, my stomach roiled with dark premonitions.

I needed a drink.

16

As I drove my little tin can up the hill once more to the Ritz, Detective Christopher's pen clipped discreetly to one side of my purse, I couldn't help but shake my head. Stool pigeon wasn't my usual M.O.

Neither was getting involved. I almost didn't recognize myself. I had always been notoriously careful to conduct my business outside of the St. Thomas spotlight, with the exception of my very public tiff with Dave the other night. No one came to me for the latest gossip, although enough people repeated it to me, grateful to have a listening ear, even an apathetic one.

Don't get me wrong. I had my opinions. But I either addressed them to the appropriate person or kept them to myself. It was the only way I figured I'd survive, by not getting involved.

So why was this different?

I heard a story in high school about a woman who was raped on the side of an expressway. Not a single person stopped to help her. The lesson? When you're in a crowd, everyone assumes that someone else will help out. That bugged the crap out of me.

It happens on the boat all the time. With big groups, unless there's a leader, most people assume that someone else is going to take care of the tip. I've gotten stiffed enough times to assure you that this phenomenon is painfully real.

It's why first responders are trained to pick out a specific person at an emergency scene and ask him or her to dial 911. Because if you just yell out "call an ambulance," the likelihood is that everyone will believe someone else is taking care of it.

Was that what would happen with Ben? Sure, Detective Christopher seemed like he had follow-through, but who knew where his real interests lay? In justice? Maybe I was a cynic, but I had a hard time believing that. It was possible. But was it likely?

Ben's face flashed in my mind. He'd scared the bejeezus out of me last night, but wherever he was, I hoped he was okay.

His face was quickly replaced by Detective Christopher's. After he explained how the recording pen worked, he locked eyes with me and told me, in no uncertain terms, that I was to stop investigating this case.

"Make no mistake, Miss Jordan. Just because I've asked you these two favors does not mean that I wish you to keep poking around. In fact, if I find you at another one of my locations, I will arrest you on the spot and we can sort things out later."

"'Your locations?'" I'd asked, a smirk turning up the corners of my mouth. "This island doesn't belong to you."

He did not look amused. "As far as you're concerned, this island *is* my island, at least until I catch this killer. I see you anywhere near anything I don't like, it's jail time for you."

"Can we at least divide up the bars of Red Hook, like a couple that's breaking up? I get Island Time. You can have Duffy's. Never really felt at home in that place anyway."

All I got in return was a cold stare.

As I drove, I squeezed the wheel in frustration. Couldn't he understand that I had a friend in jeopardy? And, frankly, I had two friends in jeopardy: Ben and my island. Detective Christopher might think this island was his, but it was my home, too. If Andrea's real killer wasn't brought to justice, I was pretty sure this island would never feel the same to me.

It had been my refuge, a safe harbor far from a place where the people you trusted the most turned on you. If it became the kind of island where a friend got locked up for something he didn't do, I didn't know where that would leave me.

But what if Ben did kill Andrea?

That would change things, too. The person who'd helped me start to trust again revealed to be a violent criminal? Might as well roll up my personal welcome mat for good. Might even have to buy a plane ticket out, find a new paradise.

I took the next turn a little too fast and tight, resulting in an angry honk from a beat-up red pickup truck. "Like you would have noticed another dent," I yelled out the window.

I should have felt righteous after my little rant, but it left me feeling hollow.

I felt my vision narrow. *No, no, no, not again.*

I saw an opening in the road on the left, a small driveway for an art studio that never seemed open. I jerked the wheel left and pulled in, my breaths coming shallow now. I blinked to try and clear the snowflakes creeping in at the edge of my vision. I felt my throat tighten. *Not now.*

I let my head drop. I tried to breathe against the resistance in my lungs. I closed my eyes. I could feel my heartbeat where my forehead met the steering wheel. Ben's face popped up along with an image of Andrea, both of them frozen together in that photograph at Duffy's.

I shooed their images away, sucking air through a throat that felt like a straw. I felt a warning bell deep in my brain. I was going to be late. Island time wouldn't do for an occasion like this. The thought only made the air in the car seem hotter, closer.

Fuck this, I thought as the air dragged in and out of my lungs. *Fuck all of this. Fuck island playboys who court a different girl every night of the week. Fuck girls who don't look out for their friends. Fuck detectives who threaten innocent people.*

"Fuck Mr. Milliken," I said aloud, but there was no conviction in my voice. The man had lost his daughter. Then Andrea's face swam up again, and I couldn't think of another person to tell to go fuck themselves. I'd reached my limit.

I'd been telling everyone I was in it for Ben and a bar tab. I'd been telling myself that story, too.

But maybe I'd thought finding Andrea's killer would save this island for me, preserve some pristine image of the St. Thomas that had opened its arms and taken me in.

There was even more to it, I realized, as I hunched in that gravel spit, pitched forward against my steering wheel.

A girl had been abandoned by her people, the ones who were supposed to care for her. I knew what that was like. But, unlike me, she'd lost her life on this island. It had taken all that she had, whereas it had given me back a lot— everything I had today. What kind of debt did I owe in return? What, if anything, could I give back—to her, to Andrea, to this girl who got left behind?

Maybe this island wasn't quite as deserving of the rosy glow I'd given it. We all came here seeking our version of paradise. Mine was a place where people chose their families, a place where loyalty extended beyond blood. But cracks were showing in the surface. Ben, the person I counted as a friend, was not who I thought he was. Whether or not he was a killer, he dabbled in something that had destroyed my life. Sure, he hadn't held a knife to me, but who knew what else had he done? And Dave hadn't been the innocent, puppy dog lover I'd believed him to be. He'd been sneaking around, and he, too, was tangled up in something I hated, deep in my core. And here I was, smack in the middle of a messy situation, deeply entwined in something I would normally have shied away from.

But, somehow, I knew I was where I was supposed to be.

Yes, it was complicated. And, no, I wasn't sure there were going to be black-and-white answers when this was all done. And I had certainly been more frightened in the last 36 hours than I had been in a long time.

But I didn't want to turn back. I didn't want to run way, hole up at home, curl into a ball and let someone else deal with this. Or hop a plane to a new, pristine destination.

This was my island. It might not have been the island I thought it was, but I wasn't ready to throw it all away, not yet. I'd take a stand for what happened here. And I'd find out the truth about Ben, even if it meant discovering that he was a killer. The pot—well, I wasn't ready to go there yet.

Baby steps, Lizzie.

I felt something loosen in my chest, like a knot pulling apart.

My head was no longer throbbing. I lifted it, blinked my eyes and saw the studio clearly in front of me. "The Color of Joy," the sign read.

"I could use some of that. If you were ever open," I said. I laughed, surprising myself.

I leaned back against the seat. I took a tentative breath. The air moved cleanly in and out of my lungs. I took a few more, feeling steadiness return to my body. I flexed my hands and put them on the steering wheel. I sat up straight, my shoulders lifting easily.

I checked my watch. Time to jam. I could only imagine what Detective Christopher would do if he thought I was shirking our agreement.

I put the car in gear and pulled back onto the road. I drove onto the Ritz property, parking again in the upper lot with barely a nod of acknowledgement from the guard.

I got out of my car, smoothed my shorts and paused. I looked behind me to see if Detective Christopher was looming behind me. I also didn't disguise the fact that I was doing it.

Let him see me.

The only person I could see was a short white man in a Ritz valet uniform headed toward the opposite end of the lot. Maybe the detective and his sidekicks were creeping in the bushes. The thought made my skin crawl.

I headed toward the open-air lobby, disappointed to discover that my new rush of energy was draining away. My eyes caught a view across the water through an archway. It was another snapshot-worthy day, the skies a warm blue, decorated here and there with a few cotton ball clouds. St. John sat verdant in the distance.

My eyes slid over these things, but they gave me no joy. Instead, the roiling in my gut only grew as each reluctant step took me closer to my destination.

My mind ticked ahead to meeting Mr. Milliken. What do you say to a man who's lost his daughter, someone who might even perceive you as an obstacle to his daughter's justice?

Good morning, sir. Yes, I went looking for your daughter. I thought I saw her in the woods, but it was just a deer. And then I had her phone, but I mostly used that to snoop around in her personal life. I also talked to a few people who saw her that night, but I'm no closer to knowing what happened to her than when I started. Oh, and I'm recording this conversation, just in case you're somehow involved. I'm sorry for your loss.

Sounded pretty lame to me.

I stepped off the path to let a tall woman with deep olive skin, a flowy white caftan and long, wavy black hair walk around me, a young boy at her hip. They had matching vacation tans. I would have switched places with her without hesitation—and not just because of the huge rock she sported on her left hand.

I took advantage of the pause to click the top of the pen Detective Christopher had given me, activating the recording function and triggering a surge of guilt. If I thought about it any more, I'd probably take the advice I'd given Ben: Go hide on the Northside until things cool down.

I took a deep breath, then propelled myself forward toward the Blue Water Grill.

Before I entered, my eyes flicked to the right toward the restaurant by the pool where I was supposed to meet Detective Christopher afterward to hand over the recording. All the tables were empty. For now.

I turned back and stepped into the air-conditioned restaurant. I felt the sweat immediately evaporate from my face. It would probably be the only pleasure in what would likely be a difficult morning. I tried to treasure it, but my stomach only rolled. Fuck my stomach, too, frankly.

I told the fresh-faced blonde hostess with the ivory skin— surely a recent transplant from the States to be in such pristine condition—that I was here with Mr. Milliken. She nodded with recognition and picked up a menu the size of my high-school yearbook. She turned, her blonde ponytail swishing. I followed her.

The restaurant was done up in island semi-formal: white tile floor, white walls punctuated by pleasant watercolors of typical island scenes—a boat on a beach, a woman selling mangoes—and white wicker chairs gathered around tables dressed in white tablecloths. In a different state of mind, I probably would have found it downright pleasant. But in my current state, I felt like I'd stepped into some kind of alternate reality—a sterile fantasyland.

We approached a table, where a white man stood to greet me. My first thought was that he was as tall as Dave and about as big, although the powerful shoulders underneath his navy polo shirt were probably a result of a trainer, not lifting scuba tanks all day.

I felt a pang, realizing that Dave probably shouldn't be my yardstick for men going forward.

But I couldn't think about that now. I had to focus.

Mr. Milliken's hair was dark brown with a hint of gray at the temples, swept straight back from his forehead. His eyes were an electric blue, his nose long with a round base, his lips thin. I thought I could see where Andrea got her nose, although the rest of his features were drawn with straighter, harsher angles than hers. The deep smile lines around his mouth seemed incongruous. He didn't seem like the type who smiled all that often, even under different circumstances.

Today, furrows gathered around the corners of his mouth, where his red lips went bloodlessly white. His mouth remained tight as he shook my hand firmly. "Darren Milliken," he said, his expression barely changing. He gestured at the empty seat.

"My wife won't be joining us," he said as he sat.

His voice seemed low and strong, but he spoke in hushed tones, perhaps to keep our conversation from the rest of the dining room. There were a few other families and couples scattered around, all enjoying an incredibly civilized breakfast, from the sounds of it. And here we were, smack in the middle of it all.

"She isn't taking this well," he continued.

"I don't know how you could take it well," I said, grimacing. "I also didn't know that your wife had joined you down here. Did you come down together?"

He looked at me sharply. I kept my face blank, as though I was just making conversation. And, truly, wasn't I? If Detective Christopher suspected this man, shouldn't he do his own dirty work?

He looked away. I could see him wince, as though he'd hit his funny bone under the table. A big part of me felt for this man. I imagined his wife lying in a tangle of covers up in one of the Ritz suites, refusing to get out of bed. He was alone in facing the loss of his daughter.

The other part of me mistrusted that wince, which seemed a little overdone in a man who seemed to have his emotions largely in check. It disappeared quickly, leaving his face impassive again.

I remembered the sickly look of Andrea's mother in her photos. "Was the travel difficult on her?" I asked, innocently.

Again, the sharp look. Then he spoke grudgingly. "Even though she's in remission, all that treatment takes its toll."

I nodded as if I understood, even though I didn't. I didn't know quite how to pump him for more information without seeming flat-out rude to a man who'd lost his daughter and was dealing with an ill wife. Some detective I was. I'd need to up my game—and soon.

The waiter came over, and we ordered without fanfare. I wanted the chocolate chip pancakes, but I thought maybe I should order something more solemn like eggs. I decided that this wasn't a time for denial. This was a time to accept that life was fleeting. Pancakes—and the little bit of comfort they could offer me—were what I needed.

I accepted a pour of coffee from the waiter, a tall, thin man with dark brown skin. He wore a neatly pressed orange-flowered shirt and khakis. I didn't chit chat about how he was today or where he was from, as was my usual custom. Before he left, the waiter also poured me some fancy Fiji water from a bottle that sat on the table. He replaced it in the square silver holder—they had holders for everything at the Ritz—and left.

We sat in silence for a few minutes, my guilt growing by the second. Mr. Milliken's face was downcast, and he spent a few minutes simply staring at his empty charger plate. Who was I to record this man without permission? I sipped my fancy water, but it tasted metallic in my mouth.

Finally, Mr. Milliken spoke. "I spoke with the police."

"What did they say?"

"They found her body in the marina—" He paused and swallowed. No tears, but he was clearly battling his emotions. I silently took back what I said about the man faking it earlier. Here was a father, bereft.

Finally, he swallowed again, then continued. "They have a suspect, a boat captain."

I opened my mouth and then shut it.

Then he turned his icy blue eyes on me, flat now and devoid of any emotion. "Jessie told me that he was a friend of yours."

My mouth flapped like a lake trout, but no sound came out. He held my gaze without blinking. I tried to match his stare, but I felt my hands start to shake. I should have ordered a drink for courage.

Lizzie Jordan, piss poor planner.

I wrestled with a choice. Should I appease the man and throw Ben under the bus? Or should I risk his wrath and speak my mind?

Somehow, miraculously, I was able to pause and marvel at myself for a second. Had the last two days fundamentally changed who I was? I knew what the old Lizzie would have done. She would have told it like it was. She was all I had in this world, and I couldn't afford to distrust her now.

"I don't think he did it," I said.

"And if he did?"

"Then he deserves to go jail." As I said the words, I felt an electric current run up my spine. *Did I really believe that?* But even as I questioned it, I knew that I did.

Mr. Milliken nodded once, then took a long sip of coffee.

I desperately wanted something to wet my now-dry mouth, but I knew my hands were still shaky. I squeezed my hands together in my lap, willing them to be still.

"I've never been to this island before," he said. "But I've been to Jamaica, the D.R., the Bahamas. I know how places like this work."

I furrowed my brow. *Places like this?* Interesting. I could only assume he meant the kind of places that are populated by "those people."

"We're doing our own investigation," he said quietly, tilting his head to the left where two beefy white men hunched over a two-person table that looked much smaller than ours. Or was the furniture simply dwarfed by their oversized physiques?

Ex-military, by my estimation. Or ex-linebackers. They were both sporting khaki shorts over tree-trunk thighs. The blonde one wore a short-sleeved white linen shirt that barely contained his shoulders. The darker-haired one, an olive-colored palm-printed shirt, classic Tommy Bahama. Both had coffee in front of them, no food. And both seemed quietly alert, casually scanning the room every so often. I wondered if they were allowed to eat. Maybe they had packets of jerky or other freeze-dried rations concealed about their persons.

"What are they, bodyguards?" I blurted.

"I do a lot of work in Israel and the Middle East. They travel with me everywhere."

I felt my eyebrows rise in spite of myself. Israel and the Middle East? I had assumed this was a local problem, but maybe it was more international than I could have guessed. Were we all barking up the wrong tree?

He shook his head. "No. I know what you're thinking. I'm a lawyer. I represent El Al."

I looked at him blankly.

"The Israeli airline. Where we go, kidnap is a real risk, but it's not personal. There are a lot of opportunists out there. If I happen to be in the wrong place at the wrong time, I'm toast. These two are insurance against that. I think they'll also prove useful here on St. Thomas." He smiled a bitter smile, revealing small white teeth. "I just want to bring the perpetrator to justice. I don't think we can trust that to the police, do you?"

I didn't answer, but squeezed my hands tighter under the white table cloth. Detective Christopher was going to have a field day with this.

"What have you found out so far?" Again, his cool blue eyes fixed on me.

I broke his gaze to look at his security force. Were they listening, too? They seemed casually disinterested in our conversation—but it seemed a little too studied. My clenched hands began to sweat. I separated them, then wiped them on the napkin but they still felt damp.

Where to begin? And what to leave out?

I took a deep breath. *Start with what you know, Lizzie.* "I know that she and Ben—"

"Your friend."

"Ben," I said, firmly. "He and Andrea spent some time together at Duffy's the night that she disappeared. As far as I can tell, she told Ben that she wanted to go home with him." I paused, but Mr. Milliken didn't react. His eyes stayed steady. "Then she went to tell the girls. When she didn't come back, Ben assumed that she had ditched him and gone home with her friends. The girls assumed she went home with Ben."

I paused.

"That's it?"

"I talked to the bartender and the waitress that night. They didn't see anything unusual." I swallowed. "I also had a friend at the bar that night. He doesn't think Ben did it, either, but he didn't see her go home with anyone else."

I swallowed. Yesterday's activity suddenly felt so thin. Magnus and Duncan had told me more about Jessie and her ineffective efforts at recruiting a willing partner, but I didn't think Mr. Milliken needed to know those details. Nor did he need to know that Ben had possibly known the girls previous to seeing them at Duffy's. And if I told him about the phone,

I was sure his two minions would tear up the island until they found it, and that wouldn't be good.

"I have a few more things I wanted to follow up on today," I added gamely.

"Such as?"

I sat up in my chair like a lightning bolt. I realized I was recording this entire conversation for Detective Christopher. Time for some damage control.

I jerked my foot to the right, spilling my bag over.

"Oh, shoot," I said, aiming what I hoped was a charming smile toward Andrea's father. I held up a finger and bent over the bag, cursing my inane choice of words. I was painfully aware that I wasn't cut out for this spy stuff.

I made a show of gathering the few items that had fallen out of my bag, a set of keys, a tube of pineapple SPF lip balm.

I spoke from the floor. "The police came to see me this morning and they asked me not to get involved."

As I stuffed the items back in, I clicked the pen on the outside of my purse once.

"Does that worry you, Miss Jordan?" Mr. Milliken asked, reaching for his cup of coffee.

"A little. But I'm not sure it will stop me."

"And why is that, if you don't mind me asking?"

"Ben is my friend. This is my home. Your daughter lost her life here and I think she deserves to be spoken for."

"And you don't think the police will do that?"

I sat up straighter as I felt more energy crackle up my spine. Hadn't he just said they wouldn't? Was he testing me? Or had Detective Christopher made a deal of his own with Mr. Milliken? Did he have his very own recording device trained on me? Maybe one of Mr. Milliken's buttons was a camera, broadcasting to the detective—or his friends at the next table. I reached for my Fiji water and drained the glass to stall.

Who was this girl I'd become? I wondered as the cool water slid down my throat. *Lizzie Jordan, little mouse?* This was my island. It was time to start acting like it.

As I placed my hand back in my lap, I curled it into a fist. That crackling in my spine? I was going to use it.

"I don't trust the police," I said. "The detective who talked to me seemed genuine enough, but I have a few other leads I want to follow. The girls talked to a few other people during their trip. I want to get their stories. It's rare that something happens on this island without someone noticing. It's just a matter of finding the right person."

He nodded and lifted the charger plate in front of him, under which I saw a wad of money with a one hundred-dollar bill on the outside. He put his hand over it and slid it on the table toward me, nudging it under the edge of my own charger.

"What's that?"

"I need your eyes on the ground. I need someone who isn't a part of . . . *things* down here. I'd like you to keep talking to people and let me know what you discover."

My hand moved the money under my charger while my mind whirred. Was this another test? Was Detective Christopher trying to catch me taking money? Should I turn the recording back on?

My eyes once again flicked over to the two beefcakes at the adjacent table. The blond one stared back. I'd once read the term "eyefucking" in a gritty book about Baltimore street life. I now knew what it meant.

That was all I needed. The perverse part of me kicked in and I gave the guy a big, 100-watt smile. His expression didn't change. Sheesh. Professionals. They took themselves way too seriously.

Back to the money. I lifted my hands off the table and raised my hands toward Mr. Milliken in surrender. "I can't take your money."

"What money?" he said. He didn't even crack a smile. The man was frosty. I'd give him that.

"The police threatened me. If I keep Nancy Drew-ing around, they'll put me in jail. So I can't take your money. I don't know if I can finish the job."

"I can't believe an idle threat from these inept cops would hold a girl like you back."

Oh, he was good. He was taking a page right out of Ben's book and appealing to my personal pride. Maybe they were more alike than Mr. Milliken realized.

Then the corners of his mouth sagged down into an inverse smile. "You could simply consider it motivation. No obligation."

At that moment, the food arrived. I felt a stab of panic as the waiter reached to remove my charger plate. I slapped my hand on it, palm down. "Do you mind if I keep this one?" I flashed a smile at him.

He looked confused, but didn't question me. He simply waited until I removed my hand, then put the new plate on top. It held a giant stack of fluffy pancakes, dotted with chocolate chips and topped with a flourish of whipped cream the size of my fist.

Despite my joy when I ordered, the decadence of the dish turned my stomach. Here I was with a plate full of whipped cream and sugar, and Andrea was never going to have another breakfast with her father. A father, I might add, who I was taping on behalf of the police. I should have ordered bread and water. That's what I deserved.

As the waiter put down Mr. Milliken's scrambled eggs and bacon, my mind flicked to the recording. I probably had to turn it back on. I'm not sure whether the detective would buy a little lie about a malfunction if it lasted nearly the entire conversation.

I needed a distraction. "Don't they get to eat?" I asked, lifting my nose at the goon squad.

"They eat plenty," he said, completely absorbed in the task of shaking salt out of a dispenser clogged by humidity.

Charming. I leaned down and pretended to fuss with my bag, clicking the pen back. I'd worry about the explanation later. In the meantime, I'd throw the detective a bone by getting the conversation back on track.

"Can I ask you a little about Andrea? I've talked to the girls about her, and I've asked people who met her down here, but I wondered if you would tell me a little about her."

He put down his fork and I saw him go very still.

"If it's too difficult—" I started.

"She was my only child."

Then we sat in silence, neither one of us moving. I watched a mosquito bump my elbow, then land. I let it do its work, afraid to break the spell. I sat and counted my breaths, keeping them as quiet as I could.

Finally, when I'd finished my second round of ten, he sighed, and the tension broke. His voice was matter-of-fact, as though we were discussing the weather. "I came from a family of boys. We . . . we raised ourselves like a pack of wild dogs. My mother was a nurse. My father sold encyclopedias. They both worked all hours, but we never had a lot of money. We fought a lot, my parents, my brothers, everybody. I was the only one who made it to college and eventually law school. I met Elena, my wife, there. I never really meant to have a child. It just happened. When she told me we were having a girl, I was terrified. I was terrified I would drop her, terrified I would break her . . . and then I was terrified that the world would break her."

I made what I hoped was a sympathetic noise with my mouth, but he didn't need the encouragement. He kept talking.

"My work took me away a lot. Elena was always so permissive with Andrea. She let her do anything." He shook his head. "She's not a strong woman. So when I came home, I would hit the roof. It only made things worse. She and I—" He broke off. "If I had another chance, I'd do it differently."

I nodded and took a bite of pancake while I let his words hang in the air. There was an explosion of sugar and fat on my tongue, but I barely noticed.

I cut another wedge of pancake and turned to Mr. Milliken. "Did she have a boyfriend back home?"

But the time for back-and-forth conversation was over, apparently. "Where is Andrea's cell phone?" he blurted.

My fork paused on its way to my mouth.

"I know you have it."

"I—" I stammered, my mind struggling for purchase as though it hit a patch of ice on a sidewalk. It started scrambling even faster as the blonde man got up from the other table and took two quick paces over.

"Is there a problem here, sir?"

"I'm not sure yet," Mr. Milliken answered.

I tried to look calm so Mr. Milliken would deactivate his blonde bulldog. My body tensed. For the umpteenth time in the last 36 hours, I was ready to run.

"Things will not be okay very quickly if Miss Jordan is not forthcoming about the location of Andrea's cell phone," Mr. Milliken continued.

The blonde man leaned forward a few inches.

So that's what this was all about. I had something they wanted. I desperately wanted a drink—and a moment to think. I had neither.

At that moment, the waiter glided to a stop at our table, still wearing his smile, in spite of the blonde goon looming over our table. "How is your breakfast?" he asked, deftly topping off my coffee. "Can I get you anything at the moment?"

His words snapped me out of my flustered state. I felt my mind go into gear. "I'd like an Absolut Bloody Mary," I said. "And make it a double." My tone of voice dared anyone to argue with me.

The waiter nodded and moved off to fill my order.

One down, many more to go. *Small victories*, I told myself.

When I spoke, my voice came out hard. "Threats aren't going to work against me," I said, returning to my pancakes and cutting a triangle out of the stack with surgical precision. "The police already know everything there is to know about me, including the fact that I'm here with you." I shrugged. "I don't really know what you have for leverage at this point." I put the pancake wedge in my mouth and chewed thoughtfully.

My Bloody Mary arrived unexpectedly quickly. This was the Ritz, so they served it in a smaller, tulip-shaped glass, rather than the pint glass you often saw down here. However, I could see a nice clear bubble of liquid at the bottom of the tulip. Absolut to the rescue.

I thought I saw the waiter wink at me, and I offered him a small smile back. At least I had one ally in this dining room.

I took a long sip and winced as vodka with a hint of tomato juice hit the back of my throat. It wasn't the best palate cleanser for chocolate pancakes. But as it slid down my esophagus and started a warm fire in my belly, I didn't care.

I leveled my gaze at Milliken. "The police have Andrea's cell phone. Nothing we can do about that. They *do* have leverage against me."

I took another hit of my drink. "As for the rest, I'll consider it, but not if you continue to threaten me."

I took one more bite of my pancakes, then put my fork upside down on top of the stack of plates. I slid the stack toward me, dangerously near the edge. As I'd hoped, I felt the pile of money drop softly into my lap before I deftly returned the plates to their original location.

I took another long sip of my Bloody Mary, sucking the concoction through the straw until I heard that satisfying ice-sucking sound.

I reached down and pulled my purse into my lap. I slid the money quickly into the front flap.

"Now, is there anything else I can do for you?" I asked.

The two men simply stared at me.

Finally, Milliken spoke. "I'm very sorry to hear that Andrea's cell phone is in the hands of the police," he said.

The dark-haired man got up and joined his colleague at the table. I imagined them rushing me from both sides, hands clamping on my shoulder and wrists. Would Detective Christopher come to my rescue if these guys decided to get rough? Or would I have to appeal to the other Ritz-goers in the room? I clamped a hand on my purse, prepared to knock back my wicker chair and run like hell.

I think it's fair to say that my paranoia had reached another peak.

"I expect you to stay in touch, Miss Jordan," Milliken said.

I felt the men retreat an inch or two. Nothing for them to do here.

Milliken reached in his pocket and withdrew a white business card, embossed with black lettering. He put it down on the table and slid it toward me. It had only his name and cell phone on it.

"This is my personal cell phone number."

I nodded, even though I was a little tickled by the absurdity of his statement. Rich people were so funny. Whose cell phone did I expect him to give me? Someone else's?

I contained my mirth as I tucked the card into my palm, embossed side out. I ran my fingers over the letters. Milliken had expectations of me, and this card was a reminder of them.

Without confirming or denying them, I simply rose without a word. I turned and walked out of the restaurant, planting each step with extra care to ensure I made it out of the restaurant without stumbling. I had an image to maintain.

I waited until I was around the corner to find a surface to collapse on. The vodka had propped me up temporarily, but I was shaking like a leaf. I couldn't believe I'd pulled that off.

I felt a sting on my elbow. When I investigated with my fingers, I felt the itchy lump the restaurant's mosquito had left behind. It was the only mark on me. I felt lucky.

My hand rested on the bulge in the front flap of my purse. I'd decide about that later. I could always return it. Or I could spy for him.

But first, I had to find the detective and get myself off the hook.

I sat for another minute until I thought my legs could hold me, then I went to find the detective.

I found Detective Christopher under a straw fedora. I have to admit, it looked smart with his beige suit. I also wondered if his fashion sense lost or gained him points with his fellow officers.

The detective's arms were draped casually over the arms of his seat, a red drink in front of him. You would have thought he was a tourist. An over-dressed one, albeit.

"Where do you do your shopping?" I asked, dumping my body in the chair across from his.

"Puerto Rico," he replied, rolling his Rs perfectly like a gentle purr. "I've got family there." He held out a hand, palm up. The message was clear. He wanted his recording device.

"What, no drink first?" I asked, pointing at his.

"Cranberry juice."

"No fun."

"On the job."

"Milliken has two bodyguards with him."

"The pen, Miss Jordan."

"I'm trying to hand it to you in a more subtle way, you dummy. Just in case they're watching."

The corner of his mouth twitched upward and I realized I was studying his mouth way too intently. I couldn't possibly be thinking of what it would be like to kiss him, was I?

Lizzie Jordan, desperate for comfort.

Did I have a rule about consorting with police officers? I might need to establish one—and fast.

He interrupted my thoughts. "Trust me when I say that I am not worried about those two. The pen?"

"What if they decide to pursue some vigilante justice?"

"The pen."

I pulled it off my purse and slid it across the table under my hand. "Did I already mention that you're no fun?"

He shook his head at what I figured he would call foolishness. He put the pen in the inside pocket of his suit jacket, a gesture I'd only seen in the movies. "This is the last time I hope to lay eyes on you for a while," he said, his eyes skipping over me and toward the beach beyond.

"And here I thought I amused you."

A smile spread across his face quickly, as though he couldn't stop himself. His eyes slid over to mine and I suddenly felt a fire in my belly that had nothing to do with that Absolut.

"Take good care of yourself, Miss Jordan."

He stood with easy grace, grabbing his cranberry juice and weaving his way through two young boys in colorful swim trunks chasing each other on the pool deck. He didn't even break stride. He had style, that Detective Christopher.

I couldn't help but watch him until he disappeared out of sight. What was the matter with me? That man threatened to put me in jail, I reminded myself. But he did have a rather pleasant face.

I shifted in my chair, feeling a slick of sweat under my thighs. Another hot one. I leaned back and contemplated the day ahead of me. Since I wouldn't be spending it in jail, my options were wide open.

I could even order another double Bloody Mary, funded by the cash in the front of my purse. Then I could order another and watch all the rich people of the Ritz get fuzzy right in front of me.

My phone buzzed in my purse, breaking the dream. This thing would be the death of me.

I debated ignoring it. But curiosity got the better of me and I reached into my purse.

I had a text message from a 567 area code: "I need to talk to you. Meet me at the bar at Coconut Cove."

My heart beat a little tattoo. Coconut Cove was the bar and restaurant on the Members' side of the Ritz resort. I was back in the game.

I glanced up. No sign of Detective Christopher. I was ready to bolt out of my seat, but I paused. Could this be a setup?

Nah. He had better things to do, right?

With the vodka continuing to give me more courage than I was due, I slipped out of my seat and took the short flight of stairs down to the beach. Even if someone spotted me, maybe it would just look like I wanted a stroll on the beach.

I weaved in and out of blue beach chairs. They were fitted with shades that reminded me of the canopies you used to see over old-fashioned baby carriages. The chairs even had little flags bolted to them that you could swivel upward to signal your desperate need for a beachside cocktail. What a way to live.

At the end of the beach, I picked up the concrete path that led to the residents' area, which gave me a clear view of the Members' Club side of the bay. I saw long limbs far from shore cutting through the water with a purpose. I wondered if it was Jessie. I watched her strong stroke, clocking that split second in which both of her arms were in the water and she was invisible from the shore.

It was a good thing that it was almost eleven o'clock. If she were swimming out that far earlier in the morning, she'd be liable to be run over by one of the charter boats picking up their Ritz guests for the day.

I continued to stare. Today, the cove's water boasted what seemed like at least ten different shades of blue. Despite the fact that I'd been pressured with jail time that morning, executed surveillance on a man who had just lost his daughter and accepted questionable money, I felt a little smile creep onto my face. If nothing, the physical beauty of this place was truly astonishing.

I broke my reverie. I needed to get moving.

For the second time in two days, I crossed over the volcanic rock separating the two sides of the resort, the sun pressing heavily on my shoulders. As I passed the lounge chairs on the resort's second beach, I realized that they lacked canopies and drink flags. Were people who owned a Ritz timeshare somehow less entitled to shade and succor? It seemed like something rich people might riot about.

Manicured landscaping rose at my left, then dropped away to reveal a restaurant and bar, charmingly named Coconut Cove, although, to my estimation, there was nothing particularly coconut-y about it. At the center of the restaurant was a square bar with a roof to protect its patrons from the Caribbean's intense sun and brief rain showers.

I scanned the bar, but its stools were empty. However, I noticed that the bartender on duty was a man of around fifty. He was wiping his hands on a blue towel. His orange flowered shirt was crisp but loose on his thin upper body.

When I got closer, I saw that his nametag read, "Grady." I nearly did a little dance right there and then. This must have been the bartender who served the girls.

Things were looking up.

My mind flashed to the promise I'd made to Detective Christopher. I wasn't detecting. I was merely getting a drink to calm my nerves after a stressful morning.

I leaned against the cool white tiles. "Grady?"

"Yes, indeed," he answered, eyes brightening in his deep brown face. His words were melodic with a light Caribbean accent. What island, I wasn't sure.

He wasn't a man with a lot of spare flesh to him, and his head was shaved bald, both of which emphasized his square jaw and his large, dark eyes. They looked kind, but maybe I was just projecting hopefulness. He smiled quickly, showing a flash of big teeth. He slid a white-and-blue Ritz logo cocktail napkin toward me. "What can I get for you today? A rum punch?"

"Thank you," I said and watched him as he pulled out a tall tulip glass even taller than the Bloody Mary I'd received at breakfast. I liked this man already. He added a healthy pour of dark Cruzan rum, then topped it off with a pink punch mixture that I knew was made in-house. He dropped in a cherry, then carefully placed an orange slice on the rim before sliding a straw into the glass.

"Enjoy," he said.

I took a sip. I hadn't had one of these in quite a while, not since a boat guest had treated me to dinner at the resort a few years ago. The sweetness of the fruit punch hit my tongue, followed by the sharp note of the rum. I nearly shivered in delight. I had to hand it to the Ritz. They did rum punch right. I slid onto the tall seat in front of Grady.

"Charge it to your room?" He flashed that smile again, his hand poised over the computer to complete the transaction.

I was tempted to lie to him, just like I'd lied to myself about what I was doing at this bar. But I lost my nerve. I couldn't deceive this man. After all, hadn't I dealt in enough deception today?

"No, I'll pay cash. My name's Lizzie. I'm looking into the disappearance of a girl who was staying here." I held out my hand.

His smile faded as he shook my hand, his grip warm and his handshake a little damp. "I heard about that."

"You did?"

"The police came here. I hear her father is on his way, may be here by now." He shook his head and looked down at his hands. "I can't imagine losing a child."

"Do you have kids?"

His face lifted. "Two. One girl and one boy." He reached into his back pocket and pulled out a brown leather wallet, worn at the edges. He flipped to a picture of two kids. The boy was about four, his skin the same deep brown as his father's. He had his father's bright eyes, but his expression was solemn above his little suit, complete with red bow tie. His big sister sat next to him in a bright white dress with a red bow, her chubby face lit with a brilliant smile.

"They're beautiful kids."

He nodded. "They're not young anymore." He flipped over to show me a picture of them as teenagers, standing next to a palm tree in front of an orange sunset. The boy was just as solemn as his first picture. The girl's face had slimmed with puberty and its expression was annoyed, her posture impatient.

"They're in St. Lucia," he continued. "I want to bring them here, but I don't have the money yet." He laughed and shook his head. "Maya hates having her photo taken. Fifteen years old and getting defiant."

I hated to follow up a discussion about his kids with immediate questions about death and disappearance—but I had to do it. Such was my lot.

I took a breath and dived in. "Do you remember meeting Andrea, the girl who disappeared?"

He sighed and the joy leaked out of his face again, creating hollows underneath his high cheekbones. "The police asked me the same."

Damn. Still, I pressed on. "The girls told me they drank at your bar. It would have been . . . Monday night."

He looked a touch annoyed at my prompt. "I remember them. I remember everybody. It's my job. I made them Bushwackers. First time for them—except for that one girl, who's been here before, Jessie. She made sure I knew her name. Gave me a nice big tip."

"Was there anyone else at the bar that night?"

"Two fisherman. One young, one older."

My ears perked up. The girls hadn't mentioned this. "Do you remember what boat?"

"Their boat has the name of my daughter—*Maya*. The older one went and got me one of their T-shirts when I told them."

"Did the girls talk to the guys?"

"They did, until it was time to close." He paused and I watched his eyes flick up in recollection. "No, the other girl with them went home early. Jessie and Andrea stayed." I felt my eyebrows lift. He didn't know Becky's name?

He must have read my face because he shrugged. "The third girl, she didn't talk much. The other two did all the talking for her. More than enough for her."

"What happened when you closed?"

Grady's mouth twisted and looked down at the rack of bottles below the bar. He turned one a few degrees so all the plastic spouts pointed the same way. "I don't talk about my guests' movements. I'm sure you can understand that."

I nodded but kept silent, hoping the fact that he had a daughter would loosen his own set of personal rules. I took another sip of my rum punch and savored that heady mix. You could barely taste the rum, but it was there—a dark, delicious undercurrent. I heard once that the secret ingredient in the Ritz punch was guava juice, but it couldn't be that simple. Maybe it was the posh atmosphere that made the real difference. Or the posh price.

Grady still hadn't budged. I'd have to get creative. Maybe I could appeal to his paternal side with a little white lie.

I leaned forward, lowering my voice. "The reason I want to know is that I'm working for Andrea's father. He thought I might be able to help him find out what happened to his daughter so he and his wife can find some peace."

Grady looked away for a moment, out over the pool and its surrounding chairs, which were starting to fill with guests. He pressed his lips together, then he turned back to me. "I don't see what harm it can do to tell you what I know. It's not much. The third girl left as soon as she ate. She didn't say anything. I just looked up one moment and she was gone. Then, when I closed out their check, the girls went back to their rooms and came back with swimsuits. The four of them, the girls and the two fishermen, went off together toward the beach."

"I would have thought Jessie knew better. She's been here before," I said.

He tilted his head slightly but said nothing.

"You know—fishermen. Not the best guys to get involved with? A different girl leaving their boats every day of the week?"

Grady shrugged, his expression neutral. "I wouldn't know anything about that. Jessie came back through here soon after while I was cleaning up so I don't think she got into much. Andrea . . ." He shrugged again. "She could have come back through, too, but I didn't see her."

"How long after they left did Jessie come back through?"

His mouth turned downward as he thought. "Maybe five minutes. Not long."

I felt a wrinkle form between my brows. Why had Jessie left so quickly? Magnus had implied that she was looking for some action. But maybe she was like the dog that caught the school bus and didn't know what to do with it.

I turned back to Grady. "What did you think of them?"

He squinted at me, as though he hadn't heard me right.

I tried to sound casual. "You see people come in and out all day long. I'm sure you had an opinion about these girls."

He looked back out at the water and tapped the bar with long fingers.

"They appeared to be nice girls," he said, grabbing a towel and wiping a small water splash off the bar tiles.

A waitress with brown skin a few shades lighter than Grady and a thick, low ponytail of dreadlocks walked up and placed a slip of paper on the rubber mat at the side of the bar. Grady glanced at it, then reached for a blender. His movements were precise yet easy as he poured an eight-count of rum plus piña colada mix into a blender. He added four scoops of ice and started the concoction mixing.

As the machine whirred, I took the opportunity to eat my cherry. I never knew what to do with that damn stem. Leaving it on the napkin seemed so gauche. I tucked it under a corner of the napkin instead.

Grady poured the contents of his blender into two hurricane glasses, then topped them each with whipped cream and a cherry. His only fault so far, I thought. Whipped cream with alcohol gave me the willies.

When he was done, I could see him pause before he turned back to me. I let him take his time. Waiting was a skill that I acquired and honed in St. Thomas. If you weren't good at it, you wouldn't make it on island. I'd put my time in at the bank, at the grocery store, at the Bureau of Motor Vehicles, at the counter to buy tickets for the ferry to St. John. I was confident that could outwait anyone, Grady included.

Finally, he rested both hands on the bar in front of me and leaned in, his eyebrows lifted.

"Is it true they found her?" he asked.

His eyes were so dark, it was hard to see where his pupil ended and his iris began. I nodded. "In Red Hook yesterday. In the water. I'm surprised you didn't hear."

"I hoped it was only talk."

He let out a sigh and shook his head, leaning heavily on the bar. I noticed wrinkles in his forehead that I hadn't seen before. "You asked me what I thought of them. Three young, beautiful girls on vacation at the Ritz-Carlton where you have all of this—" He waved his hands at the manicured palm trees, the landscaped pools and the perfect lines of lounge chairs. "Shouldn't have a care in the world. *Too bless to be stress*, you know?" He closed his eyes briefly. "Still, something was not right. Maybe the curse of having too much given to them. I couldn't say. When the two girls stayed, I thought they might tell me." He picked up the dirty blender and began to rinse it in a stainless steel sink behind the bar. "And now one of them is gone."

We sat in silence for a few minutes.

When I reached into my bag to pay for my rum punch, using Milliken's money—expenses, right?—Grady waved his hand at me. My rum punch was on him.

I dug into the proletariat side of my purse where I had small bills and left him a five. He tried to wave that away, too, but I insisted.

"Thank you," I said.

He nodded and offered me a wan smile. I wondered if he was thinking about his children.

I finished the rest of my drink, then lifted the orange off the rim.

I turned away from Grady, toward the beach. I was lifting the orange toward my mouth when a claw closed around my left bicep and shook my arm with alarming force.

I could feel fingernails digging into my flesh, and the morning's indignities flared up. I ripped my arm out of the grip and swung around, ready to fight. I wasn't much of a physical fighter, I confess, but I hoped that the pure adrenaline coursing through my veins would be enough.

As I reared to my full height and finished my spin, I saw my assailant cringe, her hands flying up to cover a face half-covered by a perfect wall of dark bangs.

It was Becky.

"Jesus Christ," I hissed. "What the hell are you doing?"

My limbs were absolutely vibrating with energy. This was the kind of day that shortened your life, no question.

"What took you so long? And what were you talking to him about?" she asked, her eyebrows pinched, her lips pursed in a pout. She wasn't wearing sunglasses, and I could see bags under her dark eyes. Someone wasn't sleeping well.

"What do you think?" I demanded, taking a step backward to reclaim my personal space.

She was silent.

"I'm guessing you're the one who texted me?" I asked.

She nodded and her face went slack. She looked like she'd been through the wringer.

I sighed. "I'm sorry. It's been a hell of a morning, and you startled me."

"We have to hurry," Becky said, reaching out and tugging on the hem of my shorts like a child.

I hesitated a second, but Becky's claw closed around my arm and she dragged me over to a deserted infinity pool. Apparently, the Ritz had so many pools that some were entirely empty. Incredible.

She chose a grouping of two lounge chairs, each padded in a burnt umber fabric. I freed my arm from Becky's clutch and stretched out, sinking into the warm cushion. The heat sank into my bones like a balm. This morning had taken a lot out of me. If I could just shut my eyes for thirty seconds—

"Hey," Becky hissed.

I let my head fall to the left to see her perched on the edge of her lounger, her talons wrapped around the side of the chair, their knuckles white.

She was wearing a brightly-colored cover up in vivid shades of green, orange, yellow and pink in a floral pattern. The bright colors were meant to look festive, but they washed her out, leaving her looking wan. The whole thing floated loosely on her frame like a caftan meant for a much larger woman. Her gaze dropped somewhere between her knees and my chair, then darted toward the shoreline. In other words, it went anywhere but my face.

"You wanted to talk to me?" I prompted.

She nodded and pressed her lips together. I felt my frustration rise.

Time to shake things up.

I glanced out at the water. "Maybe we should wait to talk until Jessie gets back. That was her in the water, wasn't it? You girls left out some pretty important information and I'm starting to wonder why you're lying to me."

I waited for a reaction. Her mouth fell open into a small O, but still no words came out.

Then, quick as a flash, Becky's hand shot out and grabbed my wrist, her bony fingers a manacle. "Did you see her? When they found her?"

I shook my head.

"Her parents are offering a reward. I heard Jessie talking about it this morning."

Her hand tightened even further, and I winced. Becky couldn't clock in at more than 115, but she did have a grip on her. Suddenly, she released her fingers and sat back. I swung my legs toward her and sat up. I was too vulnerable lying down.

Who knew what she would grab for next?

"Are you ready to talk now?" I asked her.

"Talk about what?" A shadow passed over me, taking the warmth of the sun with it.

I turned to see Jessie behind me, her blonde hair in long shanks around her shoulders, their tips drizzling salt water. The sun was behind her, leaving her face in darkness. I wasn't shocked to see her in one of the most functional bikinis I'd seen in a long time: a top with a high neck that dampened even the slightest premonition of breasts, plus a bottom whose matronly cut was usually seen on women over fifty. I could barely see her belly button, which was a shame. The girl was built more solidly than waifish Becky, but there was something decidedly wholesome about her athletic figure. It deserved better than that drab suit.

In a way, I was glad to see Jessie. It was time to start asking the tough questions of both of these two. I plastered a big, shit-eating grin on my face. "Oh, I just wanted to have a little chat about why you girls have been lying to me."

"What do you mean?" Jessie said, her tone wary. She made no motion to join Becky and me. I couldn't help but wonder if she was just going to take off running. Maybe she could make it a triathlon if she stumbled on a bicycle.

"I thought you might say that." I dug around in my purse until I found my little notebook and pen. I flipped it open to the relevant page with a flourish. "Let's start with . . . Tuesday. You didn't meet Ben for the first time at Duffy's, did you?"

"I never said we did," Jessie shot back.

I still couldn't get a good read on her face and it was pissing me off. "Look, can you sit down? It feels like I'm talking to *Attack of the 50 Foot Woman* and it's bugging the shit out of me."

I could sense a retort forming, but she contained it and sat next to Becky, her shoulders slumped in protest.

"Thank you," I said.

All I got was a fish-eye stare in return. I barged ahead anyway. "First, Ben. Did you or did you not meet him at Duffy's for the first time Wednesday night?" My eyes flicked to Becky, but, once again, she was mute, her eyes focused on some fascinating spot on the ground.

I looked back at Jessie, who was squinting in the sunlight. "Fine. I met him on Tuesday at the water sports desk and he took us sailing with him for like an hour. But you already seem to know that."

"I saw the pictures." I paused, trying to gauge reactions. Nothing from Becky. Jessie stared straight at me, but I thought I saw her eye twitch.

"What about Monday?"

"Monday?" Jessie shrugged. "I don't know."

I leaned forward, my elbows on my knees. "I'm a little confused here. I thought you wanted to find Andrea."

"Obviously."

"Then why not just tell me what happened?"

Jessie's eyes were ringed with angry red lines where her goggles had been. She looked at me coldly.

The three of us sat without speaking. Together, we listened to the pool filtration system mutter.

The silence lingered. I fell back on my island training and let it stretch.

I blinked as two children ran by in long maroon jackets. One was wearing an eye patch and the other carried a plastic sword. Must be time for the Ritz's weekly mock pirate battle on the beach. Neither of the girls took notice.

Jessie finally shifted, dropping her shoulders and straightening her back. "What does Monday matter? She disappeared on Wednesday."

"Forget it. I'll go to the *Maya* myself and get the answers from those guys. What's the deal with salsa?"

Jessie made a face. "I'm not sure why you keep asking questions if you think you know all the answers. Go ahead. Talk to those guys. You'll find out."

I was puzzled, but I didn't let it show. Was salsa some new thing the kids were doing? "Who's Zack?" I fired back.

I saw two patches of red appear on Jessie's cheekbones. I had her there, I thought.

But then she stood abruptly. "You're a bitch," she said, and took off, fleeing the infinity pool area. I saw her zag around a bougainvillea bush, then duck between two beige buildings. One thing I could say for her bathing suit: It was equipped for a fast escape.

"What the hell was that?" I asked Becky.

Her mouth twisted briefly. "She's kind of touchy about that."

"I can tell. Who is this guy?"

"He worked at Jessie's office."

I made a circling motion with my hand. *Spill it.*

"He was all she could talk about. Zack this, Zack that. Then she took Andrea to her office Christmas party and, before she knew it, Zack and Andrea were, uh, dating."

"That sounds kind of shitty."

"Jessie was a mess. She won't speak to Zack."

"And Andrea?"

Becky shrugged. "She got a pass."

"Why?"

Becky shrugged again. The girl seemed to have no other gestures at her disposal. "Andrea is Jessie's friend, not mine," she said.

"Meaning?"

"Jessie's the one who invited her on this trip."

"I thought all three of you were friends."

Again, the shoulders went up and down. "I met Jessie in high school. She met Andrea when we were all in college together. Andrea lived with us senior year, but she was never really my friend, not the way she and Jessie were friends. They studied together, went out together, binged together and dieted together. The week they were on that apple cider vinegar diet thing? So gross."

"Not you? You weren't out there, partying with them?"

"I had to study," Becky said. "School was hard for me. My parents expected good grades. I had to work for them. Jessie used to want that, too, but not senior year."

Her face screwed up quickly, and I thought she might cry. "I don't know how Andrea pulled something like the Zack thing and still got invited to St. Thomas. She got away with everything."

Not this time, I thought.

"Almost," Becky said, as though she could hear my thoughts.

But something still bothered me about Becky's account. "Andrea didn't even seem that into Zack. He kept texting her long after it was clear that she wasn't really that interested."

Becky sniffed. She'd gotten control of her emotions again, or so it seemed. "She was always like that. She likes being chased, but once she catches her prey, she either gets bored or bails or both."

"It doesn't really sound like you're close with her at all."

The shoulder routine again.

"Any idea why she might be taking sad selfies?"

"I'm not sure she needed a reason. She liked the attention." Then Becky paused, maybe to reconsider speaking ill of the dead. "I think her mom was sick," she added.

"You don't seem to know much about Andrea."

"I already told you. We're not really friends." Her words came out petulant. At that moment, I thought I understood Becky's standoffishness, as well as why she kept disappearing into the background. She was the third wheel, and she knew it.

"Becky, why did you even come on this vacation?"

She didn't move. Maybe she had been asking herself this same question.

When she finally spoke, her voice came out in a whisper. "I guess I thought it would be different."

I nodded. And, man, had I heard that one a million times. People showed up on island every day, hoping that a change of scenery would bring about a change in their lives.

It usually works—for about three months. After that, it becomes clear that your problems hitchhike a ride down to paradise with you.

I turned back to Becky. "So if you're not 'really friends' with Andrea, why did you text me? Do you really care what happened to her?" *Or did you just want a sympathetic ear?*

"I'm not some kind of monster. Of course I didn't want her to *die*."

"Well, it's a little too late for that."

I saw her face contort. I knew I had to rein it in or I would lose her. I leaned forward with what I hoped was empathy in my eyes. "Becky, you can at least level with me. Then we can find out who killed her."

Becky turned even paler, if it was possible, and her hand flew to her mouth. I thought she might puke. I watched waves of emotions crash over her face. I put a hand out to comfort her, but we were too far apart. I ended up giving her knee two awkward pats.

With a strangled cry, she stood, then bolted like a spooked gazelle.

So much for reining it in.

Becky headed in the same direction as Jessie, but at the last minute, she made a sharp zig to the left and headed back toward the hotel side of the resort.

I thought about following her, but I stayed put. It felt like things were shaking loose, but I wasn't exactly sure why.

I was tempted to go back to the bar and get another drink, but I suspected the sticker shock of that place was enough to turn me sober. I could have shelled out one of Milliken's hundreds, but I didn't feel ready to spend his money yet. As it stood, I could still give it all back intact.

Plus, I knew I could get a rum with twice the punch at half the price down in Red Hook.

So for the first time in a long time, I skipped the drink. I didn't plan on making it a habit.

Instead, I reached into my purse and pulled out my notebook and the Bad Ass Coffee pen that was now mine. I guess in addition to "amateur private eye," "possible accessory after the fact to murder," and "accomplice to a fugitive," you could also add "thief."

I glanced at the "Lies Ben Told Me" list and started a "Lies the Girls Told Me" list on the same page. Maybe it was a bit strong, but I was feeling a little self-righteous. I added a few notes:

-Tuesday (Ben + Hobie cat)
-Zack (and weird text)
-Monday with fisherman

That seemed to cover it, but it didn't do anything to soothe a growing sense of discomfort. This had all started out so simply. Go up to the Ritz and snag a glimpse of the girl who had eluded Ben, the One-Man Tourist Trap.

That thought felt too flip. The girl in question was dead. Her friends were lying to me. And the person I had formerly trusted most in this situation, Ben, had had left a few things out, too.

Taken by themselves, each of these pieces of information seemed innocuous—a Hobie cat ride, an illicit invitational with a few fisherman, a series of odd texts—but taken together, I felt like they had to mean something.

What was I missing here?

My mind flicked to that cache of pot in Ben's apartment. Maybe I'd been looking in the wrong place.

I would have loved more time to contemplate this possibility, but a hand clamped around my arm. Expecting Becky, I simply swiveled my head lazily in the direction of the clamper. Maybe I could get the real truth out of her now.

I started violently when I found Detective Christopher's face about six inches from mine, his face contorted with anger.

17

I desperately tried to pull back from the detective's grip, but he held me close.

In fact, I was so close that I could see a bead of sweat on his upper lip over a hint of dark stubble. I didn't know how it was possible, but he still smelled like fresh laundry.

"Miss Jordan, you are going to tell me exactly what's going on here." His dark eyes flashed in his face.

I smiled as sweetly as I could. "Taking advantage of my being a welcomed guest on the Ritz-Carlton property to work on my tan?"

He shook his head.

"What? All I'm doing is writing in a little notebook. There's nothing illegal about that." I was giving him my best, but my words rang hollow even to me.

He kept his grip on my arm and held out his other hand, palm up.

The notebook was in my free hand. I held it out in the opposite direction. "No, that's my private property."

He raised his eyebrows at me.

"I thought we were in this together," I said, weakly.

"I believe my words were, 'You get near anything I don't like, and it's jail time for you.'"

"But that was just an idle threat, right?" I tried a smile.

His face hardened and I heard a clatter of metal. Before I knew what had happened, he had one wrist cuffed and was pulling me up from the chair. My notebook fell from my hand as my body went numb with shock. I was being arrested. Me, the girl who had cooperated, albeit reluctantly, now had her arms behind her back, her wrist locked in cold handcuffs.

With a flourish, the detective bent over and retrieved my notebook, which he placed in his breast pocket. He reached down again to grab my purse by its strap, holding it out from his body like a man carrying a bear trap.

He took hold of my bicep again with a hot hand. "Walk," he said tersely.

Son of a bitch.

The handcuffs made me compliant, and I found my legs moving under me as he guided me around the infinity pool and down one of the Ritz's neat paths. Two women in workout clothes carrying Ritz-Carlton coffee cups stared as the detective frog-marched me by. I felt my face grow hot.

He guided me past the bar and I caught Grady's eye. His brow furrowed. I tried a wan smile and a shoulder shrug. Inside, though, humiliation frothed. I thought of all those people I'd seen on TV, covering their faces with their handcuffs. I finally understood why.

Despite the hard expression on his face, the detective's hands were gentle as he guided me into the back of a black SUV. He placed me behind the passenger seat and belted me in carefully. I got another whiff of laundry as he bent over me and found myself foolishly hoping I smelled okay.

The things that go through your head when you get arrested.

I expected a cage between the driver and me, but it looked like a normal SUV. If this were a TV show, I would have worked my hands around to the front of my body and placed my cuffs over the detective's head, tightening the chain around his windpipe. It seemed to happen in cop shows all the time, but I couldn't for the life of me see how it was humanly possible. Maybe if I were a wet noodle.

I was going to have to rely on my ability to talk myself out of a tough situation. I started up as soon as the detective turned the ignition.

"The girls have been lying to us," I said. *Ben, too*, but I kept that to myself.

"I don't want to hear it."

"They didn't meet Ben at Duffy's. They met days earlier."

"Giving him even more time to plan. So what?" the detective shot back as he pulled out of the Ritz and onto the road. We passed a pickup truck with a bed full of men in the back and I gazed at them desperately. With their coveralls and long-sleeved shirts, they looked like they were headed to a work site. With the exception of one white guy, the rest all had skin of varying shades of brown. They were laughing and talking over a reggae beat that blasted out of the front of the truck. Not a one gave the SUV a second look.

"If they've been lying to us about stupid stuff like that, what else are they lying about?" I blurted out.

He didn't respond. The SUV kept rolling down the road, offering a tantalizing glimpse of shimmering baby blue waters to our left. I guessed we were headed for the lockup in Tutu, but I couldn't be sure, so I had to talk fast. But what to say?

"They weren't all friends," I blurted out. "Becky didn't really like Andrea. Andrea was really Jessie's friend. And yet she was sort of shitty to her."

The detective didn't respond as he continued to navigate the road. He took the turns hard, and I had to brace myself against the passenger seat with my legs. The belt didn't do much.

I frantically shuffled through my brain for earth-shattering information. I didn't think that hot tub hanky-panky was the stuff I was searching for, although maybe fishermen could be a good distraction—

"'Shitty' to her in what way?" He said the word as though it were foreign.

"There was a stateside guy who Jessie had a crush on. Zack. Andrea took him from her."

"And?"

"And what? You grabbed me before I could get anything else."

His lack of response suggested that he wasn't impressed.

As we approached the turn for my cottage, I felt the car slow. Maybe he was going to take me home. I craned my neck for a look. I saw a single orange traffic cone, then a man working on the left side of the road. He held a machete and wore a navy handkerchief across his dark brown face. His eyes were covered by sunglasses. As we passed, he paused his work, a pile of recently-cut brush sitting next to him. He didn't acknowledge our passing, except to stare at the vehicle as it gave him a wide berth.

The turn to my cottage came and went, taking my dreams of house arrest with it.

"Where are you taking me?" I asked.

The detective turned the vehicle right, down a steep incline then onto the main road. We passed the Red Man's shack, but it was shut. No fish, no produce. This time of day, in the direct sunlight, the peeling paint was even more obvious. It almost looked abandoned.

No answer from the detective.

We rolled through Red Hook in silence, past the high school, past the place on the sidewalk where I took my momentous header just yesterday, and past Duffy's Love Shack, the scene of Andrea's disappearance and her momentous "gift" to Ben.

My mind kept sorting through what I knew, but I couldn't

quite grab onto anything that I thought would stop this car hurtling toward lockup.

I wished for some kind of weekday traffic jam—a broken down water truck, maybe—to halt our progress, but we slid smoothly along, past the pizza place I never ordered from, the market where I bought my $7.99 gallons of milk and the ferry terminal, quiet since we were coming through in the middle of the hour.

I had to stop this car, but how? I looked at the door handles. They looked normal enough. Maybe this wasn't a cop car at all, but Detective Christopher's personal vehicle. The assembly looked pretty standard: a rocker button that locked and unlocked the door and a bar handle that I had to pull toward me.

As the island's East End resorts started to roll by the windows, I gauged the distance between the door handle and me, my flexibility and the detective's vigilance. His eyes were focused on the road. Now that I had stopped babbling, his eyes rarely flicked in the rear view mirror.

I turned my head to make it look like I was staring out the window. We had two speed bumps to roll over, then we would be in Smith Bay. I had driven through here just yesterday after dropping Ben off. It seemed like a lifetime ago. I hoped he was far, far away from here by now.

Unless, of course, he did it.

I couldn't think about that right now. I had my own problems to worry about.

When the car went over the first bump, I used the momentum to inch closer to the door, leaning my head against the glass as though I were close to a female faint. *More like a female feint*, I thought, the pun cheering me slightly.

I eased my right foot out of my flip flop, trying to keep my upper body stationary. A thought flashed through my head.

Even if I got out of the car, I was still handcuffed. What was I going to do about that?

I'd have to figure that out on the fly. One step at a time.

First, I had to get the door unlocked. I could only assume the detective had locked me in, so first I needed to move the rocker switch to the other side.

Keeping my eyes ahead, I lifted my knee, hugging the door to keep it out of Detective Christopher's view. We were now leaving Smith Bay, passing an on-again, off-again gas station that was usually off-again, but occasionally was worked by young boys with off-kilter baseball caps and gold teeth. I peered over at a building that promised to be some kind of grocery store, but it wasn't one I'd ever stopped into. The paint on the building was peeling and their tiny windows offered little light. I couldn't take shelter there, but maybe I could find another place to hide if I managed to roll out of the car. Beyond the building was bush, which might offer me a chance. That was what I needed: cover. I had to act now. Once we got to Tutu, it would be much tougher to disappear.

As I fumbled for the switch with my toe, we passed another gas station and a tiny strip mall, the same one that housed El Cubano.

We started up a hill, and it gave me a little extra leverage to bring my toe up to the rocker switch. As I leaned back in my seat, my arms protested. *Just a few seconds*, I promised them.

I planted my big toe on the rocker switch and pushed, praying it wouldn't make a huge sound when it clicked. Once I got it open, I had to time the pulling of the handle just right. If I waited until—

"You're child-locked in, Miss Jordan."

I instantly dropped the heel of my foot to the seat, as if this stork-like position were the most natural in the world. To be frank, it was making my shoulder muscles scream.

"I'm sorry?" I asked in my most innocent voice.

"You can't get out. The doors are child proof."

"What makes you think I want to get out?"

"That can't be a very comfortable position."

I let my leg flop down with a sigh. "This is just wrong!" I blurted. "How can you be taking me to jail? There's obviously something weird going on with those girls, and we don't know what. It might even clear Ben's name. But you grabbed me before I could get enough to put it together. But at least I was doing something."

I saw his eyebrows lift in the rear view mirror. "So you think I haven't been doing anything?"

I paused.

"You think I'm that typical island cop you stateside transplants love to talk about, who knows nothing and doesn't care." He sighed and shook his head. "I thought you knew me better than that."

"You want my opinion of you to change? You could let me out of these handcuffs."

"The thing is, Miss Jordan, I can't afford to have any more interference into my investigation, and you've proven yourself to be something of a wildcard. You already made both girls cry this morning."

"I didn't realize that was a crime on this island."

"It's certainly not helping anything."

"But what about the fisherman? And the lies I uncovered?"

"And what has that led to?"

"I don't know yet. Why don't you turn around and take me to the marina so we can find out?"

He chuckled. We were now heading down the long hill that would lead us into the bustling area called Tutu, home to Kmart, Home Depot and a number of other smaller stores that formed the commerce center of the island. Tutu was also the home of a small police outpost. It wasn't my favorite place to go on a day off—the lines at Kmart were notoriously slow—and I certainly didn't want to be there now.

"No need to go to the marina," he said. "I already know what 'salsa' is—or, rather, who he is, and he has nothing to do with the case."

"What do you mean?"

"'Salsa' is the nickname of one of the fishermen who work the fishing boat *Maya*."

I found myself at a brief loss for words.

"Surprised?" he asked.

I was, but I certainly wouldn't admit it to him.

"Salsa is a regular at Caribbean Saloon. We cross paths on occasion."

"At Saloon? You go to Saloon?"

He didn't respond.

"And he's not a suspect?"

"He was at the fishing tournament party that night."

"Wasn't that party at the Ritz?"

"And?"

"So what if Andrea really did get a cab home, met up with Salsa and things went sideways?"

"Did the texts in her phone support that?" he asked, a challenging tone in his voice.

I thought back to the single word, *salsa*. "He texted her and she didn't text back." Then, a flash of inspiration hit me. "But isn't that even more of a motive? Maybe he was upset and decided to take it out on her."

"You have quite an imagination, Miss Jordan." He paused. "And, incidentally, you led us astray on Miss Milliken's phone. It wasn't at the bar, but we'll talk about that when we get to the station."

"Wait, what?" I asked. "You didn't find her phone?" That explained a little more clearly why I was on my way to the pokey. Christopher thought I wasn't playing fair.

But why hadn't they found the phone? Maybe Tower had taken it home to keep it safe. Maybe he played dumb, or maybe someone else was working. I guess I hadn't really greased the wheels of justice to ensure a safe delivery of the phone into the police's hands.

But something was bothering me, something else. My mind ticked through a few more bits of information. *Wait. They didn't have Andrea's phone.*

"So how do you know about Salsa?" I asked, my eyes fixed on the side of his face.

He shifted in his seat and he didn't answer.

"And you knew I made both girls cry."

Something was wrong, very wrong. I could feel my pulse start to pick up. How in the hell could he know about Salsa without Andrea's phone? He hadn't had time to go through my notebook. My eyes fell on my purse, which he had placed on the seat next to me. I thought of the moments he had been alone with it in my apartment while I had been changing.

I went cold. "Did you bug me?"

He stared straight ahead.

I shivered. He knew everything. Had that pen even been a recording device, or had the Detective simply delivered me a booby? Did he know about the money, too?

I had been playing this all wrong. Was I actually a suspect? Was that the real reason Christopher had bugged me and was now locking me up? I let a long string of expletives loose in my head.

It was at that point that I started babbling. "What about the rapey Coasties?"

"Pardon?"

"The Coast Guard guys she talked to at the bar. One of them has a history of rape."

"I'll check that out."

"What about Andrea's dad? Is he a suspect?"

"You know I can't discuss that with you."

"They say the Red Man was there that night."

"Who is 'they?'"

"A friend."

"In that case, your friend was there, too. Doesn't that make him a suspect, too?" The light turned green and the SUV moved forward, putting us about half a block from the police station.

"He wouldn't hurt a fly," I shot back.

"Like Ben?"

"Please don't do this," I said.

"Miss Jordan, you'll be in capable hands and out of my hair. I have no choice."

"You're going to anger Mr. Milliken."

"I gave up caring what people like that think of me a long time ago."

From there, it was a quick right past a faded blue cement-block building—a car wash that I understood was a fencing operation. You pulled up and placed your order at the same time you told them whether or not you wanted Turtle Wax. If they had it, it would be in your car when you took it back again. How it was allowed to operate next to a police station was beyond me, but obviously, many things on this island were.

Christopher pulled up to a freestanding white cement building with black lettering that read, "Mariel C. Newton Command." The front of the building featured a large plate glass window and a glass door, through which I could see a man in a police uniform sitting behind a tall podium.

The detective took a moment to straighten his shirt, then walked crisply around to my side of the car. He popped the door, put his hand on my bicep and guided me out. He reached back in for my purse, then shut the door. Then he pulled me through the front door of the station, his grip tight on my arm.

He nodded to the man at the tall desk, who looked to be in his early twenties. He handed him my purse. I had just enough time to get an impression of the man's round face, his medium brown skin, scuffed beige linoleum floors, two metal framed chairs with thin cushions covered in navy vinyl and the low hum of what sounded like a television behind the desk.

The detective pulled out a ring of keys and unlocked a metal door with a small window in it. We went through a white-walled hallway, past a few open doors. I couldn't bear to look in. If I made eye contact with someone, I'd turn into a pile of Jell-O. I kept my gaze forward.

At the end of the hallway was a jail cell door with an officer stationed at the entrance. He was a few inches shorter than me, but built sturdy. His light blue shirt was stretched tight across his chest, his sleeves outlining carefully chiseled biceps. One sharp move and I was sure he would tear his shirt open like the Incredible Hulk.

His pants seemed to be a different story. Although the blue fabric draped crisply over his legs, I couldn't see the outline of muscles below the fabric. Maybe he was the kind of guy who skipped leg day. His hair was cut in a fade close to his dark brown skin, the lines precise.

He stared at us as we approached. I couldn't gauge his age because he wore dark aviators, even indoors. I thought Christopher would say something, but he didn't. Apparently, it wasn't against regulation. Normally, this would have struck me as odd, but my arrest had moved the bar for normalcy. I simply absorbed this as one more fact.

As we approached, he pushed off the wall and nodded at Christopher. I noticed his nametag read "Williams." Short & Sturdy pulled a ring of keys out of his pocket and opened the door, swinging it toward him. Then he handed the keys to Christopher.

The detective herded me through the door. I smelled the first man on the left before I saw him. He reeked of burnt hair and years' worth of sweat. He was hunched over on the floor, his head resting on his knees. All I could see of him were a pair of legs so dry they looked more gray than brown and a head of matted salt-and-pepper hair that hadn't seen care in years.

The detective walked me past two empty cells, where the smell of the man was much less pungent. At the final cell, I heard a jingling, then my arms jerked as he unlocked my handcuffs. He guided me into the open cell with a firm hand.

"Count yourself lucky. It's been a quiet weekend so far."

I shrugged and took a few steps into the cell so I could turn and face him. I expected him to back out immediately, but he stood where he was, his eyes meeting mine. Much of the fire from earlier had gone out of them, and they now looked dull and tired. Mine probably did, too.

"I have to leave you here," he said, looking almost apologetic.

I waved a hand at him. I didn't want to get into it again.

"Do I get a phone call?" I asked. I should call Alex, even if he couldn't do anything but start next year's taxes.

"They'll give you one once they get you processed."

I nodded and turned to survey my cell. Cinder block walls painted a flat gray. Gray cement floors with a stain in one corner that might have been blood. I looked away quickly. I couldn't go there right now. A metal shelf jutted out from the wall—my bed and my couch for now. A metal toilet sat squat in the other corner, a tiny sink next to it.

As I stood in my new abode, I realized how cold it was. The St. Thomas movie theater had a reputation for being a meat locker, but it had nothing on the Mariel C. Newton Command. I suppose it kept the smell down from my friend a few cells away, but it was also raising goosebumps on my forearms.

I clamped my arms around my body. This wasn't good. Being cold was as good as torture for me. I shivered once, mostly at the thought, but I didn't have long before it would become uncontrollable.

"I'll get you a blanket," the detective said, backing out of the cell and closing the door. He locked it, then disappeared down the hallway.

I didn't marvel at his cooperativeness. Instead, once he was out of sight, I jumped up and down to get the circulation flowing. I wasn't sure it helped, but I had to try.

I heard footsteps and I froze in place, then tried to look casual. It was the detective, bearing a gray blanket. He began to feed it through the bars.

I debated making a crack about playing good cop, but I couldn't afford to lose this luxury, such as it was. I glanced behind me as I heard a whirring sound. I felt a blast of even colder air on my shoulders. I was going to need that blanket.

I stepped forward and put a hand on the blanket, the fabric scratchy under my palm. I pulled it toward me, but it was stuck on something. Detective Christopher still had his hand wrapped around the other edge.

"The phone, Miss Jordan?"

"I'm sorry?" I asked, my hand tightening on the fabric.

"Where is Miss Milliken's phone? You misled me once, and I won't let it happen again.

I tried to look casual as I increased the pressure on the blanket. "I told you where it was."

"To be accurate, you told us where it wasn't."

"I told you where I left it. I don't know what more I can do."

"I'm only interested in results, Miss Jordan."

My mind ticked as I tried to maintain my grip. I could ask to call Tower, but that would likely scare the crap out of him—and maybe even result in the weight of the VIPD coming down on my friend. That wasn't an option.

I was already in jail. I'd take the weight. What more could truly happen to me?

I loosed my grip suddenly, holding up my hands in a gesture of surrender. The detective stumbled slightly as the blanket shot through the bars. It gave me a sadistic little jolt of pleasure, but it faded as the detective quickly regained his perfect composure.

"I told you what I knew. I don't know what more I can do." I gestured at my holding cell. "It's not like I can go out and look for it."

His shoulders glided upward, then he lowered them slowly. "Then I can't help you, Miss Jordan."

I wanted to tell him he was an asshole, but I didn't want to give him the satisfaction of getting to me.

Instead, I turned my back to him and stepped to the metal shelf. I swiveled and sat, suppressing a gasp. The metal was painfully cold against the back of my bare thighs. I felt the chill seeping through my shorts, but I wasn't going to let the detective see that. I scooted back so I could lean against the cement wall, then crossed my legs like a pretzel and pulled them close. I shrugged as slowly as he had, although I'm willing to admit that he might have had me beat in the physical grace department.

I thought I saw flash of a little smile, but the detective didn't say anything more. He lifted the blanket in front of the cell and folded it with military precision, then laid it across his arm and left without another word to me.

Well, crap.

18

Once Detective Christopher was out of sight, I slouched down on my spine.

Holy hell, did it feel like an ice chest in here.

My rear was already a little numb from the cold of the metal slab. I shifted my weight, giving all the cold to my left bum cheek. I brought my knees close to my body and hugged them, warming the tops of my thighs against my trunk. I knew I was only robbing Peter to pay Paul. Soon, I knew my whole body would settle out to the same wintry temperature.

I felt another shiver go through my body. I hated being cold.

People wonder how one can truly be cold in the Caribbean. Well, let me help you count the ways. Try getting knocked off the thin and slippery gunwale of a boat on a cloudy day in twenty-knot winds. You drag your drenched self onto the transom after the captain who threw you off is kind enough to stop the engines so you don't get ground up into chum. You're left with the choice of rotting in a soaking wet cotton shirt that steals heat from your body degree by degree, or letting that persistent wind wrap its frigid fingers around a bare torso protected only by a bikini top.

Okay, it's no Alaskan crab fishing scenario, but, trust me, you would have been miserable, too.

Another shudder ran through my body.

That was the thing about the cold. It wasn't just the temperature. Sitting there on that arctic slab of metal, I felt utterly alone. Inconsequential. This wasn't a new feeling, I knew. My mind skittered back to that day on the sofa, when disbelief washed over me as I listened to my father tell me that it was time for me to face reality. It had been cold, too.

I pulled my knees tighter, trying to stop myself from shaking. I loosed my hair from its bun and dropped my head onto my knees, letting my hair fall like curtains around my legs.

Well, this sucked.

Ben's face flashed behind my closed eyes and I cursed him silently. Couldn't he just have skipped Ladies' Night, just that once?

Of course, if I'd stuck to my guns and simply stayed home yesterday, I wouldn't be here now.

And I'd done it all for what? A notebook filled with stupid musings about Hobie cats and a fisherman named Salsa.

I had squat. *Bubkes*, as they used to say on those cop shows I watched on TV as a kid.

I had uncovered a few simple lies—a blow job in a parking lot, a burgeoning tourist romance that started earlier than anyone was willing to admit and two girls who had been less than forthcoming in finding their friend. I wondered if they'd been as belligerent with the imposing Mr. Milliken and his entourage of muscle men.

How ordinary life had seemed just a few days ago, when Ben and I took those people on their tour the BVI. What if I my boss finally wanted me to work tomorrow? Was I going to have to call in "arrested?" That would be a ridiculously stupid way to spend my one phone call.

There was nothing I wanted more than to put on my cheesy logo T-shirt and make fruity rum drinks for tourists while the salty wind blew through my hair. Out on the water, I could leave all of this drama, nonsense and death on land.

I should return Mr. Milliken's money. What had I been thinking in the first place? It was ludicrous to believe that I was getting anywhere or even making the slightest bit of difference. The whole time, the detective had been one step ahead of me.

Some detective I was. I was just a snoop—and not a very good one. And not only was I a snoop, I was a single snoop, one who was doomed to rot in this cell. No one would be looking for me. Dave would be off cavorting with Christie. As for my friends, it would be the Andrea scenario all over again. Everyone would assume I was with someone else. Maybe if I did get on the schedule for work and failed to show, people would start to wonder. Or maybe they'd just fire me and move on to the next warm body.

I let my body flop to the side, curling it up into a tight ball and wedging my left elbow underneath my head to make a bony pillow. I wrapped my right arm over my bare legs, running my fingers over the sharp goosebumps on my legs. My throat started to close up.

Yep, folks, I was about to cry. I swallowed to try and stop it, but it wouldn't be held back. My nose started to sting and I felt pinpricks at the corners of my eyes.

I was alone. Utterly alone.

I squeezed my eyes shut and felt the hot tears building beneath my lids. My throat tightened and I swallowed hard. I squeezed my eyes tight and laid there in darkness, feeling utterly alone.

I heard some footsteps. I heard something shoved between the bars, then fall to the floor. I didn't move until I heard the footsteps retreat. I fluttered my eyes open and saw the gray blanket crumpled on the floor. On top of it was a paté—we pronounce it "patty," FYI—in wax paper.

I scuttled forward and grabbed my provisions, then resettled on my slab. Had Detective Christopher changed his mind? Or did I have some kind of strange friend in this place?

I bit cautiously into the paté. It was cold, but so was everything else in this damn place. I discovered a mixture of flavored ground beef inside the fried dough. Not the best I'd had, but also not the worst. Three bites and I'd devoured the whole thing. I crumpled the wax paper and set it underneath my slab.

With a morsel in my stomach, I curled myself into a ball, then covered myself with the blanket, tucking as much as I could under my body to trap the heat. The blanket smelled a little like mold. I wondered how many other people had clutched it against their skin. I banished that thought quickly.

I lay staring at the bars for a long time.

At some point, I fell asleep.

I woke up to the sound of a door slamming. Footsteps squeaked toward me, and I pushed myself up to a seated position, dashing at the crusties in my eyes. I swung my legs over the ledge of the shelf, planted them firmly on the cement and waited, the blanket beside me as though I'd never needed it. I sneaked a look at my watch. It was nearly five o'clock.

The footsteps hesitated a moment while the person was still out of sight, then they started up again. As the owner of the footsteps came into view, my eyebrows popped. It was Williams, the officer also known to me as Short & Sturdy. He was still wearing those aviators. My eyebrows popped again when I saw that he was carrying my purse.

"Come," he said, the keys jingling in his hand.

What was going on?

"Come," he said, louder this time, clearly impatient with me. His eyes were inscrutable behind his sunglasses as he swung the door open.

I stood and stumbled toward him, my legs clumsy from the cold. I hesitated at the door, confused. He gestured impatiently, and I twitched forward. Anything to be out of that cell.

I expected us to turn right, back toward the front of the station, but he shooed me to the left. He used his keys to open another door with bars, then we were in a hallway. Off to the left, a room opened, furnished with a scarred wooden table and chairs. It smelled like stale coffee. A TV played quietly. On the table sat a plush frog wearing sunglasses. I stopped and stared at it. It grinned back at me enigmatically.

"Come," the officer repeated to me, gesturing me forward.

I turned away from the frog and walked with Short & Sturdy until we reached a glass door set into the wall. He released my arm, flipped a thumb switch lock, pushed the door outward and poked his head out. After a 180-degree survey, he leaned back inside. He shoved my purse into my hands. I fumbled to get a grip on it.

We stared dumbly at each other for a second, then he pointed out the door.

"Go," he said.

I paused. Clearly, he wanted me to go outside, but I couldn't quite grasp what was going on. Why was I leaving through the back door? Were they taking me somewhere else? I looked out the door to see if I could spot a police car.

"You slow?" he asked. "Go."

Then, I felt him put a hand on my back as he shoved me out the door.

I turned around to ask one of the multitude of questions in my head, but he slammed the door shut behind me. I heard the lock click shut.

Holy shit. I'm out.

I probably stood there for far too long as I oriented myself. I still had questions—so many questions—but I had the creeping feeling that a) there was no way that this was official, and b) standing here in the parking lot, I was very, very exposed. I needed to make the most of whatever had just happened and get the heck out of Tutu.

I glanced around. The station sat near the road at the edge of a huge parking lot. At the other end was a white concrete strip mall containing a furniture store and a place called "Cash & Carry." I'd never been in there, probably because the name confused me. Wasn't every store the kind of place where you could offer cash and carry out your goods? I guess I must be slow, just like Officer Williams had suggested.

In between the store and me was a sparse smattering of cars, which offered little cover. I guess there weren't a lot of people cashing and carrying things that day. I put a taxi van between myself and the Mariel C. Newton Command, then I cautiously peered toward the two-lane road that ran through Tutu.

I caught sight of a maroon safari bus about a block and a half away. One dollar, and I would be on my way to freedom. I speed-walked in the safari's direction, using a line of parked cars parked as cover.

At the end of the line of cars, I zagged left, keeping a beige Ford Explorer between me and the police station.

My mind whirled again. *Was my release a mistake? Were cops going to come pouring out of the station at any moment, like fire ants protecting their hill?* If Detective Christopher found out about this, I was sure he'd be leading the charge.

I couldn't think too much about that. I was out, and I needed to get as far away from the station as possible. Just in case. I peered through the windows of the Explorer at the safari as it lumbered closer.

The safari was a converted Ford F-450 pickup, custom altered to hold five benches in the truck's bed, all covered with a hard rooftop to keep the occasional rain shower out. Many of the island's safaris were charmingly tricked out with airbrushed beach scenes, cartoons like Sponge Bob or the Simpsons and even portraits of the owners and their families. This one was a plain dark red, but it was the most beautiful safari on the island, as far as I concerned. It was my ticket back to the East End, my home base. These safaris made loops around the island all day, offering cheap transportation for those without a car. I'd hop it at around eleven o'clock on its loop and ride it right around to my side of the island at about five o'clock.

My chariot's benches were sparsely occupied. Through the front window, I could see a brown-skinned man in a black Kangol cap behind the wheel. Salt and pepper hair peeked out from below his cap. Although I couldn't tell for sure at this distance, he was likely from here. Most of the taxi and safari drivers were. These safaris were essentially our unofficial bus system, since the public buses never seemed to run with any kind of regularity. I saw maybe one a year. Each time, it felt like spotting a unicorn.

A flash of movement at the police station drew my attention. Two officers stepped out of the side door. Were they looking for me? I searched their body language for clues, but I couldn't say for sure.

I flicked my gaze to the safari. I had to get out on the sidewalk early enough for him to stop for me, but not so early that I got spotted—if they were, indeed, looking for me and not, say, taking a breath of Tutu's finest fresh air.

I glanced back to the officers, one of whom was the young desk attendant with the round face. The other was a tall, well-built man in uniform who I hadn't seen before, his skin also brown, but with more yellowish undertones than his fellow officer's.

I squinted, trying to make out their expressions. Did they seem like they were looking for something?

The safari was still half a block away. It seemed to be in no particular hurry. The two officers had put a few steps between them and the door, their faces scanning the nearby cars. The tall one began to gesture with his hand toward the large parking lot. He pointed in one direction, then in the other. Were they splitting up to search? Oh dear Jesus, would that safari hurry up?

I blinked. Was that snow at the edge of my vision? I felt my breath catch in my chest. *Not now. Not now.*

I blinked again to clear my vision and glanced back to the safari. It had crept a few feet closer, but not quite close enough. However, if I waited much longer, he'd probably roll right by me, and I'd be stuck.

As the snow began to narrow my vision, I knew that it would eventually block out my sight. It was already getting harder and harder to suck in air. I mentally pushed back with every ounce of strength I had, widening my eyes, as if that would help. I had to go now.

I took in a gasp of air, pinned my eyes ahead of me and took three strides forward. I lifted my hand to wave to the driver and, through the creeping snow crowding my vision, I thought I saw the dark head nod slightly through the windshield. However, the safari didn't show any signs of changing its meandering pace.

I restrained myself from dancing in place—anything to dispel the energy coursing through my body—and kept my eyes fixed to the maroon cab. I saw a large scratch in the paint on the driver's side door. I wondered if it bothered the owner, or if he wasn't that kind of guy.

The safari rolled to a stop at a glacial pace, in sharp contrast to the sense of urgency that had invaded my body.

I shouldn't have done it, but I glanced back. Through my fuzzy vision, I made eye contact with the young officer from the desk. It was hard to see much at that point, but I thought I saw his mouth pop open in surprise.

I whipped my head around and fixed what was left of my vision on the first row of seats. I took two quick strides and grabbed a bar to hoist myself in.

I sat down next to a solid lady of about sixty. By the look of the plastic bags around her, she had just made her monthly run to Kmart. She had planted herself on the seat like a queen. She wore a purple T-shirt that clung to her heavy breasts and solid middle. Her shirt was tucked into a long, black skirt that she had spread out on the seat around her. Her tawny cheeks were speckled with small moles. She was wearing a black wig shaped into a bob with the ends tucked under her chin, giving her an almost youthful appearance. Her eyes, though, were watery and pouched.

I desperately wanted to sit farther inside the safari, but the floor was covered with her bags. I had no choice but to sit on the very edge closest to the officers and their jail. I perched on the edge of the seat, tense, the snow nearly covering my vision now.

She didn't acknowledge me, but I was okay with that. My chest was squeezing tightly now, and I wasn't sure I could have mustered a greeting, not even the "good afternoon" one usually offered when getting on the safari.

I thought I heard a shout, but I couldn't turn. I couldn't watch myself get re-arrested. The safari didn't move.

I wished I could see the driver, see what was ahead of us, but my vision was still crowded with snow. I wanted to pound on the wall between us, but I knew it was futile. Stuff like that never made things move faster down here. It could also get me kicked off the safari, which could send me straight back to that arctic cell. Not an option.

I thought I heard voices again, closer this time, and I closed my eyes, waiting for the hands to grab me.

I wasn't sure, but I might have felt the safari move forward an inch. My stomach clutched, and I felt like throwing up.

I vowed to aim to the left. No sense in ruining this woman's Kmart trip.

I felt the safari jerk as the driver hit the gas. We suddenly careened forward toward the intersection, taking the turn at the light so sharply that I had to grab the edge of the vinyl seat to avoid falling out.

We straightened out and roared up the hill, the engine sounding like a freight train in my ears. I dropped my head between my knees.

I was free.

I felt the pain in my chest start to loosen, but, for now, I just let my head hang, the sides of my face slick with sweat against my thighs.

I focused on my breathing, feeling the air roll in and out of me, deeper and deeper, until I felt my lungs ease.

I felt a hand on my back, and I jumped. I lifted my head. The woman was leaning toward me. I could still see snow at the edge of my vision, but it looked like it was retreating, not growing.

"You alright, baby?" she asked.

I nodded once. She patted my back once and removed her hand, reclining against the seat.

Of all the times I'd been a mess in St. Thomas—and there were many—I'd never had a stranger worry about me. *I must look a wreck.*

My bag vibrated, and I twitched violently.

Confirmation: I *was* a wreck.

I fumbled with the zipper a few times before I could get my bag open. It was a 340 number—someone calling from the Virgin Islands. But it wasn't one I had stored.

In my days as a citizen, I would have ignored it. But I'd become something more, so I answered.

"Enjoying your newfound freedom?" a voice said on the line. It was male, authoritative. I didn't recognize it.

"Who is this?"

"Your patron saint."

"You're going to have to be more specific."

"You've got a short memory, Miss Jordan. I'm the person who gave you that walking around money just a few hours ago."

"Milliken." The 340 number must mean he was calling from the hotel.

"Try to stay out of that cop's way. He seems to have a bit of a hard-on for you. I'm not sure he's going to be happy when he finds out."

"I'm sorry?"

"I had to use a lot of favors to get you sprung."

My mind was ticking. *Milliken* had gotten me out of jail? Was I a fugitive now? "Am I a fugitive?" I'm embarrassed to report that my voice actually squeaked on that final word.

"Don't be ridiculous. You weren't even booked. I called in a favor. What have you found out?"

"That the inside of the jail is a cold, cold place to be."

There was silence on the other end of the line. Then, he spoke. "I expect more from you, Miss Jordan."

I thought about Ben. I thought about Detective Christopher, and all the other people whose expectations were weighing on me. "Get in line," I responded.

Another silence. Then, "I expect you to make good use of your freedom."

"Glad we're on the same page," I said, and I hung up, blood pulsing in my right temple.

I looked at the phone in my hand. I had two missed calls from two unknown numbers, one missed call from work and one missed call from Ben.

Jesus, Ben. Still using your phone? Not the smartest move.

Obviously, I had some calls to return, but I had something else to take care of first.

Somehow, Detective Christopher had been listening in on me, tracking me—or both. I started dissembling my purse, looking for anything amiss. Detective Christopher had taken my little notebook with him, I saw. I took everything out of my worn wallet—driver's license, two credit cards (one with a stateside billing address, one with a VI billing address), an ATM card, $63 in cash, a card from a kind of cute software engineer I'd met at a bar a few weeks ago and $1.73 in change. Nothing unusual.

Maybe the detective had stolen his little device back? I couldn't take that chance. I dug further. I found my keys, two tubes of lip balm and a crumpled receipt from a night I didn't remember. That was it. Oh, and the hundreds from Milliken, which I took out of the zipper compartment and secured in my bra. I'm nothing if not classy.

I saw the woman next to me register that move.

I ran my hands around the lining of the purse, then up and down the strap. I didn't feel anything amiss.

The safari slowed down to pick up a slim girl with light brown skin and freckles, her hair styled into a neat bun at the top of her head. She joined the back row.

I'd never liked this purse anyway. Before we sped up, I tossed it into the bushes at the side of the road. I really was getting paranoid, wasn't I? Next thing I knew, I'd be joining the tinfoil hat club and discussing the round-Earth conspiracy.

My phone buzzed, the window showing the number for my boat job. Without thinking about it, I opened the phone and answered. Apparently, I was needed on a trip for tomorrow. Without much thought, I told the girl who was working in the office that I would be there at 6:00 am sharp.

I hung up the phone and squinted at it. I'd just gotten out of jail, and I was accepting work for the next day? That was a head-scratcher.

Or was it? Going to work could be the easiest thing I'd done all week. Lizzie Jordan, first mate? That's me. Lizzie Jordan, girl detective? Never heard of her.

My mind flicked back to the call from Ben. He was taking a huge risk by calling me, but then again, he probably didn't know what I knew, that the police did have cell tracking capabilities.

I cursed. Maybe the detective had been tracking me, too. *Stupid, Lizzie. Stupid.*

However, Milliken had told me I wasn't a fugitive. In theory, I didn't have anything to worry about. That said, he might be able to spring me from jail, but he probably couldn't stop Detective Christopher from doing whatever he thought needed to be done.

I decided on a compromise. I'd make one call and then be done with it.

I called Ben, if only to warn him to be more careful. It took two aborted attempts before I was actually able to get the call to go through. Apparently, the AT&T towers were having a rough day, too.

The phone rang long enough that I was about to hang up, but I heard someone pick up.

My voice caught in my throat. "Ben?" I asked.

It was his voicemail. I exhaled and slumped a little on the seat. I hadn't realized how much I wanted to know that he was alive and well somewhere. Even just alive would do.

Just for kicks, I listened to that cocksure voice of his tell me that "you know what to do." I rolled my eyes. How 1997 of him. But even as I pondered what a ridiculous human Ben was, I felt a pang.

I was about to leave him a message, but I hung up quickly when I heard the beep. He hadn't left me one, and maybe he had his reasons.

I cast a glance over my shoulder, peering between the heads of the other passengers, back toward the police station. No police cars, no sirens. Maybe Milliken was right. I was really in the clear.

Either way, better safe than sorry. I turned off my phone and pulled out the battery. I put them in separate pockets of my shorts.

As the safari continued to roll slowly toward Red Hook, I marveled at the events of the last two days. I'd just gotten out of *jail*. When Ben pulled me aside at Island Time the night before last, I wouldn't have predicted this.

Actually, I take that back. I'd hesitated at when Ben had asked me to go to the Ritz. I had known there was some risk involved. But then I'd seen that flash of emotion in his face. I'd thought it was disappointment, but maybe it was fear—or desperation. Was I the only person he could ask for help?

Our friendship had started with a tearful confession on my part. Maybe it had created a two-way bond, one deeper than I'd realized.

As so many confessions do, it took place on a boat trip, but Ben and I were working this one. This was back when we crewed on a different boat, a 45' Sea Ray that took six passengers max on luxury excursions that ran about $2k a day.

When we welcomed the family on board, I'd had a good feeling. As I would come to discover after a bit more experience, this was not a feeling I should trust. I was a terrible judge of character. I had a tendency to like people in the morning who revealed themselves to be real assholes in the afternoon.

The parents were in their late forties, both trim and attractive, with two girls, eight and eleven years old. They still had that fresh-off-the-plane pale white cast to their skin. The father reminded me a little of a young James Spader. He even had the floppy blonde hair and the tortoise-shell glasses.

At our first stop, I was down in the cabin, making the family's breakfast, when the dad popped down and asked for the head. After he came out, he asked me if we had any Jack Daniel's. Of course we did, I replied, and asked what I could make him.

It turned out he just wanted a belt of the stuff—no ice, just some warm Jack in a glass. My pleasure, I told him. I poured, he drank—but, then, before he headed back up top, he put a finger to his lips and asked me to keep it a secret.

He turned to go topside. I felt everything shift.

I was quivering when Ben came back down to the cabin. In fact, I was shaking so badly that he had to bring the breakfast upstairs and serve it.

He came back down and found me sitting on the cooler, my head in my hands, staring hard at the liquor cabinet through my fingers. I never drank when I worked. Another one of my little rules. I was thinking about making an exception when Ben put a hand on my shoulder. I jumped a few feet in the air and started to cry.

He sent the family snorkeling on their own—a no-no, but he could tell something was wrong. In the twenty minutes we had while they were exploring the surrounding coral reef, I told him the quick version of my family's dirty secret, about my sister's drug-dealing asshole of a husband who kept my sister just addicted enough to stay with him, who cut me when I threatened to tell, and the family who didn't believe me. The family who believed him over me.

So when pseudo-James Spader asked me to keep a secret, something in me snapped. I didn't do secrets well. Not family secrets, at least.

Ben just listened and, at the end of my story, he kneeled in front of me and took both of my shoulders in his hands.

"I'm sorry, Lizzie," he said, and I saw, for the first time, what women saw in him—a sympathetic twist of his eyebrows, his face focused and serious. Maybe it was an act, but it felt real to me in that moment. "If I met the guy who hurt you, I'd beat the crap out of him, and then I'd tell your family to go fuck themselves."

I smiled, just a little. He smiled back at me.

Then his face went serious again. "But I can't. We're here now. And I need you today. Can you pull it together, just for a few hours?"

I paused, a solid lump still in my throat. I didn't speak.

"This guy isn't that other piece of shit. He's just a well-meaning dad with a problem," he said.

"But his family—"

"His family knows. Trust me. Watch him as the day goes on. They know."

We sat in silence for a moment, both of us waiting for the slight shift in the boat that would tell us our guests had returned. Nothing.

Finally, Ben spoke. "Can you hold it together so we can get through this trip?"

I nodded once. He squeezed my shoulders again, then went up top to make sure all four family members were still cruising the reef and not, say, halfway to Tortola and in need of rescue.

That day was probably the best piece of acting I've ever accomplished. The dad kept returning for Jack. *Nothing else, just the booze*, I kept reminding myself. He slowly became goofier along the course of the day, telling more and more corny jokes with abandon. His mouth did impressive acrobatics as he attempted to pronounce his words with precision, even as his gestures got sloppier. His wife took great pains to ignore his behavior, her face set in a grim smile. Ben was right. They knew.

At the end of the day, while I was polishing the cabinets with more vigor than usual, Ben asked me if I wanted to go have a beer.

We ended up having dinner in one of XO's back booths, tucked away from the crowd. Over a few martinis, I dumped about my shitty family, and he just sat and listened without interruption.

"I'm so sorry, Lizzie," he said, when I'd finished.

"Me too," I said.

And then I felt compelled to tie it all up in a bow and move on before it got awkward. So I raised my martini glass in a toast. "But that whole mess got me here. To a better place."

"A better place," he echoed and we clinked glasses gingerly so as not to spill even a drop of the precious liquid.

The conversation moved to other places, and we never spoke of it again. In fact, he was the only person I'd ever told.

It felt cathartic, and maybe it was. But I still found myself polishing off the rest of a bottle of vodka once I got home. As I sat on my couch that night, my head swimming with booze, I told myself I'd locked the vault again. I'd be okay for a while.

And, in a way, I was, until I started looking for another girl who'd been left behind—but by her friends, not her family.

The safari jolted abruptly as it hit a pothole, bringing me back to the present. That image of Ben, his face locked on mine with no judgment, only concern, floated up once more.

I reached for the phone in my pocket. Maybe I should try him again. But I let my hand drop. What good would it do now?

I looked behind me one more time. A blue pickup truck that looked like it had been dented by a hail storm—impossible, I know, but that's what it looked like—drove behind us. A black sedan followed. The safari pulled over to pick up a tall, spare man in a cream-colored button-down shirt, his hair a tight cap of gray.

I waited for either the truck or the sedan to roar up beside us and demand I exit the vehicle. Both waited patiently behind the safari. The safari started up again and I breathed out. I was good—for now.

I needed a plan. The safari was headed toward Red Hook. Lizzie Jordan, reluctant detective, had a few loose ends there—the fishermen and maybe those Coasties. Who cared if Detective Christopher thought those leads were a waste of his precious time?

That said, Lizzie Jordan, working stiff and semi-professional bystander, saw a lot of appeal in heading straight home.

But I wasn't that bystander anymore, was I? I wasn't that Lizzie who drank her drinks and went home, the Lizzie who didn't get involved. That Lizzie would have gone home, no question. She knew what happened when you spoke up—the cold tip of a knife, the scalp tingle of utter disbelief, the heavy ache of making adult decisions, knowing the family that was once your safety net is gone.

But I didn't want to be that Lizzie anymore. I'd left her behind about 36 hours ago. Yes, I was tired. And, yes, I was filthy. But I knew I couldn't go home. I couldn't turn my back on Andrea. I couldn't just write this up as an island "oops," an anomaly that didn't fundamentally change anything. My old island clothes just didn't fit me right anymore. I had to not just know the truth, but actually look it in the face. Only then would I understand it.

And I thought I might have a shot at all of that, Detective Christopher be damned.

And Ben . . . oh, Ben. He might not be great at the small moral decisions of life, but I could only hope feverishly that he was good at the big ones.

I felt my skin crawl, as though I was being watched. I turned my head slightly to see the woman at my right peering at me curiously. She had gone from gentle to suspicious in the course of our ride. I marveled at how quickly her estimate of me had flipped. Maybe my cash-stashing move made her think I was a prostitute. Or maybe she'd condemned me as a litterbug for tossing my purse. Given the number of times I've seen people throw their trash out the window while driving, I thought the former was more likely.

Nothing I could do about that. That said, her eyes roving over me so invasively gave me the creeps.

I turned my head toward her, and her eyes darted away. She thrust her chin forward and refused to meet my eyes. It only cemented my desire to get off that safari sooner rather than later.

I looked behind me again—still the blue pickup and the black sedan. Unlike the pickup truck, the sedan was awfully shiny, much like Detective Christopher's SUV. Was it possible I was being tailed? If so, why hadn't he pulled us over yet?

I casually looked out to the side of the road, hoping to get more information from my peripheral vision. The Wyndham resort floated by and I wondered if the guests were getting their fill of the all-you-can-eat buffet and the never-empty banana daiquiri machine.

I couldn't see a damn thing. I wished I could ask my former friend next to me for an assist. But when I swiveled my eyes in her direction, her chin only rose higher. If she were working any harder to avoid eye contact, she would have broken out in a sweat.

Red Hook was my only hope. I checked my watch. It was twenty minutes to the hour. The ferry dock would be filling for its hourly ride to St. John. I knew a lot of people would exit the safari when it stopped. Maybe I could blend in—just in case this paranoia of mine had a basis in reality. I snuck a quick glance at my fellow riders to see how easily I would disappear. I saw a sea of faces of every shade of brown looking back at me. "Not well," was my answer.

I let my head loll back on my neck. If I was being tailed, I was probably screwed.

We topped the hill at Sapphire Beach. I had only enough time to pray fervently that Ben had found a good hidey hole before we all found ourselves in Red Hook.

The safari pulled over on the side of the road, stopping in front of a coffee shop I'd never been in and a seafood restaurant I could only afford during high season.

I didn't stop to see what the black sedan would do. Instead, I leapt out of the cab, handed the driver his dollar and started toward the ferry. Let them think that I was going to hide out in St. John.

On my right, I could hear the slam of dominoes on a table as the usual gathering of taxi drivers killed time while waiting to be dispatched. Next to them was a row of neatly parked vans in red, black and gray, each sparkling clean. Taxi drivers took great pride in their rides and, for once, these fancy vans were going to work for me.

I walked past the taxis, then took a sharp turn around the very last one. Instead of heading left toward the ferry dock, I ducked right, crouched and fast-walked down the line of the taxis, keeping them between me and the street traffic. At the final taxi, I paused and tried to peer through its tinted windows to see if I could see the black sedan.

"That black car lookin' for you?" I heard a deep voice say.

I looked up and saw a tall man with ebony skin wearing a straw boater and a pink Oxford shirt with short sleeves tucked into a pair of khaki pants. He was leaning against the shack that sheltered the domino game from the street. From his vantage point, he could see me plain as day. He didn't smile but, then again, a lot of people down here weren't as easy with smiles as statesiders. It didn't always mean they weren't friendly.

I shrugged and tried a half smile. "Ex-boyfriend," I said and tried to look rueful. Lizzie Jordan, spontaneous liar.

He twitched his head to the right. I took that to mean that I should vamoose behind the shack. From there, I had a neat back-door entrance to the marina, where I could evade anyone who might be tailing me.

I nodded to him and sprinted past, but not so quickly that I didn't hear him say, "When you ready for a real man, you come back and try me."

I felt my mouth twist in amusement. Some men were shameless.

Once I ducked around the shack, I was able to pick up a trail of wooden planking that led behind the fancy seafood restaurant, under a canopy of mangroves. I briefly considered trying to duck into the restaurant. A glance revealed that their current crowd was too sparse to get lost in. Plus, the last person I knew there had left a few months ago for Florida. The current staff might just as easily turn me in to spare the dinner seating a scene.

I kept moving down the wooden boardwalk behind the restaurant, until it split into two paths: I could go left into the docks or right into the marina with its shops and restaurants. It was almost noon, so the docks would be mostly deserted, with the exception of the odd fisherman polishing stainless.

I glanced behind me. I didn't see anything, but I swore I heard the sound of hard shoes on wood. Time to go.

I veered right into the marina complex, starting off at an extremely fast walk through a very open, very exposed parking lot. My sight was fixed on a staircase ahead that would take me into the first level of the marina. If I could get up that staircase and around the corner, I would be golden. The marina was like a rabbit warren, with staircases, shops and hidey-holes all over the place.

Halfway through the empty lot, fear got the best of me, and I ran like hell for the staircase. I flew up the steps then paused at the landing to look behind me. At the very far edge of the parking lot, I thought I saw a man in a suit. Detective Christopher?

No time to find out for sure. I slipped around the corner of the marine supply store, narrowly missing a collision with the older St. Thomian who worked in the shop, his shoulders permanently slumped under the navy coveralls he wore each day.

He mumbled something at me that I didn't stay to decipher. I had to keep moving. He was a cranky one, always with some axe to grind with someone about something. I never knew quite what since he talked like he had a permanent mouthful of Shredded Wheat, but I knew he had a finger he could point. I was sure he wouldn't hesitate to show the detective where I'd gone.

I trotted to the next corner, hung a left and slipped up a staircase, careful to keep some distance between me and my regular coffee shop. Better to stay as anonymous as possible.

Once I hit the top level, I headed straight for a set of bathrooms, then punched the code that was supposed to keep the riff-raff out.

I wrinkled my nose as I entered the hallway. Last night's clean-up crew had missed a few spots—maybe more than a few. Or maybe someone had gone to town that day.

To be fair, these three single-room bathrooms served two busy bars in addition to all the marina's shops. Luckily, I wouldn't be staying here very long.

I passed the bathrooms and slipped in the back door of the Caribbean Saloon, which lay just beyond. I blinked a few times as the door closed behind me to adjust my eyes. It was always dark in Saloon—dark and cool. I felt the sweat lift off my body, but I didn't feel any real relief. Not yet.

Instead of turning left into the main bar, I stepped up to a closed door in front of me. I meant to knock gently. Before I could stop myself, I'd banged on the door like Judgment Day had arrived and I was its arbiter.

When the door opened, my heart sank.

The guy who stood in the door wore the classic black Caribbean Saloon T-shirt with its eccentric slogan, "Beat it, clown!" (If you ever get the real story behind it, let me know.)

Local lore aside, I had a problem. This man was not happy with me. This did not bode well. He was tall, with a good amount of weight at his front, although I couldn't tell exactly whether it was fat or muscle, not that it really mattered. If this guy told you to go home, you would obey without question. He was bald, with dark eyes and deep olive skin. His arms were crossed in front of his chest. His tattooed forearms were massive and probably could have served as legs for a smaller individual.

He looked down at me from at least six inches above, his eyebrows raised. "Well?" he finally asked.

I could feel my mouth move, but, for once, I was at a loss for words. No convenient little lie sprung to mind. "I'm . . . Lizzie," I heard myself say.

"Mmm-hmmm," he said, nodding as though he understood, although his face said that he didn't.

"I, uh . . ." How the heck do you tell a total stranger—let alone one who looks like a villainous WWE wrestler—that you're on the run because maybe, just maybe, the cops are after you, even though you'd been assured it was all perfectly legal, and would it be possible to get an assist on a place to hide out, just to regroup?

Lizzie Jordan, tongue-tied.

Just as I was about to melt into a puddle of shame, I felt someone clap me on the back.

"Hey, Lizzie." I turned to see the bartender I knew as Smitty. I had no idea if that was his real name or a nickname. "Hork and I were just about to watch the footage of this girl who went totally apeshit last night and nearly threw a chair through the window before we grabbed her. You wanna watch with us?"

My eyes flicked back to Hork. I saw his shoulders relax a little—but not much.

I glanced back to Smitty and took in his doughy white face with its eyes, nose and mouth pinched together in the center. He wasn't a looker, that was for sure. However, I'd take his friendliness over surly hotness every day.

But before I could say, "Can you hide me in the office for a little bit?" he said something that stopped time:

"You just missed Ben."

19

I reached out and clamped a hand on Smitty's fleshy shoulder. "You're not fucking with me, are you?"

He raised an eyebrow. "Jesus, Lizzie, ease up."

I felt a meaty hand on my arm. Hork was ready to go into attack mode. I dropped my hand and Hork dropped his.

"Hell's going on with you?" Smitty asked, rubbing his arm. I opened my mouth, but before I could answer, he held up a finger that said "wait" and walked back toward the bar.

I glanced over at Hork, but he just shrugged his massive shoulders at me.

I shifted my weight. I'd feel much better in that office, out of plain sight. You know, just in case Milliken didn't know half as much about "places like this" as he thought he did.

I considered asking Hork to let me slide by, but a glance at his body language suggested I wouldn't get anywhere. So I simply shifted my weight again.

A few seconds later, Smitty returned with three Presidentes, gripped in one hand by their necks. He nodded toward the open office door, and I followed Hork in at an uncomfortably close distance.

When Smitty shut the door behind me, I let out an audible sigh. Neither of the guys seemed to notice, which was fine with me.

The office was four white walls, punctuated by two fist-size holes and haphazardly decorated with tidbits the guys who ran the place found amusing—a picture of a hot Latina woman in a bikini advertising Presidente, a postcard from Wisconsin that featured a beaver joke, a USVI calendar showing last month's perfect white sand beach, plus a few video stills of people who were banned "for life," which usually meant anywhere between two weeks to six months. The office furniture consisted of a black pleather love seat with patches of white wear at the corners and a shitty black office chair that didn't look like it would hold the weight of either Hork or Smitty. I held my breath when Hork reached for it. He sat more gracefully than I expected, and the chair held.

Behind Hork was a black metal desk with a dent in the top. I wondered if the same person who had dented the desk had put the holes in the wall. Given what went on in Saloon, I'd put my money on multiple perpetrators.

On top of the desk sat two large flat-screen monitors that showed a grid of rectangular shots displaying every conceivable angle of Caribbean Saloon and the surrounding sidewalk. On the floor, a black tower computer whirred quietly, recording every transgression.

I took one half of the pleather love seat, trying not to think about how many people had probably had sex where I now rested my weary body. Smitty distributed beers before sitting down next to me.

I didn't wait for the others. I took a long draw of the beer and nearly shivered with delight. God damn, did that taste good.

"Hork, this is Lizzie. Lizzie, Hork," Smitty said, then he raised his beer to the two of us and drank.

I raised my beer to Hork in way of greeting and he did the same, although his face still wore a grim expression. I clearly wasn't in his good graces quite yet.

I took one more long draw, then turned to Smitty. "Tell me about Ben."

"Why are you all up on Ben?" he asked. "What about Dave?"

My shoulders curled forward, as though I'd taken a punch to the stomach. Dave. Dave who used to be mine. I shook my head. "That's done." I took another deep swig of my beer.

"Oh, man," Smitty said. "You okay?"

I shrugged.

Smitty leaned forward and reached around the far side of the couch, where a small cube refrigerator squatted. He flipped open the door and came out with a bottle of Jägermeister, covered in a thin layer of frost. He angled the neck toward me. I sighed and nodded. He twisted off the cap and handed it to me. "Ladies first."

I took a big swig and passed it to Hork as I swallowed.

The herbal liqueur burned down my throat, but then the rush blew through me, sweeping the cobwebs out of my head. Lizzie Jordan, tongue-tied no more.

"Now," I said, once Smitty had put the bottle back in the fridge. "Tell me about Ben."

He raised his eyebrows at me. "You know the police are after him, right? You need a better rebound."

I rolled my eyes. "Please. Ben is not my rebound. Also, it's possible that the police are after me, too. Which is what brings me to your office today."

Smitty's face registered surprise, but it quickly bounced back to neutral. "For what?" he asked.

"They think I'm helping Ben."

"Are you?" Hork asked, his first words in a while. My head swiveled around to him and I tried to fix him with my best death stare.

"He didn't do it," I said.

"That's why he wanted the videos," Smitty said, nodding with recognition.

My head whipped around again. These two were going to send me to the damn chiropractor if I wasn't careful. "What?"

Smitty pointed to the computer monitors. "Made him a tape of that night."

I tilted my head. "When?"

"Twenty minutes ago."

I checked my own watch. It was about five-thirty, which also meant I was clear to drain my beer. I turned it upward, drank and tossed it in the small trash can next to the desk where it clinked with the other empties. Two points.

"Spill it. What did he see?"

Smitty shrugged. "Didn't have time to watch. I dumped the whole night on a disc for him, and he took it to go."

"I didn't think the girls came over here that night. You sure he wanted the videos from . . . "—my mind searched the timeline—"Wednesday?"

Smitty nodded and finished his beer, then tossed it in the trash. Two points for him, too. He pumped his fist. "You want another shot? I'm doing one."

I shook my head, distracted by my thoughts. My hand fluttered around the pocket holding my cell phone. I couldn't risk it.

"Give me your phone," I said to Smitty.

"No 'please?'" he asked, his crooked smile revealing equally crooked teeth.

I flipped my hand over, palm up and raised my eyebrows.

"Is she always this friendly?" Hork rumbled from the office chair. I had to hand it to him. He might have a grumpy demeanor, but he had a very smooth voice. Deep, pleasant.

Focus, Lizzie.

"Yours, too," I said to Mr. Smooth. "Hand it over." We stared at each other for a second, but then he glanced over to

Smitty. After a small nod from him, Hork leaned back to reach into his pocket.

"You're lucky I'm a sucker for redheads," he said.

I filed that away for future reference.

I tried Ben's number from both of their phones with the same result—voicemail. I breathed out sharply in frustration.

I leaned forward on my knees, my eyes scanning the monitors on the desk as I decided what to do next. The back of a T-shirt caught my eye. "The *Maya*?" I blurted.

Smitty lowered the bottle of Jäger from his lips. "What?"

I popped up out of my seat. "Are those the guys from the *Maya*?" I demanded.

"Who, the two white guys?" Smitty asked.

I jabbed my finger at the screen. "Those two."

Smitty cocked his head at me. "Lizzie, you need to eat something. You're getting weird."

"Are they?"

Smitty leaned forward. "Yeah, pretty sure that's Salsa."

"You know Salsa, too?"

"Who doesn't?"

"I gotta go." I gave them both a salute but didn't wait for a response. I opened the door and hustled down the narrow hallway that led to the main dining area, temporarily abandoning all worries over wandering in public.

I rounded a low wall and leapt up the three stairs. I squinted in the dim light, surveying the patrons to find the guys I was looking for. The Caribbean Saloon was pretty much a giant man cave. Its lights were always kept dim, which made for a welcome break from the glaring Caribbean sun. The dim light also made it easy to see the TVs hung on every conceivable flat surface.

I spotted my quarry. The young guy in the long-sleeved shirt with "Maya" down his left arm was slouched forward, leaning on the bar. His shirt hung loose on his skinny frame.

He had a head of tousled hair bleached blonde by the sun and a pair of sunglasses parked within his unruly waves.

He was sitting with a shorter, older guy who I guessed to be in his forties. He was solidly and squarely built. His face was cut from the same tan cloth as his co-worker, but I caught a glimpse of piercing blue eyes peering out of his. In contrast to his co-worker, his hair was dark and neatly shorn. I caught a glimpse of the older man's hands as he put them on the bar: tanned and powerful enough that they looked like they could wrestle a marlin easily.

Neither of them made eye contact with me as I approached. They were clearly off-duty in more ways than one.

"Hey, you guys work on the *Maya*?" I asked.

They both nodded. The bartender floated to the edge of the bar. They turned to him and ordered a round of Cruzan Dark and Cokes. I made it three. Why not? Happy hour was in full swing, so those babies were only $3 each.

They turned their gaze back to their plates of food. One burger, one steak with a baked potato. I'd need to get their attention somehow.

"This round's on me," I said.

That worked. Two pairs of eyes snapped up, but they still said nothing.

"You guys were at the Ritz for the big party the other night?"

The younger one looked to the older one who nodded.

The conversation died quickly.

I realized I hadn't introduced myself. Maybe that would get these guys chatting. "I'm Lizzie. I used to work over on *Splash Down* but now I work out of Sapphire Marina on *Seas the Day*."

They both nodded, but offered nothing more. This was getting painful.

"And you guys are . . . ?"

The younger one looked to the older one again.

"I'm sorry, but is there some kind of pecking order here?" I asked. "Can he not answer without asking your permission?"

There was a beat of silence and I was sure I'd blown it.

Lizzie Jordan, smooth talker.

Then a slow smile broke out on the face of the older one. "I wish that was true of this one. He never shuts up. I've threatened to leave him at the North Drop just so I can get some peace and quiet. I'm Richie." He held out his hand and I shook it. His was rougher than mine, probably because he didn't get the benefit of all that Palmolive from washing dishes in the galley.

When he smiled, white teeth flashed in his tan face. There was something about a guy with a tanned face, crow's feet and a nice smile that made my knees weak. I wondered if they made Andrea's weak as well.

The bartender delivered our drinks in plastic cups. I took a long sip and shuddered as pure dark rum came through the straw. Damn, I needed that. I also felt the Jäger working on me as a pleasant warmth collected at the back of my neck.

Richie nodded back to the younger guy, who had taken the straw out of his cup. He squeezed the plastic in his hand to create a spout of Cruzan Dark and Coke that he poured into his mouth. "We call this guy Hasty."

Hasty paused his pour briefly and nodded.

I frowned. Then who the hell was Salsa? I waited for an explanation, wondering if it had to do with how fast the younger one could finish a rum and Coke. None came.

I'd bide my time on that one, but I'd try and get some answers in the meantime. "Rumor has it that you were up at the Ritz-Carlton with a few girls the other night."

In the darkness, I thought I saw them both freeze for a second. Then Hasty looked at Richie again.

Richie shrugged and looked down at his plate. "For the party," he said. He took a sip of his drink.

"That's it?" I asked.

I got a shrug from Richie and nothing from Hasty, who also seemed really interested in his plate again.

I guess my round of rum and Cokes had its limits.

"You met a few girls at the bar on the residence side."

No eye contact.

"Look, I talked to the bartender. They have videotape. You were there." I stared them down, selling the lie.

"What's it to you?" Richie asked, his tone sharp. I was definitely wearing out my welcome, but I didn't care.

"You realize that one of the girls you were with is the one who turned up in the harbor." I flicked my eyes between them.

Neither spoke, but neither looked surprised.

"I'm just trying to figure out what happened to her. I'm not accusing you of anything."

No response.

I leaned forward, into Richie's line of vision. "Please. It's important. A friend of mine—his life is on the line. I just need to know what happened that night. It stays between us."

I made eye contact with Richie and tried to make the best soulful eyes I could. For a moment, I thought I saw those piercing blue eyes melt, but they flicked away. He shrugged.

I sighed. I'd lost.

I turned away from them to pay the bartender for our drinks and slink away in humiliation. He was ringing up another transaction, so I leaned hard against the bar, calculating my next move.

I was cursing Nickelback or whatever stupid pseudo-hard-ass rock band was blaring over the sound system for stuffing four separate clichés into what couldn't have been more than thirty seconds of music when I heard Hasty start to speak:

"We went up to celebrate with the big boss, even though we didn't do that well in the tournament."

I felt my breath catch in my throat. I didn't even turn his way. I was afraid I'd break the spell.

"He brought his wife. She's a real bitch—" He broke off, waiting for a reaction from me, I assumed. He'd have to do worse than that to make me twitch.

After a beat, Hasty continued. "She wanted to go to bed early and Alex, you could tell he felt bad, so he called down to the other bar and opened us a tab." I felt him shrug. "I do okay on the *Maya*, but I ain't doing enough for $10 Dark and Cokes."

The bartender approached and I circled my hand once, gently. One more round.

I still didn't turn back to them. I waited for Richie to stop the boy from talking, but he remained mute. I just kept my weight forward on the wooden bar, my fingers tight on the sticky varnished wood surface, my breath shallow so I wouldn't miss a word.

Hasty kept talking. "Hard to resist, these girls. They come down here, looking all pretty in their dresses with their hair done. Don't get to see much of that down here." He paused again.

I held my position. He could have maligned everything I loved in that moment—he probably could have even called *me* a "real bitch"—and still I wouldn't have moved.

The bartender delivered a fresh round of drinks. I left mine untouched.

I waited, but Hasty didn't start up again. Was there more? I didn't want to spook him. Once again, I simply waited.

Nothing.

I strained my awareness to see if I could pick anything up: a whisper, a mutter or some kind of movement. I heard the scrape of a fork on a plate. Out of the corner of my eye, I saw the plate pushed forward, to signal to the bartender to come get it.

This was it. It was now or never.

Gently, as though speaking to a wild animal, I spoke. "So you went to the hot tub?"

I waited, then heard the sound of the cup being returned to the bar. I heard a quiet, "Yep."

"Your idea or theirs?"

"The blonde girl's idea." It was Richie who spoke this time. I restrained myself from doing a dance. This was it. I had them.

"Jessie?" I asked.

"Sure," he said. "Hard to remember their names."

"Are you sure the blonde girl suggested it?"

"She tell you differently?"

"Yeah, she did."

Richie spoke again. "Tell the truth, I wasn't really that into it. Hasty's happy with anything that's not a fish." He chuckled a little, and I felt the tension ease. I could turn now.

Cautiously, I rotated to my left and laid eyes on them.

I thought Hasty would protest at the characterization, but he shrugged and grinned. Fishermen. Gotta love 'em.

I detected what I thought was a flaw in his story. "So the girls were all done up and they went in the hot tub? Clothes and all?"

Richie shook his head. "No. They made us wait for them until they got their bathing suits, then we met them at the hot tub."

"That top didn't stay on for long," Hasty said, putting his empty, crushed plastic cup on the bar. This kid would be blackout drunk before long.

I looked at Richie sharply, who held up his hands. "Look, like I said, I wasn't that into it. Before I know it, that blonde girl has her top off. The other girl asks her to cool it. She got upset and stomped off."

My mind clicked in confusion. Jessie? The Jessie I knew, pulling her top off? "You guys didn't, you know, help things along?"

Richie cocked his head. "What do you mean?"

"How sober were the girls?"

He made a face. "Please. A few Bushwackers and that girl was all over the place."

"Jessie? Not Andrea?"

He shook his head. "I don't know their names. I just remember them as the blonde-headed one and the dark-headed one."

Someone was playing me for a fool and I couldn't tell if it was these guys or the girls. I tried to imagine the Jessie I knew whipping her top off in a hot tub. It didn't wash.

But maybe that was just the Jessie I *thought* I knew.

My mind flashed back to Magnus. "All the right fire, but no clue how to direct it."

Maybe I'd seen the Jessie I wanted to see.

My mind ticked through the scenario. If the girls had to go back to the room for their swim suits, that meant that Becky also probably knew something about this adventure and hadn't said a word.

We sat in silence for a moment as I digested the implications.

"Girls go crazy when they come down here," Richie said, breaking into my thoughts.

I swiveled my eyes to him.

"They leave that stateside self behind, especially at night. You see these girls at Duffy's—or even here on the right night— you wouldn't recognize 'em. I didn't know that blonde girl was gonna be in my face like that. I mean, I didn't think she was the Virgin Mary, but I didn't think she'd be crazy." He shook his head.

Hasty snorted. "She was definitely in your face," he agreed. Then, after a pause, and to no one in particular, he said quietly, "I kinda like crazy."

"There was one point," Richie said, "where she was just ranting and raving about how she thought the other girl was trying to ruin their whole vacation. I remember it because Hasty kept saying, 'It's roo-EEE-ned!' like they do on that television show, uh, *Family Guy*. You ever see that one? With the baby and the dog?"

I hadn't, but I wasn't sure it mattered.

"We've got satellite TV on the boat. Anyway, she nearly took Hasty's head off for it. Then she bolted."

Richie's blue eyes met mine. They were clear as day. He detected my skepticism quickly. "You know I'm telling the truth," he said. "May not be what you saw of those girls, but I've got no reason to lie. We went in a hot tub with them. Girl gets naked—"

"Jessie."

"Jessie—sure, the blonde-headed one—gets naked, freaks out when the other one tells her to cut it out and runs away. We hung out with the other girl for a little bit and we left. End of story."

"Hung out? You guys talk at all?"

Richie sighed, and I could tell he was coming to the end of story time. "All we did was talk. That other girl kind of killed the mood."

"What did you talk about?"

"The usual. How did I get here. Do I like being a fisherman. What's it like to live on the island." He made a puppet with his hand who chattered as he recited the questions we all got on a daily basis. When you were new to the island, full of piss and vinegar about your stateside escape, it was fun to answer these kinds of inquiries. It got tiring as your time on the island wore on.

"Did Andrea say anything about Jessie after she left?"

"Not really, just something about being wound tighter than usual and she hoped it wouldn't be like this the whole vacation."

"Anything else?"

He shook his head.

Hasty blinked at me with unfocused eyes, but said nothing.

Richie stood. "We gotta go. I gotta get this kid out of here before he makes an ass of himself. Thanks for the drinks."

"Wait—what about Salsa? Who's Salsa? Andrea had a text about salsa."

"I gave her my number," Hasty slurred. "Never called."

Now I was really confused. "I thought your name was Hasty?"

Richie winked at me. "Think a guy named Hasty ever gets laid?"

Hasty stuck out his hand. "Trevor Salsa. That's my real name. Girls love it." Before I could shake it, he took back his hand to cover his mouth as he burped. He made a face. I wondered if vomit was imminent.

"They find out he's Hasty later," Richie said, flashing one more smile at me before hustling him toward the door.

I turned to the bartender and put down one of Milliken's hundreds on the bar. Looks like I was going to pick up the whole tab. What is it they say about money? Easy come, easy go?

A tan hand grabbed the bar next to me. It was Richie. He put a fifty on the bar. "You didn't think I was going to leave you with the whole thing, did you?"

I gave him a rueful smile.

"Yeah, lots of shysters down here. Don't I know it."

He glanced at Hasty, who was leaning precariously against the rail outside. "She seemed like a nice girl, the dark-headed one. Too nice for a hot tub foursome, you know? Pretty sure that's what the blonde girl was aiming at." He paused. "I like a good lay as much as any guy, but those crazy days are behind me." He turned the corners of his mouth down, shook his head. "Maybe I'll see you around. We're here for another month." He winked at me again. I figured it was his signature move. For whatever reason, I found it charmingly anachronistic, rather than creepy.

Then he was gone.

I ordered one more drink and shuffled some money back and forth with the bartender, a smiley white guy with short buzzed black hair named Luke. I didn't know him well but the corners of his mouth always seemed to curl upward. Maybe he did a lot of coke. I couldn't say.

I left him too much for a tip and sat for a moment, mulling over what I'd learned and taking occasional sips of mostly rum with a splash of Coke.

She was going to ruin everything, Jessie had said. Well, at the end of the day, things had certainly gotten ruined for Andrea. And yet, somehow, Jessie had escaped with her life.

We women really get the short end of the stick in some ways. We're physically more vulnerable than men. Ripe for the picking, in some cases. I didn't think many men truly appreciated that every dark parking lot, every solo hike, every isolated wander through an unfamiliar city could feel like a threat.

Or, in Andrea's case, actually be a threat.

If only, I couldn't help but think. *If only her friends hadn't just ditched her, Andrea might still be alive.*

How could they just leave her behind? How could they?

I sat, took another sip and bobbed my head slowly to some stoner rock song from the bar's speaker system.

Another thought flashed through my mind. *What if they didn't?*

What if they went back to the Ritz because they *knew* she wasn't coming home?

I pushed my rum and Coke away from me for a moment, as if its distance would help my brain function. My thoughts were picking up speed. That's the only way I would have left a friend—if I were 100% sure she were safe somewhere else.

And how would you be 100% sure? How could you possibly be that certain?

If you knew who did it—or if you did it yourself.

I heard someone call my name, but I didn't look. All along, I'd thought the girls were holding something back. I just hadn't realized how big it was.

"Lizzie." The voice was closer now.

I stared off into space. I wasn't sure what they'd done, exactly. But they'd done something. That was enough for me.

"Lizzie!" A hand shook my shoulder and I snapped back to reality.

It was Smitty, holding up his cell phone.

"Got a message for you."

"From who?"

"Ben."

20

I read the screen three, four times, trying to take it in. After the missed call to his phone, Ben had texted Smitty. Smitty had replied that it was me, and I was acting really weird. Then Ben had told him to send me to the Ritz, that he was going there to show the girls the videotape to look for clues.

He'd tried to call and text me, the message said, but I wasn't answering.

I felt my chest squeeze.

No. No. No.

He was walking right into the web of those black widows.

I would have to seriously rethink my assessment of women as vulnerable flowers, ripe for the picking.

But that would have to wait. First, I had to get to the Ritz.

I wasn't sure how, though. My trusty car was already there, thanks to Detective Christopher. The safaris didn't run all the way up the road to the Ritz, but stopped at the base of the hill and continued on along the main road.

I felt my mind start to flail, like the arms of the man I'd "saved" a few days ago.

My mind flashed back to Herb the Wonder Septuagenarian. My training kicked in. I had to slow down. I had to think. Our instincts are always to jump off the boat and into the water, but that wasn't always the smartest decision.

With hands shaky from adrenaline, I reached for the plastic cup and drained the rest of my rum and Coke.

Bad decision? Hell, I at least knew it would help calm me down enough to think.

I could call the detective. I'd probably get arrested again, but as long as they found Ben, that was what mattered. And maybe Detective Christopher would listen to me this time.

"Ha!" I barked out loud. "Not likely." I was talking to myself now. But in a place like Saloon, that didn't earn me even a glance from the other patrons.

I could just call the police and stay anonymous. But would they show up? If it involved the Ritz, probably.

But what would they do? Arrest Ben, most likely. I figured that was better than losing his life. I wasn't sure he'd agree, but I really wasn't interested in his opinion at the moment.

Before I could make my move, I saw a group of men in light blue shirts and royal blue pants appear outside the bar's plate glass windows, two of them headed for the front door and one headed for the back.

They were police officers.

I didn't even pause to find out if they were looking for me. I dropped my cup. I shoved my stool back, then ran around the mahogany bar, down the stairs and past the office door. As I opened the door that led to the back hallway, I knew I didn't have much time.

I grabbed for the handle of the closest bathroom. If anyone was inside, I was screwed. My hand was slick, and it slipped on the handle. Dammit.

I tried again and it mercifully turned.

Empty. I slipped in and shut the door quietly behind me, locking it.

Maybe the back door code would slow him down. At the very least, maybe the officer would move right past the bathrooms and into Saloon.

I heard the main door open. I held my breath.

I heard the first bathroom door open, then shut. I was wrong on both accounts. Crap.

Frantically, I looked around for options. I could climb in the trash can. If I were Spider-Man, I could leap to the ceiling and hide in plain sight. I could unlock the door, hide behind it and hope he didn't check thoroughly. Seemed like a ridiculous plan, but it worked in the movies. If I were Clint Eastwood, I could bash the guy on the head and run out. Dirty Harry, I was not. I also wasn't mentally prepared to commit an assault on a police officer.

I heard the second door open. Mine was next.

I looked around wildly and found myself eyeing the gray plastic trash can a second time. I pulled off the flat, swinging lid and looked inside. I immediately recoiled. Someone had lost their lunch in the bin, and it was ripe. It was also a bright orange, as though someone had thrown up an entire bag of half-digested carrots.

I turned my head but the acrid smell of puke stayed in my nostrils. No way.

I heard the second door close, then I heard a radio squawk. The words were garbled over the radio, but I would swear I heard the man outside say something about another "bat-room."

I looked back at the orange mess in the trash can.

It was the trash can for a minute—or a cell for who-knows-how-long.

I reached over and quietly unlocked the door, then I bunched up the trash bag and tied it tight. I stepped one leg over and into the trash can, then the other, wincing as the foot on top of the bag squelched. I bent over to retrieve the lid, then sank on top of the nauseating bag, praying it wouldn't break.

I gagged once, then pinched my nostrils closed with one

hand and breathed through my mouth. I wasn't going to get caught for yakking.

I crouched tighter—and then I had a terrible realization. I wasn't going to fit. Even with my chest pressed to my knees, my head wouldn't fit below the lip of the can.

I didn't have a lot of time to consider. I heard the officer rattle the door handle. I balanced the trash can lid precariously on the back of my head and hunched down as far as I could, desperately hoping I could pull this off. The lid didn't quite rest on the can, but I might be able to pass muster.

Or so I hoped.

It was entirely possible I looked like one of those cats who thought he was hidden under the couch with his tail lying in plain sight.

The idea made my skin prickle with fear, but I had to stay as still as possible to make the illusion work.

As I huddled, I couldn't help but remember a fact I'd heard once in a police procedural show—that when you smell particles of a substance, it's because they're actually dispersed in the air. So if you're smelling poop, your nose is actually taking in miniature molecules of poop.

My brain is a motherfucker sometimes, you know?

I took shallow breaths through my mouth, hoping to minimize the number of carrot-puke particles—mixed with God-knows-what-else—that I was taking in. I considered letting the detective throw me back in jail.

I heard the door swing open. I took in a shallow breath.

Did I mention that my knees were starting to hurt? I had the kind of knees that cracked and popped even in high school. I'd always joked I'd never make it as a major-league baseball catcher. I was testing my theory, and I'm sorry to say that I was right. I wouldn't have made it through the first inning.

Add to that the fact that my stomach was in full rebellion from the noxious garbage fumes. I was glad I hadn't taken

Smitty's advice about eating. I squeezed my body tighter, hoping I could hold back. I tensed, expecting the lid to be torn off the back of my head at any moment.

But I couldn't hear a sound. What the hell was that officer doing?

At that moment, I was sure I felt something move next to my left foot. Maybe a cockroach had made its home in the bag. Or maybe a rat. It took every ounce of self-control to keep from crying out. I dug my nails into the sides of my calves and willed whatever it was to stop moving.

I heard the squeak of a shoe on linoleum, then another. Was he walking closer?

My nails dug harder. This was going to be a hell of an embarrassing way to get caught. It also pretty much guaranteed that the dude I saw earlier was no longer going to hold the title of Stinkiest Inmate.

I heard another few squeaks, then I heard a sound I wasn't expecting. The low burr of a zipper?

I heard the sound of liquid pouring into the toilet, and I suddenly understood. The officer was taking a piss. I felt one leg twitch with a cramp. Add that to the screaming of my knees, and I knew I didn't have much time. I took a shallow breath through my mouth. The air tasted humid and fetid. A few more minutes and I would pass out, taking the can with me and spilling its disgusting contents on the floor, me included. I couldn't let that happen.

I blinked my eyes. What if the snow came?

No. I couldn't think about that now.

The water continued. Apparently, the officer in question was a well-hydrated man. As each one of my muscles began to add their distress to the crazy chorus of yelling in my head, I started counting to keep myself from letting that inner dialogue out. By the time I reached four, I was ready to burst out of the can like a stripper out of a birthday cake, but I bore down mentally and kept the numbers going. Five . . . six . . . lucky number seven . . .

Finally, I heard the stream stop, then the zipper close. No flush, as was common down here for #1. However, the neat bastard did turn on the tap to wash his hands.

I was going to score one for the VIPD and their cleanliness, but then I realized he'd need a place to throw out his paper towel. Shit. Shit. Shit.

The jig was up. I had mere seconds until I would be discovered. Frankly, they'd have to carry me out because I wasn't sure I'd have much feeling in my limbs after this.

I heard the paper towel holder roll turn and I twitched.

This was the end.

It had been a good run, capped off by a tense game of cat-and-mouse that ended in a garbage can. Dirty Harry, eat your heart out.

And then I heard a banging, like someone hitting a fist against something hollow. Then I heard the officer whisper, "Muddascunt."

I heard the handle twist and the door swing shut.

Then, silence.

I had made it. I didn't know how I'd done it, but I'd made it.

But why?

The realization hit me, and I nearly laughed out loud. For once—and just this once—I was grateful for the fact that Caribbean Saloon was perpetually out of paper towels.

Now to extricate myself. I tested my legs cautiously. Would they push me up? They indicated they might, so I stood fast, ready to be out of my prison.

I forgot the top. It clattered to the ground and I froze, my ears at high alert.

I stood in that damn trash can, waiting for the officer to bust in and grab me.

Nothing happened—but I knew I had to hurry. If they looped back around, I was screwed. Plus, with Ben headed for the Ritz, there wasn't much time.

As I stepped out of the trash can, my eyes flicked to the sink. I was sorely tempted to stop and rinse myself, even if I couldn't dry a thing. No time for good hygiene, I decided.

I opened the door cautiously and peered around its edge. The hallway was empty. I skirted the door, then slipped out the back, onto the balcony that faced Red Hook. My eyes searched the near side of the road for taxi cabs, but I didn't see one of the shiny vans in sight. Of course.

I had to keep moving. With Ben headed to the Ritz, time was a factor. I hung a left and trotted along the balcony, my head swiveling in all directions. No officers in sight. I took another left, then another and barreled down the marina stairs to the street level, where I hugged the building.

Again, I eyeballed the street, my eyes roving for options while I dodged shoppers. A stringy white guy wearing a knit beanie asked me what the hurry was, but I didn't answer.

I made it all the way to the corner of the marina property, just a few feet from the East End Café. I thought about going in to see if Christie had a car I could use. Too risky. How did I know she'd help me? The dive shop wasn't an option, either.

I guess my view of humans was pretty dim at that moment.

I cursed my decision. I should have backtracked toward the ferry terminal. Mr. Domino, my savior from earlier, might have given me a ride.

Then I caught a whiff of myself—and my opinion shifted. Most taxi drivers wouldn't take me in the state I was in. They're very particular about their vehicles, and they wouldn't take kindly to the stench I brought with me.

Besides, too much distance with too little cover lay between us. It was too much risk for very little potential reward.

I looked left at the road ahead. I could hoof it to the Ritz. It wasn't the most expedient way, but most of it was hidden from sight. If I could get through the first stretch—past the high school and into the National Park—I was golden.

I looked up at the sky. Dusk was starting to settle in on the island.

I checked my watch. It was just after six. I probably had twenty minutes before darkness provided more cover. I also had twenty minutes to make progress before my bush hike became treacherous. I wished for my trusty Maglite and the cool weight of its barrel in my hand.

I flexed my feet in my flip flops. They were fine for now. They probably wouldn't be in twenty minutes. I apologized to them in advance.

I grimaced. I was going to get to the Ritz, even if it killed me.

21

I have a lot of regrets at this point. First among them was neglecting to at least buy or beg a bottle of water from Christie. I'd lived down here long enough to know that beer, rum, Coke and Jägermeister do not count as hydration. And yet, I plunged down the road through Red Hook without a drop of water to my name.

To be fair, I was overly preoccupied with the geography of the first stretch of my journey. It was going to be tricky. I had about a quarter of a mile to traverse with very little cover. If they were truly looking for me—and not some other Red Hook miscreant—walking along this well-traveled road made me easy to find.

I didn't want to take chances with any possibility of delay. I chose to walk on the side of the road that abutted the marina, which acted as a makeshift parking lot most days. Where cars could pull straight in, they did, sheltering underneath trees. The rest of the road was parallel parking pretty much all the way down to St. Thomas's piece of the Virgin Islands National Park.

Whereas St. John across the way was two-thirds National Park, on St. Thomas, the National Park was a strange spit of land, consisting of a quarter-mile of road leading to a parking lot and a cement dock. The local chickens used the road for strutting, and the local humans used the road for exercise. It was one of the few flat stretches on the island, so people gathered in track suits and spandex, walking, running or jogging their way to better health.

Why it was a National Park and what it was preserving, I couldn't tell you. Today, the park was my path to salvation. Once I got off this main street, and after a quick hop down the road, I would disappear into the bush and head for the Ritz. If there were police officers looking for me, they'd have to follow me on foot. Not likely.

But first, I had to get there.

If I'd been feeling extra brave, I might have plunged right past the parked cars and into the bush that lined the street. It was mostly mangrove trees, which ringed the far end of the inlet past the marina. It would have been great cover. I probably could have clung to the mangroves, high stepped over their arched roots and sloshed my way through the murky water near the shoreline.

Two things stopped me.

Number one, I had been told once that St. Thomas's drug addicts—I'm not talking about casual users, we're talking about people who had no family, few friends and no resources such that crack consumed them both mentally and physically—lived back in those trees. It could have been just talk, but I didn't have the emotional resources to confront that myth head-on.

Number two, the water was absolutely filthy. This side of the bay was the end of the line. The water had nowhere to go, so it simply stagnated. I was sure it was laced with diesel and human droppings from all the liveaboards in the harbor who didn't use their holding tanks. Plus, there were numerous abandoned boats hanging around, leaking God-knew-what into the water. Going in there was sure to mean staph. And after my recent stint in the trash can, I just couldn't do abject filth again.

Instead, I decided to weave in and out of the parked cars on the side of the road, using them as shelter, just in case.

The tall grass whipped at my legs as I slid in beside a red Toyota 4Runner. I leaned a sweaty palm against the side and tried to peer through its windows to see if I was being followed. The tinting was too dark. No dice.

I took the opportunity to catch my breath, which was coming in ragged bursts. This puzzled me. I hadn't exerted myself that much, and yet I couldn't seem to get enough oxygen. Maybe the booze was affecting me more than I thought. Was my famous resilience fading?

Or was the snow coming?

I felt my chest tighten at the possibility. I had to get going before it caught me.

I looked ahead at the next car, a silver Honda many years past its prime, parked with its nose facing me. The paint on its hood had fully oxidized, leaving it a dull gray. It was parked too close to a group of stout tree trunks to allow me to slip past the passenger side. I would have to go around and expose myself to the road.

I tiptoed around the SUV, then glanced down the road to see if the coast was clear. I caught sight of a decal applied at the top of the 4Runner's windshield: "How You Like Me Now?" it read in white stylized script letters. I chuckled. Bold words to paste on a ten-year-old car.

There wasn't a single car in sight, so I skittered in front of the 4Runner's hood and around the Honda without incident.

I proceeded to bob and weave around the cars all the way to the National Park, running like hell each time I was forced out in the open. A few battered island cars passed me along my journey, but no one stopped.

Before I turned left into the park, I paused to catch my breath. I was a sweaty mess, moisture slick on my forehead, perspiration running down my sides from my underarms. I was pretty sure I smelled like rum, Jägermeister and vomit. I needed a shower—bad.

No time to bemoan the state of my body. I glanced over my shoulder one more time. I squinted. Was that a dark SUV headed out of Red Hook? I had to hurry.

Since it was after working hours—and the punishing sun was fast disappearing behind the horizon—I expected to see people exercising. To my surprise, the park road was empty, leaving me the lone, sole, exposed idiot on the road.

I'd hoped that turning off the main road would make me feel more protected. I was wrong. There were no more cars to use as shields. I was all alone, wildly exposed on this two-lane road. The grass on the left was neatly mowed and, while there were a few trees on the right, they were widely spaced, offering zero cover.

I longed for the friendly faces of my regulars—like the tall, thin man with dark brown skin who always wore a navy Adidas track suit. He had to be 6'5" and I always marveled that he managed to find pants long enough for his legs. Mentally, I had nicknamed him "Doctor J." He always offered a hearty: "Mahnin'!" when greeted, although he wasn't big on eye contact, so his greeting seemed directed to the ether. It never failed to bring a wry grin to my face.

Today, though, he wasn't here to give me comfort—or cover. My only companion was a preening rooster stalking the left side of the road, his red and green feathers dull in the dimming light.

I stood for a moment, the sound of my breath ragged in my ears.

The empty road was just too eerie. I panicked like a spooked horse, and broke into a run, knowing my knees would hate me for it later. I also had to be careful. If I blew out a flip flop, my journey was going to come to an abrupt halt. The trail got a lot rougher from here on out.

I got winded quickly, my breaths coming in ever more ragged gasps. I kept going. My body struggled to pull oxygen from the air, which was still humid even at dusk. Again, that bottle of water would have helped, but I hadn't planned very well.

I wanted to look behind me, but I didn't dare. I was running on the very last bit of willpower I had, and if I saw the detective or one of his minions behind me, I thought I might just break.

Ben, I remembered. *Ben is walking into a very dangerous situation.* I tried to lengthen my stride a little, pull my arms in and stop waving them around like a crazy chicken. If I could tighten my form, maybe I could eke out a few more minutes at this pace.

I felt the tip of my right flip flop catch on a break in the concrete and I catapulted forward. My legs scrambled to get themselves under me, and I managed to catch myself. My toe stung like a son of a bitch. I'd probably lose my toenail for that. I just hoped it would hold for now.

Every stride hurt. My knees complained, my toe whined and my lungs were waging an all-out shouting match with my brain. I didn't have much left in me. I imagined the whole VI police force gaining on me, and I pushed forward.

The parking lot at the end of the road came into sight. A few lone cars sat in spaces designated for the Caneel Bay resort employees whose ferry picked them up at park's concrete dock.

Just a few more steps. Just a few more steps, I promised myself.

I ducked behind the cars and ran along a chain link fence. My eyes scanned for the break that would take me through to the road to Latitude 18, the road that ate cars. I didn't know who had cut the original hole in the chain link. It had just always been there. A local courtesy, if you will.

I got to the break and stared at it in disbelief. Someone had bent the fence into its original shape and secured the hole with white zip ties.

What the fuck.

I glanced wildly behind me. I didn't see any cars yet, but that didn't mean much.

The loud cursing in my head rose to an unprecedented level. It hurt to think.

Inventory, Lizzie. What do you have?

I went through my pockets and pawed past my cell phone, its battery, my wallet, two lip balms. I was never one for carrying a pocket knife. I vowed to correct that as soon as this whole debacle was over. I went to my back pocket. My hand hit something solid and sharp. Keys. Keys. I had a set of keys.

I pulled my house keys out of my purse and turned the teeth to the first zip tie at the bottom of the fence. I sawed back and forth a few times, then the key slipped and dug into my left index finger.

I yanked my hand back, looking at the ragged cut the key had left. Bright red blood was welling already. Damn, that hurt.

I looked back at the zip tie. Barely a dent.

My ears twitched. Was that the sound of an engine?

I looked back at the zip ties. They were tied on at every other link in the fence, all the way to the top. It would take cutting at least four or five to make a hole big enough. I didn't have enough time.

I stood up, cradling my torn finger in my right hand. At least my toe didn't hurt so badly in comparison. That or it had simply gone numb.

I looked at the fence. The damn thing didn't even have any barbed wire at the top. I had one more idea, and I knew it was my last chance.

I took off my flip flops and threw them over the fence

I looked down at my right toe. The nail was cracked and smeared with blood.

I just need one more thing from you. I wedged a few of my right toes into the chain link and pushed upward, biting back a yelp.

The thin fencing bore into the pads of my feet and dug painful welts into my fingers. But somehow, by the grace of God, and probably from a few years' experience climbing around sailboats, I got far up enough to put a leg over the top of the fence. I laid a long scratch along the inside of my thigh bringing the second leg over. Then, against my better judgment, I let myself fall to my feet, wincing as my left foot came down on a rock hidden beneath the grass.

I scrabbled for my shoes and shrank back into the leafy brush as I heard a car approach the other side of the fence. I crouched, then duck walked back a few more steps, cursing as a branch snapped under my left foot. I paused with the twig digging into the bed of my foot, praying it didn't break off in there.

I heard a car door open, and I held my breath. It was getting dark now. I could only hope it would give cover to this crazy white girl crouched in the bush. I squeezed my eyes shut and tried to make myself small.

I heard footsteps in the grass coming up to the fence.

"It's shut!" I heard a male voice call.

I thanked whatever gods were listening that my MacGyver maneuver hadn't worked. If they'd seen cut zip ties, they would have known for sure I'd come this way.

I heard more walking around. I could only pray that I hadn't left a blood trail, either with my hand or my foot, both of which were throbbing in a slightly syncopated rhythm.

As I huddled, my mind wouldn't stop churning out crazy thoughts. I, for example, started to wonder if the difference in rhythm was due to the distance my blood had to travel from my hand and foot.

But then I heard rustling in the bush on the other side of the fence and my mind went blank.

I wanted to run. My legs twitched with the urge. I thought back to the movie *Jurassic Park*, and the *Tyrannosaurus rex* who could only see prey when it moved. I stayed put. It would be easier to see me if I moved.

I stayed in my crouch, and I couldn't help but notice how similar this posture was to the one I'd adopted earlier in the trash can. It apparently was my best defensive posture, I was embarrassed to admit.

This time, though, my knees were considerably more pissed off than they had been earlier. I went back to counting, even as every tiny piece of my body began to join in a chorus, screaming what an asshole I'd been to it today.

One . . . I was going to pitch forward any second . . . two . . . Actually, I might throw up . . . three . . . Did the rustling stop? Can he see me? . . . four . . . Maybe I should just give myself up . . .

And just as I was thinking of ways to negotiate with my invisible opponent on the other side of the fence, I heard the footsteps retreat and a car door slam.

I fell forward in the grass, my forehead, knees and feet touching the ground like a devout Muslim in prayer. My body trembled. Water leaked out of my eyes. Not now, I told myself.

But I was in no position to make demands, and soon, the sobs were racking my body and I convulsed face down on the ground, sweat, tears and saliva mixing on my face until I didn't know which was which.

The storm eventually passed, and I was able to rock back on my heels.

I felt good. Surprisingly good, especially for subsisting on a largely liquid lunch and dinner. My body felt lighter, and I saw the road ahead of me with calm clarity. I needed both arms to wipe my face clear. I wanted a shower more than ever, but there was no help for that.

I pushed myself to my feet and gingerly guided my feet into my flip flops. I stood on my right foot and looked down at my toenail. It didn't look to be seeping any more blood. My soles and pads complained, but I had to ignore them. I still had a ways to go.

I set out toward Latitude 18 at a determined pace.

I shuffled down the dirt road, the mixture of sand and dirt sneaking into my flip flops. I felt the grit grinding under my soles with each step.

I briefly thought about reassembling my cell to call Ben again, but I dismissed the thought. I just had to hurry.

Once I reached the end of the road, it opened up into a large field. At the near end was the restaurant, which didn't look like much from the outside: a wooden building haphazardly painted mostly white with an open air dining room that faced the bay. Across the water was the marina I'd just run from. You wouldn't guess that it was one of the best places to watch live music on the island—or that they served a heck of a rib eye— but that's what made it so damn charming.

Tonight, the place was just getting rolling. I saw a few people at the bar and one white-haired couple sitting at a table. I could smell dinner getting started in the kitchen, onions and garlic on the wind.

I skirted the restaurant, giving it wide berth.

I wove through the field, then stepped from grass onto Vessup Beach. I pulled off my flip flops and shook them out, barely stopping my forward motion.

The sand here was grittier than other beaches, the coarse grain scratchy as it slid between my toes. I slogged down the beach, frustrated at my slow progress. Have you ever had one of those dreams where you need to hurry, but your legs feel like lead? Then you know exactly how I felt in that moment.

You'd think the slower pace would have given me a chance to catch my breath, but the sand pulled at my feet and legs, making me work for every step. I had to hurry. Ben's life was on the line.

I shuffled past the West Indies Windsurfing shed, a 10x10 weathered wood affair.

I looked over my shoulder as I passed behind the building. I didn't see anyone tailing me, but that didn't mean they weren't after me. My faith in Milliken and his knowledge of places "like these" was at an all-time low.

I continued down Vessup to the end of the beach, my quads threatening to give up on me if I continued at my current pace. To my left, in Vessup Bay, in the failing light, I could just make out twenty or so boats gently bobbing on their moorings and anchors. I usually enjoyed running my eyes over them, but I didn't have that luxury today.

In a quick burst of energy, I hurtled up the end of the beach and over to a dirt path. I dropped my flip flops and gingerly slipped into them. My messy right toenail was now covered in sand. Gross.

I looked behind me again. No one. Maybe they would be waiting for me on the other side. The thought sent a wave of anxiety through my body, but I didn't have a choice now. I had to press on. For Ben.

I imagined him sitting on that same chair I'd sat on, next to the mating birds lamp. A shadow fell across his face.

No—I couldn't lose focus. I had to keep moving.

I looked ahead at the outcropping of dark brown volcanic rock that blocked my way. Someone had made a small path into the rock, barely visible from far away. I wondered if it was the same person who had cut the fence.

No time for wondering. The sun was nearly gone, and navigating this part of the trail would get treacherous in the dark.

I looped around the edge of the rock and picked up the path, which would guide me through the sharp outcroppings. Up I went, narrowly avoiding a catch-and-keep bush that had somehow grown up around the rock. It would have loved to dig its hooked spines into me, but I twisted away before I fell into its clutches.

Once I reached the outcropping's peak, I slowed my pace. The road was 15 feet away from where the rock path let out, and it was possible the detective was waiting for me on the other side of Vessup Beach.

I descended slowly, creeping down the last few feet, the thongs on my flip flops jammed between my first two toes from the incline. My injured toe didn't care for this angle and it let me know. More throbbing. More blood. I had to ignore it.

At the bottom, I peered around the very edge of the rock and started backward, nearly tripping over my own feet. There was a car in the trees—a black one.

I pulled back to where I didn't think I could be seen. I took a few gulps of air. Then I waited and listened. Nothing. It probably helped that we were in near darkness at this point, the sky almost its evening shade of velvety navy blue.

I inched forward slowly to get a better look at the car, keenly aware that my strawberry nose was peeking out from behind the rock for anyone to see.

I squinted in the darkness. The car looked like a Toyota Corolla. I didn't think the cops drove Corollas, but I had to be sure. I squinted harder and picked out some delaminated paint along the edges of the hood. The car's side windows were tinted a deep purple.

The passenger side door opened. I skittered back again behind my rock cover. I waited for five heartbeats, then I edged my face out past the rock, nose first.

Through the crack in the open door, I could see a body turned sideways in the seat, feet on the ground. The man had medium brown skin, and he wore a white tank top. He sat hunched forward with his elbows on his knees, his back illuminated by a weak dome light. I thought I caught a whiff of pot in the air, but I wasn't sure.

I leaned back into the rock alcove and considered my options. He didn't seem like a threat, just a guy looking for a quiet place to smoke. I would prefer to slip by him unnoticed, but I wasn't sure that was possible.

Beyond the car, on the other side of the road was the Ritz. However, that portion of the resort was closed off by a ten-foot chain-link fence with plastic strips through the links for maximum privacy and minimal climbability—if I thought I could even make it over a second fence that day. Likelihood low.

I needed to get a hundred yards down the road, where the fence ended at a sandy parking area, allowing public access to the beach.

It was kind of funny when you thought about it: The Ritz had built a huge fence to keep people off its property, then that fence just ended. Sure, there was a guard to control access, but, like the guard in the upper parking lot, he rarely seemed to do much. Maybe I had never seemed like a threat. Beachgoing while white didn't seem to trigger much of a reaction.

Although I didn't want yet another witness to my whereabouts, this guy wasn't my main problem. Detective Christopher was. He always seemed to be a step ahead of me, damn him. Would he be standing inside the guard shack, a Cheshire Cat grin on his face?

I was getting ahead of myself. I was still a hundred yards away from the guard shack. I had to continue down the beach.

I came out from my rock alcove casually, hoping that the dome light would impair the man's night vision, rendering me nearly invisible.

I held my breath as I passed in front of his windshield. I snuck a look to the side. He didn't even turn his head as I passed. Before I knew it, I was on a deserted beach again, trying to scurry like a sand crab but loping like a clumsy human.

It was all I had to offer at that moment, and I hoped feverishly that it would be enough.

22

The flat, sandy parking area at the break in the Ritz fence was oddly deserted. So deserted, in fact, that I wondered if I'd missed the zombie apocalypse, leaving only two humans on the planet—me and that guy smoking pot in his Toyota Corolla.

Or, at least, that's the way the world looked to me from my perch behind a sea grape bush. I eyed the end of the fence and the pathway that would lead me on to the resort.

It was full-on dark now, and only a few of the road's street lights were lit.

I peered at the white guard shack, which looked much like the one at the top of the Ritz. It was a spare metal booth painted white, with windows all the way around. The shack was currently dark.

I thought the guard was on duty all night. Maybe I'd thought wrong. Or maybe the zombies had gotten the guard.

Or maybe there was someone hidden there in the dark.

I was also puzzled by the lack of police presence. This really was the most obvious, non-obvious way on to the resort. They hadn't bothered to post even a single officer.

Had the detective forgotten about me? Maybe I'd finally outplayed him in our little game of chess. The idea gave me a little thrill, followed by a small wave of disappointment. I'd have to process that one later.

I saw headlights approaching. Apparently, we had another survivor of the zombie apocalypse. I once again adopted the signature Lizzie Jordan Defensive Move, crouching behind the sea grape. Through the leaves, it looked like a silver SUV. I could hear a belt squeaking under its hood.

The SUV passed without incident.

Once it disappeared around the next bend, I scanned the area. Still empty. It was now or never. I eyed another sea grape bush across the way and barreled toward it with abandon. I crouched outside the bush, keeping it between my body and the guard shack. I waited. Nothing.

I was uneasy in this position, 100% exposed to the road. I had to move.

I peered over, squinting to see if I could see anyone in the shack. From this angle, I could see that the door was closed, but one window was left open. As my eyes adjusted, I could see straight through the shack. No guard.

I took the chance and bolted past the shack like a scared rabbit, hooking a right toward the resort. If someone chased me this way, I thought I might be able to lose them in the maze of buildings, hot tubs and infinity pools.

But no one came for me.

I paused next to a carefully trimmed hibiscus bush in bloom, its orange flowers illuminated by a few dim lights. Something felt wrong. I knew that the Ritz kept its lights dim at certain times of the year to prevent disturbing turtles nesting on the beach, but it wasn't just the dimness that was bothering me. I couldn't see a single soul out and about.

I scanned the resort. I saw lights in some of the rooms. Apparently, I wasn't alone on this planet with the pot-smoking man and the driver of the SUV. I'd have some help in continuing the human race. I scanned the beach to my left. Not even a couple out for a moonlit romantic stroll. What the hell?

The whole thing gave me chills.

Instead of taking the more direct route to the girls' room, I decided to use the darkness as my cover and walk down the beach. I took my flip flops in my hand and stepped back on to the soft white sand where I could hear the water lapping quietly.

I glanced out at the water. It was a beguiling dark indigo that night. It offered to take me to depths from which I'd never return.

It was the water that had brought me here, and it was the water that would keep me here, I knew.

I turned my gaze away from the water and back to the sand in front of me. I moved cautiously, like a doe ready to bound away at any moment.

The Ritz's royal blue lounge chairs were lined up precisely like mute soldiers on the beach. Using the light of the rising moon, I gave them wide berth.

I kept an eye on the resort itself, trying to make out signs of movement, my mind churning around the eerie silence. I caught what I thought were a few flashes of movement through the trees that lined the beach, but nothing that made me break into a run.

That's how I almost missed him.

I can only wish I'd made it sooner, that I'd turned right in Red Hook and grabbed a taxi, that I'd just turned on my damn phone and called to warn him, that I'd intercepted the police and told them my suspicions, potential incarceration be damned.

I'm still carrying regret with me, and I suspect I will be for a while.

It was a gut feeling that made me pause and look harder

in the dark, some shape that didn't make visual sense with the military precision of the chairs.

As soon as my eyes resolved what I was looking at in the darkness, I broke into a run.

It was a body, curled up in the fetal position on a lounge chair.

I reached Ben's prostrate form and began to shake his shoulder. "Wake up, Ben. Wake up."

His body shook. I continued to yank at him, long after I suspected that Ben wasn't asleep.

My training kicked in. I gently rolled him to his back and jammed my fingers into his neck, looking for a pulse. I couldn't find one. *Take a breath and try again.* I repositioned and waited to feel the throbbing of his carotid artery. Couldn't. I put my head to his chest, straining to hear even the smallest sound from his chest. Didn't.

"Help!" I yelled. "Please, someone. Help me!" My voice broke. Maybe someone somewhere in strangely empty resort would hear me.

I clamped my ear to his chest again. My own heart was pounding, but I didn't hear a thing from his. My mind quickly ticked through the possibilities: 1) calling an ambulance—I couldn't even fathom how long that would take—2) doing CPR, 3) going to the nearest bar to see if they had a defibrillator.

I had no idea how long Ben had been out, but I thought the defib would be his best option, if he had any. But I desperately didn't want to leave him. I stood and yelled again, "Help, please. Is anyone there? There's someone hurt on the beach."

I turned back to Ben, my throat clenching. My father had been in Vietnam. He said once that a person looked different once they were dead, like a wax dummy. I scanned Ben's face. It was too dark to tell if he was still in there or if he'd gone already. The thought made me want to wail.

Focus, Lizzie. Go for the defib. I gently arranged him on his side, into the recovery position. His limbs were heavy and unwieldy, and it took me longer than I wanted.

I looked up. There was a break in the chairs, one that would lead me to the bar where I'd met Grady yesterday.

But as I watched, a figure walked into that break. It was Becky, with a giant kitchen knife in her hand. The blade gleamed in the moonlight. She took an awkward step. Was she drunk?

"Lizzie?" she asked. "That you?"

"It's me," I replied cautiously. "Becky, I need you to get out of my way. Ben needs help. Drop the knife."

She took two more weaving steps toward me. I got to my feet so I could prepare to defend myself and, before I knew it, she had me backing up toward the water. I mentally prepared myself to run and, if necessary, swim for my life.

I tried reason once more. "Becky, the knife. Put it down."

She swayed a little.

"Did you do something to Ben?"

"No," she said forcefully, her lips struggling to form the word. She moved forward jerkily, like a robot whose battery was running down.

"Becky, why did you guys leave Andrea with Ben that night?"

I saw a tear roll down her left cheek.

"I just need to lie down," she said, swaying to her right. She was in serious danger of collapsing right into the row of Ritz chairs. I imagined the horror of her head bouncing off a metal frame like a volleyball—but I was not getting any closer to her until she put down the knife.

"Becky, put the knife down before someone gets hurt. You included."

I swear her eyes rolled up into her head before she collapsed, but it might have been a trick of the light.

What I do know is that one minute she was waving that pointy thing around, the next, she went down like an empty suit into the sand.

I took a sharp breath in, wondering if she'd stabbed herself. I took two steps forward.

Lucky girl. The knife lay gleaming maliciously beside her on the sand.

I reached out and nudged her foot with mine. Nothing. I took a cautious step forward, reached over, grabbed the knife and flung it down the beach. I rolled her into an approximate recovery position on her side. I was much less careful with her than Ben. I knew time was ticking away.

Then I stood, ready to run for the bar and the defibrillator. I patted my pockets. It was time to reconnect my cell phone. I could call the police on the way.

I didn't have the chance to do either of those things.

I was hit immediately from the side in a flying tackle.

23

I went sprawling on the sand. Another body landed on top of me, knocking the wind right out of my lungs. As I struggled for air, I beat off a flurry of slaps and scratches from what felt like more than two hands.

Then one hand closed around my throat. A second joined it and they started to squeeze.

"You're ruining everything," my attacker growled. I wanted to reply, but I couldn't. The pressure on my windpipe had completely blocked my airway.

I frantically felt for a thumb on one of the choking hands. I'd heard it was a weak point, and I was about to find out. My fingers closed on it and wrenched it backward. I heard a yelp. At the same time, I bucked my body with all my strength, throwing off the body on top of me. I skittered away, getting my shaky legs under me. My heart was hammering. I was scared, yes, but I was also furious.

I stood and faced Jessie on the deserted beach. Yes, it was Jessie. With two bodies on the beach and one in the marina, she was the only possibility left. But there was no time for analysis. There was only time to survive.

She ran at me like a mad bull, and we went sprawling again. I didn't want her to pin me, so I kept rolling until I got my knees under me, at which point she flew into me again. Her head banged mine, and my vision went white in a flash of pain as I hit the sand.

What was this girl on? Speed? I rolled to my stomach, then popped up again. I was breathing heavily now. My mouth was gritty with sand. Physical domination was Jessie's bailiwick, I guess. I wondered if Andrea had gotten the same treatment.

She stood in front of me. Spikes of hair had escaped her ponytail and they stuck up at angles around her head. A dark shadow had fallen over most of her face, leaving only the left half dimly lit. I would have sworn then that her right eye was charcoal red, but I'm sure it was the heady mix of adrenaline and pain that was causing me to see things.

I looked subtly to my left for something I could use as a weapon.

"Why didn't you just leave us alone?" she asked, her voice low and deadly.

She took a step toward me. I took one step back. I thought of that stupid Paula Abdul song from my youth about stepping forward and back—and I started laughing.

It was probably the worst thing I could have done. In my defense, I didn't have much control over my faculties at that point. It had been a hell of a day.

Her hands curled into fists at her side and she advanced on me. "Why are you laughing?" she shrieked.

I took two more steps back and that started a fresh wave of hysterical giggles. I was in full, out-of-control spasms. I couldn't respond. It was all I could do to breathe in between staccato attacks of laughter. Somehow, I matched her step for step backward, even in full hysterics, all the while knowing that I had to get an upper hand, and quickly.

My vision blurred with tears, mixing with the sand on my face and obscuring my vision. I wiped blindly at my eyes, trying to keep Jessie in my sights. There was a constant string of words coming out of her mouth, but I only heard noise.

I wiped at my eyes with my forearm, my vision clearing as my hysteria attack slowed. I darted my eyes to the side, looking between the lounge chairs for something, anything. That damn knife I'd just taken from the other crazy in this equation would have been perfect. However, I was sure we'd left it far behind in our shuffle down the beach.

I wiped my eyes again and when I looked back at Jessie, she was an arms' length away from me. I shuffled back quickly, but my feet were hampered by the sand. I just couldn't seem to put enough distance between us without turning my back to her, which I was not willing to do.

"Stop LAUGHING at me. This is all your fault!" She was screaming as she lunged toward me again. I danced back, afraid to take my eyes off her. However, I knew we were closing in fast on the edge of the beach, where the sand gave way to rocks. I couldn't let her back me up against that dead end. My flip flops were long gone, and there was no way could I navigate those rocks in bare feet—and defend myself at the same time.

But if I could get her talking, maybe I could distract her enough so I could figure out how to end this stalemate.

"What did you do to Ben?" I asked.

She shook her head and stopped moving forward. Her face went blank for a few seconds.

"I didn't mean—" she mumbled. "I just needed time."

Then she came back to life again. She threw her hands up in the air, then sent them crashing down, like a toddler in a full-body meltdown. "And Becky wasn't supposed to have any but she always has to be right in the middle of things like the hanger-on she is." Her eyes turned to me and searched my face. "I didn't mean to."

I didn't understand what she was talking about, not then. But I needed to keep her talking. "And Andrea?"

She shook her head. "She was ruining everything."

Her face crumpled and cleared, taking on a haunted look. I think the gravity of it all was finally weighing on her.

I took the chance to wipe my streaming eyes one last time. When I removed my arm, Jessie had closed the gap between us, her face inches from mine. The haunted look of shame was gone, replaced by a terrifying twisted look of rage.

The sheer surprise made me stumble. I fell backward into the sand. My right hand flailed out and struck something solid. The knife. Becky's kitchen knife. I couldn't believe my dumb luck. I'd found it.

But when my hand closed around it, I knew I was wrong. The handle didn't feel right. I pulled it toward me and stared at it, not comprehending. It didn't look like a kitchen knife.

It was a plastic sword, one I assume was left over from the day's earlier pirate battle. It had a thin curved blade that ended in an uneven point. A scimitar, if I recalled correctly.

I heard a screech as Jessie launched herself on top of me.

I didn't really think about it. I instinctively put the sword between us. She fell on me with such force that I felt it pierce her skin.

She didn't cry out. She just gasped and rolled sideways, pulling the sword out of my hand.

I scooted away from her, crabbing my body across the sand. She was lying on her back, the sword buried in her belly about three inches deep, by the looks of it.

Her hands fluttered around the sword like butterflies. Occasionally, they closed on the hilt, but she, like I, knew not to pull it out.

Her head flopped to the side, her right eye once again illuminated. But instead of a glowing coal, it was blue once again. It looked toward me, but not at me. Beyond me.

"Now you're a killer, too," she said.

24

"Don't touch it," I said. "I'm going for help."

She gave a weak snort. "If they ever get here. You ever called an ambulance on this island?"

Even in her debilitated state, this girl was still a step ahead of me. I couldn't help but marvel a little.

But Ben would need one. Becky, too. I wasn't even sure they even had three ambulances on the island. What would they do, squeeze everyone in side by side?

I felt bile rise at the back of my throat, but I swallowed it down. I knew we didn't need an ambulance for Ben. We needed a hearse.

She spoke again. "You seem surprised by how much I know about this place. I've been coming here since I could walk. I know this island almost as well as you do."

"Better than I do." My voice came out low and raw. "You've made this island into a place I don't even recognize." I felt something inside me harden. "You've changed this place for me. Forever."

Her voice was a whisper now. "For me, too."

Against my better judgment, I raised myself up to my knees and peered at her wound. Blood was spreading slowly in a dark stain along the left side of her belly.

My eyes moved up to her face, expecting to find pain there. It was still. Her eyes were aimed at the stars, their gaze vacant. Her mouth hung open slightly, giving an odd impression of awe. I sat back on my heels.

"You know what I want to know," I said.

She didn't move or speak.

Something inside me flared. "You killed my friend," I said, my voice rising. "You killed *your* friend. I want to know why."

She said nothing. Those eyes just continued to stare at the stars.

It crossed my mind that she might be dead, but I kept at her. "You have to tell me why," I said, realizing that I was now pleading with her. "Please tell me why."

After a long moment of silence, her head slowly rotated toward me again. Her right eye stared, penetrating me. I wanted to squirm, but I didn't. I looked right back at it.

Finally, she spoke. "It was an accident."

"I don't believe that. You would have gone for help. You should have gone for help."

No answer.

It was so quiet on the beach. I still couldn't hear much from the resort, but I realized the breeze was blowing off the water. It took most of the sound with it, leaving us with only the shushing sound of palm fronds rustling.

It was a beautiful night—at least it probably would have been from someone else's perspective.

"She got everything I wanted," Jessie said, her voice flat and quiet. If I were a few more inches away, I might not have heard her at all. Her eye was unfocused again, fixed on a point beyond me.

"It's a big world. Seems like there would be enough for the both of you," I said, still on the offensive.

"I used to think so. But she didn't want the same things I had. She wanted what I had."

I nodded as though I understood, but I didn't.

"Don't do that," Jessie said.

"What?"

"Act like you know. You had no idea what it was like."

"So tell me."

"I thought it was just bad luck. Or a coincidence. This guy, Nick, asked her to senior formal. She knew I liked him. She said yes anyway. Too bad, so sad. I found out she'd been texting him behind my back for weeks. Then I told her my dad was getting me the new Volkswagen Cabrio for graduation. But everything at my house went to shit and a car was off the table. She still got hers. In silver, just the color I wanted."

Jessie sucked in a long breath, then let it out with a hiss.

Her eye focused, meeting mine. "She got everything she wanted, and even the things she didn't. She got dinners with her mom, and she complained about them. I got to call in for take-out when my dad didn't come home. Then it was my mom. Both of them. I had to keep it together for my little sisters. She took Zack, too, even though she didn't even want him."

She paused.

"She was still so pretty," she whispered, her face softening. "Even when she just woke up."

Then her face snapped to attention. "I thought bringing her here would be good. I knew this place. She didn't. I thought I could finally—"

"Get the upper hand?"

She kept talking as though she hadn't even heard me. "I even saw him first. He would have been mine. But, of course, she took him, too."

"Ben?"

She didn't bother to respond.

"So you killed her?"

Jessie twitched in what might have been a shrug. "We had a fight. I pushed her. She tripped on the dock. She hit her head on some boat and went under."

"So you left her to die?"

Her eye flicked over to me again, the eyebrow cocked. "I was right when I met you. You're not too sharp, are you? What do you need me to do, spell it out for you?"

My head throbbed in response. My body begged for a break, so I sat back in the sand. I wanted to get back to Ben, even though I knew it was too late. It was too late when I arrived. He would have needed a miracle, and that miracle was not me.

But Jessie kept talking. "This was supposed to be my trip, my turn. My island. I wanted him. But she just laughed at me. Every little thing I did, she just laughed at me like I was nothing. Treated me like I was a child, a total fucking moron." She trailed off.

When she started up again, she spit out every word like venom. "So, yeah, when she told me that they'd already hooked up, that they'd had *sex* in his car, I pushed her. Her foot caught. She went right over the side. She hit her head on the side of a boat and she was . . ." I heard her throat open and close in the quiet. Then, she whispered, "gone."

I kept my voice low and gentle. "And Ben?"

No response.

"What did you do to him?" I asked, feeling a sharp edge creep into my voice.

Her upper lip rose, exposing her teeth in a feral smile. "The two of you were just so helpful. The two-man St. Thomas Missing Girl Committee. He had a tape from that night. He wanted to watch it at our place. I couldn't have that. He didn't give me a choice."

Her voice trailed off.

I probably should have just waited, let her continue at her own pace.

But fuck that—and fuck her.

"What did you do?" I demanded.

"He didn't give me a choice," she repeated. "I needed some time. I needed to know what was on that tape." Her voice took on a whine. It made me cringe, like catching a toenail on a sock. "So I made him a drink with some Ambien I had. Becky just *had* to have one, too. Always so fucking desperate to be in the middle of everything. But something went wrong, and he said he couldn't breathe, that his chest hurt, then he just ran out—"

Jessie groaned. I got up on my knees again in time to see her eyelids flutter. The stain was spreading. My eyes tried to make sense of the shape of it, and my mind flashed to the giant granite boulders that crouched on the beach at Virgin Gorda—the famous Baths, short for "Batholith," something I was scheduled to explain to a boatful of tourists in just a few hours.

As my mind had wandered, Jessie's eyes closed. She was done talking for now.

I cast my eyes down the beach where I could just make out Ben and Becky's prostrate forms.

I had what I needed. She couldn't give me anything more than she already had, and she'd already taken so much from me.

I hauled myself to my feet. I took one more look at Jessie sprawled in the sand. She was still for now. Alive, I wasn't sure, but I didn't feel moved to find out for certain. Instead, I began to trudge toward the other two bodies on the beach.

My adrenaline rush from the fight was gone, leaving me a hollow husk. I shuffled my feet through the powdery sand. My shoulders ached. Scratch that. Everything ached.

I longed to go home and take a long bath. Too bad I didn't have a bathtub.

I fell to my knees in front of Becky and checked her pulse. Slow, but steady. I shored up the sloppy rescue position I'd placed her in, cradling her head firmly on her folded arm, just in case she threw up the pharmaceuticals that had put her so solidly out.

I crawled over to Ben and looked at him in the moonlight. He didn't look like a wax dummy. So much for what my dad knew.

I reached over and brushed Ben's hair away from his forehead. His skin felt cold to my touch.

The sobs came without warning, racking my body so hard that it folded in on itself, forcing me down into the sand, my chest on top of my bent knees.

I cried for Ben. He hadn't been perfect, by any means. But he had stepped up for me when it mattered, and that outweighed a lot of human flaws, at least in my book.

He was gone—forever. The finality of it swept through me like an icy wind. I still haven't come to a conclusion about what happens when we die, but it was something I desperately wanted to understand that night. I thought knowing that he was sitting on a fluffy white cloud, playing a harp—or returning to the world again as a wrinkly newborn with a hell of a set of lungs—might give me some relief from the very visceral pain I was feeling. I was probably wrong about that, but it was all my brain could manage in that moment, to ask over and over again, "Where are you, Ben? Where did you go?"

I also cried for Andrea, whose callousness and underestimation of Jessie got her killed. The people we think we love can be the most dangerous sometimes.

And then I cried for me, alone again, just like I deserved, battered and bruised from the effort.

(Let me have my moment of self-pity, okay? I earned it.)

That's where they found me. I heard shouting first, then I lifted my head and saw the bobbing of flashlights headed toward me.

I thought about jumping into the nearest hibiscus bush until they passed. Then I'd get in my car and drive home—no, straight to the airport, catch the early morning American Airlines flight to Miami. Maybe not come back.

I shook my head. I was done running. This island was still home, despite its busybodies, its fickle bosses, its wildly expensive produce, its pesky detectives, its frigid jail cells and, now, its cold, dead bodies.

This place had once been a cocoon for me, a place where my adopted family cared for me, a place where the worst thing to happen was some stupid feud over T-shirts, of all things. But now . . .

I cast my eyes on the three prostrate forms around me as uniformed police began to swarm. That was another thing to marvel at—the police. I'd underestimated Detective Christopher, who turned out to be a man of the law worth his salt.

My world had tilted slightly off its axis, and I suspected it would remain at that new angle, no matter how much I fought it. There was no choice but to accept it. An ache bloomed in my chest, not unlike the stain spreading across Jessie's torso. I hadn't done so well at recovering from the other big shift in my life. Would I recover from this one?

I didn't know.

But I didn't jump in the bush. I stood up. To be fair, I did it like a baby standing for the first time, planting my feet in the sand, then getting my shaky legs under me. It wasn't graceful, but I stood—and I didn't run.

I did shuffle out of the way as more police, plus paramedics, security guards and Ritz staff began to stream toward the beach.

No one paid much attention to me, and I found myself backing away from the bodies on the beach. I needed some distance.

Finally, I found myself on the cement deck near the bar and pool where Grady had served the girls their first night on island.

I stared unblinkingly at the glassy turquoise water of the pool, cheerily lit by lights underneath. A lone purple noodle floated in its water. The Ritz had a way of making concrete and chlorinated water look so inviting. I could just slide into the pool's embrace and let the noodle cradle me. I'd float on my back and try to read some wisdom in the stars before they disappeared for the day.

I felt a hand on my arm. I started and teetered toward the edge. I would have fallen in if that same hand hadn't squeezed my upper arm tightly and yanked me away.

I turned and saw that the hand belonged to Detective Christopher, who was shaking his head at me. "I can understand why you might be a little jumpy. However, this isn't the time for a swim." His face was solemn, his lips pressed together.

Was he making a joke? I didn't have the energy to figure him out, so I just shrugged.

His face was quizzical, as though he couldn't imagine a Miss Jordan with nothing to say.

A radio crackled. He left his hand on my bicep and answered with his other hand.

I guessed that the hand on my bicep meant I was going back to jail. Fucking Milliken. I wondered how much he dropped on my release, and whether he'd demand his money back. I guessed his goons would get that duty, if any of them even knew or cared what had happened to me.

I'd have to call the office and tell them I couldn't work the boat tomorrow. I knew people who'd shown up drunk, gotten sent home and kept their jobs. What about getting arrested?

On this island, I probably wouldn't be the first.

I hoped the detective would at least allow me a call—and a mercy shower—before throwing me back in my cell.

He listened to the radio for a good two minutes. I didn't even try to decipher the words. When the transmission was done, he raised an eyebrow at me.

"And suddenly our prime suspect ended up with a plastic sword in her gut?" His dark eyes looked flat in the dim poolside light.

I just looked at him.

His voice softened. "Miss Jordan, I'm guessing you did what you had to. I just need to know what happened."

"Can I at least have my arm back?"

He released my bicep. "For now."

Then I told him as the chaos unfolded behind me, people shouting and hustling Jessie past on a gurney. They brought a stretcher for Becky since the gurney was taken. I asked about the number of ambulances on the island, but the detective simply raised his eyebrow at me and told me to focus on my own story.

He dutifully wrote down all the details in his notebook, his fancy pen replaced with a plastic Bic. The fact that I didn't bust his chops about it should tell you how exhausted I was.

"I thought for sure you guys would catch me before I got here," I said.

"Catch you?"

"The officers in Red Hook, the ones you sent to chase me into the National Park?"

"Miss Jordan, you do have quite an imagination, as I've told you before. I didn't send anyone after you."

"Well, then, who were those guys I saw in Saloon a few hours ago?"

His face was placid. "There was a sighting of a robbery

suspect in Red Hook, and officers were dispatched. The man ran, but we were unable to locate him."

"I don't believe you."

The corners of his mouth turned down. "That's not something I have any control over, Miss Jordan."

My eyes roamed his face, looking for signs of deception. I thought of my desperate scramble to the Ritz, sure that the VIPD were nipping at my heels the whole way. Had it all been just a figment of my imagination? An inflated sense of my role in this whole debacle?

Questions over whether or not I was the sought-after quarry in a police chase, the route I took was still the best way to get to the Ritz from Red Hook on foot. I tried to comfort myself with that knowledge.

I felt my shoulders drop an inch, and my mouth twisted wryly. "How is it that you always seem one step ahead of me?"

He tapped his forehead with a long, elegant pointer finger.

I shook my head. "That can't be it. I'm smart."

"I'm smarter."

"Can I take a shower?"

"I'm sorry?"

"Can I take a shower? I don't know what you plan to do with me now that I stabbed someone, but I had to hide in a garbage can, I basically ran here and then I had a wrestling match on the beach with a killer. As one human being to another, I respectfully request that you let me shower before you throw away the key."

Now he chuckled. "Come, Miss Jordan." He didn't grab my arm this time. He just turned and crooked his finger.

I wanted to ask him more about my impending fate, but I didn't want to ruin whatever favor I'd seemed to curry. Instead, I followed him like a puppy dog. As I trailed him, I allowed his chuckle to give me hope. He didn't seem like he was going to put me back in that cell, but I couldn't get my hopes up.

Shower first.

We cut between two buildings and came out at a well-lit square building with a covered circular driveway in front. This was the Members' Lounge where everyone was greeted with a signature Ritz-Carlton rum punch. They had coffee and cucumber water available 24/7. I also knew they had a set of showers inside that allowed people to check out, spend the day on the beach and shower before their flights back to the states. It was just so civilized.

I nearly purred at the thought of wrapping myself in a fluffy Ritz towel. Maybe I could even wangle myself one of their rum punches.

But the detective held out a hand to stop me before we got to the swinging doors. I stopped short. "Wait," he said before he passed through the doors. Through the glass, I saw him walk up to the counter to speak to one of the employees.

My body sagged. I was a mess. I smelled like a rotten banana. I wasn't wearing any shoes. My toe was throbbing again. I couldn't even begin to think what I must look like. I wrapped my arms around myself, suddenly self-conscious.

But then I remembered—my friend was dead. Gone. I'd never trade barbs with Ben again. We'd never laugh together at the daily absurdities that spending eight hours with human beings in confined quarters presented. We'd never count out hundreds of dollars in tips, grinning not just in relief that our rent was paid but also with the mutual pride of a job well done, knowing we'd sent a bunch of tourists back to their resorts with a perma-grin plastered on their faces.

But before I could process these thoughts further, the doors swung open and the detective emerged. Again, he crooked his finger at me, and I followed. We walked behind the Members' Lounge, toward the nearest guest building. We passed two doors, then stopped at one marked 1102. The Detective held the plastic key up to the door, and I heard the lock snick open.

He held the door for me, tilting his head toward the opening.

I stood stubbornly at the threshold, even as the sweet, gentle fingers of the Ritz air conditioning stroked my skin. "I don't get it," I said, crossing my arms across my body and resisting the urge to run into the room pell-mell and throw my wretched body on one of their cushy beds.

"This will be our center of operations as we untangle the rest of this case." He gestured in the direction of the beach, where I knew police and Ritz staff were buzzing around. "You wanted a shower." He flipped his hand palm up as though to welcome me into the room. "Use the master."

I still didn't move. "Why are you being so nice all of a sudden?"

I saw the detective's lips purse, but he didn't respond.

"One minute, you were throwing me in a meat locker and taunting me with a crappy blanket, and now you're giving me the master bathroom."

A broad smile broke out on his face. The detective had very even teeth. I couldn't help but notice as they flashed at me. They were almost blindingly white. "Miss Jordan, being 'not nice' is part of my job description. But occasionally, I do get to play the opposite role. And now, given what you've told me and what I've gleaned on my own, my work is mostly done, with the exception of the paperwork."

My brain scrambled for a response.

"And may I congratulate you on making some powerful friends during the course of whatever it was that you were doing? They were more powerful than a lowly detective, that's for sure." He tilted his head. "Now come in and take your shower before I shut this door on you."

I stepped in and he let the door close behind us with a soft click. The layout was nearly identical to the girls' suite, with a bedroom to the left, a walk-through kitchen with stainless steel appliances ahead and a living room beyond with the weird mating bird lamp on the side table.

I turned to the detective. "Does it look to you like those birds are—"

"What birds?"

"Never mind."

I spotted two tall, thin bottles of rum on the end table. I wondered if this was the Ritz's usual setup, or if they saved these rooms for important guests. I walked by and grabbed the dark rum bottle on my way to the master bathroom.

"I saw that, Miss Jordan," I heard the detective say.

"You wanna share?"

"I'm on duty."

"No fun."

I hung a left into the bedroom and walked past a King-sized bed with a plush white duvet. This was the kind of room Jessie had slept in. I remembered the Ambien she told me about. I wondered how much she gave Ben and Becky.

His mother would tell me later that Ben had a heart problem he hadn't bothered to tell anyone here about. He was supposed to be on regular medication, but he'd let his prescription lapse. I didn't exactly know why, but I could guess. None of us had insurance. If you didn't have it through your job, you were screwed. It just wasn't available. Even if it had been, I could only imagine how much it would have cost him, although I guess he still had to pay the bill in the end.

Not that I blamed Jessie any less once I understood why her cocktail had killed him.

As I approached the marble bathroom, I felt a wave of emotion threatening. I unscrewed the cap of the bottle of rum and took a long swig. It burned down my throat and I coughed once.

"Don't choke on me in there," the detective called.

I didn't answer.

I continued forward, the marble floor of the master bathroom pleasantly cool under my flayed feet. Large, two-sink vanity. Glass shower stall.

Then I laid my eyes on a large, oval tub that looked deep enough and long enough to let me soak up to my neck without my knees poking out of the water.

Yes.

I put the rum down on the side of the tub. I started the water and waited to plug the tub until it ran hot.

I glanced at the glass stall shower in the opposite corner. I should probably take a shower first so I wouldn't marinate in my own filth. It only made good sense.

But first, rum.

I grabbed the bottle and went back out to the main room, hooked right into the kitchen. I found a glass tumbler in the cabinet over the stove.

"Are you sure you don't want even a little?" I asked over my shoulder as I removed two glasses.

I heard a soft sigh from the seating area with the birds.

"One finger."

I filled my tumbler with ice from the refrigerator door.

"No ice for me," he said. Then his phone rang and I heard him answer, "Christopher here."

I put the tumblers side by side, then filled mine halfway. I put two fingers in his, then took it over to the side table next to where the detective sat. He nodded a thanks before launching into what sounded like it was going to be a long explanation.

I didn't even try to listen to what he was saying. I was off duty. I took the bottle of rum and my glass back to the bathroom.

The tub was maybe a third full by now. I started the shower. Then I leaned over the vanity to get a good look at myself.

My eyelids were heavy, my eyes bloodshot. My hair framed my face in a tangled mess. My nose didn't look as sunburnt, but maybe that was because my whole face was red. I also had flecks of blood all over my shirt. I had just stabbed another human being, after all.

I felt myself sway a little, then I caught myself on the marble vanity. I took a couple of long breaths to steady myself.

I'd need more than deep breathing to recover from this, but I was wasting too much water to brood. Even though the Ritz had more than enough, on an island with so little, it was still a sin. I had to keep myself moving.

I pushed off the vanity. Then I dropped my clothes in a pile and stepped into the shower. I washed my hair twice. I scrubbed my skin raw with a white washcloth that I wanted to tell the maids to burn afterward. I still didn't feel clean.

Then I lowered myself into a tub full of scalding hot water, but not before refreshing my drink. The rum was finally taking effect, and I could feel a little bit of lightness in my head.

That was exactly where I needed it. The thoughts just wouldn't stop coming. The image of Ben's body hunched over on the beach. The sight of Jessie's face as I impaled her with a plastic sword. Becky staggering forward with a knife. I hoped someone would find that knife before the night was out.

I wanted to cry. I really did. The sadness was lodged in my chest, like a weight. I couldn't draw in a full breath, so I just sipped as much air as I could in between sips of rum. If I could only get in a good cry, I thought I could probably clear it, maybe even for good.

Who was I kidding?

Delusions aside, the tears just wouldn't come. So I drank a little bit more.

I heard a knock on the door.

"I'm almost done," I said. And I was. The water was getting chilly. My fingers had turned into prunes. My fingernails were as white as they were going to get. And no amount of hot water in a bathtub was going to change the fact that Ben had left this plane of existence, and I had been powerless to prevent it.

I unplugged the drain and stepped out of the bath. My skin prickled with the change in temperature. I wrapped myself in a fresh towel, then I surrounded that with a white bathrobe. I knew I was being a little ridiculous with my towel consumption, but I didn't care.

I at least put my used towels in the hamper in the bathroom. Cleaning up after myself was another one of those little rules of mine, I guess.

When I emerged with my glass in one hand and the bottle in the other, the detective was sitting on the couch, his glass barely touched.

"Are you staying here tonight?"

He nodded. "It will be a busy night."

"So, just to be clear, I'm not going back to Tutu?"

"Tutu?"

"To that refrigerator that's masquerading as a jail."

"Is there a reason I should take you there?"

I didn't want to give him one. "What about Becky?"

"She'll live."

More than you could say about Andrea and Ben.

"Do you think she knew?" I asked.

He picked up his glass and stared at the rum as he swirled it, but he didn't drink. "I believe she at least suspected."

"If she'd only said something . . ." My throat closed and I couldn't finish the sentence. I sat down on the couch, leaving a healthy distance between the detective and me.

"I do believe she was the person who called us in the first place. We were able to trace that initial call back here to the Ritz, but not to a specific room." He leaned back, his head resting against the plush top of the sofa.

"At least you got the bad guy," I said.

"A little too late."

We both sat with that for a moment.

"I'll need you to come down to the station to make an official statement tomorrow."

I crossed my arms. "I've gotta work tomorrow."

"Oh, you have a real job?"

"I do."

"Then after you finish work."

"My lawyer is coming with me, just in case."

I heard him chuckle. "You tell your lawyer that you've been detecting on the side?"

"I don't think 'detecting' is a verb."

This elicited a gentle snort from him.

"Besides, isn't this the part where we have our, 'This is the beginning of a beautiful friendship' moment?"

He laughed outright and, for the first time, I heard him trade his careful, clipped speech for island patter. "Doan' be vexin' me, gyal."

Ordinarily, I would have laughed. All I could muster was a smile—one that faded quickly. I felt him look at me, but I kept gazing at the glass-and-mahogany coffee table with its perfectly fanned spread of island-themed magazines.

"Don't carry this with you," he said.

My head whipped toward him. "What?"

"Being this close to death can drag people into dark places."

Our eyes met for a moment. In the lamplight, I realized that his eyes weren't as black as they'd seemed at our most adversarial moments. They were a dark, dark brown. We looked at each other without a hint of our old chess game in the air. We were just two people who had witnessed the worst side of humanity and were trying to come to terms with it.

I also had a fleeting thought about getting naked with him, but that's talk for another day.

Finally, he spoke. "And this was off-island crime, on island. They brought this thing down with them, like so many people who come here. All those problems hitchhike a ride to paradise. You've been here long enough. I know you've seen it before, although likely with less permanent results."

I let that sink in a moment, then nodded an acknowledgement and returned my eyes to the coffee table.

I wanted to believe him—that this could have happened just as easily in the girls' hometown, the catalyst some guy they met in a stateside bar.

I also knew I would be happier if I did. Then everything could go right back to normal, and my island would remain the refuge it had been.

But when I tried to grab onto that thought, I remembered that Ben was dead. Holding on to my old island paradise felt like trying to come up with a handful of that clear blue Caribbean water I loved so much. It just slid through my fingers.

No, things had definitely changed. This island wasn't some pristine sanctuary, a place where I could simply bathe in the Caribbean waters and bake under its hot sun while letting reality slip by unnoticed or unheeded.

It was a place where your past could find you, and, if you refused to deal with it, there would be consequences.

I knew what they'd been for Andrea—and Jessie. I saw the impact on Ben. What waited in store for me?

Ben. I would never see him again. Never.

I shook my head, my throat getting tight again. I didn't want to cry in front of the detective. Not now. Where was the Cruzan when you needed it?

He reached out and put a hand on my shoulder. I felt a hot tear slip down my right cheek and find its way to the corner of my mouth.

"It's better you *don't* get used to things like this, Miss Jordan. You lost a friend today. You should cry for him."

"I think you can call me Lizzie at this point."

"And you can keep referring to me Detective Christopher."

I chuckled in spite of my tears. He removed his hand and moved a silver-plated tissue holder to the couch cushion between us. I took a tissue and blew my nose with a loud honk. I laughed, a little embarrassed. A smile touched at the corners of his mouth.

"I never pretended to be a lady," I said.

"Why did you do it?" he asked.

"I'm sorry?"

"You took quite a risk, you know. There was a point at which I thought maybe you had something to do with Andrea's death."

"Me?"

"Jealousy over Ben was my theory."

"Huh. And they gave you a gold shield. Some detective you are."

He ignored the barb. "You kept putting yourself right in the middle of all of this—despite all my attempts to dissuade you." The corners of his mouth turned up briefly, then his face went serious. "It's what made me believe you were involved in some way. Why else would you keep popping up?"

I wiped my nose and took a long swig of the rum left in my glass, then I topped it off and took another slug. "I did it for Ben. He—" I paused. That lightness I'd felt in my head earlier was now spreading all the way toward my fingertips. "I was assaulted by a family member. My sister's boyfriend. He's a drug dealer. He got my sister hooked, and when I tried to speak up about it, he threatened me physically and turned my family against me. That's how I ended up here. Fresh start."

I peeked over at the detective, and he nodded once, to show me he was listening. I continued talking into my glass of rum. "Ben was the only one who knew. It came out one day while we were working. I shared my secret with him, and he kept it. Maybe it seems like a small thing, but it meant the world to me. So when he got in trouble, I felt I had a debt to pay. I owed him."

I looked up and met the detective's eyes. "But I also did it for Andrea, whose friends just . . . well, I thought they left her behind. I know what it's like to be left behind, and I thought someone should speak for her. But the truth of the situation turned out to be much worse. Much, much worse." I took one more sip of rum for courage. "But I also did it because I didn't believe you would."

The detective's eyebrows popped, but he didn't speak.

"I know I was wrong—about you. But not to do what I did. I had to try and help Ben. I've spent too much time hiding. I'm not going to do that anymore."

"I'm sorry to hear about your assault. If it happened here, I could—"

I waved a hand in the air, as though clearing smoke, and I knew I was going to cry again. The detective simply let me. He didn't turn away. He didn't cringe. He simply waited. His face was placid when I finally looked up again, and I saw a glimmer of what I'd seen in Ben's face that day—no judgment, just acceptance.

I offered a small smile. "Thank you," I whispered.

"Rick speaks very highly of you, you know."

"I think he's pretty pissed at me right now."

"You'll get past it. I'll put in a good word for you."

"You two don't seem like likely friends."

"Once a cop, always a cop."

The detective shifted on the sofa and brought out a black leather wallet. He extracted a white business card and placed it on the sofa between us.

"Call me when you finish work tomorrow." He looked like he was going to say something more, but the elegant chime of the doorbell interrupted him.

I slipped the card into the pocket of my robe.

Detective Christopher got up and admitted a uniformed female officer. She was short and curvy with dark brown skin and a neat bun at the nape of her neck.

It was time for me to go. I stood, nodded to the officer and gave Christopher a wan smile. "See you tomorrow."

He nodded once.

I went to gather my things. I emptied the pockets of my shorts before wrapping my dirty clothes in a Ritz towel. I stuffed my disassembled phone in the robe pockets, then stared at my car keys. How was I going to get home?

What dumb luck. If I hadn't been towed, my car would still be in the upper lot of the Ritz, where I'd left it when Detective Christopher had frog-marched me to the Mariel C. Newton Command.

It may be the only thing I had going for me, but I felt like I'd won the lottery.

I considered looking for my shoes on the beach, but I decided to count them a loss.

I scrounged in the walk-in closet and found a pair of white, terry cloth disposable slippers.

When I shuffled back into the living room, the police officer was staring out the window, and Detective Christopher was on his phone. I left wearing the fluffy white robe, carrying my belongings in a Ritz towel. No one said a word.

The sky was still dark, but it was clear. I traced the Big Dipper with my eyes. Then I trudged back up the long hill, the slippers dragging against the concrete.

About halfway up the hill, I stopped and looked down at the circular drive that ringed the Members' Lounge. I imagined that it had been choked with navy VIPD SUVs and emergency response vehicles—a mini-city in and of itself. All that was left were two lone SUVs. I wasn't even sure you'd find a trace of what happened on the beach by the time the Ritz guests headed out for another day of the good life.

That was the Ritz-Carlton way. It was why people paid the big bucks to stay there.

Hey, if I had 'em, I would, too.

I continued on up the hill, but instead of getting in my car, I took a left through the main hotel building, past the Ritz-Carlton Signature Store—don't make the mistake of thinking it's an ordinary gift shop—and out onto the small balcony facing St. John.

I wondered what I looked like in my stolen robe. Then I remembered that I probably looked like I belonged.

That was a knee-slapper, that one. I didn't know where I belonged. Not here at the Ritz, that was certain. But I also knew I didn't belong in the role I'd been playing on this island. My mind flicked to the idea of reincarnation, that maybe whatever part of Ben continued on—call it a soul, call it consciousness—was being reborn in those very moments. If that were the case, maybe I, too, could be reborn through this experience.

St. John was a midnight blue against a darker navy sky. A few lights winked on her western hills. I wondered about those night owls and their exorbitant electric bills.

The Ritz had set up a few couches overlooking the view. I sank into one, intending only to rest for a few minutes and gather my thoughts before heading home.

I woke a few hours later, the sky at the east starting to hint at a sunrise. I checked my watch. Five a.m. Just enough time to stop by my apartment, grab a bathing suit and get myself to work.

I stood and stretched my stiff body. I probably could have cadged a complimentary cup of coffee, but I had pressed my luck on the Ritz freebies for now. It was time to roll.

It wasn't the first time I'd gone to work on just a few hours of sleep. It probably wouldn't be the last.

25

I'd like to tell you that I simply drove off into the sunrise, but there's a little more to the story.

I never heard from Milliken again, at least not in the way that I expected. When I got home from work that night, utterly exhausted and operating on a single brain cell, I found a cream colored envelope shoved under my door.

The envelope was unmarked except for a Ritz-Carlton embossed address in the upper left corner. I ran my finger over the raised letters before using my door key to open the envelope. Inside, I found $2,000 in hundreds, no explanation.

I guessed it was Milliken's way of thanking me for finding his daughter's killer and spearing her like a cocktail onion.

I couldn't help but wonder how he decided on the amount. What's the going rate for bringing a killer to justice? Maybe he'd simply emptied his wallet.

As I thumbed through the wad, the old book smell of money wafting up to my nose, it felt like too much for doing something I would have done anyway.

But then, standing in the doorway with the weight of the last two days on my shoulders, it also didn't feel like enough.

The story didn't make national news. It barely made news here on St. Thomas. It was buried somewhere in the back of what passed for the newspaper down here. The Ritz-Carlton guard was probably the only one who read it, if he made it that far before his morning snooze.

I can only assume that Andrea's father was responsible for that. Maybe the editor got an envelope of hundreds, too.

But that wasn't to say that Ben was forgotten. Not by me. I'd catch myself thinking about him in the strangest moments, like when I stopped to let a gaggle of sundress-clad tourists cross the street in Red Hook one night. "Ripe pickings for Ben," I thought automatically. When it all came rushing back to me, the pain was a physical one, enough to make me gasp like a knife to the gut—or a plastic sword to the midsection.

The community paid their tribute, too. Ben's mother found me on Facebook, and I helped her organize a memorial at the St. Thomas Yacht Club. More people than I expected packed the main room of the club to watch the slideshow she'd put together. The room was like an oven—no A/C and no breeze that night. But people stayed to hear her speak and watch the PowerPoint slideshow of Ben's baby pictures. The captain of a catamaran who'd taught Ben to sail when he first arrived on St. Thomas got up and gave a moving tribute—or so I heard.

I really wish I'd seen the whole thing. But after I helped Barb get everything set up, I ducked over to the bar for a drink. After all, what kind of yacht club doesn't have a bar? One drink turned into four. Before I knew it, my tongue felt heavy, and I knew I was slurring.

I did poke my head in at one point to see a picture of Ben in the bathtub, holding up a yellow rubber ducky. I was thinking how much I'd love to tease about that one when heads started turning toward me. Then a few whispers started. It could have been paranoia, I suppose. You've seen enough of me at that point to know I'm prone to it.

But that, combined with the fact that I'd never be able to tell Ben I'd seen naked baby pictures of him, made me flee. I found a quiet spot on their beach, leaning up against the hull of a Laser that lost its mast at some point. The air was hot, but the sand was cool. I sat in it until I was sober—and chilled to the bone. Everyone had left by then, the Yacht Club building dark. I drove home in silence. I felt so guilty about it that I treated Barb to a blow-out brunch the next morning at the Marriott with some of Milliken's money.

Ben's story—and mine; we were intrinsically linked now by history—buzzed through the coconut telegraph in the bars, restaurants and coffee shops. I'm not sure anyone knew the whole truth. The police, the ambulance drivers, sure, but they didn't move in the same circles as the people I knew on the East End.

A few bold people asked, but I wouldn't talk about it, drunk or sober. Sometimes, I refused cheerfully and distracted the asker by ordering a round of shots. I got angry on a few occasions. The people who pissed me off will remain nameless, but they know who they are.

I'm sorry about that whole broken bottle incident, too. I really am. When I look back on the days after Andrea's disappearance, I don't recognize the person living my life.

I'm not sure I really know the person living my life now, either. I know she isn't the same girl Ben asked for help at the bar that night. So far, I like her a lot better than the other girl, the Lizzie who appeared in the days after Ben's death.

That Lizzie still peeks her head in every now and then. She popped up unexpectedly the next time I visited Secret Harbour. Tower happened to be working, and he poured me an extra-tall creation he called a Donkey Kick. I have no idea what was in it, but I know it involved a serious amount of vodka. As he poured, he apologized profusely for losing the phone I gave him. He'd locked it in his drawer, only to have it disappear mysteriously overnight. Nothing else had gone missing. My mind flicked to Milliken's goons, but before I could consider it further, I felt melancholy settle over me like a blanket. I left half my drink and a $5 for Tower, then I walked home and spent the rest of the day in bed. I went through an entire box of Kmart tissues crying for Dave, crying for Ben, crying for Andrea and crying, probably, for myself. I couldn't say for sure. I washed any analysis down with some Presidentes I'd found in my fridge.

As for deeper analysis, I made an appointment with a therapist, but I canceled it, promising to reschedule. I haven't yet.

A couple of times, I thought about calling Detective Christopher. I hadn't seen him since our cordial debriefing the day after Ben's death. His card sat in the drawer of my desk, underneath my emergency Ziploc bag stash of cash tips. Every time I picked his card up, I found a good reason to do something else, like head to the bar for a dirty martini.

Or research flights off the Rock. I've seen some good deals to Florida, but I haven't pulled the trigger. I knew a few people in Fort Lauderdale who I could crash with, mostly yachties who worked for wealthy owners and spent their days polishing stainless, making beds and cleaning heads. They called it Snort Liquordale, which gave me a glimpse into what my time there might look like. We had plenty of booze here. Why travel for it?

Besides, this might feel like the same island I landed on four years ago, but it still felt like home.

I also found myself searching "private investigator license" late at night on my little laptop. I haven't taken it further than that. Yet.

Detective Christopher did leave me a voicemail at one point, to let me know that Becky had left the hospital in one piece and that Jessie was being charged with two counts of murder. It didn't feel like closure, and I didn't ask for that update.

But you know how people are down here. Or maybe you don't. Most times, you get more information than you ever wanted.

Like the fact that Dave and Christie moved in together. I wish them all the best. I really do. I just don't want to hear how happy they are. I'm not ready for that yet.

There was another piece of information I didn't want, and yet I couldn't look away from it, like rubbernecking while driving by the scene of a deadly car crash. A few days after Ben's death, Smitty drunkenly dragged me into the office of Caribbean Saloon to show me a video of Jessie and Andrea arguing at the very edge of their outside surveillance camera. I felt sick watching them gesture at each other, knowing everything that had happened afterward. So Smitty and I sent some Jäger into our stomachs to combat the feeling. We probably took more than the recommended dosage. But we both lived to see the next day, so no harm, no foul, right?

Yesterday evening, I ran into Detective Christopher in Saloon. I wasn't as drunk as I should have been, considering that I'd been pounding Presidentes since 4:00 pm. I had been drinking alone, but there was a man sitting kitty-corner who was making eyes at me, I was sure. His black hair was longish and wavy, his eyes dark under black eyebrows. His face was tan in a way that might have spoken of extended sun exposure or possibly Latino heritage, but I didn't know for sure. I was curious to find out. There was something mysterious about him, and, from what I could see of his conversation with the bartender, he had nice white teeth and eyes that crinkled when he smiled. I wasn't ready to commit to much more than a conversation, but I was interested.

He'd gotten up and headed toward the bathrooms, so I was staring at the bar, rolling the bottom of my Presidente bottle on its edge against a battered black coaster. It was emblazoned with some kind of pirate motif and its edges were starting to peel.

I felt a hand on my shoulder. "Miss Jordan," a familiar voice said.

I knew that voice. "It's Lizzie," I said.

Before I could turn, the voice whispered in my ear. "Let it go," he said. "I could see the weight of it on you from across the bar." He was close enough to smell a whiff of his cologne—or was it Downy? Whatever it was, it was irresistibly fresh. Then I felt him pull away.

I turned and looked at him. He was dressed in gray pants, a black belt and a tucked-in white linen dress shirt with the sleeves rolled up, the first two buttons of his shirt undone. His outfit would have been casual for a club in the States, but here it seemed so formal as to be otherworldly.

But who am I kidding? He looked handsome.

I smiled—or did I bare my teeth? I couldn't say.

We locked eyes for a moment and I felt him examining my face.

"I can't," I replied. I felt my bold grin giving way. Under his gaze, the front I'd been holding up—the face I'd been showing everyone, the one that said I was fine, that I was the independent, strong Lizzie I'd always been, the girl who didn't need anyone or anything from anybody—crumbled, but just a little.

His eyes continued to search my face.

"One of my new rules." I took a swallow of my beer before I fell apart completely. I tapped a fist to my chest to remind myself of that strength I'd been projecting. I pounded myself a little too hard, but I refused to wince. "He's here. Forgetting means going backward. I'm only going forward now."

He gave a small nod. He opened his mouth, as though to reply.

"Excuse me," a voice said from beside me.

I turned. My quarry had decided to make his move on returning from the bathroom. "Is anyone sitting here?" he asked, gesturing at the empty stool next to me.

"No, go ahead." I held up a finger. "Just give me a second." But when I looked back to Detective Christopher, whatever moment we shared had passed. He blinked slowly, then turned smoothly and headed for the door without another word.

"Friend of yours?" I heard from beside me.

I swiveled back around—with disappointment, I noted. "Something like that." I glanced over my shoulder, but the detective was gone.

"Buy you a beer?"

I looked at the man's face. He was even more handsome up close. There was laughter in his eyes and stories to go with those eye crinkles, I could tell. He had a face I could fall in love with. But I couldn't, not then. I had things to do.

"Raincheck?" I said. And before he could say anything else, I added, "Have a good night."

I slid off my stool, placed some money on the bar and headed home.

IF YOU WANT MORE OF LIZZIE JORDAN . . .

Trust me, I'm working on it.

In the meantime, I'd appreciate your support in connecting with more readers! Leave me a review on Amazon.com—and please be honest.
Lizzie would expect nothing less of you.

This link will take you to the right spot:
MeganOLeary.com/amazon

ACKNOWLEDGEMENTS

I don't even know where to start on this one. However, this whole thing began with a vacation to St. Thomas in 2005, so I have my dear friends Megan Burgoyne, Colleen Egan and Lesley Hail to thank, with particular thanks to Lesley's parents, Jean and Joe Grabias, for letting us use their timeshare—I mean, Ritz residence. One boat captain in particular encouraged me to make the move, so my thanks go to Christopher Robinson, who even put me up in the AYH marina for my first two weeks. I'm also eternally grateful to my mom and dad for talking me through the decision, and ultimately, delivering their unwavering support.

On the writing side, I owe a debt of gratitude to editor Jennifer Pooley, who really understood Lizzie and her journey and provided such thoughtful and skillful notes on my first few drafts. I also want to thank Gillian Hill, who helped me proofread and poked a few editorial holes in a late draft, ones that needed to be poked!

I also want to thank Thomas Boeker, my island boyfriend turned lifelong partner. I've been looking for you for a long time, and I feel lucky to have finally found you. I'm grateful for your support, as well as your willingness to read through the draft and talk it through with me. Thank you.

On the island side, I just have too many people to thank to start naming names. I've called both St. Thomas and St. John home at certain points in my life, and the thing I miss most about it are the people who live there. This book was my way of going back and spending time in the Virgin Islands which, in all likelihood, will forever call my name. All the boat trips, bar crawls (Red Hook 500!), hikes, beach days, tipsy brunches, long talks, surf sessions, sunsets, 12-hour boat shifts, late night philosophy sessions—I am personally richer for every one of them and for the people I experienced them with. I carry it all with me.

Lastly, see you soon, VI. It's been too long . . .

Made in the USA
Las Vegas, NV
07 August 2021

27768387R00233